Author's Note:

Since *Black-Haired Boy's* initial publication in December 2021, I have received a great deal of positive feedback from readers not only in The United States, but from around the world. I had never imagined this story reaching people from places such as Germany, France, and Japan, but to my delight, readers have sent me messages expressing their appreciation of me writing such a book.

The apparent consensus of many of these readers is that I have written a book that they wish had been available to them during their school years as LGBT teens. As a gay man, I began writing the first draft of *Black-Haired Boy* at the age of sixteen when I was a sophomore in high school. This early version of the story was far different from what the final product turned out to be thirteen years later. My initial intent was to write a story based in the world I was currently living in. At the time, in late 2008, I was a self-professed fanatic of the emo music scene and I wanted to create a character enveloped in this culture that was so prevalent. There were very little, if any references to LGBT themes in this initial story as I was mainly focused on writing a story about a teen boy's first year in high school and his obsession with a fictional emo band being the primary focus.

After some quite horrendously bad first drafts, I shelved the project after graduating high school and focused on other writing projects during my college years. It wasn't until some time later, 2018, a decade after I had first come up with the idea for *Black-Haired Boy*, that the desire to return to the project came back to me. By this point, I was twenty-six years old, proudly out, had been in a relationship with my husband (then boyfriend) for six years, and saw the opportunity to turn this old story into an LGBT coming-of-age novel set against the backdrop of the emo music scene's heyday which had long since faded.

The end result took several years of meticulous writing. I'd never taken such care in every sentence, every word of any of my writing projects, but the story of Kieran Northrup, my black-haired boy, very quickly became the most important thing I have ever created. The characters of Kieran and Izzy became more iconic than I ever dreamed they would be, and it is my hope that they have since become voices for a demographic, symbols of LGBT youth from the past, present, and future.

D1519398

I have always had a soft spot for young adult literature and while *Black-Haired Boy* is certainly a coming-of-age novel, it is in no way a book for children. One of the few issues I have with young adult literature is that it is censored for its audience as the understanding is that young people will be reading these books. The unsaid truth is that teenagers are far savvier on the topics of sexuality, pervasive language, drug-use, and violence than we pretend for them to not be. I believe there is a great deal of silence that lingers when it comes to discussing real-life issues with young people, however, I have not written *Black-Haired Boy* with a teenage audience in mind, but rather an adult audience looking back on their younger years and seeing a part of themselves they were at the time not seeing represented in teen literature.

The letters of praise I receive from readers have always come from adults who more often than not comment on how Kieran Northrup reminds them of their younger selves as LGBT teens living in a not-so tolerant society. Perhaps this means there is a bit of Kieran Northrup in all of us, a shy child of fourteen masking his true form in layers of a costume consisting of hair dye and band shirts to feel more comfortable while also searching for that impossible forever friend who would accept us for that true form in an otherwise intolerant world. I think these letters also let the text speak for itself; *Black-Haired Boy* is a book best visited by the now grown-up Kieran Northrups of the world after they have had time to reflect on who they once were as questioning children.

If this is your first time reading *Black-Haired Boy*, I thank you for taking the time to dive into my life's most important work. Some scenes may make you laugh, some scenes may make you cry, and some scenes may make you feel sick. Perhaps you'll toss the book at the wall in anger because you love it or you hate it. Regardless, I warn you that this is not a book for the lighthearted as it deals with some of the most difficult situations we can imagine being brought upon us and our children. I wanted to write a realistic novel that does not hold back or sugarcoat the reality of what can happen in the lives of some LGBT youth. This is why I do not recommend the book for young people, but for adults who have had the time to understand their world and are ready to look back upon the younger versions of themselves with this new knowledge in mind.

If you have read *Black-Haired Boy* before and are now returning to it, I want to thank you from the bottom of my heart for giving my work

such love. In this new, unabridged edition of the story, you will be reading *Black-Haired Boy* exactly as I had originally intended it to be presented to the audience. The journals of Kieran Northrup are now completely intact and edited as I feel will come together to create the closest thing to the perfect version of this story that there can be.

As you read or reread, keep in mind that every piece of this story very much serves a purpose. Take note of the details, every name, every date, every mention of a song lyric or phrase that is spoken by my characters. My hope is that *Black-Haired Boy* and its intended symbols and meanings will dovetail nicely for readers to think about and discuss for decades to come.

To all of my readers around the world, I thank you sincerely as I am forever grateful for your support.

- T. LaFerriere

Forward by educator Kevin Horn:

According to a PEN America study, of the 1648 books banned in US schools between June 2021 and June 2022, "674 titles (41 percent) explicitly address LGBTQ+ themes or have protagonists or prominent secondary characters who are LGBTQ+..." ("Banned in the USA"). As a teacher of English and an ally, I find this not only appalling, but also frustrating and disturbing.

In my classroom at the high school in which I teach (in a rural New Jersey district) are three brown pine bookshelves that reach from the floor to a couple of feet away from the ceiling, and within these bookshelves sit hundreds of books. I have striven to include characters who look like the students I teach, many of them white and straight, a growing percentage of them not only Black or Brown, but also openly queer or closeted. Every day as I turn on the lights in my classroom, I wonder if this will be the day that some of these books will be removed and placed in a small, dark room because of the paranoia and hate of a small -- but loud -- minority.

For the rest of us, these books are essential reading. Essential for those who are not queer, both adult and teen, so that they may begin to develop empathy, begin to understand what growing up as a member of the LGBTQ+ community is like through many of the strong internal monologues of the characters. And, more importantly, essential for those teens who *are* growing up queer so they may find both compatriots and role models in these characters, and so that they may know that they are not the only ones feeling the way they are feeling.

I am talking about books like the one you are about to read, Tristan LaFerriere's *Black Haired Boy*. While not a young adult novel, *Black Haired Boy* is a story of first love and of growing up gay. It is also the story of the beautiful friendship that inspires that love. The two main characters, Kieran Northrup and Izzy Murraro are people with whom I wish I had been friends when I was in high school. It was a different time in the eighties, though, and I'm not sure they would even have been out. I'd like to think that they would both have been living as their authentic selves.

I have a feeling that at the very least, Izzy would still proudly be out, not caring who was judging him, eighties or not. You, too, as you read through the book, will come to care about the boys, and if you could, you'd want to invite them to hang out and talk with you. You will want

Izzy to be with you the next time something awful happens to you -- he has a way of making things better, making you feel as if you are the only existing person other than him. He would give you the space to cry or rant or just be silent and he would be there to listen to everything you want to say and then give you the help you need to snap out of whatever it is that is making you upset.

Another thing Izzy has going for him is his background. Half Italian and half Jewish, he is proud of both cultures, like he is proud of his sexuality, and embraces them as he should. He is basically a guardian angel and takes pride in being one. In fact, the name Ishmael (Izzy's given name) in the Hebrew Bible means "God will hear." Ishmael, son of Abraham, is a prophet who was to be the inheritor of the Abrahamic religions. In *Black Haired Boy*, Izzy has inherited Kieran as a disciple -- at one point in the novel, Kieran declares, "Following him made me feel important" (100). While the biblical Ishmael could not save himself (he was disgraced and forfeited by his father who instead gave his love to Isaac, his half-brother), Izzy's saving of Kieran is an important aspect of the novel. In a humorous vein, LaFerriere has given Izzy an Alfa Romeo, whose logo is "a snake eating a man," (100) to drive when biblical Ishmael has a sizable fear of snakes. Not so funny are the snakes of the other cars that appear in the novel, driven by some not-so-nice characters.

And then there's Kieran, the titular character whose name means "black-haired" in Gaelic. If you knew him, you would want to spend time with him as well, because you would want to save him. Save him from all of the horrendousness in his life and save him from self-doubt and save him from the harm that unfortunately befalls him. While reading the novel, I just wanted to give him something to eat, probably chicken soup or something else just as healing. Kieran is a tortured soul even before the unthinkable family tragedy that shapes him for much of his freshman year.

Having moved from Los Angeles to suburban King's Valley, Pennsylvania, he does not fit into the cookie-cutter, East Coast suburban landscape that many others his age have no problem fitting into and no problem not questioning. Kieran is fifteen and too analytical to accept a fate of conformity. A self-described "emo kid" (remember that this is a story of the mid-2000s), Kieran is an old soul, wanting more than the suburbs can offer him. There are many similarities between Kieran and high school aged Laferriere: their love

of music, their ability to dream, and their intelligence. I am glad that I know both of them.

Black Haired Boy, LaFerriere's first novel, will certainly not be his last, and this is a good thing: he is prolific and is one of those people who does not just *want* to write, but *needs* to write. Good news for fans of this book -- he is already crafting a sequel. I remember LaFerriere as my student in our tenth grade English class when he began writing *Black Haired Boy*.

I knew he would be a writer then.

In 1985, Frank Zappa, at the Senate hearings to determine whether or not record albums should have warning labels regarding the content within, said something like this: A rating system for movies is just that; the film is the entity being rated, or judged, if you will. But records and songs are such personal works that slapping a rating or warning label on one is like slapping a rating or warning label on the artists themselves. I would make the same argument for the banning of books. Like songs, the words in books are so often insights into the author that to ban the work is to censor the person, and that's a dangerous precedent to set.

LaFerriere's voice, and the voices of thousands of other queer writers need to be heard. In reading *Black Haired Boy*, you are about to embark upon a journey you will not soon forget.

Kieran and Izzy are waiting for you to learn their origin story and for you to fall in love with both of them.

Kevin Horn
27 November 2022

Warning: This book contains sequences depicting teen sexuality, drinking, smoking, drug-use, bullying, rape, and assault. This book is not recommended for children under the age of 18 and may be disturbing for some readers.

The stars all seemed so close to one another,

each one with its own companion while I longed for someone,

alone,

in the blackened silhouettes of suburban homes sleeping with complete content that all was well with their new lives in this new town.

In these quiet moments where I was one with

nothing,

just a boy of fourteen,

frustrated,

but not yet completely broken,

I dreamed of who he would be.

I always pictured this perfect person,

a shapeshifter who would take on the identify of my ideal,

a brother,

a best friend,

a lover...

Tristan LaFerriere

Chapter One
Saturday, August 5th, 2006

Dear Journal,

I grabbed you because I decided I'm going to start documenting my life. I've just recently realized that the "happiest" times of my life are probably over, and writing will be my only way to escape reality. Books are good for that, too, I guess, but...writing requires more thinking. If I think hard enough then maybe I can just forget about everything that's around me.

That would be ideal.

I guess I should...introduce myself...or something. I don't know. I've never kept a journal before. I like to write, but I never thought my life would be interesting enough to talk about. I mean, I guess it doesn't *have* to be interesting to write about. Like I said, this is just a distraction. It's to vent. This isn't for an audience.

...

I'm Kieran.

I'll be fifteen in December.

I start high school exactly one month from today.

My favorite band is Stay Sweet.

I'm pretty much your stereotypical emo kid. I'm really skinny, not really that tall, but...not so short either, I guess. I'm super pale and have long, black hair, but it isn't naturally black; I dye it.

My eyes are blue [but sometimes they look more green].

I'm sorry; it feels kinda weird writing about myself like this, so I don't know exactly what to say. I'm usually better at noticing the details of other people or things around me.

...

12

My family and I moved here to Pennsylvania just a couple months ago at the very start of the summer. Our house had just been built. At the time, it still smelled of the mixture of fresh paint and hot adhesive that keeps the crown moldings together.

I don't know how much this place cost my parents, but it's hardly anything to brag about if you ask me. We moved from California, a progressive, forward-thinking state with all the bells and whistles, to this vast wasteland of blandness they call King's Valley. King's Valley, Pennsylvania is a small, stuffy lakeside hamlet, a getaway for the affluent suburbanites who don't want to live within the city limits of Philadelphia, but also don't want to live in a hunting lodge out in the middle of nowhere.

Our town *is* sort of in the middle of nowhere, though, in the boondocks of Berks County, about forty minutes from Philly. It's just an exit off Route 222. If you haven't heard of it, I'm not surprised. Besides the mall and Castlegate Skate Park, we don't have any landmarks, and there aren't any notable people from the area as far as I know [*big* celebrities, at least]. In the summer, the town's population reaches its peak when the older, retired snowbird residents return from their winters spent at beachfront homes in Florida in exchange for a few hot months beside the lake. While I'm yet to experience this place in its off-season, I predict what little there is to do here now will lower to an even bleaker landscape lacking any appeal.

Our house is a federal style. With Dad's promotion from Senior Manager to Director of the Chamberlain & Reed law firm came our brick McMansion on Skyview Drive. A personalized door knocker hangs on the front door, the embossed lettering spelling out in a fancy font, *"The Northrups."* The kitchen is fucking enormous and stocked with high-end stainless-steel appliances. There's no way either of my parents have any idea of how to use all the fancy gadgets down there that are pretty much just for show. It's so sickeningly posh.

My older brother, Justin, got the largest of the bedrooms besides Mom and Dad, and his room is attached to mine via this large walk-in closet that doubles as a sort of secret hallway. If we were younger, I could imagine the two of us spending hours in there as it would make a great hiding spot, a place for two brothers to pretend a wonderland of some kind existed beyond the closet doors…but those days are long over.

Tristan LaFerriere

My room is quite different from my brother's. Unlike the dark blue walls of Justin's, mine are gray. In fact, my entire room is gray. Gray carpet, gray walls [*Smoked Charcoal* was the official name on the paint swatch], gray drapes, gray dresser. The bedspread, the sheets, the pillows, my La-Z-Boy. All gray. I even painted the ceiling gray despite Mom's wishes against it. Because she spends her days as a realtor staging identical homes to our own to sell all over King's Valley's newest luxury subdivisions, she's declared herself the expert in decorating, which is why she took it upon herself to be in charge of putting the décor together in this house.

I know what you're probably thinking: *Oh, this poor rich kid. What a shame it must be to suffer through the torture of living in the upper middle-class suburbs. How horrible it must be to be forced to have a lobster dinner at the King's Valley Country Club every Saturday night.*

It's not that; it really isn't. Mom and Dad have worked their asses off for years to give all this shit to my brother and me, so I don't want to come off as ungrateful for what they've done for us. We've always undoubtedly lived very comfortable lives.

It's me that's the problem. I'm not comfortable with myself. I don't think I really ever have been, but I especially don't like what my life has become after what happened earlier today.

I have trouble making friends. Even when we lived back in California, I didn't have much of a go-to group to hang out with or confide in. Sure, there were the few who I always paired up with for group projects and sat with at lunch, but no one who would actually take the initiative to call me first.

King's Valley has already proven to be even more of a lonely place for a kid like me. Outcasts simply don't exist here. It's a realm for handsome, successful professionals.

All this started in June just a week or so after we first moved in. My room was still littered with cardboard boxes that I simply didn't have the energy to empty because it would just remind me of what I was leaving behind on the other side of the country. I spent my whole life in one house, that same postmodern dwelling in the hills of Pacific Palisades that offered so much more character than the stale carbon copy homes of King's Valley. This transition was far too quick, and

badly timed. It also isn't easy meeting new people when you're the first house built in your subdivision and the first family to move in, too. Since that day, other houses have gone up and new families have relocated to the upscale Belmont Hill Estates community, but I don't fit in with these people.

My brother, on the other hand...

Oh, he's doing just fine here. Justin is going to be a senior next month and he's always been the foil to my existence. He's everything I'm not. Handsome. No, I can't even say handsome. Justin is *beautiful*. His dark brown eyes match his silky long hair, and his body is toned in just the right places so he isn't a skinny dork like me, but also not a garish-looking athlete who's obviously just trying to show off.

He *is* an athlete, though. He's been playing soccer since he was five, which is what has always made him a local celebrity. We've been here less than three months and I can already see that he'll be a big deal here, too. It only took him a week to make a new friend, and it was this boy, Eric Gleason, who became the gateway acquaintance to introduce him to the posse of people who would define my brother's new identity.

Eric Gleason...

Eric lives in another subdivision across town where the cheapest, "shitty" houses start in the low millions. His father drives a Lamborghini Gallardo, which Eric claims he will be inheriting by the end of the year.

Eric's father is founder and CEO of the "Gleason's" chain of supermarkets that competes with the locally known Redner's Markets. Justin's told me that Eric's mother had a recurring role on some sitcom in the '80s thanks to her father being a television executive. I guess the royalties from the show's reruns added to her inheritance from him plus the success of Eric's father's grocery business are enough for them to be lying back and relaxing with their expensive toys in the heart of King's Valley's finest neighborhood.

Like my brother, Eric's wardrobe consists of mostly polos from Hollister and Abercrombie & Fitch. Finding out that we come from Pacific Palisades made him want to be Justin's friend even more. Eric's done his share of modeling for surfing magazines and

Strawbridge's or some other northeastern department store chain. He's already supposedly been accepted to Yale to pursue law to follow in the footsteps of his father's father. I don't really see the connection between those two accomplishments, but let's just say he seems to be really fucking successful in every department. Eric Gleason may just be a step above my brother and that's really saying something.

He and Justin met at the skate park I was telling you about. Don't ask me why my brother would go there since he's never skated a day in his life, but from what I've heard, this place isn't just for skaters. It's about the closest thing to a teen hangout that you'll find in King's Valley, so it's naturally where everyone goes to chill on Friday nights.

I opted not to go when Justin invited me along that week or so after we moved in. I was surprised he even invited me. I mean, we get along fairly well as far as brothers go, but he has a reputation to keep, and having his little emo brother to drag around would tarnish his first impression in this town almost immediately.

Instead, I spent the rest of the evening watching TV in our sunroom just off the living room. While Howie Mandel repeatedly asked, *"Deal or no deal?"*, I sat at the edge of the pool table in one of our dining room chairs. I rolled billiard balls down the green surface, catching them as they bounced back while imagining what I might've been missing out on at The Skate Park.

I heard Justin come home around ten. By then, I was in bed, thumbing through the latest issue of *Alternative Press*, and rubbing my dick to the images of boy bands.

Yes, I'm gay and no, nobody knows. No one.

I found out the following morning that Justin met Eric while he stood watching skaters doing whatever types of tricks they do on ramps. Eric exchanged his cell number with my brother, wanted to hang out again [Who didn't with Justin?]. He ended up coming over to our house a few days later, dropped off in that hideous Lambo that made Mom's crystal rattle in our dining room hutch when his father drove away.

I won't lie; I found Eric to be pretty damn hot even the first time I saw him that day. His hair is medium-length, platinum blonde, and he has a bit of peach fuzz at the tip of his chin. I remember the pink

polo he was wearing while he and Justin shot a few games of pool in the sunroom [his popped collar was the only visual cue that should have tipped me off that there was a bit of douchiness underneath the surface].

I laid on the couch and pretended to watch TV while I viewed the two seventeen-year-old boys circling the billiard table with their cues.

As rich as Eric's family is, he actually seemed to be quite humble. And he was polite to me. He shook my hand when he came through our door, made attempts to include me in their conversations, even smiled at me like I was someone interesting.

That couldn't have been real.

And then the ultimate twist: did I want to play a game of pool with him? I didn't even look up from the couch because there was no fucking way that this hot blonde surfer-looking guy wanted to do something with me. But he did. And my brother even sat out the next game so Eric and I could play.

He kicked my ass, of course. I never win anything. I was probably too distracted with my eyes focusing on the short glimpses of his pelvic lines. They would briefly peek as his shirt lifted with each lean across the table to make a shot at the cue ball. Blonde hair on his head, but dark, almost black, body hair decorated what I could see above his waistline. Eric was a work of art to me, and that was what prompted me to suggest we all go swimming the next time he came over.

July 16th: Eric did, in fact, come over to go in our pool. It was my excuse to see him in a bathing suit. What a sight! I spent most of the hot afternoon laying back in one of our lawn chairs. I was wearing my Ray-Bans and letting my pasty skin sizzle in the sun [a rare occurrence]. Justin and Eric raced each other from one side of the pool to the other or fought over the single inflatable raft. Yellowcard played on Dad's boombox just over the white noise hum that the pool filter and air-conditioning unit were making while builders in hardhats put the finishing touches on the roof of the new stucco house that was going up next door.

As the sun was going down, the three of us spent about an hour in the jacuzzi sipping lemonades. Sitting so close to Eric with both of us in nothing but our swimming trunks really got me going, but thankfully the swirling, bubbling water hid any evidence of my arousal. Meanwhile, the scent of cooking burgers danced from the deck as Dad fired up his new grill for our dinner.

It was a good day. We ended it by playing Texas hold 'em at the kitchen table for a few hours. Then we sat at the end of the driveway, chatting, while we waited for Eric's dad's Lambo to come roaring up the street.

When it finally did, Eric gave me a "bro hug" before he left, and for once, I thought...

So, this is what it's like to be a part of something?

...

Tyler Kirkland stepped into the picture two weeks ago, near the end of July, when back-to-school ads started flooding commercial breaks and cardboard merchandise displays in the supermarkets were boasting of September's soon arrival.

I could have survived with just having Eric around. Even if he were technically really only my brother's friend, I wouldn't have minded one bit. He was eye candy, at least, and seemed to be genuinely nice even to an emo kid like me.

I added him on Myspace [My seventeenth friend; I'm on a roll!] and was shocked to see that he's even written some poetry after I'd admittedly stalked his profile a bit. I thought I had to be the only guy under twenty-one in King's Valley to understand the concept of iambic pentameter, but I was wrong. A beautiful, athletic blonde boy with millions in his trust fund had something creative going on in that brain of his.

Then you have Tyler Kirkland.

Tyler is the type of person who I've feared my whole life, but simultaneously never knew actually existed. I thought they only wrote these types of characters as bullies into after school specials.

18

Let me put it simply; I know I'm different, but I've never really been all that intimidated by being different if that makes sense. I might not fit in and I might be quiet, but it's never felt like such a big deal before.

Tyler, though…he's the polar opposite of me in ways that make me feel uncomfortable.

Tyler judges. Tyler's what Urban Dictionary would call a tool. Tyler's the comic relief that was written into a film that didn't really need the extra character. Tyler interrupts meaningful conversations to talk about the last shit he took. Tyler drives an old Ford Mustang Cobra with one of those "fart cans" attached to it in an attempt to make it sound more badass.

And somehow, Tyler and the seemingly much classier Eric have been friends since elementary school, years before us Northrups moved into town or before I even understood why I was different from the other boys on the playground.

I first met Tyler when Justin and I drove over to Eric's in my brother's brand-new Pontiac Solstice. Justin was blasting some new Matisyahu song on the CD player when we pulled into the driveway of the Gleasons' villa-style mansion on Coleman Terrace in the gated community across town.

Eric greeted us at the door, looking hot as ever in his athletic shorts and shirt. The black cotton outlined every shape of his physique, and I could totally see his bulge. He held a can of Rockstar energy drink like the cocktail of a fancy house party host as he brought us into the basement, which is currently in mid-renovation so they can add a full bar, wine cellar, and walk-in humidor [Yes, you read that correctly. They're that kind of rich]. This is where Tyler was sitting on a few paint cans beside his very fraternal twin brother, Evan.

I'll be honest; Tyler is actually cute. He'd be much cuter, though, if his personality didn't get in the way so much. His hair is dark brown, shoulder length, thick and wavy. He has green eyes and a slightly toned body [not the perfection that is Justin or Eric, but still obviously born an athlete]. He wears American Eagle, his skin is quite tan, and he sounds just like Jeff Spicoli from *Fast Times at Ridgemont High*.

19

I sat on some boxes that probably contained hibernating Christmas decorations while Justin and I watched the others finish a poker game before we started a new one.

I felt like too much of an outsider already. Just having Justin and Eric around wasn't so much, but four preppy guys against one closeted gay kid wearing a Secondhand Serenade shirt? Suddenly, all my traits of being an outcast were amplified. I was the serious black sheep of the bunch.

In addition to that natural tension in the room between two clashing cliques, Tyler just made everything feel so on edge. I can't describe it, but just imagine a guy who judges everything you say, every move you make. If I didn't shuffle the deck as flawlessly as he did, then I was inexperienced, and he'd have to give me a demonstration to emphasize how much better he was at it. If I hadn't listened to the latest Gym Class Heroes album, then I was living under a fucking rock, and when I answered his question of what my favorite music was, he laughed because the band Stay Sweet *"are a bunch of emo fags"*.

Then the sex stories came. Each guy in the room tried to outdo the other on how much experience they've had with fondling a tit, getting jerked off in a hot tub, etc.

Eric's story made me jealous of whoever this Jenna girl from Colorado is. Blew him. He described in detail how he came in her mouth, and she swallowed.

If only he knew how many times I've fantasized about doing the same thing to him...

Evan, who I'm surprised is even related to Tyler, told the truth. He's done stuff before, but hasn't done *it* yet. His biggest admitted accomplishment was feeling up some girl named Lauren in a fitting room at The Bon-Ton in The Berkshire Mall.

Evan is quieter than the others. I liked to think of him as a preppy version of me [personality wise, at least, since unlike me, he's good-looking] who adds just a few more words to his sentences and smiles once in a while. I was thinking I could maybe be friends with him. He didn't seem to care so much about the image and reputation

these other boys were obsessed with despite his natural success in looking good.

My brother's story made me feel slightly awkward. Justin reminisced about the time he and Courtney, a girl from back west, hooked up at the movies when he took her on a date to see *Wedding Crashers*.

His fingers are up inside her wet pussy, she's got a hand around his hard dick, he blows a load in his jeans, and she fucking licks *up the evidence...*

Tyler discussed how just last month he went to Key West for a soccer tournament, met this girl Brittainy from Miami Beach, they went back up to the hotel room while his parents were still out, she blew him on the bed, he regained his strength after one round, and proceeded to fuck her. [And the whole room applauded without clapping].

"What about you, Kieran?"

The question came from Tyler after his trump card of a story, his expression already understanding that I haven't even had my first kiss yet. There was something about his smirk that suggested he knew my secret. He knew I'd rather have my hand down a guy's shorts than up a girl's skirt.

All eyes were on me.

...

"I...haven't ever...hooked up with anyone," I responded hesitantly.

Tyler was the only one who laughed.

"Probably the only one left in King's Valley who hasn't."

And as contagious as a yawn, the others followed suit with their own laughter. The chuckles from everyone, including my brother, made me realize that I didn't really belong to this group after all, even more so after Tyler tried to get me to explain what types of girls I like. Which celebrities would I bang? He ran upstairs to grab Eric's junior

21

yearbook and was trying to get me to pick out which girls from their class I found the hottest.

Hmm...that guy Luke Griffin looks pretty cute. I'll go with him.

I don't like Tyler.

...

Last week, Justin went to Tyler and Evan's place to spend the night and I honestly felt a hint of...I don't know...emptiness...or something.

For some reason, I wanted to go...and that's really weird because I'm usually alone [and I've gotten used to that], but that little taste of being part of something from the days with Eric coming over and making me feel like anything other than an outcast for once...that was an addicting feeling even for a comfortable loner like me.

Even if I didn't like Tyler and didn't feel comfortable around him, I still felt left out not being invited. Lying on the couch that night in the sunroom and watching reruns of *Pee-Wee's Playhouse* on Adult Swim was pretty dull in comparison to what I imagined was going on at Tyler and Evan's house. Coincidentally, the episode revolved around Pee-Wee being upset that he hadn't been invited to a birthday party.

I decided to call Eric.

"Please enjoy the music while your party is reached."

My right ear was served with a low-quality clipping of Vivaldi's *Spring*, an obvious default ringback tone he had never bothered to change, while I sat on the floor between the sofa and floor lamp.

He didn't answer.

Was he at Tyler's, too?

Fifteen minutes later, I tried calling him again. Retrospectively, I see that was a pretty stupid thing to do because it probably made me look pathetically desperate to have a friend.

Again, he didn't answer.

This is going to sound really lame [and clichéd], but I cried myself to sleep that night.

...

A few days later, Tyler [Now Justin's number two friend on Myspace after Eric as I've been demoted to third] invited us all [all being a loose term here; he invited my brother and my brother invited me] to his place to chill and maybe do a little "football" in the backyard.

I enthusiastically, of course, agreed to go.

I wish I fucking hadn't...

Justin and I pulled into Tyler and Evan's gravel driveway on Orchard Road in a section of King's Valley I can only describe as "less desirable" meaning most of the houses in the area cost about half a million dollars. I'm not so sure the Kirkland house fits into that category, though.

Their house is an older split-level built in the '60s or '70s. The white paint was clearly peeling away in chips, wind chimes were tolling, a tattered POW/MIA and American flag were hanging from the front porch, and Tyler's car's rear-end was exposed in the detached garage. It was desecrated with a number of King's Valley Red Devils [the local high school mascot] bumper stickers.

I felt nervous getting out of the car. I took off my Ray-Bans and scanned the property like I had a sixth sense that this was an evil place [I should have trusted my instincts]. Even walking to their front door felt risky, like I might step on a landmine between the driveway and the porch, or the elm trees surrounding their lot might reach down to attack me.

Inside, the party had already begun without us. Tyler and Eric faced each other off in a game of *Dance Dance Revolution*. Evan was on the family computer laughing at some video called *Muffins* on a struggling-to-buffer YouTube. Their father, a middle-aged soccer coach with a ponytail, sat at the kitchen table and tried to concentrate on paying bills or something. The shirt he was wearing matched one of the

Red Devils bumper stickers on Tyler's car. A half-eaten chicken potpie sat on the table in front of him. He seemed unapproachable.

I spent the next half hour attempting to make small talk with Evan while the others continued with the dancing game. He didn't say much, but I was able to get some info out of him. Turns out we both enjoy reading, but the only reason he knows anything about Orwell is because of the required summer English class he had to take in order to be passed into the tenth grade.

After *Dance Dance Revolution* had become repetitive, Tyler showed us to the bedroom that he and Evan share at the end of the mauve-carpeted hall. We passed by open doors to other rooms: bedrooms, guest bathrooms. The basement door had a piece of paper taped to it with the words *"Keep Out"* written on it in black Sharpie, a failed deterrent that only managed to pique my interest in what could have possibly prompted the creation of such a warning.

In addition to the two unmade double beds and *Clerks II* poster on the wall, their "pad," as Tyler likes to call it, was equipped with a mini fridge and microwave stained with pizza roll insides. Several video game systems and a DVD player were all entangled within the vines of controller wires so lazily stashed away below the dusty tube TV. Next to the TV was a stack of DVDs that consisted mostly of Will Ferrell comedies.

The centerpiece of the room, however, was the large terrarium that took up a good portion of the space, housing their pet boa constrictor who peered from the smudged glass at us through its opaquely milky blue eyes.

While Justin was intensely curious about the animal, I stood stiff in the corner near Tyler and Evan's messy closet as the other boys surrounded the snake's habitat, each on their knees and leaning in close to get a glimpse of it. They all looked like a group of worshippers kneeling with respect to this sacred creature they had traveled to make an offering to.

Tyler looked over his shoulder and flashed a stupid grin at me.

"Yo, my snake's single, Kieran," he said. "Come over here and she'll suck your dick."

Per usual, his comment magically made the group laugh like he was their king and failure to chuckle would result in their executions. I kept my eyes on the carpet where I caught sight of a few cigarette burn circles near my red Converse sneakers.

"I'm good," I said uncomfortably.

I looked up and my eyes met the boa's over the shoulders of the others. It was as if she were reaching out to me in spirit and trying to tell me she was just as uncomfortable around these people as I was. I felt bad for the reptile; her existence was no different than a zoo exhibit for the same stupid patrons every day.

...

Once it was dark out, the others decided a game of manhunt would be more appropriate than football.

You know the game? Different teams go hiding and slowly hunt the others until the last person standing wins for their team. Think of it as "extreme hide and go seek." Tyler and Evan's house is perfect for it because they have a good chunk of land for a backyard that extends into the woods.

Since there were only five of us, the teams couldn't be split evenly. So, lucky me...I got to be on a team with Tyler, alone, while Justin, Eric, and Evan were our rivals. I was surprised that there weren't any protests over me being on anyone's team since I'm so used to being the last one picked in gym class. In fact, Tyler's the one who established who was going with who, so why did he choose me if he didn't care for me all that much?

"I've got a good spot," he said once the others ventured off to find their own hiding places. "Stay with me."

I went along with it and followed him through the backyard, past their mother's overgrown fenced-in garden, through the trees, and soon far enough away from the house that the back-porch light was just a flickering speck in the night. Tyler carried a flashlight that he grabbed from the kitchen drawer. I had to follow him closely since we were getting deep into the woods, and this was all foreign ground to me.

"Shit!"

A sticker bush hooked onto my bare arm, and when I pulled away, I could feel it tearing my skin.

I just knew there'd be blood on my white Stay Sweet shirt.

It felt like we hiked at least half a mile, maybe more. An orchestra of summer bugs scored the scene. The humidity alone made me feel trapped and suffocated. I was under a heavy blanket of heat.

Tyler dragged me to a little clearing through a cluster of thick trees and he set the flashlight face up against a stump so that the little space we occupied was bright enough for us to see. I sat on the slightly damp grass across from him and I could feel the wetness through my jeans while he checked to ensure his phone was silenced.

"Well, this sure is fun," I said sarcastically, resting my head against the soft bark of a tree trunk behind me. I cringed at the thought of a thousand mosquitos feeding off me. My exposed ankles already itched.

Tyler peered through the branches to see if there was any sign of the others. Not at all. It was like we were the only two people in the whole world.

"If I hear anyone, I'm turning off the light," he warned. "If I do, get down low on the ground and don't say a fucking word."

"Sure."

My ass was getting wetter from the grass the longer I sat there. Suddenly, the idea of being back in my room, alone, didn't seem so undesirable. This is the shit I was missing out on? I'd take reruns of *Pee-Wee's Playhouse* over this any night.

"So, you've really never hooked up with anyone?" Tyler asked a few minutes later.

...

"...Wh-what?"

"You've never hooked up with anyone before? For real?"

I sighed.

"No."

"Dude, you've got to find a chick. At least get laid before you start high school."

I chuckled.

"Then I've only got a month."

"It's all good. Summer's the best time to meet girls. You go to The Skate Park?"

"No."

"But you've been there?"

"No."

"You've...never been to The Skate Park?" [Sacrilegious words in King's Valley for anyone under the age of eighteen].

"Nope."

"You seriously need to go, man. It's, like, where everyone hangs out."

"So I've heard."

...

"So," I said after a long pause. "You really had...sex with that girl in Florida?"

"Yep." Tyler flicked some hair out of his eyes as a model would, as if I had just reminded him of how dope he was in comparison to a loser like me.

I laughed nervously and then made the biggest fucking mistake of my life.

"So, uh...how big is your..."

"Huh?"

...

"Your...dick...how big is it? Like...do the girls like it?" [Had to disguise it as a legit question rather than just a curiosity, because the truth is that it *was* a curiosity. Being alone with another boy in such a secluded place was like a spark that ignited inside me. I couldn't stop it.

"It's pretty big," Tyler responded.

He shrugged, checking his phone, and I started to feel sick to my stomach because why the fuck would I ask Tyler Kirkland something like that? It was basically blowing my cover to the last person I wanted to know, but some stupid compulsive urge forced the words out of my mouth.

"What about yours?" he asked.

My heart started beating maniacally.

"My dick?"

"Yeah."

I was shivering even in the summer heat.

"It's...average, I guess. I don't know."

"You never measured it?"

"...No."

"Show me."

"...What?"

"Show me."

"You want to see it?"

28

"Yeah, I mean...we can compare."

This sick drop in my gut was a rush, a combination of excitement and extreme nervousness a reaction to a pending scenario I'd not yet experienced. Tyler, the immature piece of shit he is, was still undeniably cute. And I was gonna see his dick.

"Okay," I said, literally gulping. "Hold on."

I undid my studded belt a little too quickly, unbuttoned, and unzipped my skinny jeans. My hands were visibly shaking while Tyler watched. Emo guys don't just go flashing their dicks around. The whole point of the look is to cover up as much as possible [Hence why I was wearing jeans in the middle of summer and why my hair is always in my face].

Tyler grabbed the flashlight and shined it right on my crotch as I pulled down on the front of my boxers to show my junk to him.

"Cool," he said.

"I'm...a grower," I said, trying to make up for the fact that it wasn't all that impressive looking in its soft state. Of all the parts of my body that I feel insecure about, my penis has always been the biggest [no pun intended] of my hang-ups, but unlike my face or my skinny legs, I've never had to hide my penis because it's supposed to be hidden.

"Nice," Tyler said after looking at my dick for a while. "Here's mine."

He pulled his loose athletic shorts down and his flaccid cock flopped out. I was so nervous at the thought of me getting hard at the sight of it and then he'd definitely know my secret [unless he already did, and this was all just a tease].

"Cool," I said. Seemed to be the safe response since it's what he said. I mean, what are you supposed to say when someone shows you their genitals? I don't think there's really any written etiquette on that.

I was still staring pretty intently at his dick as he ever so slightly began to...play with it.

29

"How big does yours get when it's hard?" he asked me.

"I...don't know...like...six inches?"

"I'm, like, seven."

And we didn't say a word for the next five minutes. We just started jerking off in front of each other like it was the natural thing to do.

Tyler was surprisingly not lying about the size of his dick like I would've assumed someone of his temperament would do. He *did* get pretty big as he got hard. Mine stuck out its full six inches or so and I was surprised how quickly I was feeling that tingling sensation since I can usually last pretty long. Watching another guy do it in person was just different. If you told me the first day I met Tyler that he'd be the first person I ever mutually masturbated with, though, I would've thought you were fucking insane.

"I'm gonna cum," I announced, thinking fast of where I would shoot my load.

"Go for it."

At the absolute last second, I decided to stuff my dick back in my underwear and I came into them. It felt good as it always does, my body twitched, my crotch became warm, and then, as the rush began to wear off, I started to feel really fucking uncomfortable. I just jerked off in front of a guy I didn't really even get along with that much in the middle of the woods only a few days after meeting him. What the fuck was I thinking? I was basically digging my own grave.

What made it even more awkward was that he pulled his shorts back up and started to stand while a blotchy wet circle grew in the center of my boxers.

"What are you...doing?" I asked, out of breath. Beads of sweat were dripping from my forehead, and suddenly, my senses redirected back to my itching ankles.

"We should start heading back. If they can't find us out here, we'll be here all night."

...

"Aren't you gonna..."

"What?"

"Aren't you gonna...finish?"

"Nah. It's taking too long. Come on."

I re-zipped my jeans, stumbled getting up from the post-orgasm dizziness, and followed Tyler back toward the house in a silent walk of shame.

...

"What the fuck were you jerking off in the woods for?!"

I'd never seen my brother play the role of a bully before until we were driving back home an hour after the game of manhunt was officially declared dead.

"I didn't jerk off!" I lied. "Tyler's just...picking on me."

"Tyler doesn't even fucking know you, Kieran. Why would he make that shit up? And why would you just randomly whip it out in front of him? That's just fucking weird."

"I...didn't."

Explaining how everything went down would be too complicated. Just saying it never happened was much easier. I would have assumed that with Tyler's jackass of a personality, I would be at least somewhat believable when trying to say that he was just making up stories to fuck with me.

Even my own brother didn't believe me, though. He was slowly finding ways to have nothing in common with me anymore.

...

"You just get back from the woods, dude?"

31

Tristan LaFerriere

Eric's lame remark made the rest of the group erupt in
laughter. I foolishly, again, accepted my brother's invitation to meet
with the other guys in the soccer field behind King's Valley High
School, the building where I'd soon be spending eight hours a day, five
days a week for the next four years.

I'm still not sure why suddenly Justin encouraged me to be
part of the group for a day again. I hadn't been included for a while
following the whole manhunt thing, and it shocked me when he came
into my room, nonchalantly mentioning he was meeting the other guys
to hang. I don't even want to think that he wanted me to be there just
because it was all a set-up or something.

"Shut up," I said in response to Eric, trying to make my tone
sound as if I were laughing with them rather than being laughed at, but
really, now Eric, the one who I thought might have had some
redeeming qualities...he was on their side now.

Fuck that; he was always on their side. I was just too stupid to
notice it before.

I watched Justin, Eric, Tyler, and Evan kick a soccer ball
around for a while. I just sat near the goal, plucking grass out of the
ground and going over in my head at least a hundred times why Tyler
would have even tried to make the whole jerking-off-in-the-woods
thing seem the way it was. How could he have been so confident that I
wouldn't have said he's the one who suggested I whip it out? How
could he have been so sure I wouldn't rat him out, too? Why did he
want to see my dick in the first place? Was he secretly gay or did
straight dudes do shit like that all the time? Nothing made sense to me.
It didn't matter because Tyler's, for some reason, naturally liked. They'd
always believe him over me.

"I've got a game!" Tyler said after a good twenty minutes of
senseless running in circles with the ball. "And it's called..."

He proceeded to moon the rest of us, exposing the tan lines
around his sickly pale ass.

"Butt Kicks!"

The others erupted in a locker room tone of laughter.

32

"What's 'Butt Kicks'?" I asked.

Butt Kicks consists of everyone lining up in the middle of the soccer goal. Everyone standing moons a kicker and the kicker attempts to kick the soccer ball and hit one of the mooners in the ass. Whoever gets hit directly in the ass with a soccer ball...gets pissed on.

Yes, that's correct. These were Tyler's instructions. The kicker rotates.

Fast forward a few minutes and I was standing in front of the soccer ball, unsure of why I agreed to do this shit. Probably because if I ended up succeeding, maybe I would've been accepted into this group? Was this some kind of initiation? Did everyone else in this circle of friends also have to do this before they were considered a member of the club?

The bare asses of Justin, Eric, Tyler, and Evan stared back at me. Normally, I would've been delighted at such a sight, but today, I was determined to aim that fucking ball right at Tyler's scrawny ass and then...piss on him? Whatever. I just wanted to defeat him.

I missed.

We rotated.

Evan missed.

We rotated.

Tyler didn't miss.

Guess who he hit right in the ass?

Explosive laughter from everyone as I went face first into the net. And then to my horror, Eric found an empty Snapple bottle in a nearby trashcan, a conveniently placed weapon of choice. Tyler was unzipping, ready to piss in the bottle and toss it all over me.

I started running...panicking. He was really doing this. I was really gonna get a bottle of fucking piss thrown on me. And even my

own brother was cheering him on as he chased me around the field with the bottle, taunting me, laughing...and laughing...and laughing.

I fell down once, tore my jeans at the knee.

There was blood.

I succeeded in running across the field, back to Justin's car in the otherwise empty student parking lot still deserted this time of year. I got in the car just as Tyler caught up to me. My brother stupidly left the doors unlocked. I hit the button to lock them from the inside.

I was safe.

No.

I wasn't fucking safe.

Just outside the car were four soon-to-be high school seniors laughing their asses off at me while I sat and bawled like a fucking baby. Justin could clearly see that I was crying, too, but that didn't stop him.

In fact, I'd say he was laughing the hardest.

Chapter Two
Tuesday, September 5th, 2006

Dear Journal,

A little bit about Stay Sweet: they officially became a band on January 17th, 2004, and when I say "officially," I mean that it was the day they were signed on to Fueled by Ramen and were no longer just a garage band in Baltimore that played the occasional show at a local theater.

They were formed a couple years prior by lead singer, Matt Daniels, and his fraternal twin high school buddies, Sean and Clay Stone, who are on guitar and bass, respectively. Nick Wall, the current drummer, came later after several lineup changes in the early days, and existing recordings with any of the original drummers are pretty rare unless you dig deep.

Their first studio album, *Stay Sweet*, was released just last year in October. It contains such classics as the signature song of the band, "We're All Going to Paris", "Delilah", and some weird experimental rough cuts as bonus tracks where all you can hear is Sean Stone yelling, *"Matt, get me a fucking Twizzler!"* in-between takes.

Album No. 2, *Nitro*, came out in June of this year and was less of the rough stuff that their debut was known for. *Nitro* contained a mixture of happy, *"driving-with-your windows-down"* music [direct quote from an interview with Matt Daniels about the album] and some pretty heavy material that's a bit of a stretch for most emo boy bands. "Drink This", track six, is about as close to what many would consider an "emo love ballad", but it definitely isn't a song about love...at all.

Nitro was released just around the time that we moved to King's Valley, and there's no doubt that listening to it over and over again while I was shut up in my room for the remainder of the summer is part of the reason I'm still alive. It's just something about Matt Daniels and that voice of his that makes me somehow think that everything's going to be okay despite the circumstances...after all the Tyler and Eric and Evan bullshit.

Album No. 3, *Mandragora*, is coming soon.

Friday.

35

I've been counting down the days since last month as if I have a special emo advent calendar for the event. Think of a miniature version of some gritty venue with the likenesses of Patrick Stump and Gerard Way behind the cardboard windows that they'd sell at Hot Topic.

According to *Alternative Press*, this is the album that's really going to make Stay Sweet a household name [as if *Nitro* didn't already do that for them]. They've been on the magazine's official *"List of 100 Bands You Absolutely Need to Know In 2006!!!!"* since the day that album was released. I've got the special June edition of the magazine. Stay Sweet made the front cover and now it's my bible. Even if I've read all the articles and interviews over a hundred times already, it doesn't get old to me. It's just like reading your favorite book over and over again.

I like to imagine I'm there. I'm the interviewer and Matt Daniels is inviting me on all the band's adventures. They're doing photo shoots for promotional material in a Food Lion parking lot or playing an acoustic show on the sidewalk in front of a tattoo parlor. Reading about the bands you can't get enough of is like reading fiction. There's a way these interviews make the whole thing sound like a fairytale. These ultra-cool dudes are living the life I could only ever dream of living in a square shithole like King's Valley, a place where the hottest spot in town is a former Laneco converted into a lame skatepark that sells soggy pizza in its snack bar.

Last night, I was trying to forget that it was the last day of summer. In the morning, I'd be forced to go out and discover the world beyond my bedroom for the first time in thirty days. YouTube helped me get away from that reality. I'm so thankful for camera phones and the amateur footage capturing Stay Sweet's shows as they tour the country. I don't know when I'll be able to see them live, if ever, so I'll take it. King's Valley isn't exactly a thumbtack on the map, so for now, I just get under the covers, stare at my laptop screen, and try to pretend that I'm there in whatever delightfully shitty old venue they're playing.

I often dream that I'm at one of their shows. It's always the same, too. I'm being carried by this huge crowd of people, and I actually belong with them. They all understand me even though I don't know a single one of them personally. I'm still the same Kieran

Northrup who I am in real life...and in the dream, that's okay. They don't judge me. They like me. They accept me.

The venue is cavernous and dark.

Red lights in the ceiling.

Red paint.

Red ventilation and exposed ductwork.

The red ceiling leaks.

Matt Daniels, Sean Stone, Clay Stone, Nick Wall.

The crowd carries me toward them like a group of worshippers offering a gift to their Gods.

I'm smiling...I'm fucking...smiling.

My head starts to lean back just enough so that I can see what's up ahead.

The stage, upside-down in my field of vision...and those four silhouetted figures making the crowd go wild from within the clouds created by the fog machines in the pit have materialized from the manmade mist.

I'm especially excited to finally see HIM. That very familiar shadow starts to lean down. He kneels at the foot of the stage, and I can see his long, brown hair flowing like he just took a hair dryer to it even though he should be sweating from this active performance.

Matt Daniels reaches out to me from the colorful smoke.

He's going to pull me up on stage...

He's bringing me into their world...

Yes...

Yes...

…

I woke up this morning to the sound of my alarm. The first thing I saw was the spinning ceiling fan as the red ceiling of the dream venue blurred into the gray of my bedroom's paint.

I groaned, disoriented and struggling to see the digital rainbow numbers of my Discovery Channel alarm clock as my vision slowly began to focus.

Six-forty-five. My first alarm in this new house.

I banged on the snooze button.

My first day of high school. *Welcome to Hell; I will be your guide.*

For the next fifteen minutes, I could hear the house around me, simultaneously starting up as if a large key were protruding from the garage, and every morning, at the same time, the hand of God reached down from the sky, wound it up, and us little mechanical figurines started springing to life inside. Each member of the Northrup family did their same predetermined actions at the strike of the hour.

Not me, though. My predetermined action was to stay in bed and wish I was dead.

Justin came into my room shortly after, all showered and wearing his best pink Hollister polo and tan cargo shorts from Pac Sun. His long hair was brushed impeccably as always, and the scent of whatever Banana Republic's latest fragrance is lingered as my brother nudged my shoulder.

"Get up, man."

I answered with a sleepy groan.

"Come on. I'm driving you. We leave in fifteen."

Justin proceeded to yank the cord to tear open the drapes of the large rear window of the room, letting in a sickening amount of harmful sunlight that marked an official start to the day. He did the same with the corner window next to my La-Z-Boy.

"I can't do this," I said, rubbing my eyes and struggling to sit up. My body felt heavy like I had just woken from anesthesia. Getting through this day was going to be impossible.

"Come on. I'm not fucking waiting for you. You can take the bus for all I care."

That was enough to motivate me just a tad. Fuck the bus.

Justin left the room, and I was forced to pick an outfit for my first day.

As little as I really care about much anymore, dressing has become a crucial factor in keeping up with the counterculture I follow. You want to wear something that expresses your personal association with the look, but you don't want to stand out, either, since the whole idea of an emo is being tucked into the corner shadows while you watch everyone else.

I dug through my side of the walk-in closet and flipped through the hangers until finally settling for a white Stay Sweet t-shirt with paint splatter design. Even though I hate showing off my legs, it was just too hot today for pants, so black jean shorts and my red and white Converse sneakers completed the look.

After giving myself a onceover in the full body mirror, I sprayed on some Axe [no time for a shower, and it didn't matter since I rinsed off the night before after applying a fresh coat of black dye to my hair]. I headed down the back stairs leading directly to the "open concept" family room and attached kitchen. Everyone else was already congregating around the island that also serves as a snack bar. My pre-packed backpack sat on the floor next to one of the empty stools conveniently, all that new OfficeMax bullshit inside.

Dad was on his Blackberry, arguing with someone from his office and just barely keeping his cool as Justin grabbed a Powerade from the fridge. Mom poured herself a cup of coffee with one hand and wiped down the granite counter with the other. She was dressed in her usual style of attire: cream designer blouse under a gray pantsuit, heels that clack menacingly against the floor with her stride, intense lipstick, gleaming earrings and matching necklace, gold ladies' watch, and those

perfectly manicured nails that always close the deal on another property.

I hope I don't grow up to be like her. If I have so much anxiety over doing nothing, I can't imagine what it must be like trying to keep up such an appearance. Her brown hair is dyed because at thirty-nine, she's already started going slightly gray from what I imagine is her obsession over perfection. Even Dad looks worn out by her these days.

I guess if I had to choose, I'd rather be like my dad. He's forty-one, but looks about thirty and boyish for his age behind the suit and tie. He dresses nice during the week [usually a brown Brooks Brothers suit or cashmere sweater over a collared shirt], but is all about his UCLA sweatshirt and a pair of sweatpants or shorts on the weekends. He's definitely the most Type B out of all of us.

"Morning, honey," Mom said, and then a good look at me as I sat in front of an empty, beckoning cereal bowl. "Kieran, are you really going to wear that?"

"...Yeah?"

"It's your first day of high school. You should put on something more presentable. I bought those nice button-downs and khakis for you, and you haven't even taken them out of the closet yet."

If my mom's words sound scripted, that's because I think they are. Everything that comes out of her mouth sounds like it's been carefully written out for a press release.

I didn't know how to respond to her distasteful comments on my choice of clothing, so it was safest just to say nothing. I loathe the whole WASP look and its wardrobe Mom has been adding to with each of her visits to Lord & Taylor. Every polo shirt or pair of tan shorts she's brought home still have the price tags hanging from them. I plan on keeping it that way.

"Just let him go the way he wants, Shannon."

Dad was off the phone and his tone suggested he was already exhausted even though the day hadn't really started. He gave me a little smile after rubbing the bridge of his nose. Dad doesn't smile much, but when he does, it makes him very handsome [actually, more like cute].

I'm surprised I'm saying that since so many people think I look a lot like him, and I don't consider myself good-looking at all. We *do* share a lot of features, though. My eyes are the same blue hue as his and when my hair isn't dyed completely black, it's just like his light brown [with a very slight red tint from the Irish roots].

Despite him being slightly taller than me, my father and I share an almost identical build, but he still qualifies as more of an athlete than me. Dad played tennis all four years of high school and any photos of him from that time in his life would make a great visual companion to the definition of a WASP. He was almost never seen without his letterman jacket in those days, the short, skinny, long auburn-haired tennis player from Pasadena that he was.

"Morning, Kier," he said to me. "How you feeling about today?"

He asked me this like he knew how miserable I was feeling. Did he? I felt the urge to cry because so much has built up in me this past summer, so much shit I want to say, but could never tell him or Mom.

"I...don't know," I said.

Dad waved an arm.

"You'll be fine."

"Just stay close to me and you won't die," Justin added. He was leaning against the snack bar and texting someone who I probably hate.

Mom sipped her coffee.

"Aren't you having any cereal?" she asked.

"No."

I was waiting for the cliched *"You have to eat"* follow-up speech, but thankfully, she gave up and just took the bowl away before she went on to discuss much more important matters with my father, like making sure the pool guys would come by next Saturday to close it

for the season, or to have the check written out for the weekly cleaning ladies tomorrow.

Justin and I climbed into his Pontiac after breakfast. When my brother opened the garage door, it was like the gates of Hell were engulfing me. The groaning hum of the motor pulling the spring only managed to magnify the threatening image.

This was it. I was no longer safe within the walls of our "suburban castle" I'd taken refuge in for so long.

I was hoping to listen to the new Cute Is What We Aim For album that came out in June to at least give me some comfort, but Justin insisted on that Matisyahu CD, *Youth*, again…the same thirteen songs he'd been listening to all summer. I wouldn't have minded so much if his music didn't remind me of his stupid friends.

My brother backed out of the garage, dumped the clutch, and darted down the driveway where he very nearly smashed into our brass lawn jockey. I looked out the window as we sailed down Skyview Drive, out of Belmont Hill Estates, and started going through town. We passed kids and teens waiting for their busses, people walking their dogs, female joggers with pink hats and their iPods. A line of cars waiting for their McDonald's coffees stretched out from the drive-thru onto the street.

Despite the busy atmosphere of downtown, this was King's Valley in the beginning of its off-season. Within a few weeks, these streets would be practically desolate with the arrival of fall.

We pulled into the chaos of King's Valley High's student parking lot about twelve or so minutes prior to the start of homeroom. I felt my blood pressure rise upon seeing the modern, anxiety-inducing architecture of the high school at the top of the hill, the perfect setting for the latest Disney Channel sitcom. The last time I was here was during the whole "Butt Kicks" fiasco last month. Now it was jam packed with local rich kids showing off their hand-me-down sports cars, and unlike a real Disney Channel sitcom setting, this place would have no laugh track.

"Hey!" my brother announced. "There's Tyler!"

My heart sank. There he was, walking across the lot with his usual douchebag stride. The son of a bitch...

Justin pressed on the horn a few times to get his attention, and I wished I could have turned invisible.

"Northrup! My man!"

Justin killed the engine and I struggled with the car door while he and Tyler gave each other their bro hugs as if they hadn't seen each other all year. I think Tyler had been over at the house only a few days ago with Evan for one of their long nights of Texas Hold 'Em at our kitchen table. While I avoided the group at all costs when they came over for the remainder of the summer, it seemed to me that Eric wasn't around quite as much anymore.

Tyler was growing on Justin. The two of them were more like brothers now than we were.

"Hi, Tyler," I said, and then immediately wondered why I said anything.

He thankfully ignored me, and I followed the two of them toward the high school's courtyard while they babbled about the World Cup, Italy's victory over France, and the shock that I, the vampire, had finally emerged from my keep after a month of seclusion.

I let the two of them wander off. I wasn't going to let Tyler bring me down any further. He's already done his damage. Just avoiding him is my best bet now even though I'd love more than anything to punch him in the face [as if I'd ever have that kind of courage].

Cliques of every kind were at every corner in the school courtyard. There were the skater dudes in their skullcaps playing hacky sack, a long-haired modern hippie with a septum piercing and a beanie playing guitar against one of the potted plants, the football players all huddled together and getting pumped up for the homecoming game this Friday.

I don't belong with any of these people. No other emo kids. No All Time Low shirts, fingerless gloves, or Tripp pants. No dyed hair, black fingernails, or snake bite piercings.

43

Tristan LaFerriere

I am alone.

The chaos that was the courtyard amplified to a million once I tripped through the frameless glass doors of the main entrance to this brand-new, puked-up mixture that was probably designed by a few quirky architects as some weird experimental collaboration.

Immediately to the left was the main office, another room unconcealed by its massive glass doors and windows. The ancient female secretaries seated at their desks inside were miserably typing and answering phone calls in what closely resembles what's going on in the background of those PBS pledge telethons on TV.

An even older, should-have-retired-thirty-years-ago hag with short, ghostly hair and large glasses was screaming at the end of the atrium lobby for people to take their hats off.

King's Valley High School is a maze of too-narrow hallways with too-brightly-lit skylights and fluorescent lights. Red and black vinyl floor tiles that go in zig-zag patterns to represent the school mascot, Red Devils, already make me uneasy. They remind me of the weird carpets from the hotel in *The Shining*.

The freshman wing, tucked off to the left of the atrium, is hilly and narrow. The floor slopes up and down without any handrails and, if you look all the way down the long corridor, the ceiling that slants up, down, up, down gives the claustrophobic tunnel a funhouse-like sensation.

Whoever put this place together was inebriated.

My homeroom teacher, an older and seemingly strict male history teacher, instructed people as they walked in to find their assigned seats by looking at the schedules laying on the desks. I'm thankful that my desk for the next year will be in the back of the room. I sat down, sighed, and listened to the various conversations whispering in and out of being indistinct.

"I saw The Wedding Singer on Broadway! It was fucking amazing!"

"How was Cancun?"

"I can't believe Steve Irwin died. I was, like, crying for hours yesterday!"

This was my first glimpse at the real demographics of teenaged life in King's Valley since my summer had been confined exclusively to meeting the "Tyler Gang."

One thing I noticed right away of people in this town today was that everyone here is dressed nicely. Even the skater kids are wearing name brand board shorts and sneakers. The preps are sewn into their Vineyard Vines and Tommy Hilfiger. Even riding through town, I could see kids waiting for the bus to take them to the third grade, still dressed better than I am in their little Ralph Lauren outfits. Who the fuck is everyone around here trying to impress?

You'd think the second coming of Jesus was coming up in this town.

A few minutes later was the flag salute and the principal's announcements over the loudspeaker congratulating the class of '07 for making it this far, his excitement for another great school year in our brand-new building, and most importantly...the homecoming football game this Friday at 7 pm, of course. What else?

My first class was English. It was a decent way to let me test the waters since it's a class I actually don't mind. I like books and I like writing.

The teacher, Ms. Carlson, told us we'll be reading *To Kill a Mockingbird* and *The House on Mango Street* to name but a few on the syllabus. *Romeo and Juliet* will come later in the year. Two whole months will be dedicated to the play.

Next came French. I decided to take French because my dad did in high school, and it might be something he can help me with. Also, you know, "We're All Going to Paris". If I ever do get the chance to meet Matt Daniels, I'd like to impress him with some knowledge of the French language. I imagine he has some sort of inspiration with France's culture to prompt him to write a hit song about dreaming of making it to the City of Lights.

45

Tristan LaFerriere

We were instructed by Madame Carver to come up with ten good reasons why learning French is a good idea. I was partnered up with a preppy senior girl who's just taking the class for credit, and she spent most of the hour bragging about how she enjoyed her summer in Maui. Her blonde hair, lime green sweater, and designer tortoise shell glasses clashed a bit too much with my washed-out emo colors. By the time the period was over, I was practically choking from the fragrance she had obviously bathed in earlier that morning to impress her own preppy peers.

Third period was World History. Not much to say about this class except that our teacher, Mr. Campbell, seems pretty chill. Claims he doesn't give a lot of homework and doesn't like assigning group projects. Likes to just get to the point. I think I can handle this.

Fourth period was Journalism. Upon coming to the high school in the middle of July to sign up for classes, Journalism sparked my interest because it's a class where you can actually write about what's on your mind. It also gets published in the school paper four times a year if approved. Once a marking period, the school puts out *The Red Devils Gazette* with articles, interviews, and media reviews written by the journalism class that's mixed with freshmen, sophomores, juniors, and seniors.

I can at least maybe have somewhat of a voice here if I find myself brave enough to write op-ed pieces about what's really on my mind.

Our first edition of the paper is going out in the middle of October, so we're already getting started with brainstorming ideas and researching current events, politics, the entertainment industry, and all that stuff to prepare. The few of us freshmen in the class were paired up with sophomores who are in their second year of journalism for some guidance This is one of the few classes that you can take each year if you're that into it...and that good at it.

I was paired up with this kid, Thomas, who our teacher, Mrs. Kinney, introduced to me as *"The Red Devil's Gazette's most valuable asset since its formation in 1982."*

Thomas is a nerdy, but still cute guy who just moved to The States from Australia three years ago. His accent isn't traditional Australian, though. It seems to be an odd mix of several different regions. He was fashioning a light blue sweater, khaki pants, and

conservative rectangular glasses that fit over his dark brown eyes. His hair is dark brown, too [almost black], slightly long, but not the shoulder-length that mine is. His skin has a mild tan, but in comparison to my ghostly white complexion, he practically looked like a bronze statue. Instead of a backpack, he carries a brown leather messenger bag which completes his European schoolboy look that I'm surprised he hasn't been picked on for [or maybe he has]. But then again, this is a rich town. No reason to be picked on for looking like you have money here.

"Any ideas for your first article, Northrup?" Thomas asked.

"I already know," I said as we sat in front of computers at desks next to each other in the windowless computer lab in the back of the library, the room where our class meets.

"So, what's it going to be?"

"Stay Sweet's releasing a new album Friday," I explained as I clicked on a link to go to the band's official website. "I'm gonna do a review on it for the entertainment section."

"Stay Sweet?"

"They're a band."

"Ah, I see. What genre is their music?"

"Emo."

"With lyrics primarily about death and dying, I presume?" Thomas said with a smirk that seems to rarely leave his face.

I rolled my eyes, automatically clicking on Matt Daniels's personal biography on the website's main page as if it were instinct. I've visited it probably well over a hundred times in just the past month.

"They're not all about death and dying," I said. "These guys make good music. It's emo pop, not emo...death music or whatever you think it is."

"Perhaps you're an exception," Thomas continued. "But my understanding is that all emo kids want to do is sit in their room all day,

listen to these sad, sad anthems, and write poetry about how they cut themselves to feel alive."

I rolled my eyes again, slightly offended, as I scrolled through information about Matt Daniels: birthdate, height, weight, hair color, eye color, etc. It's not like I didn't know all these things already. Matt Daniels was brought into this world on November 10th, 1984, in Baltimore, Maryland. He's 6'1", 155 lbs. with long brown hair and green eyes [however, his hair is sometimes dyed black, which was my inspiration to start coloring my own in the first place].

"Well, I write poems sometimes," I said. "But not about death."

"What *do* you write about?"

Boys, boys, boys. Penises, penises, penises. Let me artistically describe all the senses of what it would be like to bend over and let Matt Daniels stick his huge, hard cock up my ass.

"I don't know," I said. "It's…it's hard to explain. It's kind of like a customized genre."

Thomas's smirk remained, and it worried me that he had me completely figured out already. Sometimes I wonder if maybe I'm wasting my time pretending that I wouldn't rather be spending every second of my life in the arms of another boy. I wish I could see myself, my interactions and mannerisms, and just how easy it might be to decipher who I really am.

"What are you writing *your* first article on?" I asked just to change the subject.

Finally, a different kind of smile. Thomas was ready to pounce with the information. Perhaps I was the first audience to his intellect.

"The mid-term elections, of course."

"*Of course*," I imitated him.

"I sense a hint of distaste in your tone, Northrup."

"You do."

"And why would that be?"

"Because that shit bores me."

"We may just be hitting a milestone in November, Northrup. Numbers are looking promising for Pelosi. First woman speaker of the house will cause an uproar in the conservative corners of this neighborhood for sure. I still see a fair number of really faded Reagan bumper stickers from time to time on the old cars around here."

"This is all a foreign language to me," I said. "How the Hell do you know so much about American politics if you've only lived here for, like, three years? I couldn't even tell you who the Australian president is."

"*Prime minister.* John Howard."

"Oh. Sorry."

...

Lunch is different here than from what I understand most high schools do. There *is* a designated cafeteria, but you can pretty much eat anywhere in the building that you want to [within reason; trust me; my initial thought was that at least I could lock myself in the janitor's closet to have my lunch and stay away from everyone, but I can't do that. The fucking hall monitors here are like the Gestapo]. If not the cafeteria, you can eat in classrooms, the library, the courtyards, or even in the hallways if it's in one of the approved areas.

King's Valley High has two gyms [the competition and auxiliary gyms]. Tables are set up in the competition gym during lunch where they put out little hot dog, pretzel, and cookie stands in the corners. I would've chosen to eat in there since there aren't any windows. It's quite dark despite the hot industrial lighting and it would've been a good place for me to blend in, but Thomas insisted on just outside the cafeteria in the hallway [Yes, it looks like I may have made a new friend despite us having little to pretty much nothing in common].

We sat in the wide hall where about a dozen or so other people were also eating. An open container of store purchased sushi from

Gleason's was sitting alongside Thomas, including the cheap, disposable chopsticks.

Joining us was his other sophomore friend, Athena, who greeted him by jumping on his back while we were in the lunch line in the competition gym so I could get a Coke and a pretzel. Athena appears to be the only other emo person in all of King's Valley that I've seen, which surprises me because her personality suggests the complete opposite of what Thomas's assumptions of emo people are. Athena is black, wears boy Tripp pants she's practically swimming in, "zipper" earrings from Hot Topic dangle from each of her lobes, and she eats from a My Chemical Romance lunchbox. Each of her fingernails were painted a different color today, and she was fashioning a Cradle of Filth t-shirt with several gel bracelets around her wrists. Her hair is braided.

It hasn't been confirmed, but I'm pretty sure the cafeteria is unofficially reserved for the popular kids. I only came to this conclusion because I could make out my brother in the distance, sitting at a table with Tyler and Eric while the three of them laughed along with the two girls they were sandwiched in between.

The girls were Melissa Grandstaff and Ashley Fielding, two people I haven't even said hello to, yet they've bumped me down to number seven on my own brother's top 8 Myspace friends. I haven't been on his profile for several weeks, so I wonder if I even make the cut anymore.

"So, when did you move here, Kieran?" Athena asked me in between bites of her turkey wrap.

"June."

"Where'd you live before?"

"California."

"Oh! Cool! Were you in, like, Hollywood?"

"No." I chuckled at the usual assumption. "L.A., but not Hollywood. Pacific Palisades."

"That's so awesome! I've never been there, but I really want to go."

"One of the few places in the world I've never been to," Thomas added. He was jotting down notes or something in one of his composition books. From the angle he was at, I almost could've mistaken him for a younger Justin Long, the actor, with glasses.

"What are you doing?" I asked him. "Homework?"

"He's always doing homework," Athena said. "Even when we're hanging out, he brings homework to do. He was fucking working on calc problems when we went to see *Final Destination 3*."

Thomas rolled his eyes as he adjusted his glasses.

"No one could ever burn to death in a tanning bed," he said. "That movie was fucking stupid. And to answer your question, Northrup, just some ideas for my first article. I think it'll be particularly interesting to see if we'll have a Democratic Revolution in complete contrast to what happened in '94. I'm going to conduct a survey with the student body to see where they stand. You have any research done for your article?"

"I don't really need to do any research. Stay Sweet's my life. A majority of my 'research' will be listening to that album as soon as I get it."

"And when will that be?"

"As soon as it's released on Friday. I'm gonna pick up a copy after school. I'll have the whole thing listened to and a rough draft of the review written for class on Monday."

Thomas nodded, approvingly, as he took a sip of his iced tea.

"Fair enough, Northrup. Just remember this isn't some amateur newspaper. We put out a better paper here than some universities do, so make sure it's pristine and professional."

"It will be."

"Good."

...

While my morning classes aren't so bad, whoever's in charge of scheduling decided it would be a good idea to throw me into Freshman Science, Algebra I, Health, and Gym all into the later hours of the day so that I'll want to kill myself over one, big clusterfuck of bullshit by the time the final bell rings.

Algebra and science didn't end up being so torturous, but fucking science...my science teacher is this obnoxious woman who's probably on drugs. For half the class, she stood on top of her desk, acting like it was a pep rally in order for us to understand that all energy on earth comes from the sun in two forms of light and heat and that the light shines on green plants which contain chlorophyll...blah...blah...blah. We must have recited this cycle over a hundred times as if we were being brainwashed in some sort of religious cult on photosynthesis.

Last period...gym.
Short explanation: I fucking hate gym.

First of all, I'm not an athlete. I've never liked sports, which is why I don't understand how Justin and I are even related. I can't get into the game, and this always pisses the rest of the class off [especially the team I've been assigned to, which is always the captain who has the unfortunate luck of getting to choose the last person standing].

Gym periods here consist of one large class with a mix of people from each grade. Thank God Thomas and Athena are in my class because so is Evan Kirkland. If I didn't have my new friends to distract me, I'd probably be focusing on the fact that I'm in a class where just one little mention of me being the kid who jerked off in the woods would make me the laughingstock of the year.

...

After doing a warm-up run around the auxiliary gym, we went outside to play a game of flag football.

Again, a bit of unusual luck for me with Thomas and I on the same team. Athena didn't bring gym clothes with her because, in her words, *"Fuck gym,"* so she was forced to sit on the sidelines with the

few others who didn't dress out while she scribbled anime drawings in her notebook.

Thomas and I ended up spending the rest of the period on defense, letting everyone else take care of the game while we stood and talked wearing those gross sweaty-smelling nylon pinnies to distinguish us from the opposing team. Meanwhile, the echoing lyrics of some Vengaboys song drifted through the wind from the football field. The cheerleaders were already practicing their big routine for Friday's homecoming game.

My eyes focused on the grass under my sneakers for a moment, and then I realized I was standing only a few yards away from where I was last month when Tyler tried to throw a bottle of piss all over me. In fact, Athena and the other "rebels" who hadn't dressed out were sitting right alongside the goal where Tyler hit me in the ass with the ball.

I turned to Thomas.

"You haven't heard any...rumors about me, have you?"

He shook his head.

"Nah."

"Are you sure?"

Thomas laughed.

"You're so uptight, Northrup. I told you I haven't. Even if I did, who the fuck cares? You seem to be quite awesome people."

"I...do?"

"You haven't given me any reason to think otherwise."

I smiled...can you fucking believe it?

"Thanks," I stuttered.

...

53

I found Justin after last period, leaning up against his car and flirting with Ashley Fielding. She's really just your basic clueless preppy girl. Her hair is curly, blonde, and she wears designer sweaters. My brother looked to be pitching some pick-up line to get her to let him cop a feel after the game this Friday. It's not that Justin would have to work hard to get that sort of access granted to him, though. All he has to say is *"I am Justin Northrup"* and it magically melts away girls' panties.

Ashley gave me the world's tiniest smile when she noticed me approaching.

"Hi," she squeaked.

"Hi." I turned to Justin. "Let's go."

My brother did his little farewell routine, explaining that he'd be on AIM tonight to chat with her before she hurried over to her car. For sure a lucky girl in the eyes of all the other envious females in town who want my brother to fuck them.

"So, how'd your first day go?" Justin asked me with a gleam in his eye like he was expecting, and hoping, for a negative answer.

"Can we just go?"

Even when we were back on the road, I felt tension because the wave that was my first day of high school still left me sore.

"So, it looks like you didn't die," Justin said under Matisyahu's beats pulsing from the car speakers.

"Shockingly."

"You meet any new friends?"

"As a matter of fact, I did. *Two*, actually."

"See? It wasn't all bad."

"Sure."

"How were your classes?"

"You sound like Mom."

"What do you think of the school?"

"I hate it."

"Dude!"

I thought Justin was about to run off the road. His entire demeanor changed instantly.

"Will you stop being so fucking negative all the time! You're really starting to piss me off. All you do is fucking whine. Seriously...why do you think Eric and Tyler and Evan all think you're so fucking annoying?"

For some reason, I felt butterflies in my stomach as if this weren't already news to me. The confirmation that his friends didn't like me hurt worse than I imagined.

"If you'd stop feeling so fucking sorry for yourself all the time then maybe people would actually like you."

I kept quiet. I wasn't in the mood, and it seemed like Justin forgot about anything he was talking about by the time we pulled into our driveway since when he pushed the garage door opener on his visor, the middle of the three doors that's designated as his didn't open.

"You fucking kidding me?" he said, jamming his thumb into the little button over a dozen times before finally quitting and killing the engine. "Nothing works here."

"It's these houses," I sighed as we got out of the car. "They built them too fast. They have a lot of flaws."

We started up the flagstone walkway to our front door, Justin two steps ahead of me and walking with a fussy stride that reminded me of a child who was just told they had to go finish their homework.

"Mom and Dad never have issues with theirs," Justin complained. "It's no fucking wonder they gave me the middle door."

Tristan LaFerriere

"I thought we weren't supposed to be so negative."

Justin gave me a dirty look and went back to fumbling with his keys.

I sighed and let my eyes wander around the cul-de-sac. I noticed a moving truck in the driveway of the stucco house next door, Number 2714, as my brother started unlocking our front door. Sleek, edgy-looking furniture was being brought into the house through the garage.

Our house, the conservative federal façade of brick that it is, clashes quite a bit next to the Spanish design alongside it. 2714 looks more like something you would see in our old California neighborhood.

"Looks like we've got new neighbors," I said, nodding toward the house.
Our front door clicked.

"Great," Justin quipped. "Just what we need. You know that bitch, Mrs. Gray, up the street?"

"Maybe they'll be nice."

"That doesn't sound like your usual optimism."

He opened the door and I followed him inside as I rolled my eyes.

Justin headed to the kitchen and went straight for the fridge to grab another Powerade, humming a Gym Class Heroes song while I hurried upstairs to my room. I shut my door and slumped down on the bed so damn hard I thought the springs would break. I felt like I was hit by a train, and I was relieved to be back in the room I had hardly left for thirty days.

But I still wasn't comfortable. I wasn't comfortable anywhere anymore. Not in this house. Not in this town. Not in this state. Not on this side of the country. Maybe not even in this country at all. I'll be eighteen in just a little over three years. Maybe I can move to Canada then. Three years, though? Can I seriously wait that long?

Once I regained the slightest bit of energy, I popped in the Cute Is What We Aim For CD I had hoped to play in the car and let myself cry into my pillow while the lyrics to "There's a Class for This" covered any evidence of me weeping.

...

Dinner was at seven as always. We all sat at the kitchen table in silence. The only sound was the occasional *clack* of a fork against a plate when one of us would cut into a piece of Mom's roasted cauliflower or scoop up a mouthful of brown rice. While Mom seemed to be very aware of every bite she took [ensuring her lipstick wouldn't be smudged], Justin was already nearly finished and taking a swig of Powerade in between each swallow of food. I was surprised that Mom hadn't scalded him for texting at the table since she's usually all about having a nice "family meal" each night like we're in a '50s sitcom, but it would have been hypocritical of her since she was working out commission figures on a notepad right at the table while she occasionally sipped her glass of merlot.

Dad and I had hardly touched our plates. As usual, I wasn't all that hungry, and Dad seemed mentally exhausted from work. He eventually broke the ice by throwing at me the question I was most dreading.

"How was your first day, Kier?"

I stared at my plate, the cauliflower and rice still steaming. Our orange and white cat, Larry, rubbed his head against my legs under the table. We've had Larry since he was a kitten a few years ago. He's the only living thing I've come out to, and, so far, he hasn't treated me any differently [I say *living thing* because I came out to the fridge a few weeks ago and it kicked on with a hum of disapproval].

"It was...okay..."

"Just...okay?" Dad asked.

I shrugged.

"Yeah?"

"It'd be a fucking tragedy if something went well for him for once," Justin chimed in.

"*Excuse* me." Mom was not pleased.

Dad was still looking at me. Maybe he really was concerned. I don't know. Dad and I don't really talk that much, but I feel like he and I are probably the most alike. Like me, he doesn't seem comfortable in his own skin half the time anymore. He also isn't so talented when it comes to disguising his feelings.

"Why don't you join a sport, Kieran?" Mom suggested as she stabbed a piece of cauliflower with her fork. "It'll give you something to do after school. You hardly even came out of your room all summer. You could do tennis or golf. Dad and I could help you practice. They have some beautiful tennis courts here and our golf course is ranked the nicest in the county."

I cringed at her attempt to connect with me, but only managing to sound like the script she has written for a real estate sales pitch. And really? Golf? I golfed with my dad and brother in Palm Springs a few years ago and I'm still surprised I didn't fucking kill anybody.

"I think I'm good, Mom."

...

After I cleared the table and loaded the dishwasher, I flicked on the patio and pool lights. Through the kitchen's sliding glass doors, I could see the pool illuminate from underneath the water. I stepped outside, down the deck steps, and stood at the edge of the pool for a few minutes before I sat at its edge, took off my shoes and socks, and dipped my feet in the shallow end. While I moved my legs back and forth in the cool water, I looked around the dark backyard, at the fence separating our house from the stucco place next door, at the diving board where Justin and Eric Gleason attempted [and failed] to do flips into the deep end a month ago. I wanted to take in every last moment of the summer heat that I could. As a native Californian, it worries me how I'll react to the winter months here. I'm not so sure I'm ready to be cold for so long.

I made my way back up to my room when I realized the kitchen lights had been shut off and everyone was upstairs for the night. I put the TV on while I read through the same Stay Sweet interviews in the *Alternative Press* magazine that I keep in my drawer. You'd probably think I keep gay porn in there or something, but nope...just magazines with Matt Daniels on the cover. My imagination does the rest.

Already, some lights were on in the newly inhabited house next door, and through my window next to the La-Z-Boy, I could see that there were boxes upon boxes piled high in one of the upstairs rooms. It looked like a stocked warehouse.

Justin came into my room at about nine-thirty just as the contestant on *Deal or No Deal* revealed the million-dollar case. The moans and groans of the audience on TV just happened to coincide with his entrance. It all fit too well for how I was feeling about him. I was also planning on jerking off, so here he was interrupting my session.

"What?" I said coldly, my eyes not leaving the page showing Matt Daniels in a behind-the-scenes photo of the "We're All Going to Paris" music video where they were shooting at the Baltimore airport.

"Hey," Justin said.

"What?" I repeated in the same tone.

My brother sighed, and even though I didn't look up at him, I could sense he had rolled his eyes.

"Now you're just being negative to be negative, dude."

Justin slammed my door shut and walked over to the side of the bed.

"Kieran, seriously. You really need to quit all this emotional bullshit. You're acting like a little kid, and you can trust me that shit isn't gonna get you anywhere in high school."

"As if you act like an adult," I scoffed. "Ever since you've been hanging out with those scumbags, you're just a fucking bully."

"Why do you always have to attack my friends? What did they ever do to you?"

I had to hold myself back from screaming. Was my brother really this blind?

"Do you seriously need me to answer that? You just told me they don't like me."

"Because of the way you act."

"So, it's okay to spread rumors about me and try to throw piss on me?"

Justin wanted to argue, but he couldn't, and I could see his frustration right before he plopped down on the edge of the bed. He knew I was right, but he'd never admit it.

"I'm not fucking saying you have to be friends with my friends. Just do me a favor, though, and stop being this big fucking black hole of negative energy. You'll never make any friends."

"I made new friends today."

"Yeah. We'll see how long that fucking lasts."

Shit, that hurt.

"It...will." I heard my voice cracking like I might cry. He really was being a fucking bully.

"Okay, but you can forget about ever getting a girlfriend."

"You got that right," I muttered, and immediately regretted it.

"What?"

I changed the subject quickly.

"Why do you even care about me?"

"What?"

60

"I mean, why do you even care? You don't even like me anymore."

"Kieran..."

I put the magazine down and sighed, folded my hands at my belly, and fought back the tears.

"You're not the same anymore," I said. "This place is turning you into an asshole."

"I don't know what you want me to do, but I can't just stop being friends with my friends and be more like you to make you happy."

"I'm not saying you should be more like me."

"Then what are you saying?"

"I don't fucking know!"

I looked away from him, waiting for him to say something or get up and leave, but then he was...climbing in bed with me, getting under the covers with me, and I didn't know how to react because he'd never done anything like that before. It was the last thing I expected him to do. It caught me off guard.

I could feel his leg against mine as I reached for the TV remote and muted it. This left us in a great deal of awkward silence except for the crickets outside my cracked window. The air conditioner kicked on for probably one of the last dozen or so times of the year.

I couldn't find myself with the emotional energy to roll over and look Justin right in the eye. Oh, I fucking wanted to, though. I wanted more than anything to face him, cry, and let him take me in his arms while I screamed at the top of my lungs that I'm gay, and that no one would ever understand or accept me, and why the fuck did we have to move to this horrible place, and why did his friends have to be so mean to me, and why, just why couldn't he stick up for me instead of going along with everything those fuckers say?

But I didn't do any of those things.

I couldn't.

I *did* roll over and face him, but that was it. The words that came out of my mouth shouldn't have, but it was the only way to move stuff along. It was the only way to pacify him.

"I'm sorry."

Justin patted my shoulder after staring into my eyes for a while, and then he leaned back in the bed.

"You worry too much, Kieran. You need to fucking relax, man."

"Yeah. I guess so."

We were both lying on our backs now, facing up and looking at the ceiling. He didn't smell like his Banana Republic fragrance anymore, but adolescent underarm odor.

"We should…go out and do something," Justin said after a while. "You and me."

I looked at him like he was crazy. It was so out of character for him to say, and especially with his ever-growing douchebag of a personality, but they were just about the best words I could've heard. It actually managed to brighten me up a little.

"Really?"

"Sure." He faced me. "We can go to the homecoming game on Friday."

I sighed.

"I don't want to go to the fucking homecoming game."

"Dude, I have to go," he said defensively.

"You don't have to do anything, Justin. Maybe it's what you jocks are *expected* to do…"

"I'm inviting you. You should be happy about that."

...

"I'll tell you what," I started. "I'll go, but first, you have to take me to the mall so I can get the new Stay Sweet CD."

Justin shrugged.

"Fine. But I'm not paying for it."

"I didn't say you have to pay for it."

"Then it's a deal. We'll leave here at five-thirty. That'll give us enough time to be at the game."

"Alright. Cool."

"We can go to the dance, too."

"What dance?"

"The homecoming dance."

"When's that?"

"Thursday night."

"Who the fuck has a homecoming dance on a Thursday night? And the first week?"

"Apparently it's a King's Valley tradition," Justin explained. "Back in '86, they had to have the homecoming dance on the Thursday night after Labor Day because for some reason, it was the only time they had to fit it in that year's schedule. The Red Devils went on to be undefeated that year, so now it's a tradition. The homecoming dance is always the first Thursday of the school year and the homecoming game is always the first Friday."

"That's fucking stupid."

"Well, that's what Dennis told me. And this is the twentieth year, so it's kind of a big deal."

"Who's Dennis?"

"Dennis Folton. You don't know him."

Ah, his No. 6 Myspace friend who recently surpassed me.

"Do I want to know him?"

"He's chill."

"I'm sure he is," I said sarcastically as I shivered. Goosebumps had formed on my arms in just the last minute.

"You cold?" Justin asked.

"Yeah," I nodded and pulled the blankets a little higher. "This air-conditioning works too well. And it smells like glue."

"I can go turn it down."

"Mom will fucking kill you if you touch that thermostat."

"So what? It's our house, too. I'll turn it down."

"No. I'm fine."

Justin was staring at me as I shivered again.

"Maybe…you just need a hug," he said.

I looked at him like he was crazy again. Did my brother, the king of jocks, the king of preps, the boy who was becoming a douchebag more and more as he matured each day…did he just suggest that I, his little emo brother, needed a hug like he actually wanted to hug me?

"…Okay," I said, almost uncomfortably.

He didn't hesitate to hug me.

It probably lasted all of five seconds, but it felt way longer than that, and I really tried to take in every moment of it because I can't remember the last time he hugged me like that. We were probably still

in our single digits, back in the days when we shared a bedroom and would on occasion play GI Joe with each other [where I would strip the Joe action figure naked and be disappointed that there were no genitals under those tiny pants].

"What…what was that for?" I asked him as soon as the hug broke.

"You were cold," he said. "So, I hugged you."

I didn't know what to say. The look in his eyes really spoke to me, like he was trying to say, without using words, that he loved me, and I really wanted to tell him, with words, that I loved him so much, but that hug was like the best thing that happened to me in a long time, and it felt best just to leave it that way.

"I'm hittin' the sack," Justin said as he climbed out of the bed. "See you in the morning."

I let out a long, overdue yawn that was in response to the whole day. My brother went out the door, and I was alone again with a muted TV and some flickering lights next door.

I switched off my bedside lamp and was plunged into a lonely, but comfortable darkness. This house is still a new place to me. Each night feels like staying in an unfamiliar hotel with the indistinct noise of Justin's unwinding through the walk-in closet. It's not unlike strangers on the other side of the wall as you try to get accustomed to a bed that isn't your own at some Holiday Inn.

I decided to jerk off like I had originally intended before Justin came in. Images of a naked Matt Daniels rewarded my thoughts as I slid my hand beneath my boxers and touched myself, took my time to ensure that it was a worthwhile session.

Matt Daniels…

His perfect body, or at least what I imagine that body to look like under those clothes.

His broad shoulders…

His toned arms…

65

Tristan LaFerriere

His hip bones protruding...

His dick...

I imagine Matt Daniels fucking me...

But not just fucking me...

I imagine him touching me in places I've never been touched before.

What would it be like to be touched so intimately by such a beautiful boy?

He faces me from the wall over my desk, within the poster I picked up from Hot Topic back in L.A. It depicts him, with closed eyes, arms outstretched on stage and his head tilted slightly to one side as beads of sweat drip from his forehead [glistening in the red stage lights as the rest of the band plays behind him]. The screaming fans reach out from the pit below.

He watches over me each night and he's the last thing I see before I close my eyes. I hope to God that I'll dream about him again tonight, hearing the sweet sound of him singing his signature lyrics to me like a lullaby, like his voice making love to me...

"You know you're right, we're gonna take a flight,

We're gonna leave you all behind,

It'll be something to see,

Old gay Paree,

And we're gonna leave you all behind.

We're all going to Paris,

We're all going to Paris,

We're all going to Paris now."

Chapter Three
Thursday, September 7th, 2006

Dear Journal,

The homecoming dance was held in the competition gym tonight. For a school supplying education to such an "elite" group of students, the decorations were pretty fucking deplorable. A badly-painted banner sagged forlornly over the folded-up bleachers, stating *"Homecoming, '06!"* Other than a few sparse dollar store party streamers and balloons set up in the corners, there wasn't much different about the room than what it is during a gym class, except that the lights were dimmer, and a very less than average DJ was set up in the corner playing the latest Hellogoodbye song.

Justin and I, of course, separated the instant we entered the room, as I suspected, despite his suggestion for me to come along in the first place. To his delight, Tyler, Eric, Evan, and apparently this other recently joined member of the group, Dennis Folton, were already there and hanging out in the middle of the crowd.

The kings of King's Valley, I thought.

I took refuge in the back near the bleachers after getting a plastic cup filled with a diabolical medicine-tasting fruit drink at the refreshment table. I instantly regretted saying yes to coming since my brother wasn't spending any time with me and standing alone was just a reminder of how rejected I was in this new town.

I must've looked like a complete idiot standing there, holding my drink, and sticking out like a sore thumb amid all the other beautiful people. Mom had protested my choice in dress for the occasion on our way out the door: a red long-sleeved The Academy Is... shirt, black jeans, and my Converse sneakers, rather than something "nice" like the Guess jeans and button-down shirt from The Gap that Justin had chosen.

I watched my brother dance with Ashley Fielding while James Blunt screeched out "You're Beautiful" for the one slow dance of the night. Alongside Justin and Ashley were Tyler and Melissa Grandstaff, Eric with some girl Kayla I've only heard of who apparently has a reputation for being rather promiscuous, and Dennis Folton with a girl I've never seen.

I wondered what it would be like if two guys started dancing in the middle of the room. I could just imagine the scowling PTA members shaking their heads in disapproval and demanding the nonsense stop. Such a distraction to this exclusive establishment that isn't about to tolerate such an immorality.

You know what isn't fair about that, though? If someone like my brother were to grab hold of another guy and dance with him, there wouldn't be a single sign of disapproval. There would be laughter, of course, but not in the same way there would be if I were to do it. It would be funny because it would be a joke. If you're prominent and well-liked or even just attractive, you can get away with just about anything.

"Northrup, I didn't think a true emo would be caught dead at a function such as this."

You guessed it. Thomas. And while I didn't admit it or show it, I was damn glad to see him. I'm not sure if it was a relief that an actual friend of mine was there, that I wasn't the absolute biggest outcast attending, or a little bit of both [I guess that isn't accurate; Thomas isn't really a true outcast. He isn't like other people in this town, but he doesn't care, and not caring has in a weird way made him fit in].

"Hey," I said, trying not to sound too excited while I flipped my long hair like suddenly having someone to talk to made me hot shit. "What's up? I didn't think I'd see you here, either."

"Just making my rounds, Northrup. Decided to take a break from pondering over domestic affairs and straining my eyes in front of the computer. It can get quite tiring."

"You mean you really have a life outside of keeping up with the latest from the Bush Administration?"

I wish I could never take offense to anything in the way that Thomas literally does not give a shit even when you tear into him [all in good humor, of course, but still, he takes everything lightly in a way that I envy].

"Ah, Northrup, I would ask you the same about your life and that 'Stay Sick' band you're so devoted to."

"Stay *Sweet*," I corrected him.

Thomas cocked an eyebrow.

"Where did they come up with a stupid name like that?"

I blinked hard. If I were being truthful, I'd say he's actually right. I decided to educate him in Stay Sweet 101.

"The lead singer, Matt Daniels, was trying to figure out a name for the band while he was looking through one of his old high school yearbooks. A girl he was friends with signed it and wrote *'Stay Sweet!'* and the rest is history. He wrote a song about her that's on their first album."

I held the cheap cup of punch to my lips, hearing the lyrics in my head.

"*Delilah*," I said, breathy, as I tried to imitate Matt Daniels and his seductive rendition of the song. Then I frowned. "A certain other band totally copied them earlier this year."

My eyes were on Justin, who was still dancing with Ashley. They looked like they would eat each other's faces off at any given moment. They'd probably end up fucking later tonight in his car or in his room if he could sneak her into the house.

"I see," Thomas finally said in response to the explanation of my favorite band's name origins. He sounded very unimpressed.

"Have you ever even listened to any of their songs?"

"Nope." Thomas crossed his arms, looking proud of this declaration.

"Maybe you should before you judge."

"Not judging, Northrup. I just think we're in a terrible trend of horribly named bands that are trying far too hard to be edgy. I mean...'Death Cab for Cutie'...what the fuck?"

69

I wasn't really paying attention to what Thomas was saying.
For some reason, I was bothered by seeing Justin dancing with Ashley.
I guess I was sort of jealous...like I wanted to be able to experience that
with someone.

"Northrup?"

"Uh...yeah...'Death Cab for Cutie' is actually named after the
song by The Bonzo Dog Doo-Dah Band."

I took a sip of punch, still staring at my brother and his friends
dancing with their girls. I wondered what would happen after the dance.
Would everyone come over to our house to hang out around the kitchen
table and play Texas hold 'em again while I hid upstairs? If that *did*
happen, would Tyler tell this Dennis Folton all about what I did in the
woods if he hasn't already? Simply existing in King's Valley was
walking on eggshells for me now. I was a moron for whipping my dick
out in front of someone whose favorite word is "faggot."

"So, they named their band after a song?"

"Yeah. It's from the '60s. And that song's name comes from
the title of a pulp fiction crime magazine story or something."

Justin and Ashley were leaning in close to each other, going
for the big kiss as the song built up to a climax.

"Which," I struggled to continue, "is thought to have
originated from a Richard Hoggart book, *The Uses of Literacy*..."

"Ah, yes," Thomas cut me off.

Meanwhile, The Soca Boys began babbling out "Follow the
Leader" from the speakers in the corner now that "You're Beautiful"
was over. There were a number of nostalgic screams from the crowd.

"*The Uses of Literacy*," Thomas continued. "That would be the
classic study on the influence of mass media in The United Kingdom. It
was a key title in the origins of cultural studies."

I cracked a smile.

"Of course you'd fucking know that."

Various conga lines were assembling in different corners of the room and slowly beginning to group together into one, massive swarm of horny teenagers. Oh, the DJ loved it and encouraged everyone to keep going. Even the grumpy chaperones seemed to be enjoying the show.

Justin was in there, his hands on Ashley's shoulders.

I shook my head and sipped the last of my drink. I let the cup clatter to the floor where I smashed it with my sneaker like I was putting out a cigarette. Such a rebel.

"So stupid," I muttered, sick at the sight of the insufferable festivities.

…Man, I really am negative…

"Come on," Thomas motioned his eyes toward the party.

"WHAT?" I asked, louder to be audible over the increasing decibel levels.

"Let's join in."

"Oh, no, no, no, no," I protested, putting my hands up. "Fuck that. I don't dance."

"Come on, Northrup!"

He was motioning for me to join him, and I have to admit that it was tempting as the groups of people standing on the sidelines were getting smaller and smaller, meaning whoever was leftover looked even more immensely pathetic.

"Come on, Kieran!"

…

I finally grabbed onto Thomas's shoulders and became the final person in a line of about forty or more promenading in a circle to the '90s hit. The line curved and contorted like a snake, and soon, the

front was passing us in a parallel form like two side-by-side inverse escalators.

Dennis Folton passed...then Eric...Melissa Grandstaff with her permanent bitch face...that girl, Kayla...Tyler...Ashley Fielding...

Thomas's shoulder blades protruded and shifted with each bobble. I could feel his sweat under my curled fingers that gripped onto him.

...my brother passed by...

Somehow, in this long chain, I was connected to him.

...

"Thanks for paying," I said to Thomas as his father drove me home. After a while, Thomas and I decided to ditch the dance, so we walked to the nearby Friendly's and finished off the night with some ice cream sundaes before Thomas's dad came to pick us up.

Mr. Burnham was dressed in a plaid button-down shirt and khaki pants. He looked to be about fifty with his graying hair and glasses. He's a handsome and friendly soft-spoken man who's aging well. Thomas has also told me that his father probably has over a dozen publications at this point in his career. He's been an anthropology professor for over twenty years, teaching in "a menu" of countries, but now he's tenured at Kutztown University. I'm starting to see where this runs in the Burnham family. You know what I say? Fuck Eric Gleason. Thomas will be a true face of success.

"No problem, Northrup," Thomas said as he turned to face me from the front seat. "You should come over this weekend and we can go swimming."

Wait, what? Someone was inviting me to hang out? Fucking pinch me.

"I'd...I'd like that."

"Which number is it, Kieran?" Mr. Burnham asked as he drove. We were on Skyview Drive now, going uphill at an incline that I've only recently realized gives our street its namesake.

"2716. It's the brick place in the cul-de-sac."

Thomas's dad pulled the car up to the end of our driveway where the lawn jockey greeted us. Justin's garage door was open, and the light was flooding out like a halo around the rear end of his parked car. I hadn't bothered to find him at the dance before I left. He ditched me, so I figured I'd just go ahead and ditch him. And it's not like he texted me when the dance was over to make sure I was okay.

Thomas got out of the car with me to say goodbye to me. It was a polite gesture that I could never imagine my brother's friends doing.

"Thanks for the ride, Mr. Burnham," I said to Thomas's dad through his open window.

"You're welcome, Kieran. We hope to see you this weekend."

Thomas gave me a pat on the shoulder.

"See you tomorrow, Northrup. Get some rest. Remember, we're doing a mock layout. And you've got that new album to listen to."

I perked up a bit after Thomas said this. It had nearly slipped my mind that in less than twenty-four hours, I would have already listened to each of Stay Sweet's new songs.

"I will," I said. "See you tomorrow."

Thomas got back in the car and they drove off. I sighed, alone on the quiet street as they disappeared. I rubbed the goosebumps on my arms and started up the steep driveway. The front lawn's sprinklers started going off, sending a trickling stream down the side of the driveway that disappeared into the drainpipe near our mailbox.

Distant music was approaching.

I stopped about halfway up the driveway, looked over my shoulder, and noticed the glow from two headlights of a red sedan driving up toward the end of the cul-de-sac. The amber turn signal started to flash as the car, now revealing itself to me as an older Alfa Romeo, began pulling into the driveway of the stucco house next door.

73

Tristan LaFerriere

Something drew me to this mysterious vehicle crawling up the otherwise quiet street at this late hour. Green Day's "Jesus of Suburbia" was pumping from the open windows as I tried to make out the driver, one of the new residents of this new house.

The car stopped in front of one of the three closed garage doors. The brakes squeaked, and a second later, the door began humming open while the driver waited for access to their home. What appeared to be a male hand hung from the open driver's side window, tapping the car door to the beat of the song, but otherwise, this person was just a silhouette to me from within the dark interior.

Finally, there was enough clearance for the car to enter the garage as the door rose, and it disappeared into the house. As the large door began to close, Billie Joe Armstrong's voice became muffled, and once again, the end of the street was blanketed with near silence.

...

Larry immediately greeted me in the kitchen when I entered through the garage, rubbing against my legs in hopes of a late-night treat. I fed him and pet him for a while before I headed upstairs. Everyone else was in bed already. I could hear Justin typing away furiously on his laptop as I passed his room. I assumed he was sending sexy messages or something to Ashley Fielding on AIM while he jerked off.

I stood there for a moment, my head down and focusing on that little crack of light leaking from under his bedroom door as I listened to him typing. After a while, it was quiet, and the crack of light went dark.

I didn't bother to say goodnight.

Chapter Four
Monday, September 11th, 2006

Dear Journal,

If there is a God, FUCK HIM!

It's as if he looked down at the world, looking for a pawn on his giant game board to knock off the table when it was already fallen over.

Just go ahead and spit in my fucking face when I'm already down, why don't you?

Fuck this world.

Fuck God.

Fuck life.

I wish I were fucking dead.

FUCK

FUCK

FUCK

FUCK

FUCK

FUCK

…

I just read back what I've written, and I didn't realize I was capable of being this angry. I'm actually scaring myself.

I also just noticed today's date. It's perfect, really…a perfect example to further accentuate my argument on what an abominable fucking reality we're in.

75

Tristan LaFerriere

September 11th.

It's been five years and it's still as fresh as yesterday...just as this past Friday will be to me for the rest of my life. I have my own 9/11 now, but it's 9/8.

September 8th, 2006.

...

"This is Today..."

The fucking *Today Show* theme down the hall from Mom and Dad's TV. It was the first thing I heard when I woke.

My first thought as I rolled out of bed and forced myself into the shower was that, at least in less than twelve hours, the weekend would officially commence, and with that weekend would come twelve new tracks from the brilliant lyrical mind of Matt Daniels as it was the official release date of Stay Sweet's newest album, *Mandragora*. I'd have so much to keep me occupied until Monday, and it would pacify Thomas for him to know that I would have no trouble banging out a draft for my review.

I'll never forget the outfit I wore that day. When tragedy strikes, you always remember the clothes you had on at the time as if it were a soldier's uniform, a relic still stained with the blood from battle of a long-passed war.

I decided on a pair of jeans with holes purposely torn at the knees. I threw my red Stay Sweet hoodie on over the very first Stay Sweet shirt I ever got from Hot Topic at The Del Amo Mall in Torrance last summer. The last time I had worn the shirt was the "jerking off in the woods" night. It made me hope it wasn't forever cursed or something.

Hmm...

My brother and I were quiet for the first mile or two while he drove us to school. I was admittedly still a bit pissed at him for abandoning me at the dance. The awkward silence was made even more uncomfortable since the radio was appropriately tuned to "Bad Day" and Daniel Powter's voice reverberated from the speakers with gloomy lyrics to match my mood.

"Don't forget we're going to the mall tonight," I said.

"The mall?"

"You seriously didn't forget, did you?"

"What are you fucking talking about?" He sounded tired…or hungover…or stoned…or all three.

"You promised me the other night!" I groaned. "You promised you were gonna take me to get the new Stay Sweet CD!"

"That's today?"

I was so fucking mad I felt dizzy.

"Yes! You said we could go before the game tonight."

"Oh," Justin said in an even more stoned-sounding tone. I could swear a hint of Tyler's voice was in there somewhere like he was being possessed by him. "Right."

We were stuck behind a slow, old grandma car with its vintage blue license plate declaring, *"You've Got a Friend in Pennsylvania"*. Sure…

"So, we're going, right?" I asked.

"Yeah," he sighed. "I guess so. Just don't keep me there all fucking night. I don't want to miss the kickoff."

"I'm just running in and out. I need that CD."

"You don't *need* it."

"Actually, I do. I'm writing an album review on it for our first edition of the paper. I need to have the whole thing listened to and a draft typed up by Monday, so…"

"Okay!" Justin interrupted me as we finally pulled into the school parking lot. "I'll take you. Just fucking lay off it."

I stared at him. This was not my brother.

"What the fuck is wrong with you?" I asked. "You're so fucking edgy."

Justin yanked violently on the parking brake.

"You're one to talk, dude."

Our conversation ended with that. I never did find out what, if anything, was bothering him that morning.

I never will know.

...

In Journalism, we did a "mock layout" as Thomas had reminded me the night before. He questioned me once again to confirm that I'd have my hands on *Mandragora* by the end of the night.

"As long as my brother follows through," I said as I struggled to resize a stock photo to fit into an article template.

"Is there any reason to think he wouldn't?" Thomas asked.

"I'm just worried he's not gonna drive me. He's, like, obsessed with the idea of missing a microsecond of the game."

"Typical jock," Thomas said. He didn't laugh, though. I think he was genuinely worried I wouldn't be prepared with a review.

"I'll get the CD," I said. "If I have to, I can always download it from iTunes."

"Why don't you just do that in the first place?"

"I don't like downloading music. I'd rather have a CD. It feels more permanent, you know? Besides, I'd have to borrow Justin's iPod since I don't have my own, and he'd probably give me even more shit for that."

"This all sounds very complicated," Thomas said. "Don't get too caught up in this one. Make sure it gets done. We have to start thinking about the next project."

"The next one? The second marking period doesn't end till, like, Christmas."

"It never hurts to get ahead, Northrup. The next article will be a bit more challenging, too."

"How do you know?"

"It's going to be just the same as it was for us last year. The second article has to be interview-based. You have to conduct an interview with someone."

"Really?"

I didn't like that idea. Who the hell in King's Valley would I interview and about what? Eric Gleason's father and how much a walk-in humidor costs?

"Yes," Thomas said. "So, start thinking."

"And who are you planning on interviewing?" I asked. "Dick Cheney?"

Thomas's mischievous smirk returned.

"It would be particularly interesting to dig up some more info on that Harry Whittington incident," he laughed. "But no, I plan on speaking with Walter Peters on the whole debate of tearing down the old bowling alley to put up those luxury condos. It is, after all, the biggest 'scandal' going on around here right now. Rumor has it that Peters would light a match himself to burn down some of the older, protected landmarks in this town in the name of urban renewal. In fact, we're going on a year today since the infamous fire that destroyed..."

"Who's Walter Peters?" I interrupted.

"Ah, I forget you're even newer to this town than I am, Northrup. Walter Peters is the mayor of King's Valley. A true, card-carrying Republican."

I was honestly a bit impressed.

"You're gonna interview the mayor?"

"I'm certainly going to try. The idea of a fifteen-year-old coming to him with questions regarding the mysterious fire that destroyed the old hardware store last year just a few months before they broke ground on the same location for the new shopping center may not sit well with him. I may be chased away. We'll have to see. I have backups if this doesn't work out, though. You always have to make sure you have backups."

"I'm surprised you'd even attempt that. Don't you have to, like, make a meeting with town hall and everything?"

"Yeah, so what? It's not impossible. You should shoot for something bigger and better. What if you interviewed that singer you like? Matt Daniels?"

"I wish I could," I swooned, and then caught myself because I said it in just about the gayest tone possible. Thankfully, Thomas didn't seem to notice.

"Maybe you can, Northrup. What if you caught him at one of their shows? Are they playing around here anytime soon?"

I shook my head.

"Nope. Believe me. I check their website all the time. They *are* starting a tour next month, but none of the locations are anywhere around here."

"Ah, a shame. Perhaps you could email him interview questions and hope for a response while you try your hand at something slightly more accomplishable."

"I think anything would be more accomplishable."

"That attitude will get you nowhere, Northrup."

I shrugged.

...

I finally relaxed a bit at six-thirty that night when Justin started driving us to the mall before the game. We got off to a late start because his garage door took thirty minutes to open completely, and since Mom and Dad were out at the country club for the evening, we wouldn't have been able to get a ride from either one of them.

The Berkshire Mall greeted us long before we were even close to the parking lot entrance. Glowing, fluorescent globes atop each pole illuminating the exterior of the building let off halos of light that could be seen all the way from the highway prior to getting off the exit for the shopping center. The parking lot lights reminded me of thin mushrooms with bulbous heads sprouting from the cracks of the concrete.

Justin parked the car just outside the entrance to Sears where the distant scent of spices wafted through the air from a nearby Applebee's reaching its peak hour of dinner business. People were waiting outside for tables to become available.

"Hurry up," Justin said. "We only have, like, half an hour."

"I'll be right out," I said, slamming the car door behind me.

I darted into Sears like I was in desperate need of a bathroom with the world's biggest shit trying to squeeze its way out of my ass. I nearly ran into and knocked over a group of mannequins showing off new autumn apparel as a nearby cashier eyed me suspiciously from behind the jewelry counter. A woman standing by the fragrance counter tried to hand me a sample of some new perfume, but I darted right past her to the store entrance and out into the mall that was surprisingly not too busy for a Friday night. Everyone must have been at The Skate Park or that stupid fucking home game.

I ran forward from Sears, over a wooden bridge that stretched out over a large fountain where a bunch of plants and some lampposts decorated the area to make it look like an outdoor park. Nearby, I could smell baked pretzels and greasy hot dogs from Auntie Anne's as a teenaged couple that probably goes to King's Valley gawked at me when I ran past them. They were probably wondering what this emo loser was doing trespassing onto their preppy hangout territory, but I

81

tried not to care. I was on a mission to get that CD even if it meant making myself look like a total idiot.

Thankfully, FYE, the store where they sell CDs and DVDs, wasn't far off from Sears. I rushed in and felt relieved that, like the rest of the mall, the store wasn't busy. Besides myself, there were only a few other customers, and the section I needed to get to wasn't blocked by anyone. No more obstacles that I could see. My mission was almost complete.

S.

Simon and Garfunkel, Carly Simon, Simple Plan, Ashlee Simpson, Jessica Simpson, Frank Sinatra, Siouxsie and the Banshees, Sir-Mix-A-Lot...

Come on! Where the fuck is it?

I madly flipped through the sea of jewel cases like they were cards in a Rolodex until I finally found the tab for Stay Sweet. There were two copies of their first album, quite a few more of *Nitro...*

...

One copy of Mandragora.

...

I snatched it, but handled it carefully as if it were the Holy Grail. Hell, it *was* the fucking Holy Grail to me.

The cover art took my breath away despite its extremely simplistic approach. It was a much different direction than the previous two albums. *Stay Sweet* was a simple, grainy Polaroid-like image from a photo shoot with the band posing around a decrepit old Plymouth Horizon, the license plate on the car spelling out the band name and the self-titled debut album.

Because *Nitro* came out following the band's growing success, the cover art looked much less "rough", and its depiction of Matt Daniels in cartoon form biting down on his index finger was highlighted with rainbow colors to coincide with the second album's somewhat lighter vibe. It reminds me a lot of the cover art for The

Postal Service's *Such Great Heights* single album with the crying child who has just dropped his ice cream cone.

Mandragora was a step away from both of its predecessors. Rather than a photograph or a doodle, it was simply all black with white letters spelling out in all caps *"MANDRAGORA"*. Nothing else except for the explicit content warning label. It almost passed for a bootleg CD found in an underground record store by an unknown, but brilliant best-kept secret band.

I cradled the little plastic square, scanning the back of the jewel case only to find that it was blank. They were really going for something outlandish here.

Mysterious. No track listing. No special thanks. Nothing.

Just blackness.

...

"Nice, dude," the cashier said when I went to pay for it. He was kind of cute, looked like a skater. His lip was pierced. Probably named Alex.

"Have you listened to it yet?" I asked him, half-serious about striking up a conversation about Stay Sweet and probably also subconsciously flirting with him. *Definitely* flirting with him.

"Nah, but it's supposed to be fucking epic. You ever see them live?"

"No. I really want to, but they never play around here."

"I saw them last year when in Scranton," he said. "Hands down one of the best shows I've ever been to. They're fucking dope."

I sighed with jealousy. I was probably the band's No. 1 fan, but still felt no hopes of seeing them live. What kind of devoted fan doesn't even see their favorite band in concert?

The cashier skater boy scanned the CD, I paid him, he gave me my change, and slipped the new album into a bag that he had already taken out and unfolded onto the counter. Each step seemed so

ceremonial, so ritualistic, like a priest spreading out the linen corporal over the alter in preparation for the holy sacrament of the eucharist.

As he handed me the bag and my receipt, my eyes wandered over to the various life-size cardboard cutouts of different celebrities of the music industry on display next to the magazine racks.

Brendon Urie of Panic! At the Disco, Sonny Moore of From First to Last, Billie Joe Armstrong of Green Day, Hayley Williams of Paramore...

...Matt...Daniels...of Stay Sweet.

The cutout was the "in the flesh" version of *Nitro*'s album cover, Matt staring seductively and biting down on his index finger. It caught me off guard, the closest I've ever been to seeing him in person.

"Are these things for sale?" I asked.

The cashier looked up from his issue of *Thrasher* and nodded.

"Yep."

I approached the artificial face of Matt Daniels. Despite its obvious indication that I was infatuated with the image of this famous figure, another boy, I surprisingly felt no shame when I reached out and brushed the top side of my hand along the rough edges of what in real life would be the soft skin of his cheek.

How could anyone be this beautiful?

...

"What. The. Fuck. Is. That?"

Justin stared at me in disbelief as I hauled the life-size cardboard cutout of Matt Daniels to his car. Walking back through the mall and through Sears with it felt rather awkward, but I couldn't pass up on the opportunity to have this amazing relic.

"It was only twenty-five bucks," I said. "It's going in my room."

Justin shook his head as I carefully set cardboard Matt along the center console between us, bent at the "hips" so that it was as if Matt Daniels were sitting there [the parking brake looked rather phallic as it stuck up between cardboard Matt's crotch]. Then I climbed in, next to Justin, with the new album in my hands as I marveled over this new piece of Stay Sweet that belonged to me.

"We have, like, ten minutes before kickoff," Justin said as he fired up the car. The Pontiac's 4-cylinder rumbled to life...for the last time. The digital clock on the dash told us it was 6:49.

"We'll make it," I said, clicking in my seatbelt. I immediately began tearing the plastic packaging from the new CD.

"We fucking better. I just texted Tyler. He wanted to know where the fuck I am. Told him you dragged me here to get your dumbass CD and he's fucking pissed."

"Can we listen to it?" I asked, ignoring him, and holding up the now-unwrapped CD case.

My brother shrugged. We were pulling out of the mall parking lot, past the crowded Applebee's, and blending in with the traffic on the highway. A sea of cars was now fighting to get from the congestion of Route 222 to their good times on a Friday night.

"You're only gonna get through, like, one song," Justin said.

I didn't care. This was it. It was a *new* song, a new melody to add to the collection of lyrics that never failed to bring me out of a depression, even if it was just ever so slightly.

I popped the disc out of the case and slid it into the CD player. The little digital characters on the readout switched and adjusted as it began to read the disc.

...

Guitar riff begins.

Yes! I immediately recognized Sean Stone's playing style. No one could match his signature sound.

Tristan LaFerriere

Track one of *Mandragora*. I didn't even know the title of this new song yet.

I still don't.

The traffic was changing from less of a stop and go, but a slow and steady line of glowing red taillights that drifted along in an orderly, uniform fashion. The mushroom orbs of the mall's parking lot lights faded behind us.

"Here we are in your unmade bed,
fully clothed and with a feeling of dread..."

The sound of Matt Daniels's voice...

"You have your suitcase...
and I don't know where we're going from here,
is this really what you want to do, my dear..."

Justin drove onto the exit ramp for King's Lake Road, the winding bend that hugs the edge of King's Lake. It's a direct route, a sort of "back way" scenic shortcut to the center of town and then to Carlton, where the high school is. He was driving fast, presumably to ensure we didn't miss the kickoff of that stupid fucking game.

Unlike the highway we had just come from, King's Lake Road was practically desolate, and horror movie-scene dark.

"The tears in your face tell me all,
the sudden gasp in your voice is a call...
I can't let you go now..."

So fucking epic...

As the lyrics poured from the angelic voice of Matt Daniels, I looked over at my brother who was staring ahead at the dark, empty road only illuminated by the car's headlights.

"Under my sheets!
It's where I find you,
all we have
are the memories left between them..."

Justin looked over at me for a moment.

I smiled at him, trying to encourage him to crack one, too.

He had been so miserable that day. I'll never know why he was, but I didn't want him to be. I just wanted him to be the optimistic Justin I knew.

I wanted him to be the Justin who climbed into bed with me only a few nights before and hugged me just because he wanted to.

I wanted him to love me and not be afraid to show it just because he was putting on an act for his friends.

> *"I still dream of you,*
> *I still dream of you,*
> *I still dream..."*

Justin smiled, but it was a disappointed kind of smile, like he felt bad for something he had done, and this expression was making up for whatever it was.

> *"I find you under my sheets..."*

And that was when the headlights illuminated the deer standing stupidly in the middle of King's Lake Road.

That was when Justin's first instinct was to jerk the steering wheel sharply to the right.

That was when the tires of the Pontiac screeched, and the nose of the car went diving into the guardrail that separates the road from the edge of the now infamous lake that will forever be associated with the tragedy that struck this town.

That was when my brother slammed on the brakes while we both screamed...in unison...to the sound of crunching metal as the car slammed through the rail and dangled over the edge.

The airbags deployed, a deafening shotgun sound that exploded into our faces violently. My ears were left ringing after the deafening blast, the skin of my face burning.

The car's busted radiator hissed as it leaked steam. Rocks and stones tumbled down into the water. I could hear them splash violently, a warning of what was about to come.

The stereo had seized. Matt's singing voice was reduced to a skipping, distorted chanting speaking in tongues that coincided with our grunting as we attempted to escape the crippled car.

I howled in pain, wincing from the sharp cut that the seat belt had dug into me on impact. I managed to untangle myself from it, kicked open my door, and started to climb out as Justin attempted the same on the driver's side.

I caught a glimpse of blood on the dashboard, on the steering wheel, on the deflated airbags…dripping like thick syrup. The red glow of the dash lights flickered and flashed like some hellish lightshow. This fucked-up image was only further provoked by what was once the sound of the seat belt warning chime, now a long, drawn-out whine that played over the scene. The car was screaming in pain.

Cardboard Matt Daniels had been thrown up against the severely cracked windshield, his head torn from the body and now resting against the blood-splattered dashboard. His seductive gaze was still present. The face was bent, a crease permanently folded from the top left side of his head to the bottom right of his chin.

I tumbled out onto the grass just at the edge of the lake, dizzy and disoriented in a pile of broken glass as my brother struggled with the jammed driver's side door. Then he was climbing over to my side, blood on his forehead, reaching for me…

…and calling out my name…

I wanted to reach back to him…

I wanted to pull him out…

…but like a dream where you're trying to escape something, it was as if a force were paralyzing me, pushing me down on the ground and holding me back.

Something wasn't letting him stay.

My brother's car slid over the edge and plunged upside down into the lake below. Its thunderous splash is the last thing I remember before I blacked out.

Tristan LaFerriere

Chapter Five
Monday, September 25th, 2006

Dear Journal,

On the night of Justin's funeral, I had a dream.

Justin and I made it to the homecoming game.

The accident never happened.

We arrived at the football field just in time to hear the last few notes of The National Anthem. We received glares of disapproval from conservative-looking fathers because we didn't stop to face the flag, and then, of course, we were over meeting up with Tyler, Eric, and Evan. Dennis Folton was there, too. So were Ashley Fielding and Melissa Grandstaff.

It was crowded, and a number of people were hanging out underneath the bleachers. Some couples were making out, others were arguing. I could hear the cheerleaders doing their cheesy routine I had heard them practicing for earlier in the month while I scanned the crowds of cliques congregating beneath the seats as if it were some sort of secret underworld.

The weird thing about the dream is that it wasn't like how dreams normally are where you're in a familiar place, but it looks completely different from the way it does in real life. This really felt like the football field at the high school. I could practically smell the fresh coat of red and black paint that had been recently applied to the new digital scoreboard lit against the black night sky.

It really felt like Justin was still alive.

Dreams are especially strange when someone who died is in them. My grandma [Mom's mom] died when I was four. A few months after her death, I dreamt that she and I were spending the day together in some Florida neighborhood. I don't know why it was Florida; I've never even been to Florida, but in the dream, I asked her why she was there since she had just died.

Grandma Curran's response to me was, *"Oh, Kieran, honey, I just couldn't sleep. So, I decided to come back."*

And that made perfect sense to my four-year-old mind.

I spent the rest of that dream exploring the nearby beaches of the Gulf Coast with her like we were on our own little vacation together. Vague recollections of fighting pirates and befriending anthropomorphic fish with her also come to mind when I think back to that dream, but those scenes are fuzzy in comparison to the crystal-clear parts with my grandmother suddenly come back to life. She came back just to visit me.

Similarly, I knew Justin was gone, but...there he was at the game with me. And it was completely normal. It was just his usual routine of meeting up with his friends that I hated, me watching him from the sidelines and wishing I could still be a part of the group...

He was just...back. I didn't even have to question it.

...

I haven't written any entries in a while for obvious reasons. For the past few weeks, I haven't even had the energy to do everyday tasks.

But I have to write again. It's the only way I can really "talk" to anyone.

Justin's really gone.

It didn't fully hit me until I saw his body in the casket a week later at the funeral parlor during his viewing. It didn't even look like my brother. It looked like a sleeping wax statue. His skin wasn't that color. He had obviously been touched up with makeup to hide whatever he really looked like in death. And his hair...his hair was always so beautiful, but...something just wasn't right about it. The color...it wasn't that perfect brown anymore. It looked almost...gray...and artificial like a wig that had been sewn into his scalp.

That was when I broke down. I cried even harder than Mom or Dad [probably because they were both drugged up quite a bit on Xanax]. My grandfather came over to comfort me, and I hugged him, which felt strange because I've never really been all that close to him. He and my dad, while they're civil with each other, haven't always been

91

on the greatest terms. My grandfather used to insist to my dad and Uncle Ryan that they call him by his first name rather than "dad" so that no one would think he was old enough to have children, so yeah…that gives you an idea of their relationship.

I blubbered like a baby while I sank my face into the expensive suit that Darren, Sr. wore. He hugged me close and told me everything would be okay. He even hugged Dad that night. I've never seen them go so far as to shake hands.

Mom's just been quiet most of the time. We haven't sat down as a family at the dinner table since. It's all been takeout and eating separately in our bedrooms like we're in our own secluded apartments of misery.

Sometimes I hear Mom crying down the hall while Dad tries to comfort her. She never cries in front of me. I think it's all part of that obsession she has with trying to be professional. Being successful is an attribute that she will never give up under any circumstances. She refuses to appear weak.

I've even seen Dad cry more than her. Most recently, I caught him on the phone in the sunroom, begging his brother to return a call because he had awful news for him. My Uncle Ryan tends to disappear a lot, and, in this case, it drove my dad to tears, which I listened to from around the corner in the living room. His sobbing stopped me in my tracks on my way to the kitchen, and I froze because the rare glimpse of him crying paralyzed me with discomfort.

"Please, Ryan...please pick up," I heard him cry as he paced the room on the cordless phone. "It's Justin...your nephew. Please, just call me. Please. I don't know what to do. I just...I don't know...I don't know…I…don't…know."

Dad has yet to get through to him. He didn't come to the funeral and probably still isn't even aware of what happened. The last we heard from him, he was supposedly somewhere near Seattle and that was at least two years ago. He had some idea of re-inventing his life up there because living in Portland just wasn't working out anymore…and before that, living in Pasadena with my grandparents hadn't satisfied his "wild" lifestyle as Mom has described his problem. It seems that every few years, he just keeps going north in hopes that he'll find a place where he belongs.

I think I kind of get him. If that means Vancouver is his next destination, I wouldn't mind joining him.

...

I still have flashbacks to the accident on a daily basis. They pulled Justin's body out of that lake a few hours after the crash. Paramedics swarmed on me, asking me so many questions like if I knew my name, if I knew what time it was. They were shining bright lights in my eyes, trying to determine just how severe my injuries were. I was in shock, badly bruised, and perhaps forever will be, from that damn seat belt that saved my life. Now I wear its mark like a jagged tattoo across my chest, a hideous black and blue stripe that's still sensitive to the touch.

The Stay Sweet shirt I had been wearing has several specks of blood splattered against the band's signature logo. I've stashed it away in the closet and find myself avoiding the corner where it hangs every morning when I get dressed. I'm still not sure if that blood belongs to me or Justin, but I know both of us bled that night, and for some reason that makes no fucking sense, I can't bring myself to get rid of it. It's like throwing it away would put a curse on me.

...

Today was my first day back in school since the accident. Mom and Dad insisted that it was okay if I decided to stay home for another week if I had to, but I argued that another minute in the house would have driven me crazy. It's a lot different from the days I spent locked in my room over the summer when the most I had to worry about was one of my brother's friends calling me out for jerking off in the middle of the woods.

Such simpler fucking times...

Now my room feels like a prison for just me and my thoughts. Thoughts are the biggest bully I've yet to come across, and it's not like you can just avoid your thoughts like you can other people. You're stuck with them, so the only option I felt I had was to go back to school and try to play it like everything was back to normal even though that was far from the truth.

93

It would never be the truth. Nothing would ever be completely normal again.

This morning, I woke up to my alarm for the first time since September 8th. Unlike the previous days of my morning routine, the house was dead silent after I slapped the snooze button. No other alarms since Mom and Dad still aren't ready to return to work, no showers running, no air-conditioning or ceiling fan humming now that the outside air has grown cooler with the arrival of fall. No light or sounds outside my windows, as they were closed, and the curtains were drawn. For some reason, even the usual distant sounds of traffic on the nearby Route 222 behind our development were inaudible this morning. It was as if everything were paused.

I just laid on my back, staring up at the ceiling while I waited for Justin to come barging into my room to berate me for not getting out of bed yet. Of course, that moment never came, and I had to make the final decision that I was, in fact, going to force myself to get up.

I did a few minutes later. I tossed away my sheets and comforter and looked around my room like I was seeing it for the first time since the accident, like I'd just come out of a coma and was re-discovering the world, like I was trying to find something different in the details of my usual surroundings…as if a tragedy meant anything would be different.

It wasn't.

Everything was just as it was before. The same La-Z-Boy sat in the corner next to the window, the same Stay Sweet poster hung on the wall above my desk where the same computer was, and the same four gray walls besieged me as always.

My feet were hugging the soft carpet. I made fists with my toes, started to stand up, and felt a sharp pain across my chest where the seat belt has forever stained me. I crossed the room carefully as if I might run into a trap, and it felt like I was walking a mile from my bed to the door. I wanted to fall back, get under the covers again, and try to wake up from this nightmare that's lasted several weeks.

But, of course, I didn't.

I opened the door and went into the hall where I found Larry curled up in a ball outside the closed door to what used to be Justin's room.

Used to be...Jesus...

The doors to Mom and Dad's bedroom and the guestroom were closed. I was peering out of my room like Dorothy exploring the outside for the first time just after her house landed in Oz. I was observing my world after the storm, the post-apocalyptic suburbia that is King's Valley following the death of its well-respected leader.

I showered for as long as I could, watching the hot water swirl down the drain for an eternity. The suds ran clear, so I guess all the leftover dye that could have washed out of my hair has already.

Quickly, I slipped in and out of my closet to choose an outfit, grabbed my backpack, and headed downstairs. By the time I was in the kitchen, Dad had already gotten up, although he wasn't dressed for work; he was still wearing his blue pajamas while he sipped his coffee.

"Hey," he said, forcing a smile through his tired eyes.

"Hey. You're...going to work?"

"No." He put down his coffee cup on the counter, the ceramic clacking against the granite. "I thought maybe you'd...want a ride to school."

"Oh." I noticed his pajama top was buttoned wrong. "I, uh...I can take the bus."

Did I really want that? No, but I guess I didn't want to inconvenience him, or something. He hasn't been sleeping much and it really shows. Meanwhile, Mom has been sleeping too much with the aid of Ambien.

"Are you sure?" he asked like he was begging for an excuse to drive me.

"It's okay."

"I really don't mind. We can stop at Dunkin' Donuts for breakfast if you want."

I stood awkwardly in the doorway, eyeing the backdoor like getting past Dad was an obstacle in a video game where my first objective was to get out of the house.

I suppose that would mean the final boss would be Tyler Kirkland.

"I can take the bus, Dad. It's okay..."

"Are you sure you're ready to go back, Kier? It's really okay if you want to stay home. If you need to..."

"Dad...I *have* to go to school. I can't stay in this house anymore. It's just..."

The fridge conveniently hummed to life to break the silence, and then the sounds of Mom's footsteps could be heard upstairs. She was getting up and she'd be down in a few minutes. I didn't want to have to talk to both of them, so I made a decision quickly.

"I'm...just gonna take the bus. I'll be fine."

...

"Alright."

He looked disappointed, and I started to regret not taking him up on his offer as I headed out the backdoor, but I was just happy to be alone again once I was walking down the steps from the deck.

I passed our pool that's now closed for the season, the same pool where only two months ago, I laid and watched my brother swimming with Eric. Now it's as desolate as a water park closed for the winter. Dead leaves have fallen against its cover and diving board leading to nowhere, the lounge chairs and other patio furniture have all been put away in the basement, and the filter is dead silent.

I opened the gate and started to walk around the side of the house, next to the windows of our sunroom as I passed the stucco house next door. We've yet to meet the new neighbors, but it's probably been

awkward for them seeing a line of cars in front of the house after Justin's funeral and not knowing whether or not they should come knock on the door out of respect or wait until the storm's died down a little to introduce themselves. I don't blame them for not showing their faces yet. I certainly wouldn't want to get to know my family right now.

I started walking down the street, past other houses, past fenced-in backyards where swimming pools were either closed or beginning to turn green, toward the bus stop at the corner of Steeplechase Way. I hadn't taken the bus since we were back in California, and I was feeling myself slowly build up to a panic as I imagined what this experience would be like.

Would people know who I was?

Would they recognize me as the late Justin Northrup's younger brother?

A number of people from the high school showed up at the funeral and may have seen me sitting in the front row near the casket as they came up to pay their respects.

I don't want their fucking pity. I just want them to leave me alone.

I zipped up my red Stay Sweet hoodie, and when I saw the figures of other King's Valley High students waiting at the corner, I flipped my hood up. In my experience, an emo kid having his hair in his face and his hood over his head is the universal sign for *"Don't fucking bother me."*

I stood at the corner where a few other Belmont Hill Estates residents made small talk. I looked down at the sidewalk most of the time, so I couldn't tell if any of them were looking at me. I just eavesdropped on their conversations about their high scores on *Guitar Hero* or how angry their conservative parents are that Nancy Pelosi just might win the election.

I looked up when the bus whirred up to the stop a few minutes later, its brakes squeaking at an uncomfortably loud volume just after the red Alfa Romeo from the house next door to us sped by. What sounded like another Green Day song was blasting from its sound system.

I followed the others I didn't know up the bus steps, found a seat in the middle, but still slightly closer to the front, and leaned my head against the cold window.

As the bus filled from stop to stop, the talking grew louder, and I decided that I needed my Walkman CD player, so I dug it out of my backpack, popped in my Cute Is What We Aim For CD, and stuck my earbuds in my ears.

I started the CD on Track 7, "Sweet Talk 101". The song served as my soundtrack as we pulled up to the high school.

...

"Hey, you okay?"

Thomas greeted me in the hallway after the end of homeroom.

I wasn't prepared to say anything to anyone. I stared at him stupidly for a few seconds with the weird thought that I should've just turned and walked away like I didn't see him, but that would've been fucked up.

"Yeah," I finally said, and fuck, if I wasn't already starting to feel tears welling up in my eyes. I gave up on trying to hold it in and wiped my eyes with the thick sleeve of my hoodie.

"Oh, Kieran," Thomas said. "I'm sorry." It was about as serious as I've ever heard his tone.

We walked over to the corner of the hallway, and I turned to face the cinder block wall, embarrassed and ashamed of myself as he put a hand on my shoulder. A laminated poster urging me not to smoke pot caught my eye as I attempted to compose myself.

"It's just so...fucking...awful," is all I could spit out. I took in big breaths, the warm tears stinging my eyes. I must've looked like a fucking mess.

"It's alright." Thomas patted my shoulder. "It's alright. Just let it out, man."

My head hurt and my nose was running with gross snot.

"I don't know why I fucking came here," I snorted. "I just don't want to be in that...fucking house anymore."

Thomas still had his hand on my shoulder. I could tell he wasn't sure of where to take this conversation. I can't imagine the awkwardness on his end.

"I'm sorry I couldn't make it to the funeral," he said. "My dad was a guest speaker at Penn State, and..."

"Let's not talk about it," I interrupted. I'd finally gotten enough of a grip to at least speak normally.

"Okay." Now he really didn't know what to say. "Just...let me know if you need to talk, Northrup."

"I will."

"See you in class?"

"Yeah." My voice cracked.

He nodded and gave me a slightly uncomfortable smile before he headed off to his first class. I stood up against the wall with my red, wet eyes matching the color of my hoodie. A couple of people looked over at me as they passed by. Either they knew who I was, and they were gawking at me, or they were just wondering what this emo pussy was crying about.

...

As the morning progressed, all my teachers made it very clear that I can catch up at my own pace. They offered their condolences, and I spent each period daydreaming while my eyes wandered the classrooms.

Justin was in everything I saw, everything I heard, everything I touched. Any face I saw contained his deep brown eyes staring back at me, any teacher lecturing the class was his voice, any pen or pencil I held was his firm hand on mine.

I swore on several occasions throughout the day that I could even smell him. I would get this brief whiff of a scent that reminded me of him. I can't describe it, but it was just…him. It's as if a part of him were following me around. Was he still roaming these walls somehow?

There were a few more instances where I neared tears, but somehow, I was strong enough to struggle through the morning. Maybe it isn't so bad that the teachers all feel sorry for me and aren't expecting much effort. I don't want to sound like a typical slacker kid who doesn't do anything, but right now, I think I've earned a day or two of just sitting and doing nothing.

At lunch, I sat with Thomas and Athena like usual. I didn't get any food. I wasn't hungry. I haven't really been hungry for weeks. I may have even lost a few pounds. My belly must be practically concave at this point.

"How are your parents doing?" Athena asked me once we sat in the hallway.

"I don't know," I responded, my CD player in my hands. I regretted not putting my earbuds in immediately because I really didn't feel like talking about this. "My mom doesn't say much when she's grieving. I think she's worried it'll show…weakness…or something."

"What about your dad?"

Thomas was munching on a ham and cheese sandwich when he sort of eyed Athena like she was prying too much, probably worried that she'd set me off as he accidentally did this morning.

"He's been pretty quiet, too," I said. "Everyone's been quiet."

"Oh. Well…I'm really glad you're back."

"Thanks," I said. "I guess I am, too." I turned to Thomas. "Sorry I never got that review ready."

"You're kidding, right?"

"I *do* want to contribute," I said. "I don't want to just sit around while the paper gets written without me. I just don't know what to write about now. I'm not feeling very creative."

"Well, you can always submit the album review for the next issue," Thomas said. "But with some sort of interview with someone to go along with it. If you feel you're up to it right now, there's probably still time for this issue, too. You'd just have to have something soon, like this week, for it to be considered. We're starting layout next week and that means everything has to be edited and ready by Friday at the latest."

"I don't know if I can listen to that album," I said quickly. "It's..." *Fuck, here we go again. I'm getting more emotional by the second.* "It's what...Justin and I were listening to when..."

"Oh," Thomas said, looking uncomfortable again. "Well...you can...always pick something else."

"Under my sheets!
It's where I find you,
all we have
are the memories left between them..."

That fucking song is torturing me, and I can't get it out of my fucking head...

"Excuse me."

I stood and headed for the nearest bathroom. I needed a secluded place so I could cry in private this time.

There are bathrooms in the hall just across from the cafeteria entrance. I made my way through the crowds as lunch was starting to die down. Keeping my head down to avoid eye contact with anyone, I went through the men's room door, felt relieved to find the room empty, and headed to the stall furthest in the corner.

I stepped into the stall, locked it, sat on the toilet, and let the tears flow.

...

After lunch, I was called to the guidance office over the PA, just as I was about to go to fifth period. I almost considered ignoring it because I knew exactly what they were pulling me in for and I didn't

want to talk about it, but it was an excuse to not have to go to science. I was actually slightly happier with the idea of going to guidance to be psychoanalyzed than having to sit through a class with that woman screaming her face off about inertia.

After walking to the office, I was told by this receptionist who looked like she just downed a bottle of Valium to wait and Dr. Meller would be with me in a moment to talk.

I didn't have to wait long, but it gave me enough time to look around the room. It's like a real therapist office waiting room, only sadder. A Latina girl was sitting in a chair near mine, looking bored while she stared ahead at some generic motivational posters with stock images of nature or aquatic life. I could smell incense burning somewhere, or it might've just been someone wearing too much patchouli. A phone was ringing, and it wasn't being answered. The Windows XP startup tune sounded from one of the room's desktops.

"You're Kieran..."

…

I turned to face the Latina girl who went from staring at the wall in boredom to looking at me with an expression that said, *"Here we fucking are. What are you in for?"*

"Aren't you?" she said when I didn't say anything.

…

"…Yeah…"

She continued to stare me down harshly. That phone in the background still wasn't being answered.

"I'm sorry," she said.

And then she turned back to face the wall.

"Kieran Northrup?"

Dr. Meller called me into her office. I walked into the small room in the back of the waiting area where she told me to sit down. The

blinds were closed, and a lamp was switched on at her desk, throwing petals of soft light around the shadowy room. I sank into this overstuffed armchair directly across from her, and she sat down at her computer surrounded by various souvenirs and photographs, memories of twenty years of vacations with her family that have been paid for by the King's Valley Board of Ed.

"Kieran, I'm Dr. Meller," she said. "I'm your guidance counselor."

She flashed a concerned smile. I have to say that even though I'm gay, this woman is very pretty. I'd make a guess and say she's in her mid-40s. She has medium-length black hair, wears glasses, and today she was wearing a dark blue dress accented with a nice-looking necklace that her husband probably bought her. She typed a few things at her keyboard, the monitor of her computer shielded by one of those privacy filters, and then looked up to me again.

"So, Kieran, I'm sorry to pull you away from class, but I just wanted to talk to you for a few minutes."

She enunciated each word as if teaching one how to speak English. Every syllable was heard.

"I'm fine, really," I said, immediately feeling stupid for saying that because that's exactly what people say when they're not fine.

"Okay," she continued, slight hesitation in her voice. "I guess you probably know why I called you in here, then."

I shrugged.

"Listen," she said. Her voice was very soft. "Kieran, I understand what you must be going through right now is very difficult. I'm not even going to go into detail about it because I'm sure you've got a lot on your mind, but I just wanted to let you know that if there's anything you want to talk about at any time, you can just come down here to my office. Okay?"

"Yeah," I said.

"Are you…doing okay?"

"Yeah, I'm okay. I mean, I don't really know how to feel, I guess."

She nodded, followed by a full sixty seconds of silence.

"How are things at home, Kieran?"

"They're fine."

"Have your parents been helping you cope?"

I shrugged again.

"I don't know. I guess. They don't say much about it."

Dr. Meller typed a few more things, but she didn't take her eyes off me. And then she wasn't saying anything, but just staring me down like she was waiting for me to say something else for her to analyze.

"I don't really know what else to say," I continued. "Even though my brother's gone, it's not like anything else is really different...except that he's...gone."

"Were you and your brother close?"

It's sad that I had to think about my answer.

"We...*were*."

"So, you both got along fairly well?"

"I mean, most of the time, yeah. I don't know, I mean, he was a lot different than me."

"In what ways?"

"He was into sports and shit." I paused. "Sorry."

She let out a little laugh.

"It's alright. I think I can give you a pass on that one. My office is like Vegas. What happens in here stays in here."

Her attempted reference was painfully desperate in trying to connect with me as a young person.

"I really looked up to him a lot, I guess," I finally said. I bit my lip hard. "He was really popular."

She smiled, but it was one of those sad smiles, like the one Justin flashed me seconds before he died.

"I *have* heard a lot about him. It sounds like he was a good kid."

Hearing my brother called "kid" is weird because to me, he always seemed so much older and experienced in the world.

"Yeah."

Dr. Meller took in a deep breath. I guess this was her cue to end our session.

"Well, Kieran, I'm going to let you get back to class now, but just remember that you can come down here to talk whenever you want to, okay? I've notified your teachers, so all you have to do is ask them and they'll let you come down."

"Okay."

She stood up and opened the door for me. That overpowering incense or patchouli smell wafted in from the waiting room. That damn phone was ringing again, and it still wasn't being answered.

"Just take it easy. We're here for you."

"Thank you."

I headed for the door to the hall, but froze when I noticed Ashley Fielding sitting in a chair in the same spot I had been waiting minutes before. Tears were in her eyes as she stared blankly at the wall, but then she noticed me. Besides the tears, she was expressionless. She looked right through me.

Tristan LaFerriere

Chapter Six
Friday, September 29th, 2006

Dear Journal,

This is going to be a fairly short entry because I'm pretty busy. I'm starting to finally get back into somewhat of a routine and actually do have homework that I've decided to put the slightest bit of effort into tonight.

Yeah, I know; it's Friday, but I just know that if I don't do what's due for Monday tonight, then I'll be rushing to finish late Sunday evening or even early Monday morning. I'm trying to avoid stress even in the slightest form, so for now, I've stopped procrastinating like usual.

In Journalism, I'm doing an album review, but it isn't for *Mandragora*. Since I've been listening to *The Same Old Blood Rush with a New Touch*, the Cute Is What We Aim For album, a lot, I figured it would be a good opportunity to write about it. I've been listening to a few of the songs repeatedly to help me get just the right words out about how I want to describe the feel of the album. "The Curse of Curves" is, of course, their signature song, but I think "The Fourth Drink Instinct" and "Teasing to Please" are my favorites. "Finger Twist & Split" gets a special mention, too. It has some of the most beautiful guitar-playing I've ever heard. It's almost what I would describe as harmonic. Listening to it makes me feel like I'm right there in the recording studio with them. And the lyrics…it's pure poetry.

Mrs. Kinney has been really accommodating. While most everyone else is starting the layout process, she's giving me extra time to work on my article. She's told me that the work I've been doing so far is impressive and she wants my voice to have a space in the paper even if it means I'm not working at the same pace as everyone else. That's fine with me since the layout process bores me. I'd rather just write.

Thomas has been helping me out a lot, too. He's a good proofreader, but I'll be honest that sometimes he's a little too blunt with his thoughts on the material. I'm still thankful I've had him and Athena, though, to keep me sane this past week. It's good to not be completely alone.

Overall, things seem to have gotten sort of better since Monday. Mom's back at work now. Dad's going back on Monday, but he's been busy working from home for the past few days. He's converted the guestroom into a temporary office.

I can't really tell how he's feeling. I think he's obviously still depressed, but most of the time he's just quiet. As far as I know, he still hasn't heard from Uncle Ryan, and I think deep down, even though they're not in each other's lives all that much, it really hurts him.

...

What prompted me to write tonight is that, believe it or not, I actually went out and did something.

I went to a home game.

Even though it's far from what I'd normally do on a Friday night, it made me think of what Justin and I missed out on. I guess in a way, it felt like I was fulfilling something that was never finished. I was also sort of genuinely curious to see what a home game in King's Valley was like since it's all anybody ever talks about around here. For a school so obsessed with its athletics, particularly the football team, I imagined this would be about as intense as it could get. It was better than just sitting depressed in my room like usual. Even if I did have homework to do, it was Friday night. Fucking Friday night. I had to take Friday nights back because they haven't been the same since. I used to love Friday nights, but now that it's scarred with the memories of the accident, there's a dismal chill in the air that counts each week that's passed since Justin died.

Three weeks.

Twenty-one days.

I lived my entire life, nearly fifteen years, alongside my older brother, and after just twenty-one days, it feels like he was never here. His absence has sadly become normal.

I figured that the game would somehow throw the little bit of social life I've ever had back into motion. I've sort of gotten used to being back in school, so not being a prisoner of my room on the weekends is the next step to living a "normal" life again.

107

Dad seemed shocked when I asked him if he would drive me, but also pleasantly surprised to see that I wanted to go out. He jumped up from his chair in the sunroom, put on his coat, tossed me the keys, and offered to let me back the car out. I passed on the offer, though, and just let him do it. With my mind as distracted as it's been lately, I imagined good chances of me driving right into the side of the house.

"I didn't know you liked football," he said once we were backing out of the driveway in his brand-new Cadillac DTS that still smelled fresh from the car wash.

"I don't," I said.

He shifted into drive and started down the street, the Cadillac's V8 purring once we picked up speed. The sun was setting and the halogen streetlamps around the neighborhood were buzzing to life for the night as we went downhill.

"Well, this is an interesting choice for you, then, isn't it?"

"It's…something to do," I said. "I guess."

This was the extent of our conversation.

Dad pulled up in front of the high school a few minutes later. I opened my door and stepped out, already hearing the marching band's brass instruments and tapping of drums drifting through the air from the stadium. I walked along with others who were just arriving, some being dropped off by their parents like me, or those with their licenses pulling up in their first cars.

I was wearing my red Stay Sweet hoodie again [it's basically my uniform these days], hands in my pockets, and hood up to keep warm from the ever-growing cold. I paid my $5 admission fee at the entrance gate where a volunteer dad was working, entered the stadium, and found it to be not so much different from the dream I had where I walked through the same grounds with my brother only to be separated from him a few moments later.

In this case, of course, I was alone, and I felt even more alone here than I had when I went to the homecoming dance. I think that sports just generally make me feel like an outsider because it's never

been my thing. Thomas wasn't there to keep me company, either. It was just me and a few hundred other people who all seemed to know each other.

I got some overpriced cheese fries and a Coke at the concession stand after waiting in a forever-line, walked along the chain-link fence that separates the bleachers from the field as I watched the marching band play their rendition of "The Horse", and scanned the seats for a safe place to sit.

Unlike my dream, the underside of the bleachers is not open for everyone to roam around in real life. I was disappointed by this because it seemed like the best place for someone like me in such a setting. If anything, I may have found my King's Valley equivalents chilling under the popular crowds sitting above. Instead, I made my way up the bleachers, sat in an open space, and watched as the game began while munching on my messy fries and sipping my soda.

Twenty minutes in, I still had no idea what was going on. I understand football so little that I never really watch it; I just look at it. All I could follow were the gestures of the rest of the crowd, so when they cheered, I attempted to look pleased and when they booed, I just maintained my usual expressionless face.

"Hey, man! Aren't you in my gym class?"

I didn't even look up because I was sure no one would be talking to me. If they were directing their words to me, it'd probably be to ask how I enjoyed shooting a load in the woods at Tyler Kirkland's house.

"Hey!"

I turned to see Adam Woolf, a cute blonde jock from the senior class of my gym period, sitting at the other end of the empty bleacher. I felt goosebumps not from the cool air, but from having flashbacks to what it was like when someone as cute as Eric Gleason was interested in making small talk with a person of my status.

"Oh," I said. "Hey."

"You're in my gym class, right?"

I've never talked to Adam before. His type intimidates me now that I know what true colors can come out of the town's jocks. Tyler has really ruined the image of this archetype for me.

"Yeah," I said. "I think so."

Oh, I've noticed him. Even when I'm in my deepest depths of depression, I can't help but subconsciously pick out the guys I'd like to see naked. I've never gotten a glimpse of Adam's dick in the gym showers, but now that I'm thinking about it, I'm sure I could if I'm discreet enough.

"You're Kieran, right?"

I nodded.

"Yeah."

"I'm Adam."

"Cool."

I looked back at the game I was uninterested in, but Adam wasn't finished.

"I...I was friends with your brother, man."

I shivered.

"Oh?"

"I'm sorry," Adam immediately said. "I mean, Justin was a great guy. I mean, I'm really sorry about what happened."

"It's okay," I said, wiping the fake cheese from my mouth with a thin napkin.

"You, uh...holding up okay?"

I forced a smile while I quickly swallowed a clump of the greasy crinkle cuts.

"I'm fine."

Adam smiled, too, but it was so much more genuine than anything I could ever pull off.

"Good, man," he said. "Are you, uh, here with anybody?"

"No."

"Oh. How'd you get here?"

"My dad dropped me off."

"You want to sit over here?"

"Yeah, sure," I said as nonchalantly as I could, even though it was pretty damn thrilling that the cutest guy who had talked to me since Eric Gleason was inviting me to get closer to him.

All the reason to be more cautious; I'd see how this played out.

"So...were you here for the homecoming game?" I asked.

"Yep. Red Devils lost, though. It was a major defeat, man. Wyomissing creamed us, twenty-one to nothing."

"Guess that superstitious tradition doesn't work so well, huh?"

"Yeah, right?"

We both laughed, and then my stomach dropped as I noticed Evan Kirkland walking along a row not too far from us, down toward the middle, where Tyler, Eric, and Dennis Folton were sitting with Melissa Grandstaff and some other girl I didn't know. I worried one of them would notice me, and what an embarrassment it would be if they spotted me with Adam Woolf. They'd probably come over immediately to ensure that he was aware of the "incident in the woods".

I almost thought I noticed Tyler looking over his shoulder at us like he knew we were here, but it must've been my paranoia. I've never seen Tyler and Adam hanging out. Adam's friendship with my brother must've been only between the two of them. I couldn't imagine a scenario with Adam fitting into a group of people who played a game

111

like "Butt Kicks". He seemed, at least at first glance, too mature for that kind of thing.

"What are you doing after the game?" Adam asked me.

I shrugged.

"I don't know. Probably just going home. I've got homework to do."

"Dude!" Adam laughed. "It's Friday! Fuck that."

"I know, but I just want to chill over the weekend. It's been...rough to say the least."

"I feel ya," he said. "But me and a few friends are going to see *The Wicker Man* after this. You want to come?"

Very tempting...

"Maybe," I said. "Who are you going with?"

"Tyler and Evan Kirkland. You know them, right?"

Knew it was too good to be true.

"Oh, no," I said. "No, no, no, no."

"What?"

"I can't. I don't...get along with them. Especially Tyler. I can't fucking stand him."

"Oh," Adam laughed. "Tyler's just Tyler, man. I've known him since the fourth grade. He's harmless, just a character."

"A *very* unlikable character," I said. "I'm sorry, but I can't. He doesn't like me. He likes to...spread rumors about me."

Adam waved a hand in the air.

"Who cares what Tyler says? Just come to see the movie. If he starts shit with you, just tell him to shut his mouth."

It sucks because I really did want to go, but the idea of seeing Tyler especially sounded bad right now. I wasn't sure if he'd start anything with me. If he did, that would be true evil considering he knows what I've been through, but I just didn't feel like risking it.

"I'm...sorry," I said. "I'm probably just gonna go home."

Adam shrugged, and you know what? He actually seemed genuinely disappointed.

"Suit yourself, man."

I'm still punching myself in the face for declining. I've been sitting here at my desk for the past hour trying to figure out why the fuck I can't stand up for myself. It's no wonder I'm not good at making friends. Even though it's all I want, I'm just too afraid to do anything. It's like I'm stuck in a shell that's so cramped and I hate being in it, but the idea of breaking from it is even scarier.

I'm heading to bed now. Homework is done and I'm struggling to keep my eyes open. Goodnight, journal.

Tristan LaFerriere

Chapter Seven
Thursday, October 5th, 2006

Dear Journal,

In English today, we were finishing *To Kill a Mockingbird*. Ms. Carlson urged the class on in a long discussion once we finally got to the end of the last chapter of the book. I was relieved because this meant that tomorrow, we would be watching the film in class, and I could listen to Gregory Peck for the period instead of another lecture or classmate reading at their own painfully slow pace.

"Let's take a look at Scout's development throughout the novel," Ms. Carlson said as she addressed the class. "What do we see about her that's changed from the beginning of the story?"

No replies.

"How has she developed?"

Nothing.

"How has her attitude changed in chapter thirty-one?"

Still nothing. It was painful.

I twirled my pen in my hand, the ink making light marks on the blank page of my notebook. You were sitting on my desk, too, journal. I was thinking today that maybe I shouldn't bring you to school because losing you and having you fall into the wrong hands would basically be signing my death warrant.

"Anyone?" Ms. Carlson asked.

I felt like I was an extra in *Ferris Bueller's Day Off*.

My eyes wandered to the bank of windows to the left of all the desks. The room where my English class meets faces one of the school's many courtyards, and I found myself to be the audience to a family of ducks gathered alongside the skinny trunk of a recently planted elm.

"Come on, guys!" Ms. Carlson said in a slightly annoyed, but still chipper classroom tone. She looked around the room, making eye contact with different people at different moments to persuade someone to speak. "Don't any of you have anything to say?"

...

"The trial."

...

I'm the one who spoke.

It must've come as a surprise to everyone. They were the first words I had spoken in class since returning to school. Now that I think of it, it very well may have been my first time speaking in class all year so far.

"What's that, Kieran?"

I immediately regretted saying anything. I hate speaking in class, but I just blurted out an answer like I was thinking aloud. The failure to get anyone to say anything had driven me crazy.

"The trial," I repeated, licking my chapped as fuck lips.

I looked forward and brushed some hair out of my face. People were looking at me like I was a different species of human. I tried to ignore them. This was one step, I suppose, in me trying to function like a normal human being. So far, I didn't like it.

"What about the trial, Kieran?"

Ms. Carlson looked hopeful, like she had finally struck gold. I would be excited, too, if I got someone like me to talk in class.

"It's a representation of her growing up," I said. "In the beginning of the book, she's...a completely different character. The whole book is about growing up and the trial represents her loss of innocence."

Ms. Carlson's eyes wandered up toward the ceiling as she pondered my interpretation.

115

Tristan LaFerriere

"Can you expand a little more on that, Kieran?"

Fuck...why did I open my mouth?

"She's...more grown up afterwards because she sees how harsh reality is. The things that were important to her in the earlier chapters aren't important to her anymore. It's like the whole trial opened her eyes and she's symbolically an adult now. And...Boo Radley symbolizes the way she views things as a child in comparison to an adult. As a child, she fears him, but as an adult..."

I took a deep breath.

"...she pities him."

I focused on the duck family again momentarily, each of the petite babies following their mother in a steady stride as she began introducing them to the world.

No one had responded to my explanation, so I continued.

"She doesn't fear him anymore because she sees the world as a different place now. The trial made her see how the world isn't always right. She isn't sheltered from reality anymore."

...

"She finally sees all the ugliness."

The definition of awkward silence would be a description of this moment if I could define it myself. The exact feeling I never wanted to experience materialized there, that discomfort of being noticed that I always imagined I wouldn't take so well.

Ms. Carlson's expression was a bit puzzled, and she was staring at me with a concerned type of analysis like I was the controversial book she was trying to explain to the class.

"What does she see all the ugliness in, Kieran?"

...

116

"The world. The world is an ugly place."

"Is it?"

...

"Yes."

"Is that how you think Harper Lee felt? Or is that how you feel?"

...

"Ms. Carlson asked for me to speak with you."

I was sitting in that same overstuffed armchair in Dr. Meller's office during lunch. I was clearly fidgeting, extremely annoyed that the school decided it was a smart idea to pull me away from my lunch because they suspected I might be cutting myself or something.

"Is there anything you'd like to talk about, Kieran?"

"No."

"Ms. Carlson mentioned that you seemed to be giving off a negative vibe this morning. She said you were discussing a book in class."

"To Kill a Mockingbird."

"Right. She said that you seemed to be expressing frustration in your response to a discussion about one of the characters. She said you mentioned that you felt the book was about seeing the world for its ugliness."

"Yeah, so?"

She gave a little shrug.

"I think it's just curious to explore what you meant by that. There seems to be some speculation that this isn't how you were necessarily interpreting the book, but how *you* feel about the world."

117

I stared at the carpet. I had to be careful in how I presented myself here. I've heard horror stories of school counselors simply suspecting that a student might feel depressed and that was considered valid enough evidence to throw them into involuntary therapy. That shit really fucking scares me. If you're depressed, you can't even tell anyone because they'll just throw you into shit that'll make you even more depressed if you admit it.

"I don't get it," I said sharply.

"What don't you get, Kieran?"

"What's the point of discussing a book if we can't interpret it? Isn't that what we're supposed to be doing? It's a book!"

Dr. Meller nodded, her sign to reassure me that she was listening and understood even if she didn't.

"I understand, Kieran. I'm not saying that there are any complaints about your contributions to discussions. As a matter of fact, Ms. Carlson mentioned to me how your vocabulary is…" She paused as she glanced at some handwritten notes in front of her. "Impressive," she said to finish the thought. "You appear to be very well-read."

Because I wasn't raised by morons, I thought.

"You've used words like *diatribe* and *gaucherie* in your written assignments."

Because I know how to use a fucking dictionary.

"So, if anything, I'd say you're one of our brightest students."

"Then why I am I here? This is so stupid. You can't say anything anymore without being accused of something. It was the first time I talked in class all year and the first thing that comes out of my mouth has to be interpreted like I'm a fucking basket case or something. This is bullshit!"

"Now, Kieran." Dr. Meller held up her hands. "Let's just talk about this calmly. I can understand your frustration, but we must take all concerns here very seriously. Especially with someone who has

recently experienced trauma. That's why we felt the need to talk to you."

I was rubbing my hands together, working my fingers around each other as tears boiled inside of me. My AFI sweatshirt was itchy and irritating my left nipple. *Everything* was fucking bothering me.

"The last time we spoke, we were discussing your relationship with your brother."

I looked up.

"What about it?"

"I think we should take another look at how his death is affecting you, Kieran. Sometimes we don't see just how much of an impact the loss of a loved one has right away. Those thoughts and feelings tend to manifest in other ways that subtly interfere with our everyday lives. In this case, I think that your response to Ms. Carlson about the book may have something to do with that. I also think it's important to have your teachers understand what types of triggers can cause you to have these feelings. In this case, maybe a discussion about the book was a negative trigger for you...and your feelings about your brother."

...

I sighed. It was clear that my only way of getting out of this was to talk.

"We were close, okay?" I said quickly. "But my brother's been dead for nearly a month now. And there's no point in anyone trying to talk to me like it never happened, but...whenever I see someone, they just know me as the kid whose brother was killed in a car wreck, so they talk to me like I'm a baby and it's like they're walking on eggshells the whole time. Everyone's afraid that what they say might set me off."

Dr. Meller was scribbling notes furiously.

"And that's all pointless," I continued. "People don't have to say anything to 'remind' me about what happened. I was there. I was in that damn car. I have the fucking scar to prove it."

I clutched at my chest through the sweatshirt, and the stinging at my nipple was further irritated by the faint soreness of the still-remaining seatbelt scar.

"I hate how everyone thinks that if they don't mention anything then I forget about it. I'll never forget about it. I think about it every day. Every. Single. Fucking. Day. I think about it from the minute I wake up to the minute I go to bed. My brother doesn't come in my room to wake me up. He doesn't drive me to school. I don't see him in the halls here. I don't see him hanging out with his friends. He doesn't meet me in the parking lot after class. He doesn't drive me home. The house is quiet without him playing *Call of Duty* or *Halo* or whatever he'd play in his room. Everything reminds me of the fact that he's gone, so people can stop worrying about setting me off because, if anything, I'm already set off." [Bad choice of words in a counselor's office. Had to correct it]. "What I mean is...I'm already feeling as bad as I can feel, so I think if people would just...leave me alone then that would be best."

Dr. Meller jotted down a few more notes, such a finality in the way she dotted her i's and crossed her t's like she was just finishing up a masterpiece. I expected there to be another long, uncomfortable silence between the two of us while she tried to write a response in her head, but she almost immediately had an answer to my rant.

"Are you familiar with our peer support program, Kieran?"

I shook my head.

"Peer support is a program we have here where freshmen who are struggling to adjust to high school or simply having general difficulties are partnered up with a junior or a senior for the rest of the year. They meet once a week with each other, and the upperclassman gives you advice so that you're getting direction from one of your own peers rather than an adult. We've found that the experience of another student can be extremely beneficial in assisting those who are struggling."

"...Okay."

"I think that you'd benefit greatly from this program, Kieran. I'd really like to pair you up with someone. It's been a great help to

some of our students, and for someone like you, I think it'll be a good way for you to try interacting with your peers a bit more, too."

...

"Is this something you'd be interested in?"

...

"Yeah. Sure."

Did I have a choice?

Dr. Meller smiled.

"I'm very glad to hear that, Kieran. I have a junior who just moved here last month who's volunteered to be a peer. He's a very nice boy, and I think you'll find that he'll be able to help you with some of the struggles you're having."

It could've been worse. I'd take this over being thrown in a mental institution for sure, because apparently now that's what can happen if a teacher translates your interpretation of assigned reading the wrong way.

"Okay," I said. "Fine. When do we start?"

"You can start today," she said as she started typing on her computer again. "I'm looking at your schedule now. You have gym last period?"

"Yeah."

"I'm going to contact Mr. Best and let him know you won't be in class this afternoon because we'll be starting your peer one-on-ones. Would that be alright?"

I nodded. At least I got to miss gym. Maybe this would be a positive experience solely for that reason, although that would mean Thomas and I wouldn't get the chance to talk. In a way, I felt like I was "cheating" on Thomas by using another student to talk to about my problems, but then again, that wasn't what Thomas signed up for.

Whoever was crazy enough to volunteer to help some emo kid with his issues only had themselves to blame for what they were getting into.

"The two of you will meet in the theater room. That room is open during last period, so you can get to know each other and discuss things privately. You know where the theater room is? Behind the auditorium?"

"Yeah."

"Great." More typing. "So, for last period, you'll go to the theater room instead of gym and your peer will meet you there. I'm going to let you go now, Kieran. Make sure you get some lunch."

I stood up, clutching my backpack.

"I'll be following up with you tomorrow to see how things went," Dr. Meller added.

She stood up, too, to see me out the door.

"Thank you," I said flatly. "What's his name?"

"Pardon?"

"My peer. What's his name?"

"Izzy Murraro."

…

The theater room was dark and empty when I arrived.

I flipped on the lights. They flickered to life one by one like dominoes falling across the ceiling. It felt less like a theater room, but more like a morgue. It's one of the only classrooms in the building without windows, a cluttered, but pretty vast space that looks like it's held together by Broadway show posters and advertisements of past King's Valley drama club productions.

There were messes of props overflowing from boxes of items to be used for a variety of different scenes or improv games that I

assume are taught in the curriculum's drama class that doesn't seem to be very popular here.

Why is it that there's always a fucking red feather boa? It seriously never fails.

Something I found weird about this room was its lack of desks. Instead of your typical classroom desks set up facing a white board, there were different kinds of seats like old sofas, armchairs, and plush beanbag pillows.

I made myself comfortable on one of the couches that looked like it belonged in a 1970s grandma house, set my backpack down on the floor, and let my eyes wander the room while I waited for my peer to arrive.

In this area of the school, there isn't a lot of hallway foot traffic, so the sounds of people heading to their last classes of the day were muffled and distant through the open door. I found it relaxing to be somewhat separated from that world of chaos, the hectic knot of this town and its obnoxious characters. Besides my room, I rarely have the chance to be alone anywhere.

It was nice to have some quiet for a few minutes to just take everything in, all the bullshit that's paraded through my life in these recent months...some time to reflect on what the fuck is going on.

Why'd you have to fucking die on me, Justin?

...

"Kieran?"

About a minute after the bell rang to remind everyone that the final period of the day had officially started, I looked up to see my peer, Izzy Murraro, standing in the doorway.

Izzy Murraro

Izzy was medium height and ever so slightly taller than me. He had very dark brown hair that was almost black and vaguely curly, which he had styled long, but not as long as mine, in an "organized messy" fashion.

123

"Hey," I said, standing up slowly. "Izzy?"

His eyes were the same color as his hair and there was something almost artificial about them. The soft brown circles appeared to be full of thick, brown paint that I wouldn't notice until a moment later when he was closer to me.

"Yeah, man!"

Izzy tossed his black backpack that appeared to have seen better days on one of the empty armchairs that was leaking stuffing. His slightly exposed forearms revealed quite a bit of dark body hair growing from his pale skin. He extended a hand to mine, a big and friendly smile spread across his cute face. His eyebrows were very expressive.

"Dr. Meller told me about you, dude. How are you?"

He was wearing a black and white long-sleeved Vans shirt, black skinny skater jeans, and black and white checkered Vans sneakers. A Nixon watch was hooked around his skinny wrist, slipping up and down his forearm as he moved.

"I'm...good," I said, and shook his hand. It was so bony and cold that the sudden feeling of freezing fingers on my own startled me. He had a firm grip. "Nice to meet you."

He was very thin [almost frail looking], a skinny boy even more twiggy than me.

"Nice to meet you, man!" Izzy nodded toward the sofa I had just been sitting in. "Sit down, man. I'll pull up a chair and we can chat."

Izzy's face was clean shaven, but he looked like he could grow some serious facial hair rather quickly if he let it go.

I watched him grab another armchair. He dragged it closer to the couch and sat down. I sat, too, and we faced each other as any sort of sounds emanating from the hallway traffic elsewhere in the building ceased completely.

124

"So," he said. "Dr. Meller said I should explain exactly what we're gonna do. Um...did she tell you how the peer program works?"

I nodded.

"Awesome!" He talked with his hands a lot. "So, basically, we'll meet once a week. We can keep it on Thursdays if that's cool with you. You'll have to miss one class and it'll rotate, so next week, you'll come to peer instead of your first class, the week after that your second class. You get it?"

"Yeah."

"Alright, cool!" He slapped his hands together. "And we'll basically just talk about anything you want to talk about. Any topics are open. Nothing's off limits. I just try to help you out so everything's going as smoothly as it can for you. Makes sense?"

"Yeah."

"Great! So, I guess we should start by introducing ourselves. I'll start. So, I'm Izzy and I'm a junior. I turned sixteen in July, and I just moved here with my dad from Mt. Olive, New Jersey."

"Cool."

"What about you, Kieran? Tell me more about yourself, man."

"Well," I said. "I'm Kieran. I'm a freshman. I'll be fifteen in December."

I paused, thinking. To be honest, Izzy's cuteness was a distraction, and holy shit what a personality he had! Normally, I'd be worn out by so much fun energy, but his vibe was so positive that I couldn't help but be charmed by it.

"Sagittarius or Capricorn?" he asked.

"Sagittarius. December 4th."

"Cool, man! Cool!"

"I also just moved here," I continued. "In June. I'm from L.A. I was born and raised there."

"L.A.? Awesome! How do you like Pennsylvania so far?"

…

"I...fucking…hate it."

Izzy laughed.

"Dude, I feel ya.' I'm just from one state away and I fucking hate it, too. I can't imagine going from L.A. to out here in the sticks. That must've been some serious culture shock."

I was relieved that it was clear I could be completely honest with Izzy without him judging me. Everyone else who lives in King's Valley seems to worship its ground for some stupid reason.

"It sucks," I said, exhaling. "I really don't like it here."

"Me neither. I've been living here for less than a month and I already miss Jersey, but hey, I'm only planning on living here for another year. I really want to go to college in New York. I want to live in the city."

"Nice," I said. "You like New York?"

"Love it, man. Fucking love it. My parents are from Brooklyn and my dad worked in Manhattan for years. I really want to be right in the heart of all of it all, you know? I love the city life."

"Yeah," I sighed. "I'm more of a city guy, too. I miss L.A."

"Dude, I envy you! I've never gotten out there, but I've always wanted to go."

"You'd fit right in," I said, studying his attire. "The skate scene is pretty big out there."

"So I've heard, man. You into skating?"

"Not…really."

126

"I've been skating since I was ten."

"Have you ever been to Castlegate?" I asked. "The Skate Park?"

"Yeah, but it sucks. It's not a real skate park; it's just, like, a hangout place and it's really shitty. Nobody really skates there. The one time I went, all I saw were a bunch of girls fighting about their boyfriends and this one girl went in the bathroom and came out and threw a cup of piss all over this other girl in the parking lot."

I chuckled. That seemed to be the thing to do to your enemies around here.

"I've never been there," I said. "My brother went a few times, though."

For the first time since Izzy appeared, there was silence. The sound of the building's heating system kicking on made a shudder that caused the lights to flicker momentarily.

"Dr. Meller told me you've been going through some rough times," Izzy said. "You want to talk about it? She didn't go into detail or anything."

"She didn't?"

"Nah. She can't. It's confidentiality stuff."

"Oh. Well, yeah. It's been...pretty rough."

I licked my chapped lips.

"My brother was in a car accident last month. He died."

"Dude..."

Izzy unfolded his legs and stared at me intently, but still with a sense of warmth that I had never felt from anyone my own age before. This is when I really noticed his eyes.

"I'm so sorry, man," he said. "That *is* rough. I am *so, so* sorry."

I shrugged.

"It's over," I said. "But...I miss him."

"Were you guys close?"

"I...*think* we were."

Izzy put a hand on my forearm and squeezed it.

"I know exactly how you feel, man. My mom died last year from cancer."

"Oh. I'm sorry."

"It's okay, man. That's one of the reasons my dad and I moved here. They lived in our old house since my brother was born, and the memories were just getting really painful for him, so he wanted to start over somewhere else to try to help him move on. My brother's in college now, and without him and my mom, the house just didn't feel the same anymore. It was this big, empty place, you know?"

I nodded.

"...Yeah."

Izzy threw up his hands as if presenting the room to me like Vanna White introducing the puzzle board on *Wheel of Fortune.*

"And, so, he chose this lovely fucking town."

We both laughed. It felt really good to share a laugh with someone.

...

We spent the rest of the hour talking about our shared hatred for King's Valley and Izzy's life back in New Jersey, but a great deal of the time was his fascination in my connection with L.A. I offered him stories about Justin and I spending many of our childhood weekends at The Del Amo Mall, how we both got lost in Robinsons-May at The Sherman Oaks Galleria when I was four, the delicacy of In-N-Out

128

Burger, scenes from the Mr. Bean movie being filmed near our old house ten years ago, and my experience of being terrified on the Santa Monica Pier roller coaster when I was seven.

We didn't linger on Justin. I think that was what made the session feel good. I was just having a conversation with someone who wasn't treating me like I was fragile. Izzy was just being himself to me. Everyone else seemed to be wearing this mask of caution while they talked to me [even Thomas and Athena at times], but not him.

"We'll meet next Thursday, first period," Izzy said as the final bell rang. He shook my hand for the second time and gave me another big smile. I was admittedly a little disappointed that our meeting had to end. I felt like I could've talked to him all day.

"Thanks, Izzy."

I stood up with him and we both swung into our backpacks. In the distance, we could hear classroom doors bursting open, several, then dozens, and over a hundred conversations intertwining into one overwhelming mix of chatter. It was the immense exhale of the building as the day ended.

"No problem, man!" Izzy said. "It's my pleasure."

We headed for the door.

"So," I said, nearly interrupted by the final loudspeaker announcements of the day. "How many other, uh…'peers' do you have?"

"Just you."

"Oh. Really?"

"Yep. Dr. Meller said it's best to just assign one freshman per upperclassman. It's supposed to make the peer relationship more…I don't know, intimate, I guess."

He chuckled.

"But I think the reasoning behind that is just so we don't end up getting to skip, like, five classes a week."

I laughed with him as we went out into the hallway.

"You got a bus to catch, Kieran?"

"Yeah. Do you?"

"Nah. I drive."

"You have a car?"

"Yep."

"Oh. Sweet."

"Why? You want a ride, dude?"

"No, that's alright."

"You sure?"

I almost protested again, but then I realized I was making the same damn mistake over again like when I declined Adam Woolf's invitation to go the movies. Here was someone who was actually offering me hospitality in a place that was otherwise so unwelcoming. Why the fuck wasn't I just seizing the moment?

"I mean, if you want to," I said as we started down the hallway. Not too much longer and we began to blend in with the sea of students rushing for the exits in every which way.

"Why not, dude? I mean, I'm supposed to be a good peer, so it's the least I could do."

He laughed again and, damn, was it contagious. Each time he let out his boyish giggles, I was drugged.

"Alright."

We stopped near the cafeteria at one of the school's many banks of vending machines where Izzy grabbed a bag of M&Ms and a bottle of Dr. Pepper. Then he led me to the nearest exit, through the main courtyard, and toward the student parking lot. Following him

made me feel important. Even if he was as new to this place as I was, he carried a sense of status with him.

We reached his vehicle parked at the far end of the lot underneath a few trees that were beginning to shed for the season. The plates on the car were still from Jersey and appeared to be original from twenty or so years ago.

"Hold on," Izzy said, and he leaned over the hood. "Let me get some of these out of here."

He yanked some of the crunchy leaves that were stuck within the windshield wipers, and that was when I realized I recognized this car. It was an older, red Alfa Romeo sedan. The logo was distinct…a snake eating a man?

"An…Alfa Romeo?" I asked.

"What?" Izzy was still leaned over and cleaning up the leaves from the windshield.

"This is an Alfa Romeo?"

"Yeah, dude!" He stood back up and brushed his hands against his jeans. "It's an '87 Milano. It was my mom's. She and my dad bought it brand-new. He gave it to me when I got my license. It's old, but it's unique."

He smiled at me.

"There's nothing more fun than driving an Italian car."

"Where do you live?" I asked.

"Over in…oh, what the fuck's it called?"

He paused, thinking, and then snapped his fingers when it came to him.

"Belmont Hill."

"Skyview Drive?"

131

Izzy looked at me.

"Yeah, man. How'd you know? You live over there?"

"I…think I live next door to you."

"Really?"

"Yeah. I've seen your car. You're 2714, right?"

"Yeah!" His face lit up. "Holy shit! You live in 2716?"

Oh my God

"…Yeah."

Izzy laughed.

"Dude! That's crazy! I can't believe I've never seen you."

"Well, I…don't really leave the house much."

He unlocked the car. I climbed in on the passenger side and sank into the seat.

An array of band stickers that adorned the sun visors caught my eye. Some were familiar: *Taking Back Sunday, Dashboard Confessional, We the Kings, A Day to Remember, Boys Like Girls, Green Day*. Others I had never heard of: *The Cum Guzzlers, Hanging Weirdo Ass Fucking Dolls, Where Tragedy Sleeps, P.R.Y.D.E….*

"No CD player?" I asked when I noted the original cassette deck.

"Nope, but who needs one?" Izzy inserted the key in the ignition. "I've got this tape adaptor thing for my iPod."

He turned the key and the car's engine strained.

"Shit."

Izzy pulled the key out and turned it again. The dash lights came to life, the analog gauges twitched, and the seat belt chime sounded, but it wouldn't start.

"Damn!" He gave the horn a little punch and it let out a plaintive whine. "I'm sorry, dude. This thing really needs a new fucking battery."

He gave the key one more try, but no luck.

"I'm gonna have to call my dad. It needs a jump."

"Oh. Okay."

"You need to get home soon? I don't want to, like, hold you up or anything, man."

"No," I said. "I'm good. I'm in no hurry."

"Cool. Hold on."

He dug his Nokia flip phone from his pocket and started dialing his dad's number. I watched his thumb press the buttons furiously.

"I'll have us out of here soon, man. Don't worry."

"I'm not worried," I said, relaxing in the seat. "I'm in no rush to get home. There's nothing to do at my house."

Izzy smiled and then he got through to his dad. Their short conversation played in the background to my point of view of the reflected image of the parking lot in the passenger sideview mirror.

Was that Eric Gleason walking by? With Evan? Yes, the two boys started climbing into that familiar Lambo. Apparently, Eric had been truthful with his claim of inheriting the beast.

"So," Izzy said once the conversation was over. He slapped the phone shut and sighed. "My dad's not gonna be able to get here till like five. The jumper cables are in the garage and he's still at work."

"Oh."

133

"You sure you don't need to get home sooner, man? I could, like, ask someone here to help out or I could call AAA."

"No," I said. "It's fine. I'll just walk home."

"Dude, I'm so sorry. I feel so shitty leaving you stranded."

"Don't be." I waved my hand. "It's no big deal. I don't mind walking."

I opened the passenger door and unhooked my seatbelt.

"I'll walk with you," Izzy said. "If you want. I mean, we live in the same place."

…

"Okay."

I had to contain myself from showing how fucking happy I was to hear him say that. I really wanted to throw my arms around him.

"You ever been to Sal's?" he asked.

"Sal's?"

"It's a pizza place in town."

"No."

"Let's stop there. They've got the best fucking pizza. It's almost as good as Jersey. My treat. You game?"

I wish I could have seen my expression when he said, *"You game?"* I can only imagine this tired shadow of a boy slowly coming out of a depression coma and finally remembering what it felt like to smile a real smile again.

"Yeah," I said. "I'm game."

Izzy and I ditched his car and started our long walk into town. I zipped up my red Stay Sweet hoodie and Izzy did the same with his

black Vans hoodie that he grabbed from the backseat of his car. He offered me some of the M&Ms he bought, and we shared the bag as we walked.

Eventually, we were walking along the side of the road. The school was out of sight and distant behind us while we passed rows of stately homes that had the unfortunate luck of facing the busy Carlton Street. Groups of other people who lived more locally were walking home, too. For once, I felt like I belonged in this town with everyone else since I was actually walking and talking with someone instead of shuffling alone like a zombie to my bus like usual.

"So, is Izzy your real name?" I asked.

"No," he said, taking a sip from the bottle of Dr. Pepper. "I hate my real name."

"What is it?"

"I can't tell you."

"Why not?"

He widened his eyes and made hand motions to me like a parent making faces at their newborn child.

"It's a...*secret*! I'd have to kill you if I told you."

"Oh, come on!" We walked over a pile of crunchy leaves. "It can't be that bad."

"It's too embarrassing. I'm not telling you."

"Come on!"

"No!"

He pulled his hood up and jokingly hid his face from me as he crossed his arms.

"It's just a name!" I said. "I probably wouldn't have picked *'Kieran'*."

He flipped his hood back down to reveal the playful smirk on his face.

"Kieran's not a bad name at all, dude."

"It's okay, I guess."

"What does it mean?"

"My name?"

"Yeah."

I shook my head.

"I'm not sure. It's…Gaelic, I think."

"Cool."

"Seriously, though. What's your real name?"

Izzy bit his lip and looked off in the distance, contemplating with a gleam of mischievousness in his eyes.

"I'll give you three guesses."

"Oh boy."

He shrugged.

"Can you at least give me a hint?"

"It does start with an 'I'. I'll give you that."

"That's not enough!"

"That's all you get."

I groaned, trying to think of a male name that starts with "I" and also not wanting to waste any of my guesses.

"You have to give me something else. That's way too vague."

"It's biblical."

"Biblical?"

"Yep."

"I literally know nothing about the bible."

"Oh well."

…

"Isaac?"

"Nope."

"Fuck!"

"Two more guesses."

"You're still gonna tell me, though, right?"

"Only if you can guess it.”

"Dude!"

"Like I said, two more guesses."

“Just *one* more hint.’

…

“*Moby Dick*.”

…

"Ishmael?"

"Yay!" Izzy clapped.

"That's it?"

"Yep."

"Oh, come on. Ishmael's a nice name."

He laughed.

"I fucking hate it!"

"Why?"

"I just do! It's so…I don't know…"

"It's Jewish, isn't it?"

"Yep."

"So, you're Jewish?"

"You got a fucking problem with that?"

I froze.

"What? No!"

Izzy started laughing and he patted my back.

"Relax, bud. I'm just fucking with you."

"Oh," I laughed, sighing.

"But yes, I'm half Jewish. My mom was Jewish."

"Oh. What's your dad?"

"Italian. Like, *really* Italian. He could be Christopher Moltisanti's twin. People have actually walked up to him because they thought he was Michael Imperioli. Sometimes he just goes along with it. They have the same voice and everything."

"They think he's who?"

"You've never seen *The Sopranos*?"

"No."

"Dude, you need to watch it! You got HBO?"

"Yeah."

"Watch it! It's ending soon. The last season just started. You can get the older seasons on DVD. Trust me. It's worth it. It's, like, the best TV show ever."

"Oh. I don't watch much TV. I'm more of a music guy."

We turned and started walking down Arbor Avenue, a residential street that eventually connects with the main road going through town. There were still people walking home from school around here, girls chatting it up with their friends and guys from the lacrosse team who I only recognized because of the stupid pep rally they forced everyone to attend a few days before.

"What kind of music do you like?" Izzy asked me.

"Well, Stay Sweet's my favorite band."

"Dude, I love Stay Sweet!"

This was the first time anyone said those words to me in person. Man, I *really* wanted this guy to be my friend.

"You do?"

"Hell yeah, dude! They're amazing."

"I don't think I know anyone else who loves them as much as I do. As well-known as they are, their fan base isn't really that strong out here. I guess it was different in California. They seemed to get more attention over there."

"They were pretty popular back in Jersey. I found out about them through my friend, Vicky. She had this party and she put on their songs for us to listen to. I was hooked instantly."

"What's your favorite song by them?"

139

"Hard to say, dude. I'm partial to anything from *Nitro*, but I really am liking 'Marionette' the more I listen to it."

I stopped walking. Izzy stopped, too.

"Marionette?"

"Yeah."

"By Stay Sweet?"

"...Yeah...?"

I stared at him.

"You know," he began, and then sang quickly, "*You are my blood and sweat. I'll be your marionette.*"

"I...don't think I know that song."

"Well, it's a new one. It's off their new album, *Mandragora*. It just came out, like, last month."

Then I remembered; I had only gotten through half the first song on that album before Justin crashed. I hadn't listened to anything else on that CD and the CD was, of course, gone now. It had sunk to the bottom of King's Lake and was either part of the cube that Justin's car had been presumably crushed into after they towed what was left of it away, or it was still floating around underwater somewhere.

"I...haven't gotten to listening to it," I said, not wanting to think too much about that song and those lyrics that led up to the crash.

"It's a great album, dude," Izzy said. "There was a lot of hype about it. I'm surprised you haven't checked it out yet."

"Well...I'll get around to it."

I put my hands in my pockets and we started walking again. By now, most of the other little groups of walking commuters had branched off onto various side streets or developments, so it was just Izzy and I heading into town while the occasional car passed us.

140

When Izzy and I got to Sal's, we sat in an orange booth near the front window. Izzy ordered a Dr. Pepper, I ordered a Coke, and we each got a slice of pizza that came out on thin paper plates sitting on brown plastic trays. The place had a lot of brown paneling and those faux Tiffany lamps hanging over each table.

"So, you said you have a brother?" I asked.

"Yep."

"In college?"

"Yep. He goes to Penn State. He's studying sociology."

"Cool. What's his name?"

"Giovanni," Izzy said, and he went on to annunciate his brother's full name in the most Italian accent he could give. *"Giovanni Antonio Murraro!"*

I chuckled.

"And," Izzy added. "Since our grandparents on our dad's side couldn't survive without it, he's technically got a Catholic saint name in there, too, so he'd be Giovanni Antonio Xavier Murraro."

"Jesus," I said. "What's yours?"

"My what?"

"Your saint name."

"I slipped through the cracks on that one, thankfully," Izzy laughed. "No saint name. I'm just Izzy Ya'akov Murraro, or, if you want to get technical, *Ishmael* Ya'akov Murraro. Jewish as fuck until you get to my last name. I'm a total pizza bagel, officially bar-mitzvahed and baptized."

He laughed again and I joined him as I looked out the window.

"What's your middle name, Kieran?"

"Donovan."

"That's a really cool name."

"Thanks. So, are you and your brother close?"

"Yeah. Really close. He's pretty much, like, my best friend."

I rolled my straw wrapper up into a tiny ball and moved it around at the base of my thumb and index finger.

"Well, that's nice."

I took a few napkins from the booth's chrome dispenser and attempted to soak up some of the grease that seemed to be more than half of what made up the single slice of pizza on my plate. Izzy just started digging in, and for a moment, I was struck funny by how a boy with such an Italian last name was scarfing down a slice of pizza so quickly. The stereotype was perfect.

"You seem like you're never negative about anything," I said, intrigued by just how happy-go-lucky this boy came off.

He laughed and wiped his mouth with a napkin. For a moment, the light glistened off one of his fingernails. I don't know why I remember that or why it even caught my eye, but it's just one of the many little details I want to hold on to from today.

"You'd be surprised," he said. "But hey, I try to stay positive."

"Well, you make it seem so easy."

I took a sip of my soda and was disappointed to find that there must've been a crack in the side of the straw. I pulled the lid off the cup and sipped directly from it. The cold, crushed ice hit my chapped lips.

"It wasn't easy when my mom died," Izzy said. "I was actually a mess for a little while. I cried a lot."

The thought of someone like Izzy crying broke my heart. He seemed like the happiest person on earth, and to think of him being a crying mess was just a disheartening visual.

"I'm sorry," I said.

"Hey." Izzy put his hand on mine. Never before had I felt such a strong drop in the pit of my stomach. "*I'm* sorry. I can't imagine losing my brother."

I bit my lip.

"…Yeah."

"But, look, man," Izzy continued. "If you ever need anyone to talk to or anything, just let me know. I'm here for you, dude."

Don't cry, Kieran. Don't cry. Don't fucking cry.

"Why...are you being so nice to me?" I asked.

Izzy looked at me strangely.

"What?"

I shrugged, my eyes moving to the window again.

"You're just, like…*so* nice to me."

"Why wouldn't I be?"

"I'm sorry. I shouldn't have..."

"You're a nice guy. There's no reason I wouldn't be nice to you."

"People aren't normally that nice to me."

"Fuck those people, dude. They don't matter." He paused for a moment as he studied me. "You okay?"

The tears were coming back again, and this time it actually hurt to fight them. They just started leaking from my eyes and I was trembling.

"Fuck..."

Izzy grabbed another napkin and handed it to me to use as a tissue.

"It's okay, man."

I started wiping my eyes. Izzy's hand was on mine again. His grip never loosened.

"Don't cry. You're okay, dude."

It was time.

"Izzy," I said, my voice quivering and my heart pounding at a really uncomfortable rate. "I…I have to tell you something."

"What is it, buddy?"

The way he said "buddy" almost made me cry more. I just wanted to move over to his side of the booth and have him hold me tight for the rest of my life. Who was this angel that just dropped out of the sky on me today? How could it be possible that a lame school program had just successfully changed my life by bringing this boy to me? How?

"I'm…gay," I said in a loud whisper. It was followed by gasped breaths and more tears. I felt sick and terrified. It was out. I had actually told someone.

"Kieran…" Izzy's grip tightened on my hand. "It's okay, man. I am, too."

…

"You are?"

"Yeah, man." He giggled, and now it was even cuter than it had been before I knew the truth about him.

"Really?"

Another cute giggle.

"Yes."

"Does...does anyone know?"

"Yeah. A lot of people know."

"A lot of people know?"

"Yep."

"Like who?"

"My dad and my brother. My friends back in Mt. Olive."

It amazed me that someone could be so comfortably open about it. I still wonder what Justin would've thought if he had ever found out about me.

"Your dad and your brother know?"

Izzy nodded.

"Mm-hmm."

"And they're cool with it?"

"Yeah. They don't care. They're both chill. My mom was, too. It runs in the family."

I laughed a little, sniffled, dabbed my burning eyes, and finally stopped crying. I didn't want to cry anymore. I wanted to hug this beautiful boy. I wanted to kiss him.

"I can't believe I just told you that," I said. "You're the first person I told."

Izzy let out a little gasp. It was fake, but still cute, nonetheless.

"I'm the first person you came out to?!"

I shushed him, looking around to make sure none of the other restaurant patrons had heard him.

"Sorry," he giggled.

"It's okay," I said. "But yeah, you are."

"Aww." He held his hands to his heart, another fake, but ridiculously adorable gesture. "I'm so flattered!"

"You're...so nice," I said. "You're, like, the only person who I could tell wouldn't judge."

"Well, if I did, that would be really fucking hypocritical of me since I like dick, too."

We both laughed together again. We laughed a lot this afternoon.

"So, are you worried about telling your parents?" he asked.

"I don't know," I said. "I just...don't think I'm ready. You know?"

"I feel you, man. I was nervous, too, but..."

He stopped, and I could see in his eyes that he was searching for the right way to say what he wanted to say without being offensive.

"I'm just really lucky," he finished. "My family's good people."

"Did your mom know?" I asked. "Shit." I shook my head, feeling stupid. "I'm sorry..."

"No! It's okay! I don't mind talking about my mom. I never mind talking about her. But yes, she knew, and she was so fucking happy when I came out to her."

"Really?"

Izzy nodded, sipping up the last of his Dr. Pepper and gulping it down before he spoke again.

"Oh my God, yes! She was so excited. She used to tell me all these stories about her friends in the gay scene in New York in the '80s, all the crazy parties and clubs they used to go to."

146

He looked out the window.

"She lost a lot of friends, though," he went on. "To AIDS. She told me how one year she lost, like, fourteen friends, all from AIDS. They were, like, dropping off the face of the fucking earth. She and my dad were good friends with Keith Haring, you know."

I was dumbfounded.

"Really?! Keith Haring? The artist?"

"Yep," he smiled. "We have some of his originals."

"Wow...that's...amazing."

Izzy grabbed his straw from the now-empty glass of Dr. Pepper and held it between two of his skinny fingers. It almost looked like a long cigarette.

"Get this," he said. "So, you know Keith Haring's work, right?"

I nodded.

"So," he went on, and his eyes looked so passionate about whatever he was about to tell me. There was something oddly hot about that. "Get this. You know that one series he did over and over, *The Radiant Baby*? It's, like, a baby that's got these lines coming out of it like it's glowing or...radioactive or something."

"Yeah."

Izzy smiled and his shoulders shrugged up as he giggled.

"So, when my mom got pregnant with me...he painted one of those for her right before he died. So, he made a *Radiant Baby* just for me and called it *Radiant Ishmael*. It's supposed to be me."

"Whoa," I said. "That's fucking awesome."

I didn't know what else to say. I really was amazed.

147

Izzy looked out the window again, still smiling with pride after his story. God, if I could only describe the way the afternoon sunlight hit his face through the smudged glass. It would make the perfect album cover.

...

After we finished our pizza, Izzy and I made the longer part of the walk to Belmont Hill Estates until we finally reached the incline of Skyview Drive. The whole time, we talked about bands we're into. Izzy filled me in on all the concerts he's been to, and his stories really made me feel like I've missed out on so much. His life sounded like so much of an adventure.

"I can't believe I haven't been to a single concert," I said as we neared our houses at the end of the cul-de-sac. "Unless you count some shitty local bands from where I used to live that would play at the theater."

"Hey, though, Cali must've had some pretty sick bands."

I chuckled.

"California has more entertainers than it has people and not all of them are good. I've never seen a big band like Stay Sweet, though."

"I don't want to rub it in, man," Izzy said.

He walked a few steps ahead of me, turning around to face me like a student giving a college campus tour. Then he stopped when we approached the bottom of my driveway.

"You really need to get out and see some shows, though, dude," he continued. "When I saw From First to Last, they just had this fucking amazing energy. It really depends on the audience you're with, too, though. Sometimes you get stuck with a dull group of people, but if everyone's into it, then it's just like a big party. You fucking lose yourself in it, man."

I imagined my dreams of being in the crowds of Stay Sweet's audience and those frozen moments in my head becoming realities. The multicolored stage lights, crowd surfing toward the microphone where Matt Daniels would be reaching out to me, the lyrics of "We're all

Going to Paris" or "Drink This" or "Delilah" or "Hollywood Sign" dousing me with a feeling of ecstasy as I would lose myself in their world, this massive venue where, regardless of how ugly you may be, you belong.

"Nice place," Izzy said as he looked over my house, even though he had probably seen it a hundred times by now. He stood beside the lawn jockey and attempted to imitate its conservative pose.

"I...guess."

"You guess," Izzy laughed. "You've got, like, the nicest house in the neighborhood, dude."

"Thanks," I said. "Do you, uh...want to come in?"

Izzy glanced over at his own house, the stucco house, and then looked back to me.

"Well, my dad still isn't home, so yeah, I guess. I just don't want to be a bother to anyone."

"You won't be. No one else is home, anyway."

I had just checked the time on my phone. 3:51. Mom would be home in approximately half an hour, possibly a little longer if she stopped for a workout at the community fitness center like she sometimes does after work. I didn't see the big deal if anyone came home to find I brought a friend over, but I also didn't feel like having to introduce him to anyone. I liked how so far, this whole afternoon had just been a private moment between the two of us.

I led Izzy up to the front door, unlocked it, and let him into the foyer. He looked up at the hanging light in the center of the tall ceiling, nodded as he scanned the entryway and its contents: the grandfather clock, the artificial palm adjacent to the stair banister, the framed school photos of Justin and I going up the wall to the second floor [my painfully dorky fourth-grade photo of me showing off a mouth full of metal haunts me every time I walk past it].

"Nice," he said.

"I guess."

149

I shut the door behind us and noticed that the potted ferns in the floor planters on either side of the front door were beginning to wilt. The leaves were turning brown.

"You want to see my room?" I asked.

"Sure, dude!"

We headed upstairs and went into my room. The bed was unmade, piles of clothes on the floor. The usual.

"Sorry it's a mess," I said. "The cleaning ladies don't do this room."

Izzy made a face like I was crazy.

"Dude, you should see my room."

He noticed the Stay Sweet poster over my desk.

"Oh, sweet."

He walked up to the image of Matt Daniels, his hands folded. He blew into them.

"Are you cold?" I asked.

"I'm anemic, so I'm always cold."

"I can turn up the heat."

"Nah, it's okay. I'm fine." He continued to examine the poster. "He's so fucking hot."

"Matt Daniels?"

"Yeah." Izzy blew into his hands again to warm them. "I've had a big crush on him ever since I saw the "We're All Going to Paris" music video. I can't tell you how many times I've jerked off to him."

I felt a rush at that remark.

"Me too."

It felt weird saying that. I almost forgot that I had come out to Izzy less than an hour earlier, so speaking the words that confirmed I lusted over this boy band singer still felt forbidden.

"I like the paint color," Izzy said, running his hand along the gray wall. He looked toward my closet doors, which were slightly opened. "What's that, another room?"

"Sorta. It's the closet, but it leads into…Justin's old room."

"…Oh."

"You want to see it?"

"Oh, no." Izzy said, shaking his head. "You don't have to…"

"No," I interrupted. "It's okay. I'll show you."

I walked over to the closet doors, parted them, and peered into the dark forest of clothes that separated us from the room that hadn't been touched in so long.

"You sure?"

Izzy was right behind me, and I could feel his breath on the back of my neck as I moved the hangers to make way.

"Yeah. Come on."

I yanked a row of hanging band shirts to the side and moved forward to what was once Justin's side. His colorful polo shirts, soccer uniforms, Nike sneakers…all still in the same place.

The closed doors to his room beckoned to me. Once I opened them, we were greeted with darkness, as the blinds and curtains had been drawn in Justin's bedroom weeks ago. Almost no sign of the late afternoon light was able to seep through.

I crossed the room and flicked on the ceiling fan light switch while Izzy stood in the closet doorway, looking around at the place like it was an exhibit, pieces of history behind glass that you weren't

151

allowed to touch. If this exhibit had a plaque explaining its significance, I imagine it would describe in some way that what you were looking at was the bedroom of the late Justin Northrup, short-lived King of King's Valley, his domain preserved exactly the way it was when he was still alive right down to the Hollister cologne bottles sitting on his dresser. Textbooks were still lying closed on his desk where a framed and autographed photo of Andriy Shevchenko sits up against a now slightly dusty gooseneck lamp. His laptop remained on the desk, too, closed and the battery drained long ago.

"Well," I said, throwing my hands up. "This was Justin's room."

Izzy stayed in the doorway like touching his feet to the carpet of the room would be toxic, but his eyes scanned the only bit of my brother that he would ever know.

"He was a big athlete, huh?" he asked, eyeing the various soccer trophies displayed on the shelves high up on the wall.

I nodded.

"Yeah."

Izzy inched back into the closet just as light raindrops started to sound against the windowpane.

"You don't have to show me this," he said, almost looking uncomfortable. "I don't want to make you…"

"No," I said, interrupting again. "I want to be in here." I sat on the edge of Justin's bed. I could smell him in the unwashed sheets. "It reminds me of him."

Izzy slowly stepped in. It was starting to pour outside, and the white noise of the rain broke the uncomfortable silence as I imagined Izzy tried to figure out what to say or do in the bedroom of his new friend's deceased brother. Now that I look back at this afternoon, I probably made things pointlessly awkward bringing him in there. But still, he didn't complain. He just looked around like he was trying to get a feel for who my brother was, and, after a few minutes, he sat down on the edge of the bed next to me.

"I'm sorry, buddy," Izzy said, and again he slipped his hand into mine, holding it tightly. "I know you must miss him a lot."

...

"...Yeah."

I started to cry again, and it almost poetically coincided with the hard rain bouncing off the roof.

"You're so nice," I said. "Just...so...nice."

...and I exploded into tears.

"*Shhhhhhhhhhhhhhhhhh.*"

Izzy hugged me tightly. I hugged him back and just let it all out. I cried and cried and cried while this boy, this beautiful, beautiful boy, held me as if I were his own brother. And here I only had known him for a few hours. Who was this angel? Who could ever be this kind to me? Who could ever be this kind to anyone?

As Izzy broke the hug, he stared at me and gripped my hand even tighter to stop me from trembling. The rain was a monsoon now.

"Have you ever kissed a boy?" he asked me.

I shook my head and he started to cry, too. In a weird way, I found his tears to be beautiful. You know how some people ugly cry? Izzy beautiful cried. It was almost inhuman.

"No," I said. "Have you?"

"Yeah."

We were quiet for a moment while he continued to stare at me.

"Do you want to kiss me?" he asked.

I nodded, and almost before I even made a move, his lips touched mine. For the first time in my entire life, I kissed a boy.

153

Izzy's lips were soft, and he kissed me so gently and delicately that it took me by surprise. I was used to seeing people my age kissing furiously and so intensely, but my first kiss wasn't like that. I think it was probably so much better than that.

...

"Hey, Dad! This is Kieran. He lives next door."

Izzy introduced me to his father, Vincent, in the kitchen of their house next door. Both of us were soaked from the rain after we ran from my house, and Mr. Murraro was in the middle of spreading yellow mustard onto a slice of white bread as he made a sandwich at the counter.

"Hey, Kieran. How are you?"

Mr. Murraro licked a dab of mustard from his finger and shook my hand.

Izzy's dad is a handsome man with longish graying hair. He is, as Izzy described him, very Italian-looking. His New York/New Jersey accent-mix was obvious, and despite his friendliness, there was a slight trace of aggressiveness from his city upbringing that lingered in his demeanor, which was quite the opposite of his son. I could sense a lifetime of success, but sadness buried into this man who had recently lost his wife. He seemed lost and out of place in this new house, like he didn't really want to move here, but the memories of losing Mrs. Murraro were much more difficult to deal with.

He was wearing a gold chain around his neck, which Izzy later told me was an anniversary present from his mother that hadn't been unclasped in nearly twenty years. It was partially hidden by the tufts of graying chest hair peeking from the unbuttoned top button of his white shirt, and I imagined that upon arriving home from work, he had torn the tie from his collar to let his neck breathe.

"Nice to meet you, Mr. Murraro," I said, probably sounding nervous.

I was taken aback by the stark contrast of the interiors of their house from what ours is like. Everything in the room, including the appliances, was white. Fluorescent lighting in the all-glass ceiling gave

the room a washed out, sterile appearance. I didn't even know they still designed kitchens like this. Was this a custom job? The side-by-side fridge had obviously been brought over from their previous residence as it was clearly an '80s model with its sleek black handles, solid state technology that was so advanced for its time, and aged font proudly declaring that it contained an *"electronic monitor and diagnostic system"*.

"You guys met at school?" Mr. Murraro asked. He tossed the butter knife into the sink and started to rinse his hands.

"Yeah," Izzy said. "I'm his peer in the peer program. Just found out we lived next door to each other."

"Ah." He smiled for the first time since I met him. "You'll have to introduce me to your parents sometime, Kieran. I've yet to meet any of the neighbors. Seems like a pretty quiet neighborhood."

"I will," I said. "And yeah, it is."

"Would you like to stay for dinner?" he asked. "I was just gonna throw together some penne for Izzy. You can have some if you'd like."

"Thanks," I said. "But that's okay. My mom's cooking tonight."

"Okay, no problem," Mr. Murraro said. "You're always welcome, though."

"Come on," Izzy said. "I'll show you my room."

He led me not upstairs where I expected him to bring me, but down the basement steps through a door in the hall just off the kitchen. Before we made our descent, I noted that the hall between the kitchen and foyer was, as most of the rest of what I had already seen of the house, stark white, and the walls were home to a number of original Keith Haring prints Izzy had told me about, which were illuminated by track lights in the ceiling. I wanted to mention them, but Izzy was already halfway down the stairs, eager to show me his domain, so I followed.

"Your room is down here?" I asked.

"Well, sort of."

He pushed open a second door at the bottom of the steps and switched on the lights to the next room. Both of us were bathed in a wave of warm recessed lighting. I entered the carpeted room with him to find that a majority of the house's finished basement had been converted into a "pad" for Izzy, complete with a sleeper sofa, mini fridge, microwave, stereo, flat screen TV, various video game systems, racks of CDs, DVDs, a giant stuffed Spyro, and stacks of old board games like Chinese Checkers and Parcheesi.

The walls were papered with band posters for October Fall, Phantom Planet, 3OH!3, and Mayday Parade, to name only a few. A black and white Jay and Silent Bob poster hung on the wall over the washer and dryer, which were tucked away in the corner next to the bottom of the laundry chute in the next room. An old *Super Mario Bros.* pinball machine from the 90's and a *Sega OutRun* arcade game from the 80's topped off everything in addition to the two guitar hero controllers hanging from pegs on the wall. If I had no other context, I would've taken this image as a professionally decorated set built specifically for a teen film, but not your typical cheesy teen film. This was fucking spectacular.

"Dude," I said, literally lost for words. "This is fucking incredible. This is your room?"

"Like I said, sort of. I have a room upstairs, but I just hang out down here most of the time."

"So, it's, like, your second room?"

"Basically."

Izzy pressed the play button on his stereo's CD player, and a song I've never heard started playing at low volume. He sat down on the edge of his sleeper sofa, which was already unfolded to its bed form.

"What band is this?" I asked, intrigued by the insanely awesome vulgar lyrics to the song.

"The Cum Guzzlers."

156

I recognized the band name from one of the stickers in Izzy's car. I mean, who wouldn't remember that?

He grabbed a CD case sitting on a side table next to the couch bed and handed it to me.

"That's them. They're from Mt. Olive where I used to live. I used to hang out with the lead singer a lot. He and I were tight."

I looked over the front of the case, the cover art a group of four guys standing in front of the outside entrance to a Sears, all dressed in black with long, black hair like mine covering their faces. They were each giving the middle finger to the camera.

"That's at The Rockaway Mall," Izzy said. "It's near my old house. I used to hang out there all the time. It's where *everyone* hangs out up there."

"So, you and the lead singer were friends?" I asked. I put the CD case back down on the table.

"Yeah. Nate's awesome. He graduated last year. He was pretty much, like, the most popular guy there. So many girls were crazy over him. He and the band used to play at private birthday parties for girls who were having their sweet sixteens and it was, like, such a big deal. Last summer, you almost couldn't go to anyone's house without hearing them playing in someone's backyard."

"Nice. So, uh, is he gay, too?"

Izzy laughed.

"No. He's not. Despite the band name. Trust me; I know. I've seen him hook up with so many girls. I mean, I'm not for sleeping around and shit, but he definitely gets a lot of girls."

He paused for a moment. It seemed like he was hesitating to tell me something.

"We *did* make out once," he finally said. "But it was during a game of truth or dare at this party we went to, and we were both really drunk. It didn't mean anything."

157

"...Oh."

"What?" Izzy laughed, patting me on the shoulder.

I shook my head.

"Nothing. I guess I just envy anyone..."

I hesitated, realizing I was about to say something I shouldn't have started.

"What?"

"...I guess I just...envy anyone who's gotten to hook up with you because...I like you."

"Dude." Izzy gave me a sideways hug. "We just made out, like, twenty minutes ago."

"I know, but..."

"But what? You don't know if it was genuine or if I was just doing it to make you happy?"

...

"I guess," I said. "I'm sorry. It's just...I have trust issues. Every time I think I've met a decent friend, they let me down."

I thought of Thomas and how he's never let me down, so that really wasn't a fair statement, but this feeling I had for Izzy was a lot different. He was the type of friend I felt like I could actually maybe get on another level with...if you get what I'm saying. That would obviously never happen with Thomas.

"You don't have to be sorry," he said. "I get it. I'm sorry for kissing you. Maybe I shouldn't have done that."

"No," I said quickly. "I...I really liked it."

There was that beautiful, hypnotic smile again.

"I liked it, too."

We were quiet for another minute, but then my curiosity got the better of me. I just had to know more about this boy.

"So, have you ever, like, done anything else with a guy before?"

"Like besides making out?"

"Yeah."

"Yeah. I hooked up with a guy at my old school."

"So, you guys, like…did it?"

"No. It didn't go that far. We made out, gave each other hand jobs. I gave him a blow job."

I felt myself getting hard as I imagined Izzy, naked, and his head between the legs of another boy. I wanted so badly for that boy to be me.

"Nice," I said, my voice trembling a bit. "So, you've never actually had sex?"

"I have," Izzy said. "But it was with a girl."

I lost my boner even faster than it came.

"You…had sex with a girl?"

"Yeah, but trust me; I wasn't crazy about it. I mean, it felt good, but I wasn't into her. She was a friend who always had a crush on me and this one night we were just hanging out at her house in her room, and she started making a move on me. I was pretty horny, so I figured I'd just let things happen."

"…Oh."

"Don't worry, though," he laughed. "I didn't get her pregnant or anything. I used a condom."

159

I tried to smile.

"Well, that's…good…I guess. What was it like?"

"Sex with a girl?" He shrugged. "Like I said, it felt good, but it wasn't for me and things got kinda awkward after that night. We didn't really talk much after that and I think it's because she knew I was gay, but she had feelings for me, so sometimes I feel bad about it. I probably should've just told her it wasn't a good idea."

I envied this girl so much that it almost made me angry.

"I'm still a virgin," I said, and it must've shown that I was ashamed of it because Izzy immediately put his arm around me.

"Sex isn't really what it's all hyped up to be, bud," he told me. "It's not like you're missing out on anything out of this world. It's better to wait for the right person to come around. Trust me. I wish I waited."

The question I wanted to ask began to rise slowly from my subconscious. I knew it was there all along, but I was afraid to cross that line. Here I was, though, alone with a boy who I knew liked me enough to kiss me, and who liked me enough to take me under his wing just to be my friend because he wanted to be nice to a stranger. Here we were in his room, on his bed, talking about sex. Why should I have to repress the obvious question?

"Would you have sex with me?"

I held my breath.

Izzy kissed my cheek and for a second, I thought it was his way of politely declining.

"Maybe," he said, and I relaxed a little. "Not right now, though. I think we should wait it out so we're not being too impulsive. Like, let's get to know each other a little better first. You know what I mean?"

"Yeah," I said, looking away and feeling like I could cry again. "I guess so."

"Don't worry," he said, patting me on the back. "We're still friends. I just don't want to make any bad decisions, you know? I'd love to have sex with you, but I want it to be right. We just met and we already made out, so let's take it a little slower now. Okay?"

I nodded.

"Come here, bud," he said, and he hugged me again.

And you know what? That's really all I needed.

Before I went home, Izzy showed me his other bedroom upstairs, which was still fitting to his personality, but didn't have the same amount of character that his basement hangout had. His upstairs room was more of a representation of the "skater boy" side of him with the Tony Hawk poster on the ceiling and Vans clothing everywhere. He wasn't kidding when he said it was messier than my room; the floor next to the bed was littered with empty Dr. Pepper cans. I discovered that the window in this room faced my house, and even more specifically, the window next to the La-Z-Boy in my bedroom.

We exchanged numbers [Thank God], and then I walked back home before Izzy and his dad headed over to the school to jump-start Izzy's car. By then, the rain had subsided enough that it wasn't coming down in buckets, but a light drizzle, and as I've sat here tonight and written all of this, I continue to take glances out my window, knowing that the warm glow of light coming from the upstairs of the stucco house next door is my new best friend, Izzy Murraro.

Chapter Eight
Saturday, October 21st, 2006

Dear Journal,

I've been spending a lot of time with Izzy these past couple of weeks. Just the morning after he and his dad jump-started his car, he texted me and offered to drive me to school. The text was already waiting for me when I woke up, and I quickly sent him a message back to tell him I was game.

I don't think I've ever taken a shower and chosen an outfit so fast. I even grabbed a granola bar from the pantry for breakfast, which must've confused Mom and Dad since I darted out the back door, explaining that my new friend would be driving me.

I can only imagine the thoughts going through their heads [Kieran has a…*friend*?!].

I met Izzy in his driveway just as he was opening the garage door.

"Hey, bud!" he greeted me. "What's up?"

"Not much," I said. I was so fucking happy to see him, but tried not to act too overly excited. It took me hours to fall asleep the night before because I was thinking about him so much and how close by he was in his own bed in that awesome arcade basement bedroom of his. "Thanks for driving me."

"Hey, it'll make up for me making you walk last night," he said with a wink. "Battery's all good now." He patted the hood of the Alfa. "Should be alright for a while, but I definitely need to replace it soon before she leaves me stranded again."

He unlocked the car, we got in, and he successfully started the engine this time. During our short drive to school, he used that iPod cassette adaptor thing he was telling me about. To my delight, he chose a Stay Sweet song from his playlist, and it wasn't just the song that put the rare smile on my face, but the thought that he did it just to make me happy. I know he likes the band, too, but I could tell from the smile on his face as he was backing out of their garage that he was excited to play the song for me.

162

This is how it's been every morning. Izzy drives me to school every day. Sometimes we even leave a little early. We'll stop at Turkey Hill on the other side of town to get hot dogs and fries for our lunches while he gets gas for the car. He always insists on paying for me and I'm never successful in talking him out of it.

We always hope that this cute, lanky guy [Kody, according to his nametag] with long black hair, tattoos on his arms, and snake bite piercings will be behind the register. If he is, Izzy and I will check him out and then go on about how hot he's looking when we hop back in the car. It's so awesome to finally be able to share my appreciation of other cute guys with someone else. The idea is slowly becoming more normal...and wonderful.

Izzy's been sitting with me, Thomas, and Athena at lunch. I was happy to see that Thomas and Athena seemed to take an instant liking to my new friend. Even though he's never shown the slightest trace of interest in the arts, Thomas has been pretty open to listening to the stories Izzy has to offer about how his father was a financial advisor and friend of New York artist Eric Fischl back in the '80s. It led to their family having close ties to the scenes of Jean Michel Basquiat, Julian Schnabel, Andy Warhol, and, of course, Keith Haring, in addition to other prominent faces in the Manhattan art movements at the time.

I still haven't come out to Thomas or Athena, and I guess that's pretty fucking stupid because I don't think there's any way either of them would give the slightest shit about me liking guys. I guess just having Izzy know is kind of like a thrill to me or something. It's like I want to give him the privilege of being exclusive in that way. Izzy promised me that my secret would be kept just between the two of us until I felt I was ready to tell anyone else. He's even gone so far as to keep it from Thomas and Athena that he's gay so that the subject won't come up and wouldn't make things any more obvious about me.

I swear he's a fucking saint...

Afternoons in the recent weeks have become a routine for Izzy and me. I meet him in the parking lot after school, he gives me a ride, we sometimes stop for pizza at Sal's or grab a couple of burgers from the Burger King drive-thru, and then he drives me home where I run upstairs so that only about thirty seconds later, he's calling me once he's settled inside his own house. We'll spend the next hour or so

163

chatting on the phone about anything and everything that I'd normally never dare bring up in front of anyone else, like which guys at school we find cute, who else in King's Valley we think might be gay, who our biggest celebrity crushes are, etc.

These conversations go on at least until I hear Mom's car pulling into the garage, and then, usually after dinner, we'll call again and sometimes even watch each other from our bedroom windows before we go to sleep. Regardless of whatever discussions we have, I always tend to climb into bed with a feeling of content that I haven't felt in a long time.

My Stay Sweet dreams have even evolved into fantasies of Izzy, me running into his arms and him holding me while I sink into his chest that slowly, and sadly, changes into the pillows on my bed when I wake up.

The dreams go further than that sometimes. I've imagined him naked, imagined what it would be like to have sex with him. It's been difficult for me to not bring up the sex thing again, but after he made it clear that he doesn't want to be compulsive about that, I've decided that it's best not to talk about it since it might make him feel uncomfortable. The last thing I need would be to scare him off and lose the one thing that's been distracting me from Justin's death, the one thing that's made me happy. I don't know if I've *ever* been this happy, honestly.

So, I've been taking it slow with him. Our conversations in the car on our ways to and from school and the long talks on the phone at night have been fulfilling enough. It's just really nice to have a friend who, for whatever reason, is so devoted to me. It's taken me a while, but I'm finally starting to accept that this is for real and not just another "too good to be true" situation that will eventually fade like the kindness Eric Gleason initially offered me before showing me his true form.

Izzy's different. I *know* he's different.

...

Today, or yesterday, rather, since it's after midnight now and technically Saturday morning, Mrs. Kinney congratulated us on a very successful first issue of the school paper. She reminded us that the

second marking period would be over in a flash, so it was already time to start preparing for our new articles.

Thomas called it. This would, as the first article was, be about whatever we wanted, but an interview would have to be conducted as part of the requirements.

"Still planning on interviewing your man?" he asked me.

"My...*man*?"

I nearly choked on the glazed donut I was finishing, one of several dozen Mrs. Kinney brought as a treat for us to celebrate the first issue's release.

"You know, that singer guy from the band. Mark Daniels?"

"*Matt* Daniels." I relaxed. "And no. I wish."

"Remember what I told you, Northrup. Always go big. Just have some backups."

"What about you?" I asked. "You still gonna question the mayor?"

"That one unfortunately fell through."

"Did you try?"

"I made multiple attempts. Left several emails and voice messages with Town Hall. No luck." He waved a hand in the air. "Doesn't matter. That alone reinforces my suspicions on what local government's true colors are. Won't even return a kindly student's call on a class project. That says it all. They're far too busy trying to cover up their crimes."

I sighed, my cursor hovering over the Google homepage while I tried to look busy. I didn't know what to write about. Even if I came up with a topic, it didn't mean I'd have a decent candidate to interview.

"What are you doing instead?" I asked.

As if he were waiting for me to ask, Thomas slapped his worn-out notebook in front of me, opened to a colorful page of extravagant notes detailing not only the mayor project and the subject of the scandalous fire which were now crossed off, but also multiple backup ideas numbered in order of undertaking. I'm not even going to get into what these backup topics were, but it was somewhat exhausting to hear all the material Thomas has gathered in preparation for an assignment I haven't even yet considered.

I obviously wouldn't admit it to Thomas, but my time with Izzy has been distracting me from thinking about anything related to the paper.

And that's totally okay with me.

…

"Yo, Kieran!"

I stopped at the exit to the school's main courtyard when I heard someone calling my name. I turned to see Adam Woolf making his way through the afternoon locker crowd, smiling as he waved to me.

"Oh," I said. "Hey. What's up?"

Adam responded by putting up his fist for me to bump. I did, and then he was reaching out to give me a hug.

"What's good, man?" he asked, giving me a quick squeeze. "What's new? How you holding up?"

I shrugged.

"Not much. I'm doing okay."

"Great, man! Great! Listen, I'm going to see a movie tonight. You want to come?"

…

"Um…I don't think…"

"Don't worry, man," he interrupted. "Tyler's not gonna be there, so no one's gonna start shit or anything. It'll all be good."

"Oh. What movie are you seeing?"

"*The Grudge 2.*"

"Oh. Well, I would, but I...kinda..."

Adam's face started to fall.

"...made plans," I finished.

"Oh."

Again, Adam looked surprisingly disappointed that I was declining another one of his invites.

"Shit," he said, and he started to fidget a little. "Well, you want to hang out tomorrow or something, man? We could, like, go to The Skate Park and chill."

I nearly felt nauseous at the thought of going to that place.

"I...I don't know if I really want to go there."

"Well, we could do whatever, man. I just thought it'd be cool to hang."

I was confused. Adam was being so persistent. Why didn't this ever happen when I was actually looking for someone to be friends with? I guess that isn't true since he *did* invite me to hang out before, but...that was before I met Izzy...and now I *only* wanted to spend time with Izzy.

"I don't know," I said, standing there awkwardly while dozens of others walked around us to get out of the building. "I think I have plans tomorrow, too." I looked down at the floor.

"Sorry."

Adam shrugged.

"It's all good, man. Don't worry about it. Let's hang soon, though. You got my number?"

"No."

"Here, let me give it to you. You got your phone?"

"Yeah."

We stepped to the side and I pulled out my phone. Adam grabbed it and added his number. As he handed it back to me with his disappointed smile, I weirdly felt sort of good about all this. It was nice to be the one who had to turn down someone else's invite for a change instead of waiting by the phone with the hopes that someone would reach out.

"Thanks," I said. "I'll, uh, hit you up soon," I added for good measure.

"Cool, dude. Have a good one."

He headed out into the courtyard and I watched him go, that pretty blonde boy with his backpack bouncing behind him. He wanted to hang out with me...one of the hottest guys in school...and I passed for the second time. Did that mean I was somewhat significant now?

I opened my phone, and since Adam's name comes first alphabetically in my short list of contacts, it appeared immediately as the first name. He added a colon and parenthesis to make a little smiley face next to his name.

I slammed my phone shut and stuffed it back in my pocket, feeling slightly, but not too guilty, as I headed out the door.

...

"Hey, bud! Where you been?"

Izzy greeted me, standing up against his car as I came walking across the half-empty lot. He looked so fucking cool in his black denim jacket and Blink-182 shirt underneath. His hair has gotten slightly longer since we first met, the Jewish/Italian curls beginning to take

form as it fills out. Sometimes, though, before school, he'll take a straightener to it, and his hair will have a slick wave.

"Sorry I took so long," I said. "Fucking…"

I stopped in mid-sentence when I noticed a lit cigarette stuck between two of his skinny fingers, most of it already smoked.

"Fucking…gym class."

"No worries, man! I wouldn't have left without you. Hop in!"

He dropped the cigarette to the blacktop and stomped on it with his Vans sneaker. I opened the car door and sat down in the passenger seat. Izzy got in behind the wheel and started the engine.

"You smoke?" I asked.

"What's that, bud?" He hooked in his belt, silencing the warning chime. We were left with the rattling of the Alfa's aging engine.

"You smoke?"

"Oh. Yeah." He laughed. "I didn't tell you that?"

"No." I hooked in my belt.

"I only have one once in a while." He put the car in gear and started driving.

"I'm not judging," I said. "I'm just surprised."

"Surprised?" he chuckled. "Why?"

"I don't know. I guess you just seem so…pure."

Izzy laughed louder than I've ever heard him.

"Me? Pure? You've got a lot of surprises coming to you, buddy."

I brushed some hair out of my eyes, smiling at the thought of a "bad boy" side of Izzy that maybe I was yet to meet.

"You ever smoke?" he asked me.

"Nope."

"You want to try one?"

He pulled a pack of Camels from the pocket of his jacket and held it out to me while he steered with the other hand. I stared back at it, at him like he was the antagonist in one of the many short films they showed us in elementary school where we were basically told we were guaranteed to be offered free drugs from just about everyone when we got older. The script called for me to respond with a simple, *"No, thanks."* Nancy Reagan's campaign had successfully trickled down to my generation.

...

"Oh, fuck it. Why not?"

I grabbed the pack and slid one of the cigarettes out. It felt weird because it was my first time ever even holding one.

"You, uh, got a lighter?" I asked.

I caught a glimpse of the speedometer. We were doing about thirty on Carlton. Izzy tried reaching into his bottom jeans pocket for his lighter unsuccessfully, his foot still on the gas while he attempted to maneuver his butt out of the seat enough to reach around to grab it.

"Shit," he muttered, and nodded toward the center of the dash just above the air vents. "Use the car lighter there."

I stared stupidly at the contraption for a moment, realizing I had never used one in my life and had absolutely no idea how to.

"Press it in," Izzy said when he noticed I was confused.

I felt myself turn red.

"Thanks."

170

I pressed the lighter in and waited.

"I was thinking," Izzy started. "It's Friday. We should do something tonight."

I looked over at him and felt happy butterflies in my stomach.

"Yeah?"

"Yeah, man. Why don't you stay over at my place?"

Staying over...at Izzy's house...possibly sleeping next to him...

"Really?" I said.

"Yeah. My dad can make us dinner and we can stay up late and do whatever. I've got N64 and Super Nintendo. We could play *Mario Kart* or *Donkey Kong Country*. I've got the *Silent Hill* games for PS2, *Banjo-Kazooie*..."

"Yeah," I said, quickly, like if I waited to respond, the opportunity might slip away. "Let's do it!"

Izzy smiled and then held up his hand for me to grab it. I did, he gave me a squeeze, and that was when the cigarette lighter popped out to tell me it was ready.

That was when I stupidly pulled it out and grabbed it so that the hot coils burned the palm of my hand.

That was when I yelped at the sudden pain, tossed the hot cigarette lighter, and it landed on Izzy's crotch.

That was when Izzy reacted by quickly taking his hands off the wheel to brush the lighter away from him and doing so caused the car to start aiming toward the opposite lane of incoming traffic.

Izzy hit the brake and jerked the steering wheel violently to the right to avoid a collision with an oncoming SUV. He lost control for a moment. I could hear the tires squealing as the car took a dip onto the soft shoulder of the road and managed to run into some shrubbery.

171

We finally slowed to a stop in the shallow ditch on the side of Carlton, near the turn for Arbor Avenue.

"Shit," Izzy gasped. He let out a sigh of relief as he pulled his hands from the wheel and sank back in the seat to catch his breath. "I'm sorry, man. You okay?"

I sat stunned for a moment, staring out the windshield at the branches and leaves that had fallen onto the hood of the car after we dove into the greenery. The seatbelt had tightened against my chest in the same place where my bruise from the accident with Justin still is, and the similarity to that experience forced me to bury my face into my hands.

"Oh, no!" I heard Izzy say.

There was the sound of him unclicking his belt, and then I felt his arm around me while I started crying really hard. My palms were already wet with tears when Izzy brought me in for a sideways hug.

"I'm so sorry, buddy," he said, patting my head as I whimpered. "I'm so sorry. Are you okay?"

Still whimpering with my hands over my eyes, I shook my head.

"Oh, buddy," Izzy said. "It's okay. We're okay. I'm sorry. It's alright."

My nose running, I unhooked my belt, pushed away the restraint, and hugged Izzy back. I let him hold me while I cried into his shoulder. He shushed me gently until I calmed down.

…

I think about fifteen minutes passed. My face was still pressed up against the denim covering Izzy's shoulder while he held me. We were both quiet, and only the sounds of passing cars filled the background of the moment when I stopped crying, but stayed in his arms because that was what I really needed. I needed to be held.

"You okay?" Izzy asked.

"Yeah," I said hoarsely. "I'm sorry I cried. I just..."

"I know. I know. It's okay."

He patted my head and we separated. I wiped my eyes with my hoodie sleeve while Izzy reached down to the floor near his feet where he retrieved the fallen cigarette lighter. He held it up between two of his fingers. It had grown cold again.

...

Izzy drove to Skyview Drive, pulled up to the garage of my house, and let me out so I could run in to pack an overnight bag to stay at his place. In the few minutes I was inside packing my bag and feeding Larry, Izzy had taken out his iPod and started playing an unfamiliar, but sublime song that hit me the instant I opened the car door.

"All set?" he asked.

"Yep."

"Awesome."

He started backing out of my driveway while the ambient music continued.

"What band is this?" I asked, picking up his iPod.

"Slowdive," he said, looking over his shoulder as he backed up. "Why, you like them?"

It took me a moment to respond. It was like I was being hypnotized by this music...and him. There was something about his one hand firm on the steering wheel and the other clutched around the knob of the gearshift that made Izzy look sexier. He was in complete control, and looked so mature...like an adult, but I still felt like such a kid.

"I...*love* it," I finally said. "I can't believe I've never heard of them."

"They're a '90s band. My brother got me into them. It's, like, the best chill music ever."

"Catch the Breeze," I said, reading the name of the song from the iPod description. I closed my eyes and let the song capture me until I could hear the sound of Izzy's garage door opening.

I didn't even want to look back at my house. I just wanted the rest of the night to be with Izzy and his world inside 2714 Skyview Drive.

After the garage door shut behind us, Izzy turned up the volume, and the two of us sat in the car while the hauntingly beautiful sounds of Slowdive filled the space in an almost dreamlike manner. Izzy's hand found mine, and any trace of the anger or sadness I had with the world completely vanished.

...

I wasn't able to completely relax until an hour or so later when I received a text back from my mom, responding to me asking if it was okay if I stayed over at Izzy's. She thankfully agreed, even though I had been worried sick that she would decline since she and Dad still haven't met Izzy, but I guess the fact that he lives right next door was enough for them to let it happen. Maybe my absence from the house for a little while will give her more time to cry or something.

I was so relieved, and by the time Mr. Murraro started cooking hamburgers for us after he got home, I was feeling a rush of excitement…a good excitement that's been rare to me these days. I felt like something epic had to happen tonight. Something amazing was on the agenda. I just didn't know what it was yet.

Since it was too chilly to do the burgers on the grill, Mr. Murraro broiled them in the oven, and they came out amazing. The three of us sat at their high-top kitchen table [I almost felt like my head would hit the glass ceiling]. The table was laid out with bottles of ketchup, mustard, mayo, a jar of bread and butter pickles, and a plate of baked golden-brown French fries. There was potato salad, too, and for drinks we had the option of Coke or Dr. Pepper. I chose Coke and Izzy Dr. Pepper like usual, but there was a bottle of red wine for Mr. Murraro.

Izzy's dad had this Italian singer, Ryan Paris, playing on his sleek Beomaster stereo in the other room. Mr. Murraro looked absolutely entranced by the music in a way not so different from how I had felt about Slowdive a few hours earlier. He bobbed in his seat to the beat of the song, reaching across the table for the mustard as he mouthed the words.

"Dad, could you be any more stereotypically Italian?" Izzy laughed when he noticed his dad's theatrical reaction to the '80s hit, "Dolce Vita".

"Hey!" Mr. Murraro started using his hands in an exaggerated way to speak. "What-a do you mean? I'm-a just trying to enjoy some of the 'Dolce Vita', my Ishmael."

Izzy groaned and looked legitimately pissed off at the sound of his real name.

"Don't call me Ishmael!"

"That is-a your name-a, is it-a not, Ish-a-mael?"

"Dad! Stop!"

Izzy pounded a fist on the table, and for a second, I was scared that this really was a fight about to break out between the two of them, but I relaxed when I realized they were both laughing. It suddenly felt like I was watching a sitcom about a father/son duo. This was the first time I had seen Izzy's dad in such a lighthearted tone, poking fun at himself and almost resembling someone our own age, maybe even younger. I could see a peek of where Izzy's personality stems from when Mr. Murraro's laughter began.

"Did you know Ishmael is his real name?" Izzy's dad asked me.

"I told him," Izzy answered for me.

"Oh, you told him?" Mr. Murraro turned to me. "You must be a *very* special friend. He doesn't tell many people his real name, you know."

175

Izzy was staring at his plate with an expression of embarrassment. I wasn't sure if it was because of the whole conversation about his real name, or from Mr. Murraro referring to me as his "*very* special friend".

"Yeah," I said. "I don't know why, though. I like it."

Mr. Murraro squeezed some mustard onto his burger.

"Do you like your name, Kieran?" he asked.

"I don't know. I never really thought about it before."

"Are you named after anyone?" Izzy asked.

"Not that I know of."

"Vincent's a family name," Mr. Murraro said. "Vincenzo. It's my name, it's my father's name, it was my grandfather's name, and my great grandfather's name. My older son, Giovanni, is the first of five generations not to be named Vincent. I felt like it had to end somewhere. It was already getting very confusing at family gatherings. My father wasn't too happy about me ending the streak, but he came to like the name Giovanni since we named him after Giovanni Bosco."

"Giovanni Bosco?" I said.

Mr. Murraro nodded.

"The Italian saint."

"*I* would've rather been named Vincent," Izzy interrupted.

His father shrugged.

"Well, when you're eighteen, you can go to the courthouse and have it changed, okay?"

Mr. Murraro slid the open bottle of wine down the table toward me.

"Would you like a sip, Kieran?"

"Um…no…that's okay. Thanks, though."

He passed it to Izzy, and I watched him take a swig of the expensive wine straight from the bottle, gulping it down like a marathon runner would with water.

"Hey!" Mr. Murraro laughed and grabbed the bottle from his son. "A *sip*, Ishmael! A *sip*!"

Izzy made eye contact with me from across the table, giggling as he held a hand to his mouth to not spit out the wine from his laughter. I laughed a little, too, looked down at the burger I was finishing, and when I looked back up, Mr. Murraro was smiling at me.

"Kieran, you remind me so much of Andy," he said.

"Andy?"

"Andy Warhol. Did Izzy tell you his mother and I knew him?"

"Oh. Yeah. I…remind you of him?"

"So much." He took another sip of wine. "You have his mannerisms, his voice. You have the same modesty Andy had. You aren't shy, but…private."

I smiled a little, assuming this was a compliment. The only other time I had ever been compared to a celebrity was when my grandmother told me I reminded her of a very young Arlo Guthrie.

"But," Mr. Murraro continued. "Just like with him, I can tell you're brilliant. You're a good kid. I miss Andy, so it's nice to have someone like him in the house again."

"Thanks," I said. I almost felt like I could cry, but a good cry.

I loved it in this house. At that same moment, I pictured Mom and Dad sitting at our table next door and being miserably quiet while Mom cut the silence once in a while to complain that our supposedly high-end washing machine wasn't successfully getting a certain stain out of one of her designer blouses.

Even though the Murraro house had also recently experienced a death, there was a much less gloomy vibe about the place. Izzy and his dad are just so open with each other. It's like they actually know each other. It's like they're friends.

...

After dinner, I helped Izzy wash the dishes at the kitchen sink while his dad retired to his "study" for the evening. Mr. Murraro's "study" is a room that's really just a den with a big-screen TV, desk, and the Beomaster I was talking about. Everything looks so "Wall Street" '80s in there: sleek, black and white, edgy, and modern for what was modern twenty years ago. Even though it was cold and urban at first sight, it felt more inviting and unique than my mom's idea of staging our house to be a copy of a 21st Century yuppie home décor catalog. Hell, I wanted one of those stainless-steel floor tree lamps like Mr. Murraro has next to the fireplace. I liked the Patrick Nagel paintings that were hanging up all over their house and the framed "blown away" Maxell logo print on the wall over the stereo. The bookshelves were lined with baby blue neon lights that looked like they belonged in the ceiling of an '80s mall food court, as did the artificial weeping fig trees framing the windows. It didn't really fit with the rest of the neighborhood, and I think that's why it was so appealing to me. There was something almost utopian about this fun, accepting place in the middle of such a brusque subdivision.

"You ever have sushi?" Izzy asked as he handed me freshly washed dishes to dry off with a hand towel. The sound of John O'Hurley saying *"Survey said!"* in between dings and buzzers faded in from the study TV while Mr. Murraro watched *Family Feud*. Izzy sipped from a can of Dr. Pepper now and then that was sitting on the counter.

"No, I haven't."

"My dad and I do sushi once a week. We get takeout from Kasai Kitchen. It's so good. You have to join us sometime."

"I don't know how I feel about eating raw fish," I said.

"Ah, you don't have to worry about that, man. It's safe. It's really good. I love sushi."

Izzy pulled the food catcher from the drain, and the soapy water started to lower with a loud, sickly gurgle.

"There isn't much you don't like," I said. "Except your name."

He laughed and dried his hands with a paper towel.

"You got that right, man. You want to play *Mario Kart*?"

"Sure."

We headed downstairs to his basement room. He fired up the N64, and we spent the next hour playing *Mario Kart*, a game I hadn't played since Justin and I faced each other in the late '90s. It had been so long that I almost forgot what the game was like, but Izzy made it more fun by blasting Green Day on his stereo to go along with our races. "American Idiot" was an excellent soundtrack to go with the final Rainbow Road track.

By 10 pm, we were both lying on Izzy's sleeper sofa and watching *Family Guy* on Adult Swim. I wish they made a candle of what Izzy's house smells like because I'd love more than anything to smell that all day. I can't even put into words what the aroma is reminiscent of, but it must be some kind of mix of whatever body spray he wears and Mr. Murraro's cooking fumes that travel through the air vents from the kitchen.

"Thank God it's Friday," Izzy said, yawning and stretching. He was still wearing his Blink-182 shirt and jeans. "It's been such a long fucking week, man. I had a chemistry test *and* an Algebra II test. I'm sure I fucking failed one of them."

"Every week is long," I snorted. "But then on the weekends, I don't do anything, so I don't know what's worse."

Izzy sat up and adjusted his shirt. I was dying to see what was under it, but so far, the night didn't seem like it was headed that way. I was slightly disappointed that the flirtatious Izzy who had kissed me several weeks earlier didn't seem to be active tonight, but I was also just thankful to be with him. It had been years since I had a sleepover with any friends, and even then, none of them were "personal" ones that I was invited to solely. They were always a group event where a

kid in the class must have been obligated to throw my name on the list of invitations.

"Don't think that way," Izzy said. "You have to go out and do more, bud."

"I know, but what is there to do in King's Valley? This town is so fucking boring."

"I hear you, man. We gotta get out to New York sometime."

"You and me?" I asked.

"Of course, bud."

Izzy smiled and moved his stocking foot to playfully nudge my hip.

"You'll take me?"

"Dude, yes! Why wouldn't I?"

"I don't know," I said. "I guess I'm just still surprised someone cool like you would want to hang with me."

Izzy laughed.

"Cool? Is that what I am?"

"I think so."

His laugh turned into a boyish giggle that made me want to kiss him again. Oh, why am I bothering to censor my real feelings here? I wanted to fuck him.

"I don't think I'm that cool," he said. "I don't try to be. And why wouldn't I hang with you? You're so sweet."

"Sweet?"

"You're very sweet. And the world needs more sweet people."

180

I never thought of myself as being sweet. To be honest, I always figured I was an antisocial asshole.

"You're cute, too," Izzy said.

I was starting to get hard. Maybe Izzy *did* have other plans for us tonight.

"*You're* cute," I said. "I don't think I am."

"Just take my compliment," he laughed, but it was an annoyed laugh, like I was driving him crazy with my low self-esteem. "You need to relax more."

"Yeah," I said, disappointed with myself for being such an idiot in front of him. "I know. I'm, like, anxious all the time. That's why I'm always listening to music. Stay Sweet calms me down."

"Whatever works for you, bud." He smiled and looked me up and down for a moment. "You want to know what I do?"

"What you...do?"

"To relax."

"Oh. What do you do?"

He stood from the sleeper sofa and reached out his hand.

"Come on."

"...What?"

"Come on. I'll show you."

"...Okay."

I took his hand and he helped me to my feet. We both went back up the basement stairs and through the kitchen, which was now dark except for the eerie glow of the light over the stove. Izzy went ahead of me, tiptoeing up the carpet of the steps as I followed him. I didn't know what we were doing, but it felt like we were getting away with something.

The doors to Mr. Murraro's bedroom far left at one end of the hall and up a few carpeted steps were closed, and I assumed him to be asleep. Izzy led me to the right, past a heater baseboard that was letting out a throaty exhale as the furnace did its job of heating the house. It also managed to blow around a hanging Basquiat tapestry in a ghostly way.

Izzy opened a door at the right end of the hall, revealing a linen closet stocked with fresh towels, an old bulky Electrolux vacuum cleaner that was probably around before I was born, and some extra sets of bed sheets. He reached up to the top shelf and grabbed a handful of various bath towels before kicking the door shut and leading me across the hall.

"This'll be nice," he whispered. "It's gonna seem weird, but trust me. You'll love it."

He opened the door to the guest bathroom, a room that was sparsely decorated with the exception of another one of those large artificial weeping fig trees that reached toward the ceiling's skylight hanging over the circular jacuzzi tub. Izzy shut the door behind us, flicked a switch, and several track lights in the ceiling lit up. Soft, amber light pointed down onto the tub. The flick of a second switch started the groaning sound of a heater in the ceiling.

I watched him start to unfold a couple of the bath towels he grabbed, laying them out like blankets along the tiled floor against the rounded edge of the tub that was large enough to fit two people. The tub itself was encircled by a brass railing and situated into a corner "turret" with windows facing the backyard, but the view was blocked by closed blinds that were a dusty mauve color that matched the floor tiles.

"What are we doing?" I asked, the slightest trace of nervous laughter in my voice. The way he was laying those towels out reminded me of teen movies where couples would sneak into the woods to have sex on a blanket. Was that what this was going to be?

"You'll see," he said.

He turned the glossy handle for the hot water, pulled the little metal nose to plug up the drain, and the bathtub started to fill. The tub's

182

tiles were a deep, dark blue that the clear water made look all the more refreshing in the way that it bent the light.

Izzy sat down on the floor at the edge of the tub so that his head was resting up against it. He patted his hand against the second towel spread out next to him.

"Come here," he said. "Lay next to me."

I laid down on the fluffy towel next to him, and then he was grabbing the other towels he tossed in front of the sink, draping them over us like big blankets, and it was as if we were lying in bed together. The right side of his body was so close against the left side of mine that we were practically conjoined twins.

"Well, this is…comfy," I said, still unsure of what exactly we were doing.

"Isn't it?" He slipped his soft hand into mine and sighed. "This is what I do every night to relax."

"You lay on the bathroom floor?"

"Yep. With all these towels over me and the water running. I just lay here, close my eyes, and let the sound drown out anything else so it's like the rest of the world doesn't exist."

It was like Izzy was speaking for me. This was something I would've come up with on my own, but I never speculated that someone else could ever find beauty in such a simple idea. Here I was, though, lying on that floor with layers of towels covering both of us. The sounds of the bathroom were doing just as Izzy explained, making me forget the rest of the world was even there. I wondered if I would ever be able to get as comfortable in my own room again. This seemed to trump everything. This was my safe space now.

"Isn't this nice?" Izzy asked me after a few minutes had passed.

"Yeah. It is."

"My brother told me about this."

"What?"

"My brother…he told me about doing this. I learned it from him."

"Oh. Really?"

"Yep. He used to disappear in the bathroom for hours and it annoyed the shit out of me since we shared the same one and he was always hogging it up, but eventually he told me the reason he was in there so long was because he was relaxing, and this is what he was doing. So, I figured I'd try it and I've been doing it every night for, like, the past two years now. I guess it's kind of like meditation."

He stared at the ceiling, at the black sky and stars beyond the glass over the tub.

"It really helped when my mom died. I'd just think about her and try to bring myself back to something I did with her when I was little. Sometimes, I use even more towels and put some over my head so it's like the rest of the world is really gone. I really get lost in thought. If I'm feeling shitty during the day, this is like a detox. It's a cleansing, you know?" His eyes widened as he continued speaking, a more than passionate look taking him over. "It's, like, no matter how shitty the day might be, this is something *I* can completely control. You know what I mean?"

I clutched his hand tighter and almost instinctively cuddled my head closer to his. He accepted it.

"You're so…philosophical," I said.

"You think so?"

"Yeah."

"You should meet my brother."

"Is he philosophical, too?"

"I think so. He's just, like, really chill. I wish I could be more like him."

Hearing Izzy say he wished he could be like anyone else was just about the most surprising thing I had ever heard. In my eyes, he was perfect, and I wished I could be everything that he was.

"I wish," I started, hesitating because I didn't want to be weird with continuously complimenting him, but then decided I had to finish the thought since I opened my mouth. "I wish I could be more like you."

"Like me?"

"Yeah."

"Why like me?"

"Because...you're, like, the friendliest person I know."

"If I'm the friendliest person you know, then we must live in a pretty fucked up world," he said.

"Why do you say that?"

"Because being friendly just comes naturally to me. There's literally nothing difficult about it."

I meditated on that thought for a while.

"This house," I said, taking in the unconventional interior design. "It's...interesting."

"You mean the décor?"

"Yeah. It's, like...I don't know, like..."

"Like, really fucking outdated?" Izzy laughed. "Like a fucking mall in 1986?"

"I...guess so, but...I like it."

"That's my dad's doing," Izzy said. "He designed all this. He ordered it. He had a vision in mind when he had this place built for us. He worked as a stockbroker for The Memphis Group in the '80s and

that sort of became his thing. My mom never liked this style, though. Our old house was a lot more traditional."

"Memphis Group?"

"Yeah. They were this Italian design company that basically designed furniture that looked like it belonged in an N64 game."

"Oh. Well, I like it. It's different. It's...fun."

"Yeah. We're basically living in a giant piece of pop art," he laughed. "I think he just wanted to make this place look as different as possible from our old house. He wanted moving here to be like stepping into a new world."

The running water was starting to let off a bubbling, glurping sound that reminded me of throwing large rocks into a river. The sound temporarily paralyzed me with a sudden drop in the pit of my stomach. I remembered hearing a similar sound just before Justin's car...[really had to literally shake my head to get that shit out of my head].

"Sounds like it's almost full," I said, feeling a rush of adrenaline as I tried to forget about the memories of the accident that had suddenly creeped their way into me again. Sometimes I wonder if I'm mentally fucked up for life because of that.

Izzy sat up, leaned over the tub, and twisted the faucet handles to stop the water. We were left with only the continuous roar of the heater.

"That's a lot of waste, isn't it?" I asked.

Izzy had dipped his finger into the tub water, swirling it around. For a moment, he seemed mesmerized by the steaming liquid, like he had never seen water before in his life and this was the first time he was experiencing it. Then he looked up at me with an innocent smile.

"What do you mean?"

"I mean, that's a lot of water to fill the tub with just for background noise, isn't it?"

Izzy laughed, sat on the edge of the tub, and started rolling the sock away from his left foot.

"I'm not wasting the water," he said, taking off the sock. He peeled off the right one a second later. "I'm gonna take a bath."

Before I could comprehend what was going on, Izzy was pulling off his shirt. For the first time, I was able to take in the sight of his bare chest, the skinny torso of pale skin overcast with black body hair that was growing around his very pink nipples and trailing down to his navel. Izzy's underarms were each sprouting their own tufts of black hair that were exposed as he lifted the shirt over his head and tossed it to the floor next to me. A slight aroma of whatever flavor of Axe he wears caught my nose when he began undoing his belt and pulling his jeans down to his ankles.

His legs and thighs, like the rest of his body, were skinny and hairy. I was actually taken aback by how thin he looked without clothes on. The little bit of extra layer that his clothing provides apparently hides just how frail-looking Izzy actually is. It's not that this bothered me, though. I loved what I saw. I loved the way his body looked.

As his fingers began to grab the rim of his navy-blue boxer briefs, Izzy stalled briefly, looked down at me with a slightly mischievous smile, and chuckled. He was about to show me everything. It was the first time I sensed any bit of nervousness from him, but that smile never faded.

Izzy pulled down his underwear, stepped out of them, and stood naked before me. He didn't hesitate to get in the water, though, and I watched him sink into the tub where he sighed with a slight moan that almost sounded sexual [as if I needed anything else to turn me on in that moment].

"Ahhh, this is fucking awesome," he exhaled.

My heart pounding, I slowly started to rise from the floor. I didn't want to waste another second at the chance of being able to see him. Who knew if I'd ever get to see him naked again? Up until this moment, I had barely seen an inch of his skin. Now, I was seeing it all at once, every part.

187

Tristan LaFerriere

"Looks...nice," I said, peering over the side of the tub at him, and then instantly cringed. "The bath, I mean. The bath. It really looks really nice."

Izzy laughed, his eyes wandering down to his own body with an expression that almost suggested he was admiring his anatomy.

I could make out the slightly distorted image of his body beneath the shimmering water, his pubic hair, his penis that was circumcised like mine. The dark blue tiles of the tub clashed to the whiteness of his skin.

"So," I said, a tremble in my voice as I clutched the brass railing around the tub. "You're not...embarrassed?"

"Embarrassed?"

"...Yeah."

"About what?"

"About...being...naked...in front of me."

Izzy shook his head.

"Not with you." He smiled through the curtain of steam, raised his arms, and rested his hands behind his head. "Besides, we're both guys. We've got the same parts."

A few drops of water dripped from the spigot into the tub.

"You ever take baths?" he asked me.

"Not in a long time."

"You should more often, dude. They're so relaxing. They make everything okay."

We were quiet for a while. It was hard for me to think of anything to say when this boy I had been dreaming of seeing naked for weeks wasn't only undressed, but taking a bath before my eyes. As much as I tried to be polite, I couldn't stop staring.

"Enjoying the view?"

This was followed by the signature Izzy giggle. The spigot dripped again.

I took in a deep breath just to say, "Yeah," and I was startled by how hoarse my voice sounded.

"You can get in here with me if you want," he said.

I instantly felt dizzy.

…

"Okay."

…

I lifted my shirt up slowly, just my belly button exposed, and already I felt modest, but Izzy's smile encouraged me to keep going. I pulled it up over my head, of course getting it stuck around my ears before I clumsily tossed it to the floor.

Izzy's sensual gaze grew at the sight of me shirtless, and besides the few boys in the locker room at school, he was the first person to witness the fading bruise that still marks my chest as a reminder of the accident. His eyes definitely caught a glimpse of it, and I could tell in his changing expression that he knew what it was.

I took off my jeans and my socks and stood in just my boxers for a moment while he still looked up at me. This was it. I was about to be completely naked in front of someone…for the first time, really…for the first time with this developing body of mine.

Like when I had partially exposed myself to Tyler in the woods, my hands were shaking as I pulled at my underwear.

"It's okay," Izzy said. He must have thought I was scared to death by how much I was trembling. "You don't have to be embarrassed in front of me. It's just your body. It's *you*. It's how you were made."

I smiled. He always knew the right things to say.

I pulled my boxers down to about my knees and let them fall on their own the rest of the way to my feet. I was naked and standing at the edge of the tub, Izzy looking me up and down with an admiring gaze that made me even harder than I already had been.

"Look at you-ooh," he said in just about the cutest gay pitch. "You look great."

I chuckled nervously and looked down. My hands seemed to instinctively cup over my genitals to hide them, but I fought the urge to do that.

"I'm...pretty sure I don't look...*great*."

"Take my compliment," he said. "Yes, you do." There was a pause as he continued to look me over. "You have a nice body."

I turned red.

"I'm a skinny dork," I said.

Izzy laughed and looked down at his own body, flicking the surface of the water with his hands.

"Um, do you see this shit? I'm, like, a fucking skeleton. You can see my ribs."

"So?" I said. "You...um...you look...really...*really* nice."

Izzy winked and smooched at me, bringing my boner to its full salute. Then he nodded toward the empty space in the tub in front of him as a signal for me to get in.

My heart continued to pump gallons as I stepped into the water. The tub was large enough so that we weren't on top of each other [as much as I would've enjoyed that], but our feet teased at each other as I sat down on my end. Then the realization sank in...I was taking a bath with Izzy Murraro. Our naked bodies were so close to each other.

...

190

"So, have you ever…taken a bath with another guy before?" I asked after a few minutes. I had to break the silence.

"No," Izzy laughed as he stretched his arms from side to side and grabbed the brass railing. "Have you?"

I shook my head, thinking about how Izzy has already been so many "firsts" for me. My first kiss, my first real sleepover, the first boy I'd ever taken a bath with…

Izzy sighed again. He held his nose, dipped his head under the water to wet his hair, and rose back up to the surface. He looked so different with his hair all wet, but, in a way, almost even cuter than usual.

It's weird, but you know what? I think the way he smiled at me in that moment was what made me realize it…

I love Izzy Murraro.

…

After we soaked in the tub together for a while, we tossed the wet towels into the laundry chute out in the hall once both of us had dried off. Izzy drained the tub, and we left the bathroom, both running down the steps naked in a hurry, to return to the basement bedroom. Izzy immediately grabbed the towels from the bottom of the chute and threw them in the washer. He twisted the chrome knob of the aging appliance that sounded like it was attempting to hock up spit as it filled with hot water.

We dressed into our night clothes after that; both of us were wearing just underwear and band shirts as we climbed under the sheets and blankets of the sleeper sofa. Adult Swim was still on TV, but had moved on to an episode of *Robot Chicken*. After a few minutes, the wash cycle on the washer kicked on, and we were given a concert of sounds from the agitator chugging in circles.

Izzy's hairy right leg interlocked with my left one, our toes met, and something like a childish game I may have played with Justin under the kitchen table when we were both little seemed like such a moment of affection between the two of us.

191

"What are you thinking about?" he asked me after we had been watching TV for a while. I wanted to tell him how I really felt, but I was afraid it would scare him away. I had to be so careful not to fuck this friendship up. Was it even a friendship anymore? It felt like so much more than that. I wanted it to be so much more than that.

"Just…how happy I am that we're friends," I said. It was about as toned down of an answer as I could muster.

"I'm glad we're friends, too, bud."

He hugged me and I hugged him back, but when I started to pull away, he didn't let go, like he didn't want it to end.

"You know, you're my best friend," I said, still hugging him. My leg was pressed up against his bare thigh. I could feel his goosebumps.

"Aww!" Izzy responded as we broke the hug, his voice starting to sound tired. "Am I?"

"I think so."

He held my hand under the sheets.

"I think you're my best friend, too, buddy."

Tears welled up in my eyes at almost the instant he said that.

"Why are you crying, bud?" he asked.

I snorted.

"I don't think anyone's ever called me their best friend before."

Izzy didn't say anything, but gave me a light smile as he used his fingers to wipe the tears from my eyes.

"Well," he finally said. "People don't know what they're missing."

A fucking saint…

192

Izzy kissed me on the forehead, and we left the TV on since he likes having background noise to fall asleep to. I didn't mind because I wasn't interested in sleeping, and this, mixed with the lulling sounds of the washer running in the other room, were actually quite relaxing to me now that Izzy has introduced me to this whole new world of soothing white noise.

I just laid there and watched him until I was certain he wasn't awake anymore. He looked so peaceful and beautiful as his chest rose and fell with each breath, a vague satisfied smile still evident over his expression even as he was dreaming.

It got me wondering; what do beautiful people dream about? Whose arms do they imagine falling into? Would Izzy be dreaming about me in the same way that I've dreamed about Matt Daniels pulling me up on stage? Would he be dreaming about me in the ways that I've dreamed about him?

I've spent the last few hours writing about today while lying next to him as he sleeps. It'll be morning in just a few hours, and while I haven't said this aloud to anyone, I'm going to say it again here and now; I think I'm in love with this boy.

I *know* I'm in love with this boy.

I love Izzy Murraro.

I fucking love Izzy Murraro.

Chapter Nine
Sunday, October 22nd, 2006

Dear Journal,

I was awake for most of Friday night while I slept over at Izzy's. I passed out not long after I finished my last entry. I don't remember my dreams, so it must've been a deep sleep, and time didn't feel like it passed at all when I opened my eyes later.

I must've woken from Izzy's stirring because the first thing I saw was him rising from the blankets and ruffling his bedhead. The TV was still on, and because Adult Swim ended hours earlier, we were tuned in to a show for younger kids as the Saturday morning cartoon marathon had already begun.

"Good morning," I said, my voice groggy. I cleared my throat.

"Good morning," Izzy repeated, stretching and yawning. "How'd you sleep?"

"Pretty good. What time is it?"

Izzy reached for his phone on the end table and opened it.

"Almost eleven."

My eyes adjusted. There are no windows in Izzy's basement, so it could have been any time of day and we wouldn't have known.

"Seriously? It doesn't feel that late."

He stood up, stretching more. His messy morning hair was so fucking adorable.

"I'm gonna take a shower," he said. "Gotta wake up. You want me to make you some breakfast?"

"Sure." I smiled. "I've never, uh…been to a bed and breakfast before."

Izzy giggled as he walked over to the washer, unloaded the spun towels, and tossed them in the dryer.

"Well, welcome to *Izzy's Bed & Breakfast*. You can get anything you want."

I followed him up to the kitchen and he went upstairs to take his shower. While I sat alone at the table, I opened my phone and noticed there was a missed call from Thomas. I called him back just when I started to hear the running water upstairs.

"Morning, Northrup."

"Hey. You called?"

"Yeah. Where've you been?"

"It's…Saturday. I was sleeping in."

"Ah. Well, I was thinking since we had such a successful first issue of the paper, we should celebrate. You want to come over?"

"What are we gonna do?"

"Swimming, of course."

"Swimming? It's, like, almost November."

Thomas laughed.

"I guess I never told you. We have an indoor pool. Open all year."

"Indoor? Wow…"

"It's not that big of a deal, Northrup. It's a small pool in this room off the garage. We're not talking about a YMCA in the house."

"Still, though. That's pretty cool."

"So, you want to come?"

"…Sure. Is it okay if Izzy comes, too?"

I'm not gonna lie; I kind of didn't want to go. I wanted to just spend the rest of the day alone with Izzy, but it felt wrong to just abruptly toss Thomas aside.

"I don't see why not. You seem to be taking a particular interest in this Izzy fella, huh?"

I swallowed hard.

"Yeah. I mean, he's cool. You know?"

"Never said he wasn't, Northrup. I find him to be particularly interesting. But yes, he can come. Are you with him now?"

"Yeah."

I started pacing the room, walking back and forth past the patio doors. I wasn't sure if Thomas would catch on or not if I mentioned that I slept at Izzy's house. From the tone of his voice, it was almost like he was suspecting what was going on between us.

"I...slept over at his place last night," I said. "He invited me over to hang out."

"Ah, nice."

...

"So, can you be here around one?" Thomas continued when he realized I wasn't talking.

"Sure. I'll just make sure that he didn't, like, have any other plans for us or anything."

"Fair enough, Northrup."

Thomas gave me his address, and right around that time, I heard footsteps coming down the stairs. The sound of the shower had stopped, and I was expecting to see Izzy enter the room, but it was Mr. Murraro who came walking into the kitchen. He was wearing a red satin kimono-style bathrobe over his long underwear and sleeveless shirt. I hate to use the term "wife-beater", but that's really my only way to describe the garment.

196

"Hey, good morning," he said to me as he scratched his side.

"Good morning, Mr. Murraro."

"Please," he said, grabbing a box of Raisin Bran from the pantry. "Call me Vince."

"Okay."

"You sleep well?" His hair was so stereotypically "dad on a Saturday morning style".

"Yeah. Thanks for letting me stay…Vince."

"No problem, Kieran." He opened another cabinet to retrieve a cereal bowl. "Would you like some breakfast?"

"Izzy said he'd make me something."

"Hey, I'm the better cook. What would you like?"

I shrugged.

"Whatever's fine."

"I could throw some bacon and eggs on the stove." He opened the fridge to grab the milk. "Maybe a cheese omelet?"

"Sure."

"I can put in some diced ham and toss some green peppers in it, too, if you want. That's how my mother used to make them all the time for me when I was a kid."

"Okay."

Before I knew it, Mr. Murraro was throwing strips of bacon on a skillet, cracking eggs on another, and chopping green peppers to whip up a morning meal for me. Once the bacon started sizzling on the stove, the room smelled like a country diner that my family and I stopped at near Wyomissing shortly after we first moved to King's Valley. All that was missing was Mary Chapin Carpenter playing on the radio. I'll

197

forever associate the song "He Thinks He'll Keep Her" with my first moments in Berks County.

I was relieved to see that it seemed Mr. Murraro liked me. I don't know why, but the first time I met Izzy's dad, I felt a sense of indifference to me, and it had me worried that we wouldn't click. From what I've learned, though, it seems like Mr. Murraro goes through phases of being quiet and distant and then will turn around suddenly to be nearly as playful and friendly as Izzy. I've never brought up the subject of Izzy's mom to him, but I assume the reason for these mood swings comes from the emptiness hanging over the house now that she's gone.

Izzy joined us a few minutes later, all showered and dressed in a pair of skinny black jeans and a gray sweater with a beanie for headwear. He complained to his father that he wanted to cook breakfast for me, but Mr. Murraro insisted that his omelets were a far better delicacy. This led to more of that playful banter between father and son that I witnessed between them at the dinner table the night before.

This all made me smile. I never wanted to leave this house. I wanted to live here with these two forever and be a part of their family with their playful antics, big, delicious breakfasts, hot bubble baths, and video games in the basement.

This was Heaven.

Mr. Murraro finished his breakfast first, cleaned his cereal bowl in the sink, and then headed upstairs to take his own shower. The sound of the water running prompted me to ask Izzy about going to Thomas's for the day.

"Thomas called me," I said as Izzy finished his last strip of bacon. "He invited us to his place to go swimming."

"Swimming?"

Izzy looked confused.

"That's what I thought, but apparently they have an indoor pool."

"Oh, nice!"

"So, you want to go?"

"Sure."

"You didn't, like,…have any other plans for us, did you?"

"Well, I was gonna say let's go to the movies or something, but that's okay. Swimming will be fun."

"Shit," I said. "I'm sorry…"

"It's fine," Izzy laughed. "We can catch a movie anytime."

"Are you sure?"

This was my subliminal plea to get him to tell me let's just skip going to Thomas's and have an afternoon at the movies alone. I imagined him putting his arm around me in the theater, us sharing a popcorn, and maybe even sneaking a kiss or two when we thought that no one else would be looking. It would be like a date. This is what I really wanted, and I suddenly regretted even bringing up going to Thomas's. I should have just told Thomas I had plans today and left it at that.

"Yeah, I'm sure," Izzy said, much to my dismay. He took one final sip of his orange juice and then stared at me like he was about to declare his love for me or something [I could only be so lucky].

"What?" he asked, his voice going up in pitch as he said the word.

I shook my head, looking down at the table because I felt like I might cry.

"Nothing," I said.

"Hey, what's wrong?"

I looked up at him with my watery eyes.

"I just…kind of wanted to spend the day with you."

Tristan LaFerriere

"You *are* spending the day with me!"

"I meant…*only* you."

"Aww." Izzy grabbed my hand. "That's very sweet of you, bud, but Thomas is a good guy. I don't think we should ditch him. We can go to the movies tomorrow."

"Really?"

"Sure. Why not? I'm not busy tomorrow. You can stay over again tonight if you want."

"I can?"

"Of course."

"Your dad won't mind?"

"Dude," Izzy laughed. "No. He thinks you're a nice guy."

"Really?"

"Of course, he does. So, don't worry! We're gonna have a good time today. I promise."

I finally smiled. If I was spending another night in Izzy's house, there was a possibility of us going further. I had thoughts of us maybe having sex later that night, and if by tomorrow morning I'd be able to officially declare that I was no longer a virgin. I'd be able to wear that pride in school on Monday without even having to say a word. Just had to get through the rest of the day and look forward to the potential events that were to come in the evening.

"Okay," I said, and stood up. "You have a bathing suit?"

A few minutes later, Izzy grabbed his bathing suit, a t-shirt, and sandals from his upstairs bedroom closet and stuffed everything into a black Hot Topic bag. He stopped at Mr. Murraro's open bedroom door to let him know we were headed to a friend's house for the day. Then we walked next door to my house so I could fetch my own swimming supplies.

"You want to come in?" I asked him as we approached the back door on the deck. The glass kitchen doors with a view of the inside obstructed by its translucent curtains were a cold invite to return to my own home. I didn't even want to go inside because nothing could compare to Izzy's world next door.

"Do you want me to?"

Some weird feeling was making me nervous to have Mom and Dad see him. They have, of course, known that I've become friends with the new boy next door. Otherwise, I'd have some serious explaining to do for having suddenly the interest to go out all the time, but our relationship felt private or something to me. I could tell my family in passing that Izzy and I were friends and we were hanging out a lot, but seeing us together was like a forbidden thing, a confirmation that the two of us were a bit more than friends. I wanted to separate the dismal world in our house to that of the positive vibes that Izzy was gifting me each day.

"I mean," I started. "I'm just gonna run in real quick."

A neighbor's dog barked in the distance.

"Okay."

Izzy smiled, and his innocent demeanor made me feel bad. I felt like there shouldn't be any secrets between us, and not giving him the whole scoop as to why I felt slightly uncomfortable with my family seeing us together filled me with guilt.

"I'll be right out," I said, feeling defeated by my own insecurities as I opened the kitchen door.

"Mom?" I called, shutting the door behind me. It was after noon by now, and there wasn't a single trace of breakfast remaining in the room. Nothing on the table, nothing on the snack bar, nothing in the sink. The place was almost too clean, an exaggerated staging as if our house was the model home Mom would be showing to a new, eager family.

"Mom? Dad? Are you home?"

Quiet.

201

Tristan LaFerriere

I stepped into the adjoining "great room" that, too, like the kitchen was almost too clean. Carpet recently vacuumed, furniture dusted. I looked up at the tall ceiling, the fan watching over me in the vast family room that dwarfed me.

While staring up there, I bumped into Dad's chess table that sits in the corner. A king and queen fell to the floor while a few of the pawns tipped over on the board. I put the pieces back in place and then started up the nearby back steps.

Upstairs was even more painfully empty and silent. I passed the closed door to Justin's old room, and then went into my own where it felt like I hadn't been in so long even though only a day had passed. Matt Daniels watched over me from the wall as I entered the almost unfamiliar room and went into the closet. My bathing suit was up on one of the shelves somewhere with other summer clothes that weren't expected to be used until June, so I started digging.

A white shirt that looked as though it had been crumpled up like a scrap piece of paper tumbled onto the floor as I reached for the familiar texture of my bathing suit. I grabbed it and unfolded it to see what had been stashed away up there.

My heart sank when the old Stay Sweet shirt, tarnished with dried brown blood, stared back at me through nearly two months of wrinkles.

Two months.

I immediately folded it back up and stuffed it back on the shelf not far from where the invisible line was drawn that designated one half of the closet as mine and the other as Justin's. I could see piles of his clothes still up there, his bathing suit that probably still smelled faintly of chlorine as mine did, enough socks to last a month before needing to do the laundry again, and nearly a dozen folded pairs of boxer briefs.

I heard whimpering from through the louvered doors leading to Justin's room.

My first, and foolish, thought was that someone had broken into the house. I had an instinct to dart back downstairs and run outside before the burglar noticed me, but after a few seconds of listening and

202

rationalizing, I realized the soft crying was Mom. As I've said before, Mom never cries in front of anyone, so the sound was unfamiliar to me.

I peered through the door slats to see her sitting on the edge of what had been Justin's bed. She was clutching one of his soccer jerseys close to her nose. I froze at first, didn't want her to see me, but then decided to make my presence known since she may have thought the same of me being an intruder if she heard rummaging through the closet without an explanation.

"Mom?"

I slowly opened the folding door, but her attention was still drawn to that blue and white Palisades Dolphins jersey that Justin used to wear all the time, even here after we moved and before he suddenly hopped on the King's Valley Red Devils spirit bandwagon that took over in the last month or so of his life.

"Mom?"

I stepped into the room and she gasped. There were tears in her eyes and her face was red. Even though it was her day off, she was still dressed in a nice sweater and pants. She hadn't failed to apply some makeup and jewelry even for a day planned to be completely spent at home.

"My God!" She clutched her heart dramatically. "I didn't know you were home."

"Sorry," I said nervously. "I was just, uh, grabbing my bathing suit. Izzy and I are going swimming at our friend's house." I waited for her confused inquiry and then added, "He has an indoor pool."

"Oh," she said, quickly wiping the tears from her eyes and setting the jersey down on the bed. She stood up. "Okay. Your father went to Wegman's. I was just, uh, straightening up a few things." She snorted. "How was your...sleepover?"

"Good. Um, I was gonna stay over there again tonight. If that's okay."

I held my breath.

"That's fine, Kieran, but I don't want you to overstay your welcome. And we still haven't met this friend of yours or his parents."

"He just lives with his dad," I said. "And it's okay. They invited me."

She snorted again, clearly congested from crying. I could sense the cogs turning in her head, assuming that my new friend having a single father must have meant they were some sort of dysfunctional, divorced family. She's so fucking judgmental.

"Well, as long as it's okay." She looked me over. "You aren't...doing anything questionable, are you?"

"What...what do you mean?"

"I mean, you aren't drinking or doing any..."

"Mom," I interrupted, rolling my eyes. "No. We're just...hanging out."

"I just have to ask," she said defensively. "I don't want to feel irresponsible just letting you go off with a friend Dad and I haven't even met yet. I know you said he's a little older than you. I just hope he's a good influence."

I was screaming inside.

"He is," is all I said. "He's a good friend."

"Okay."

Mom sighed and looked around the room, her arms folded. Her expression was not unlike that of a queen who was about to make her ruling on an execution. Time to look tough again now that she had been caught in a moment of weakness.

"I'm thinking we can turn this into a guestroom," she said.

I stared at her.

"One of the new models on Concorde Drive has some really nice paint swatches in the spare bedrooms," she continued. "I'm

thinking of a wine color or something similar. That seems to be quite 'in' right now." She nodded at the bed. "And I saw this setup in Better Homes & Gardens. A couple of nice vases with artificial pussy willows on either side of the bed would be very inviting. I was thinking of taking a drive over to Pier 1 Imports today to see what they have."

"Mom…"

"I have to throw in some laundry," she interrupted. "Have a good time."

She left the room. The force of the door shutting knocked a picture off the wall. When I went to pick it up, I found Justin staring back at me from within the frame, posing in his soccer uniform at his old high school. His face was partially hidden behind the cracked glass.

Chapter Ten
Monday, October 23rd, 2006

Dear Journal,

I was too tired last night to write about what happened Saturday night, so I figured I'd slip it in for a short entry today. I don't have a lot of time to write since I'm fucking bombarded with algebra and science homework and, of course, Thomas spent all of Journalism and lunch interrogating me on what I'll be working on for the next article.

Anyway, sorry; let me get back to the rest of Saturday night.

After our afternoon of swimming in Thomas's indoor pool, Izzy and I went back to his house, ordered pizza, and spent most of the night taking turns playing through the levels of *Banjo-Kazooie* until I was too tired and just laid back on his sleeper sofa. I watched Izzy play through a few more levels as it got close to midnight, and soon, he joined me and sat next to me while we listened to Spike Feresten through the ceiling from the TV upstairs.

"So, have you put any thought into your Halloween costume?" Izzy asked after we were quiet for a while.

I chuckled.

"No, I don't know if I'm dressing up."

"Oh, come on!" Izzy nudged me. "It'll be fun. We live in the best neighborhood for trick-or-treating. It'll be crazy. You can help me pass out candy."

I shrugged.

"What are you going as?" I asked.

"Napoleon Dynamite."

"Really?"

"Yeah! I've got this *Vote for Pedro* shirt and a curly blonde wig. All I have to do is put on a pair of my dad's reading glasses and I'm all set."

"But then you'll be dizzy."

"Nah, I can use an old pair of his. I'll just punch the lenses out."

"Oh."

"Come on, buddy!" Izzy nudged me again. "Why don't you dress up as Matt Daniels?"

That idea actually piqued my interest.

"Well," I started, not being able to help but smile. "I guess I could do that. I've pretty much already got the wardrobe for it."

Izzy smiled, looking happier already that I was considering dressing up.

"Exactly!" he said. "It'd be easy for you. You could be creative, though. You could go as, like, 'old-school' Matt Daniels from the first album era."

"Yeah, I guess so." I grabbed a strand of my hair. "I'd have to dye my hair again, though. His hair was always black back then."

"Yeah," Izzy said. "Your dye's fading. Your brown roots are starting to grow in."

"I know," I said, feeling slightly self-conscious about a bit of my true appearance coming through. "It's definitely overdue. You want to dye it for me tomorrow?"

Izzy laughed.

"I've never dyed anyone's hair before," he said. "I might fuck it up."

I shook my head.

"It's real easy. You just mix the stuff, put on the gloves…"

He started leaning in close to me.

"…and you rub it in."

He kissed me, and holy shit, did I feel like my boner was about to burst through my boxers.

Unlike our previous lip locking, this one was serious. I was caught off-guard and slightly confused by his sudden move to stick his tongue in my mouth. I had only ever heard about open mouthed kissing before from people like Justin and his friends back when I would be an audience for their sex stories. I never quite understood the concept of "slipping someone the tongue" until now, but I just went along with it, and I swear we were practically in a knot by the time Izzy broke the kiss to smile only a millimeter or so away from my face.

"You know, you looked so fucking cute in your swimming trunks today," he said to me.

I turned beat red.

"Yeah?" I giggled.

Before he said anything else, I felt his hand crawling up my leg like a spider, his fingers brushing along my thigh, and making their way up under my boxers. I shivered at the feeling, having never been touched like that before.

"I wanted to pull them down," Izzy said with a horny gleam in his eyes.

I giggled again.

He kissed me, seriously, again, and a few moments later, we heard the basement door swing open.

"Hey, Izzy?" Mr. Murraro's voice called from across the room, and I gasped as our lips separated.

"Yeah, Dad?"

I couldn't believe how nonchalantly Izzy responded, and especially since Mr. Murraro was leaning into the doorway and catching us in the act of not only kissing, but his son's hand beginning to slip up into the leg of my boxers where my more than just a little noticeable erection was fighting to peek through the undone crotch button.

"Oh," Mr. Murraro said, and looked away. "I'm sorry, guys. Izzy, I gotta go into work for a few hours in the morning, so if I'm not home, that's why. I should be home a little after noon."

"Okay, Dad. Thanks."

Mr. Murraro didn't turn back to look at us, but wished us both a goodnight. I was shocked that Izzy's hand still rested on my balls, his lips only inches away from mine as his dad went back up the stairs and let the door shut behind him. We were left with the sounds of a Geico commercial and a disgruntled caveman complaining of the company's latest offensive ad from the TV upstairs.

Izzy went back to kissing me, but I pulled away.

"Whoa," I said. "What the fuck just happened?"

"What do you mean?"

I looked over my shoulder where Mr. Murraro stood only a moment before and then back to Izzy who still had a horny glimmer in his expression.

"*That*," I continued. "Your dad...he just..."

"What?" Izzy was giggling as if he were drunk, and his hand started to slip further up toward my dick, which was sadly now going limp.

"He didn't even care that we were fooling around."

"I told you he doesn't care about that."

...

"So, he...knows about us?"

Izzy shrugged, still smiling.

"I guess he does now."

I wish I hadn't been so paranoid about what happened because seconds later and Izzy was touching me, the first boy to ever put his hands on me there. It felt surreal having a hand that wasn't mine touching my penis. I wanted so badly to be aroused for him, but I was too pre-occupied with the idea of him not being the only person to know my secret now.

"Wait," I said, and pulled away. "Hold on just a minute."

Izzy must have been alarmed by my sudden rise in tone because he put an arm around me and rested his head against my shoulder.

"What's wrong, bud?" he asked.

My head was down, counting the threads in Izzy's blanket as I tried to comprehend the weirdness of how simplistic an event that I always assumed would have been threatening had just been. Izzy's dad was really that carefree about the situation? I knew that Izzy said he was accepting of him being gay, but this just seemed too easy.

"I just...can't...believe your dad doesn't care about that," I said. "I mean, we were practically..."

Izzy tightened his grip.

"I told you, bud. He doesn't care. He knows I'm gay. He doesn't care if you're gay. My dad *loves* you. He's not gonna tell anybody."

His fingers teased my nipple and again, any negative thoughts were washing away like magic with his touch.

"But...you weren't embarrassed? I mean, if my dad caught you and me..."

"Hey," Izzy interrupted. "I walked in on him and my mom having sex once. Now, that was fucking awkward. I saw my dad's balls."

We both laughed and things felt good again. I let him go back to what he was doing. He slipped his hand back up into my underwear and played with my balls while we kissed. He was so gentle, and it felt so good, but after a minute or two, the tears started to well up in my eyes and I was crying, which really startled Izzy because he immediately began hugging me tight and kissing the top of my head as I wept in his arms.

"What is it, buddy? Why are you crying?"

"I wish my family was like yours," I snorted. "I want to...I just...I just want to be able to...come out to them, but..."

"Shhhhhhhhhh." Izzy kissed my head again. "It's okay. When you're ready to come out to them, then you do it."

"I want to come out to them *now*," I cried. "I'm just so sick of my whole life being a fucking lie. I fucking hate it. I hate that fucking house. I just want to live here with you."

Izzy brushed some of my hair from my face.

"Aww," he said. "I'd love that, but you need to be comfortable in your own house. Besides, I'm right next door. You can visit me whenever you want to."

I didn't stop crying, but Izzy didn't stop holding me, either.

The TV went mute upstairs, and we could hear Mr. Murraro walking up the steps to his bedroom by the time I calmed down. I was tired and Izzy clearly was, too, so we both sort of just accepted that it was time to go to sleep. The lights were shut off and Izzy turned on his TV to a *Family Guy* episode to lull him to sleep. We pulled the blankets up over us and we cuddled close together. I held onto him for dear life like as long as I felt his warmth, I was protected from all the evil in the world.

Tristan LaFerriere

As I drifted off to sleep, the sound of *Family Guy*'s theme morphed into a vaguely familiar anthem, a composition I had only heard once, but continues to haunt me subconsciously each day...

> *"Under my sheets!*
> *It's where I find you,*
> *all we have*
> *are the memories left between them.*
> *I still dream of you,*
> *I still dream of you,*
> *I still dream...*
> *I find you under my sheets..."*

...

I slept for about an hour and woke up in complete darkness minus the flashing of Izzy's TV. I had to piss so fucking bad, but I tried holding it in because the closest bathroom was upstairs, and I didn't like the idea of just roaming around Izzy's house in the middle of the night. Something about that just seemed weird.

Eventually, though, I couldn't hold it in anymore, so I carefully climbed out of bed without making a sound and tiptoed up the stairs to the kitchen where that old fridge greeted me with its glowing digital readouts. Otherwise, the entire ground floor of the house seemed to be in complete darkness, and I found myself stumbling through their front living room to the foyer with a bit of difficulty to find the half bathroom near the front door.

I pissed like a racehorse, washed my hands, and left the bathroom worrying that the toilet flushing would wake someone up. Instead of going back through the living room, I made a detour and crossed into the dining room, a room I'd never really been in or taken much notice of since I started spending so much time in their house. There was a bit of light coming from the entryway, so I figured it would be easier to find my way back to the basement this way.

The source of the light were several paintings on the walls that were each lit up with their own frame lights. I recognized one of the portraits to be another work of Keith Haring's as the dog depicted in the painting was undoubtedly one of his best-known, but the other, large landscape-style canvas over the mantle behind the long table was something I'd never seen before.

212

A centerpiece to the dining room, lit with a halo of warmth from the bulb above the canvas, was a large depiction of *The Last Supper*, but far from the traditional image anyone would be familiar with. This painting, while accurate with the religious figures seated at the famous table, was done in a black and white sketch that appeared to be unfinished. Overlapping the faces of Jesus and his disciples were several logos for well-known companies. Covering most of the left side of the painting was the cursive font of the Dove soap logo in a pastel pink.

Covering a large portion of the right side was the familiar General Electric *"GE"* logo in its blue circular form, bordered almost subliminally by those white glows of what I assume are meant to be electrical charges of some kind.

"Admiring my painting?"

I nearly jumped out of my skin when I spun around to see Mr. Murraro standing in the foyer entryway, clad in his kimono and underwear. He chuckled at my startled response and then looked back up at the painting I had just been...interpreting, or something.

"Sorry," I exhaled. "I was just..."

"It's alright," he said. "It's one of my favorites."

I looked back up at it with him, and it seemed like we were both staring at it for quite some time while I waited for my heart to stop racing.

"Who did this?" I finally asked.

"Andy," Mr. Murraro said with a sigh.

"Warhol?"

He nodded.

"That's right. This one's just a print. The real one's in MoMa. It's *huge*."

He walked up to me and stood beside me, his eyes never leaving the painting. I saw a hint of Izzy's eyes in his for a moment, that same bit of hypnotic wonder I'd seen in his son's expression when he would drive with the windows down while blasting Stay Sweet or Slowdive.

"This is the only non-original I have," he continued. "The rest are all authentic, but I just had to have at least a copy of this one. He did sixty of these right before he died, you know."

"Really?"

"Yep. Sixty different versions of *The Last Supper*, but...this one always stood out to me for some reason. Only Andy could pull off something like this."

Mr. Murraro seemed to force a smile in an attempt to, what I can only imagine, hold back any tears in memory of his late artist friend. It was just in that moment that I realized...there was so much death around all of us. Over this cul-de-sac, both families were showered in relics of the deceased whether it be my brother, the late Mrs. Murraro, or any of these lost artists Izzy's parents had been so close with years ago.

There's so much death everywhere.

"What are you doing up, bud?" Mr. Murraro asked me, and I suddenly remembered that only an hour or so earlier, he had been a witness to Izzy making out with me and sticking his hand down my pants. This man was the only person besides Izzy to know that I was gay. I wondered if he would bring anything up about it.

"Just had to...use the bathroom," I stuttered, for some reason. "Sorry...if I woke you."

Mr. Murraro shook his head.

"You didn't wake me," he said. "I don't sleep much. I was just gonna grab a glass of milk."

He motioned for me to follow him. I did, and we went into the dark kitchen where he headed straight for the fridge.

"It's something I've done since I was just about seven years old," Mr. Murraro said as the light inside the fridge shined about the darkened room from its open door like a portal into some new world. I immediately thought of that scene in *Ghostbusters*. "I always have a glass of milk before bed."

"Hmm," I said, watching him grab the gallon of milk from one of the shelves. "Why is that?"

"It calms me," he said, taking a glass from one of the cabinets. "Helps me rest."

He poured himself a glass.

"I used to have a lot of nightmares when I was a kid. Could never sleep. My mother used to have to lay next to me all the time to make sure I was okay."

He finished pouring, brought the glass to his lips, and took a sip.

"I'm not proud to say this," he said with an almost embarrassed smirk. "But she probably had to read me bedtime stories until I was about twelve."

I remembered what Izzy had said to me before we went to bed: *"My dad loves you."* Is that why he was telling me all this? He was opening up to me in ways I never imagined. The man who seemed so indifferent and maybe even slightly intimidating at first was suddenly so doting.

"Would you like one, Kieran?" he asked after his second sip.

"Sure."

He smiled and poured me a glass, too. By then, the fridge was beeping and flashing to remind him to shut the door. He put the milk back and sat down at one of the kitchen table's chairs before he pulled out another and nodded toward it.

"Come here," he said, patting the empty chair. "Sit with me, bud."

215

I did, and we shared a rather long conversation while we sipped our glasses of milk. Most of the talk was about Warhol and Mr. Murraro's memories of him, how I somehow remind him so much of the late artist, and that he was really glad to see that Izzy and I are such good friends.

He didn't bring a thing up about catching us hooking up, and I think, in some way, his silence was his way of giving me a wink to say it was okay…that he approved of everything.

Chapter Eleven
Saturday, November 25th, 2006

Dear Journal,

It's getting to be that time of year when the anticipation of winter break has made everyone in King's Valley High even more uninterested in education than usual. The first snowfall of the season already made its debut last week in the days before Thanksgiving when Mom, Dad, and I spent a humdrum Thursday half-watching the Macy's parade on TV in the sunroom before we sat down to a lonely early dinner.

The meal consisted of all the usual: an oversized turkey from Gleason's that would serve us well in leftovers for several days, Stove Top stuffing, jellied cranberry sauce, green bean casserole, and mashed potatoes with gravy crowded our dining room table while we all continued to do our best at not addressing the elephant in the room. That lone chair at the end of the table was still empty, and here, even three fucking months later, none of us had anything in the slightest to say to each other.

I wished the whole time that I could've gone with Izzy and his dad to his grandparents' house in Brooklyn, a brownstone in Crown Heights where Mr. Murraro grew up. The setting that Izzy described to me made the whole thing sound like one of those feel-good holiday movies, a total inverse to the immensely drab forlornness of a cloud that seemed to forever be lingering over our house. 2716 Skyview Drive continued to be a black sponge still soaking in any of the remaining grief leftover in town from the loss of my brother.

Now, in the beginning of winter, it seems that most of King's Valley has buried the once strong bereavement in response to the death of its once prominent epitome, Justin Northrup. Even the memorial sprays of lilies that once flourished aromatically around the perimeter of his locker at school have long-since wilted to a doleful rot that are merely wispy shadows to the passing hall traffic today. I no longer see the school's popular kids, the girls of Melissa Grandstaff status or jocks who would have known my brother, wiping tears from their eyes as they walk the halls [something that was common when Justin's death was fresh news].

I suppose other events and the general passing of time has made everyone move on. The new talk of the town is still over the House of Representatives elections, the fact that our country, for the first time, has a woman speaker of the house, the arrival of the winter holidays, and the hype surrounding the recent release of the Nintendo Wii.

I feel horrible about this, but…I'll admit that even I find I tend to forget sometimes.

…

I spent the half hour or so after Thanksgiving dinner assisting Dad with the dishes by loading them into the dishwasher after he gave everything a pre-rinse in the sink, the sleeves of his white button-down dress shirt rolled up as he ran the various bowls and cups under the hot water.

Mom had retreated to the sunroom to unwind to an episode of *Deal or No Deal*, still finishing off her second glass of wine, and she had already transitioned from Thanksgiving to Christmas by playing our Brenda Lee album on the living room stereo. Meanwhile, a brand-new artificial Balsam Hill tree was waiting in its box in the basement for us to unpack and let dominate the front bay window until the end of the year.

Mom has also started decorating, and her hideous snow baby figurines have taken over the dining room credenza while those creepy caroler dolls sit on top of the piano. A fancy wreath has already been hung on the front door, but Mom's decided to leave the exterior lighting to some professional company that's going to come out to make sure we have the nicest-looking house in the neighborhood.

I was heavily anticipating a promised phone call from Izzy that was supposed to come after he was finished with his own family meal. I was starting to worry he had forgotten or fell asleep while "Rockin' Around the Christmas Tree" echoed from the other room.

"No Izzy this weekend, huh?" Dad asked before handing me a plate.

"He'll be back tomorrow," I said, setting the oval plate between some of the prongs of the dishwasher rack.

"He's with family?"

"Yeah, his grandparents in Brooklyn."

Dad was washing Mom's gravy boat now, one of the few artifacts from our Pacific Palisades house that survived the move. He nodded.

"That sounds nice." He was quiet for a moment. "You never said where you two met."

"In...class." I didn't want to have to explain the whole peer program thing and its origins. "History."

"Oh."

"Yeah. We were paired up for a project." I felt my blood pressure rise, and it suddenly made perfect sense to me how lie detectors work.

Dad squinted like he was trying to pin down the answer to a confusing thought while he sloshed the hot sponge around the curved porcelain.

"I thought Izzy was a junior."

Fuck...

"Um...he is," I said, my voice quivering. "It's just he, uh, because he came from a different school, he didn't...meet...all the requirements here, so he had to, uh...take freshman history instead of an elective. I guess the, uh, curriculums are different in Jersey or something."

"Oh, I see."

I relaxed just a tad.

"He sounds like a really nice kid."

"Yeah. He is."

219

"I'd like to meet him sometime."

Dad squeezed the bottle of green dish soap into the gravy boat and a few fugitive bubbles floated through the air as he struggled to scrub a deep stain.

"They've been living next to us for a few months now," he continued. "The least we could do is say hello to each other, especially since you two spend so much time together."

I didn't say anything.

"You guys really are close, huh?"

 . . .

"Yeah."

"Well, that's good." His eyes were glued to the sink. "It's nice you've got someone to hang out with."

He slowed down with his scrubbing technique, and it seemed so pointless to have a dishwasher if we were working that hard for just the pre-rinse.

"I was starting to worry about you," Dad continued. "I mean, when we first moved here, you hardly came out of your room. It was like you lived up there."

I stayed quiet. The Brenda Lee album continued in the other room. "Santa Claus Is Comin' To Town" probably never scored such an awkward scene before.

"What do you guys do when you're together?"

He finally handed me the gravy boat while I tried to think of a safe, but not completely untrue answer that would just snowball into another obvious lie.

"We just…hang out. Play video games and stuff."

"Oh. What games?"

"Like...*Mario Kart*...*Banjo-Kazooie*."

"That's all?"

"That's all what?"

"That's all you guys do?"

I shrugged, pushed the dish rack in, and closed the dishwasher door.

"I mean, we watch TV. We listen to music."

I chose the settings for the wash and pressed the start button. The dishwasher motor started groaning as Dad dried his hands with a paper towel. He hadn't bothered to shave that morning and it showed in the red five o'clock shadow that was forming at the surface of his pale skin.

"What's his dad like?"

"What?"

"Izzy's dad. What's he like?"

I shrugged again.

"I don't know. He's nice."

"Yeah?"

"Yes." I must've sounded annoyed.

"What's the matter?"

"What do you mean?"

"The way you said that."

"Said what?"

"Yes," he repeated in a tone like mine.

221

Tristan LaFerriere

I rolled my eyes.

"Dad, why are you asking me all this?"

He shook his head, got defensive.

"I'm just asking. You're with Izzy all the time. I think I have a right to know a little bit about your friend and what his family's like."

"Well, I don't know what you want to know. We're just friends and we hang out. His dad's a nice guy. Okay?"

"Okay. I was just curious…"

"Curious about what?"

I closed my eyes, already sensing the scuffle that was coming. I should've just kept my fucking mouth shut. I was an idiot to keep the argument simmering.

"Just curious what it's like over there. You spend more time next door than you do here now."

"Yeah. Because I like it there."

"Are you saying you don't like it here?"

"I never said that!"

"Alright, alright. Forget it."

I started to let loose. It must've been a long time overdue because the way I suddenly blew up with a torrent of complaints even startled myself.

"You and Mom never bother with me, but then all of a sudden when I start hanging out with somebody who actually gives a shit about me, you want to know what I'm doing every waking moment like it's illegal for me to have fun."

"Kier, come on! There's no need for this."

"For what?"

"You're being ridiculous! You're coming at me and I was just asking you a few innocent questions."

"Innocent questions? You're fucking interrogating me!"

"Kieran!"

He said my full name. He really must've been pissed.

I was, too, and it made me say something very unexpected.

"You never made a big fucking deal over anything Justin did!"

...

My father took in a deep breath, the words ready to come out, but he stalled after processing what I actually had the balls to say. Shit, did I regret it, too, because I've never seen such pain in my dad's eyes. He looked to be on the verge of crying, and I couldn't handle seeing that, so like a completely weak wimp, I avoided the whole thing by turning and running up the back stairs. Suddenly, my dad had looked so vulnerable, dwarfed by this oversized house and its gluttonous features while he stood helplessly there in the kitchen.

I slammed my bedroom door behind me and collapsed onto the bed, waiting to hear the footsteps approach and the knock that would soon follow to be the lead-in for resolving the fracas that just happened. I prayed that Mom hadn't heard our argument because she'd make no hesitation to berate me for not keeping up the professional Northrup image even when there weren't any guests over to witness it.

I sulked in the worrisome anticipation and decided to try distracting myself. I turned on my TV to find *It's a Wonderful Life* already beginning its many airings for the holiday season. Only a few minutes in and the massage of my phone vibrating in my jeans pocket conveniently interrupted my dread. I quickly retrieved it to answer it.

"Hey, buddy!"

It was Izzy.

"Hey," I said, rolling over on the bed so I was on my stomach and facing the door with my feet up in the air. "Done eating?"

"Yeah," Izzy said. "I was just helping my grandma clean up. How was your dinner?"

"Alright," I said. "Nothing to brag about."

I didn't want to spoil the conversation I had been waiting for all day with explaining what just happened between me and my dad, so I decided not to bring it up. I was too happy to hear Izzy's voice to be upset about it anymore.

"Did you watch the parade?" he asked me.

"Yeah. It sucked like usual."

Izzy giggled.

"Well, I didn't mind seeing The Jonas Brothers. Nick was looking pretty cute as usual, but, yeah, it's basically all, like, musical numbers now. They don't even bother to show the balloons anymore."

This summoned a long-forgotten memory of sitting on the floor of the TV room in our old house as a kid, and me being nearly traumatized by the images that became headlines the day after Thanksgiving in 1997.

"You remember years ago when the Barney balloon popped from the high winds?" I asked.

"No!" Izzy laughed. "For real?"

"Yeah. It, like, almost killed people."

Suddenly, my door swung open and Dad let himself in without a knock. I audibly gasped because unlike Mom, it was extremely rare for him to cross such boundaries even at his most pissed off. I was completely unexpecting his abrupt entrance.

"Dad…"

"Get off the phone, Kieran."

I held the phone to my chest so Izzy wouldn't hear anything, and I mouthed, *"What?"* to my dad with an annoyed expression. What I was feeling under the surface was far less annoyed, though, but terrified at the thought of him being legitimately pissed at me.

"Get off the phone," he repeated. "We need to talk."

"Dad, I'm talking to Izzy!" I said in a loud whisper, the phone still pressed against my chest. I heard the desperation in my voice, the sudden coward I could easily become at the scolding of one of my parents.

He walked slowly toward me, his hands in the pockets of his dress pants.

"Tell Izzy you'll call him back. I need to talk to you."

"Dad…"

"Right now."

The funny thing about my dad is that he never yells, even when he's angry. He just annunciates his words in a way that isn't like him, and it lets you know that he's serious. His Arctic eyes really have the ability to be fierce and frightening if he wants them to be. I've never really given him reason to show that side, but on occasion, Justin would drive him to the edge when we were younger, and I would witness the subtle, yet terrifying transformation of Darren.

I put the phone back to my ear while my mind went fuzzy.

"Can I call you back?" I asked Izzy, feeling defeated.

"Yeah," Izzy said. "Is…everything okay?"

"Yeah."

He had to have known I was lying.

"Okay. Talk to you later?"

"Yeah."

I waited for Izzy to hang up first because that made it feel more like the decision to cut the conversation short was out of my hands. When the line went dead, Dad went back to my door, shut it, and then leaned against it with his arms crossed. He didn't look mad, but he clearly wasn't content. I was relieved to see any possible tears that may have come had receded because I really wouldn't be able to stand seeing him cry. Now that he was standing at my door like that, though, I was pretty much a prisoner to my own room, and the only password to get me out would be to start talking about whatever he wanted to get out of me.

"What, Dad?" I watched my tone this time.

He didn't respond for the longest time. It probably really wasn't that long now that I think about it, but damn, did it feel like an eternity while I sat there on the bed and he watched me. It was so uncomfortable, like he knew that I knew what he wanted to talk about and was just testing me to see if I'd be the first to bring it up.

I wasn't.

"What's going on with you, Kier?"

I swallowed hard.

"What do you mean, Dad?"

He sighed and walked back toward the bed. Behind him, my TV continued playing, but on mute.

…

"I know it's been hard," he said after a long, dragging interlude of silence. He bit his lip, clearly fighting a war with his emotions that wasn't completely visible to me.

"I just worry about you, Kier." He stalled. "I look at you and you…just look like you're a million miles away anymore. You…don't talk. You're never home and when you are…you just keep to yourself all the time. I feel like I don't even know you anymore."

He chuckled, but it was one of those sad little laughs that comes out when you're getting emotional.

"I feel like Izzy probably knows you better than I do now. I guess I envy him for that. You just...never talk while you're here..."

"I've always been quiet, Dad."

"This isn't just quiet, Kier. Half the time it's like you're catatonic or something. Sometimes days go by and it's hard for me to remember the last time I heard you speak. I always have to...nudge you a little bit to get you to say anything, and even then, most of the time all I get in response are these one-word answers."

I shrugged.

"What's bothering you, Kier?" He closed his eyes for a second. "Is it Justin?"

I put my head down, battling my own constant urge to cry that's only been recently pacified by my time with Izzy, but still, it lingers like a fucking bitch. Suddenly, it dawned on me that I wasn't hiding in the shadows no matter how many layers of hair dye or black band shirts I've tried to cover myself with. It might've blended me in otherwise at school or even with other people in my family, but not with Dad.

He had been watching every move I made since we moved here, noticed each tear I fought to hold back, each relentless trudging up the stairs I made every night as I retreated to my room to be alone and miserable. Even if I was successful in fooling everyone else that I was passive to the judgement of others, I could never deceive him into thinking that there wasn't something keeping me under a dark cloud. Unlike Mom, who didn't want to believe that I wasn't the embodiment of the flawless trophy child she's envisioned me to be, Dad knew I was this morose outcast with something holding me back from being happy.

I knew this because I saw the same dissatisfaction in his eyes while he forced himself to pretend that he was fulfilled with the new life he and Mom grabbed at a desperate attempt to keep up with their success. It was his worst nightmare coming to life as he realized that even a brand-new house in the most prestigious zip code of the county,

a couple of new, expensive cars, and a Rolex didn't matter in the slightest if our nest was lacking the life it once had with Justin.

"Dad," I started.

This was it. It just came out of nowhere. It's like all this time, the struggle to cough up the admission was caught in my throat and fucking finally I was able to clear it. I had waited for this moment for so fucking long, always imagined that it would be so well-thought out and planned in advance like a girl announcing she was pregnant, but the words escaped me so quickly, so spontaneously that it was as if my body couldn't handle keeping in the secret anymore.

"I'm gay."

It felt like someone injected me with adrenaline. I was shaking, and it was hard to tell from Dad's unreadable expression if he was speechless with disbelief and disappointment, or an ah-ha moment and a final realization where everything suddenly made sense when my confession came over him. The few seconds between me at last choking up the two words I had practiced a million times in front of the fridge and Dad's response were the most terrifying in my life. If I had to honestly choose a moment to relive, I think the terror of waiting for his reaction would have scared me away even more than having to be in that car accident with Justin again.

"Oh, Kier," he said softly, and suddenly his tone went from being a stern father to an amiable dad.

He sat down on the side of the bed next to me, his eyes never leaving mine as I began to tear up. So was he.

"I knew that, buddy."

"I knew that, buddy" rang through my ears on repeat for a few seconds, and then, when I understood that what was killing me inside for what seemed like my entire life wasn't going to be the death of me, I exhaled like all the anxiety obsessing over my sexuality was leaving my body at last. The disease of stress had been cured.

"You...did?"

Dad nodded and put a hand on my shoulder while his blue eyes grew misty.

Despite our resemblance to each other, I've always seen so much more of Justin in him, the handsome man who knew how to dress to impress when it mattered, the well-spoken guy who everyone seemed to genuinely like without him having to put in much effort, but the soft-spoken traits that I inherited while Justin's natural ability to be popular definitely stemmed from Mom's loins. It was like Dad grew up being me, but Mom influenced both he and my brother to be completely different from who they really were. I could tell at the dinner table, just as he could probably tell with me, that there was always a discomfort in this role of professional suburban dad that he was playing, and that's why I've always considered myself to be mostly like him out of everyone else in my family. We've both been living a lie for so long now, and neither of us could admit it to anyone.

I immediately grabbed him for a hug at coincidentally the exact moment that Jimmy Stewart hugged his children on TV. Even though the TV was muted, I could hear the music in my head, Dimitri Tiomkin's score playing over the classic movie's scene...and the scene of my dad hugging me.

It wasn't just the usual [I shouldn't say usual. We've never done a lot of hugging in this family, which is why Justin's invitation to hug him a few days before he died had confused me so much], not just the "usual" quick hug that Dad may have given me as an obligatory quota for affection in an otherwise expected uniform household, but a real tight hug that I felt like I would never escape from.

I almost felt asphyxiated as he squeezed me firmly, and then I realized he was crying with me. And that killed me because the few times I've seen my dad cry have been just about the most difficult things I've ever come across. In our family, if Dad was crying, you knew something really serious was going on. The last time I saw him devastated with tears was when I accidentally walked in on him desperately trying to get ahold of Uncle Ryan on the phone to relay the news to him of Justin's death.

"I'm sorry," I said, my voice jittery as my tears started to soak the fabric of his white dress shirt at the shoulder.

He surprised me by hugging me even tighter, something I didn't think was possible, and I could feel his wedding ring digging into my shoulder blade. It was like he was holding his breath, but then finally let it out with a sob when he realized there was no point in trying to hold in the tears anymore for me. His vulnerability had finally been exposed, and now we could both be ourselves in front of each other.

"Why would you be sorry?" he asked.

"I...I thought you wouldn't like me anymore."

I don't think this was a completely truthful response, but it was the first thing that came out. You know, as stupid as this sounds, I never really considered the details of how Mom or Dad may have felt about finding out I was gay. It was a simple conditioning from society that made me assume regardless of what the reaction was that it would almost certainly be a negative one.

"Oh, honey." My dad never called me that before.

He started crying harder, even harder than me, and then he kissed me on the cheek for the first time since probably when I was eight and I skinned my knee attempting to play basketball with Justin in our driveway [and I never dared to try a sport again].

"I could never not like you," he continued. "I love you so much."

Now we were in a contest to see who could cry harder.

"I love you so much, Kier. You know that? I love you...so, so much." He kissed my cheek again and ran a hand through my hair. "You're my baby. I've loved you since the first time I held you in my arms...right after you were born."

He sniffled and I closed my eyes as he continued to hold me...like I was that newborn child again.

"I love you now just as much as I did that day," he went on. "I...I remember watching the nurses clean you up right after you were born and...and they brought you to me. You were this tiny little thing wrapped up in this blanket and you wouldn't stop crying." He

chuckled. "But then I held you and you put your head up against my chest and...you stopped crying just like that."

I smiled even though he couldn't see me as we were still embraced. This was something he had never told me before. The story came out so suddenly, and flawlessly like he had been waiting a long time, the perfect moment to tell me.

"Really?" I said, my voice cracking over the tears.

"Yeah," he said, hugging me tighter again. "It was like you were drawn to me the moment I held you. It's like you knew who I was. It was...it was the most beautiful moment of my life. There was something so special about you. You were my beautiful boy. You're *still* my beautiful boy. Even though you're quiet...I know you're such a sweet kid and that you have such a good heart. I love you, Kier. I love you no matter who you are."

...

"I love you, too, Dad."

At this point, I was even more composed than he was.

After our five-minute hug was over, he gave me a smile through the drying tears, patted my arm, and sighed. He looked like a child who had just returned from timeout. In a way, he *was* a child. I've always known him to look far younger for his years, but it wasn't until this moment where he looked so innocent, so fragile and full of naïve youth. He was no more an adult than myself. We're both kids. We both have no fucking idea what we're doing in this world.

"Do you want me to tell Mom?" he asked.

I shook my head.

"No?"

"I don't know," I said, my heart pounding at the thought. "I don't know what she'd say..."

"I don't think she would mind," Dad said. "But I won't tell her if you don't want me to."

I wiped my running nose with the long sleeve of my gray button-down [Mom wouldn't have had it for me choosing a Taking Back Sunday shirt to wear at the Thanksgiving dinner table].

"I just feel like she'd be…disappointed," I said.

Dad put his arm around me and squeezed my shoulder in a way that reminded me of Izzy, and then he leaned in close so that our words couldn't be heard by anyone else even if their ears were pressed up against my bedroom door.

"I know how she can be," he whispered. "Trust me, I know. She gets herself so worked up trying to make everything perfect."

I nodded.

"But she loves you," he added. "She's also loved you since the day you were born, and she'll always love you."

I didn't say anything, and it must've worried him that I was doubting his reassurance.

"She loves you, Kieran. I promise you that. And if she did know, she'd still love you. Your mother's a strong woman, but…she's a very loving person. She just doesn't always show it the way others do. Okay?"

I nodded again as Dad stood up. He smiled again, and this was the first smile I'd seen from him in months that didn't feel forced or illegitimate.

It was just like the smiles he used to give me when I was little, when I would run up the front steps of our old house on Chattanooga Place after getting off the school bus and be so happy to see him waiting for me at the front door, the smiles that used to be part of the animated expressions he would give me during his readings of *Hop on Pop* by Dr. Seuss while he laid in bed with me as I got so into the story [even going so far to, of course, hop up on his chest and re-enact the scenes in the book]. It was like the smiles in the old photos of him holding me when I was just a few weeks old, my newborn face pressed up against the breast pocket of his shirt while he proudly marveled over me like witnessing my birth had been seeing God. It was just like the

smiles he used to flash me during our Saturday trips to The Del Amo Mall where he would take me for a special treat at Hot Dog on a Stick in the food court. It was like the smiles I remember him giving off as he handed me pennies to toss into the mall fountains before he'd bring me to the arcade, like the smile forever documented in the photo of him and I standing in front of Walt Disney's statue in Anaheim when I was four years old and his obvious excitement that he was showing me "the happiest place on earth" for the first time.

It was a smile that made this house feel warm for once. It was a smile that would make me associate my new room with the long hug my dad gave me when he reassured me that it was okay for me to be who I was while we cried in each other's arms.

It was a smile that let me know he loved me.

Chapter Twelve
Tuesday, December 5th, 2006

Dear Journal,

It's official; I'm fifteen as of yesterday.

There isn't much exciting about turning fifteen if you ask me. It isn't one of those milestone ages where you get any special recognition or privileges like being able to officially call yourself a teenager at thirteen, having a sweet sixteen party at sixteen, getting to buy porn at eighteen, or being allowed to purchase alcohol at twenty-one. The only real appealing thing about it is that within the next couple of weeks, Mom or Dad will be taking me to the DMV to get my learner's permit, and my driving practice won't be limited to backing Dad's car out of the garage anymore.

I came out to Thomas and Athena yesterday on my birthday. I figured if my dad was okay with it, then I was worrying for nothing about what my two progressive friends would think. As anyone besides me would've probably suspected, they were accepting with open arms. You could almost say Athena was *too* accepting.

"Oh my God!" she squealed at the bus loading area at the end of the day. I led her and Thomas over against the wall of the school, far enough away from anyone to overhear so I could tell them. I almost brought it up at lunch, but decided it was too risky with so many people close enough to eavesdrop, so I told them both I had to talk to them about something important after last period. I had to shush Athena because her reaction was to immediately shriek with accompanied jumping up and down. Learning that one of her best friends was gay was just about the best news in the world. Go figure.

"I'm so proud of you!" she said, giving me a big hug. I stood stiff, unsure of what to do. I'm not used to having girls hug me. "So, you really like dick?"

"Shh!" I shushed her, my eyes wandering over to the group of students who were standing just off the school grounds past the gates and smoking cigarettes. "Not so loud!"

"I'm so sorry!" Athena laughed, covering her mouth and still having trouble with containing her excitement. "I've just always wanted a gay friend!"

"Why?" I asked.

"Because you're basically like one of the girls now! We can talk about the guys we think are hot and we can paint each other's nails!"

"Um, yeah," I said. "I guess."

"I always knew, Northrup," Thomas said with a wink. "Happy to see you're comfortable enough to tell us now."

"You knew all along?"

"Definitely had a feeling, at least. Not many straight guys I know obsess as much as you do over an 'emo stud' like Matt Daniels, although, after taking the time to look over some of those lyrics of his, I can see why you're particularly fond of him. I've been listening to that *Nitro* album, and I must admit that it isn't quite as conventional as I imagined."

I stared at him.

"You've been listening to Stay Sweet?"

Thomas gave me an almost embarrassed smile.

"I mean, it's all you talk about, Northrup. I had to see what all the hype was about."

"And you like it?"

"It's...different. I wouldn't say it's my favorite genre, but it's kind of growing on me. For an emo band, their lyrics are certainly more political than I would have imagined."

We started walking up the sidewalk alongside the row of buses where the rancid smell of diesel mixed with the sound of those beastly engines collectively grumbling reminded me of how lucky I am that Izzy is always my ride.

We approached Athena's bus and she gave me another hug before she boarded.

"I'm so proud of you!" she said for the second time. "See you guys tomorrow! Text me!"

She disappeared up the steps and we gave her a little wave before we continued walking to Thomas's bus.

"Why didn't you tell us before, Northrup?" he asked.

"What?"

"That you're...you know." He lowered his voice.

"Oh," I said. "I don't know. I guess I just didn't know if I was ready for everyone to know."

"Athena and I are everyone?" Thomas chuckled. "I would guess that Izzy already knows?"

...

"Yeah. He knows."

"He's gay, too, right?"

I nearly tripped and Thomas laughed a little. I didn't have to say anything to confirm it.

"It was a bit obvious, Northrup. Athena and I discussed it. We actually figured he was gay long before we even suspected a thing about you."

"How is it obvious?"

"Well...I don't want to come off as offensive or assuming the stereotype is true, but I can hear it in his voice."

I stopped walking when something hit me.

"Do I...have the 'gay voice', too?" I asked.

"Not really. You just sound scared all the time."

"...Scared?"

"You're a nervous guy, Northrup."

I couldn't deny that.

"You're soft," Thomas added.

"Is that...a good thing?"

"At times, but it'd be nice if you weren't so scared of the world. Think of all the stress you could've saved yourself if you had come out to us back in September."

...

"You knew that day, didn't you?"

"What?"

"When you invited us over to go swimming. You knew what Izzy and I were doing."

We stopped at Thomas's bus as he clutched the strap of his bag.

"I don't know exactly what's going on between you two," he said. "I can use my imagination, but actually, it's none of my business. I've always noticed a bit more closeness between you two than there is between any of the rest of us, so I can only assume it's more intimate than what you lead it on to be."

I wasn't sure about how to feel of Izzy and I and our relationship being more obvious than I expected. It felt more special with the illusion that we were the only two in the world who knew about it.

"I'm surprised you never asked us," I said.

"That would just be rude," Thomas said. "I know it's quite contrary for people around here to keep their private lives to themselves, but I don't see what's so special bragging about what you do with other people behind closed doors. I don't care who's fucking who. What you and Izzy do on your time is your business. I don't need to know about any of that if you don't want to tell me. As long as you're both happy, that's what matters."

I put my head down, feeling a chill from the frigid December air. I shivered, looked up, and finally smiled despite my uneasiness in what was public now. It was like coming out to Thomas was easy, but coming out to him as someone who had something intimate with Izzy was a whole different story.

"Thanks," I said. "Just…please don't tell anyone…about Izzy and me."

"I won't, Northrup. Like I said, that's your business."

"Not even Athena."

He laughed.

"Trust me. I won't tell her anything. She tends to talk before she uses her brain." He looked up at the steps to his bus. "I have to go, but don't worry; I don't think any differently of you. It's not like you told me anything I didn't already know." He gave me another wink. "Happy birthday, Northrup."

He patted my shoulder and then started up the steps to his bus. I sighed, my breath visible in the chilly wind. I started the long walk across the campus to the parking lot where Izzy would be waiting for me.

…

"I have a surprise for you," Izzy said once we were on the road in the Alfa. He was playing "The Great Escape" by Boys Like Girls from his iPod at a low volume and smoking a Camel. He kept his window cracked just a tad to air out the space and was driving slowly to be careful not to skid on any ice. Ever since our near-miss when he crashed into the ditch, I've noticed he seems to practice extra careful driving whenever I'm in the car with him.

238

"A birthday surprise?" I asked.

"Sort of," he giggled. "I guess it could be."

"What is it?"

He blew a puff of smoke out the cracked window.

"My dad's going to visit my grandparents in Brooklyn for a few days. He's gonna be there till Thursday, so I'm gonna have the whole house to myself. He's leaving tonight."

I imagined all the possibilities of what we could do in the Murraro house with only the two of us there. If Izzy didn't care about his dad walking in on us when he was normally home, I could only imagine what he must have had in store if he was so excited about him being away.

"What are you saying?" I asked in a dazed-sounding voice, feeling a high as my horniness levels were suddenly going right through the fucking roof.

He puffed on his cigarette again and smirked as he stared ahead at the road. He was so beautiful in that black peacoat of his, and the black beanie that his growing hair stuck out of only added to his cute alternative boy look.

And...he was all mine.

"I'm saying you should spend the night tonight," he said. He dumped some ash in the ashtray. "Will your parents let you?"

"I hope so," I said, dreading the thought that I wouldn't be allowed to have a sleepover because it was a school night. "I mean, I don't see why that would be a big deal. You're right next door."

I thought for a second.

"And...they don't have to know your dad won't be there."

He giggled again and gave me a wink.

"Good boy."

I felt the hairs on the back of my neck stand straight up as his right hand found my thigh. He caressed the denim of my dark jeans for a moment before both of his hands were back on the wheel and his used cigarette tossed out the window.

This was going to be an amazing night as long as I could manage to get out of the house.

7 pm:

Mom and Dad surprised me with a cake after dinner. The three of us stood around the kitchen table, even Larry, while my parents sang to me. Red and green frosting that fit the season well spelled out *"Happy Birthday, Kieran"* across the white background of icing. Two candles topped everything off by forming the number "15" to declare my new age. I blew out the candles just before wishing to lose my virginity that night to Izzy, and then that familiar smell of freshly extinguished flames filled the room as everyone clapped.

"Happy birthday, sweetie!" Mom said, and handed me a large, bulky rectangular-wrapped package.

"Thanks," I said, and tore off the paper to reveal a brand-new Nintendo Wii.

"Whoa," I said, legitimately in awe of such a prestige gift. "Thanks, Mom. I thought these things were, like, impossible to get."

"It wasn't easy," she said. "They were sold out at Berkshire. I had to drive all the way to King of Prussia to find one."

It was Dad's turn. He handed me another rectangular package, this one much smaller and lighter than the one the Wii had come in. His eyes were full as I unwrapped it. I could sense his hopes that I'd be happy with what he got me.

It was a journal just like you, but not a composition book from OfficeMax. This was a beautiful, leather-bound journal with a black ribbon to hold it closed. Dad had customized it to spell my name across the cover in fancy cursive lettering.

"Open it up," Dad said. "I wrote a little something for you in the front."

I unhooked the black ribbon and pulled back the cover. As it had only been open once before for Dad to write his message, the spine cracked. I could smell the fresh scent of the new stationary as I read over the words he inscribed on the inside of the front cover in bold, black ink:

"Art, the beautiful expression of one through a form, free of boundaries but of the mind, or soul. The art one creates, whether for personal, commercial, or a small audience, art, may be the best gift to give to the world. If only making you feel free, the recording of one's spirit is rare, and needs to be recognized. I give you this gift to facilitate the production of your art, the expression of your creative spirit."

I must have read the short paragraph half a dozen times, confused by this unexpected poetic side of my father that I never knew was there. I wondered for a moment if the quote was taken from a famous face, but even if it was, it was the thought that counted, and I was immensely touched by it.

"Dad," I said, reading his message over and over again still. I was trying really hard not to cry. "Thank you. But, how did you…"

"I always see you writing in that composition book," he said. "And I know it can't be for school because there's no way you have that much dedication to your homework."

We all laughed. Even Mom. It was the nicest moment between all of us since Justin died, maybe even the nicest moment we had as a family since we moved.

7:15 pm:

Mom cut the cake and we each had a piece while Larry played musical chairs at our feet, making his rounds by trying to charm one of us into dropping some dessert on the floor for him.

I cradled my new journal like a relic. The night was going so well that I was almost afraid to raise the question standing at the precipice of my thoughts.

7:30 pm:

"Izzy wanted to know if I could stay over tonight. Is that okay?"

Mom and Dad looked at each other. I held my breath, figuring that it was probably too much for me to ask to make the night that much more perfect. Would I be forced to sneak out of my house for the first time?

"It *is* a school night," Mom said. "Do you have any homework?"

"I finished it all." [Total lie].

She looked to Dad while she delicately ate her tiny piece of cake. Dad looked to me, back to Mom, back to me again, back to Mom again.

"It *is* his birthday, Shannon," he said. "I think that would be alright."

"Don't go off skipping school or anything tomorrow," Mom said.

I rolled my eyes.

"Mom, we're not. Izzy drives me every day."

"He'll be right next door, Shannon." [I fucking love my dad].

…

"Alright," Mom finally said. "It's okay with me. Can you please just text me in the morning to let me know when you get to school?"

"Sure!" I said, a little too happy and loud. The excitement was real. "Thanks, Mom!"

I shoved the rest of my cake down my throat so fast I'm surprised I didn't choke. I tossed my dirty plate and fork in the sink

before I thundered upstairs to my room, sent Izzy a text to let him know I was coming, and immediately started packing an overnight bag: boxers, jeans, shirt, socks. I ran to the bathroom: toothbrush. My phone vibrated: date confirmed. I ran back downstairs with my red Stay Sweet hoodie on, said goodnight to the family now unwinding in the sunroom to some Christmas movie, and hurried out the door so fast you would've thought I was fleeing from a housefire.

After nearly slipping on the ice that had formed on our front steps, I trudged through the snow to Izzy's house as quickly as I could. Before I even had the chance to ring the bell, he opened the front door, and I ran into his arms.

10 pm:

Izzy and I stood in the window of his second-floor bedroom as we watched Mr. Murraro load his Schedoni luggage into the front trunk of his '85 Ferrari Testarossa.

I was breathing heavy, my heart pounding with anticipation while we waited to have the house to ourselves. Izzy stood beside me, wearing a Bayside t-shirt and flannel pajama lounge pants. We were both barefoot, my feet still cold from my short run through the snow.

Mr. Murraro finally climbed in behind the wheel with his black coat trailing behind him, and the Testarossa's engine roared to life. It was such a deep sound that I could practically feel my head vibrating. As soon as the tires rolled down the icy driveway and the red glow of the taillights disappeared into the distance, it was like a bell went off to let the two of us know that we could let our hair down at last.

"Happy birthday, Kieran," Izzy said.

. . .

I was given a taste of what the tone of the evening would be once Izzy and I began furiously making out at the instant realization that we were alone together. It's a good thing that nobody decided to walk past the house at that moment because if they had, they would've seen the two of us kissing, framed in the window upstairs while Izzy's hand reached up my shirt and began exploring the territory of my chest. I felt his fingers trail up my skin and rest on my right nipple, which he

243

began to tease. The sensation instantly aroused me, and I could feel myself getting hard while our tongues continued to interact.

When he broke the kiss, Izzy put a hand on each one of my shoulders, his face close to mine.

"Are you nervous?" he asked, his voice almost a whisper. He ran a hand through my hair.

I nodded.

"Yeah."

He took my hand and squeezed it.

"It's okay," he said, and then he kissed my fingers. "You just tell me what you like. Let me know if you like what I'm doing."

The back side of his hand brushed along my cheek. I shivered and closed my eyes. There was something very strange going on with my body. It was like it knew I was going to lose my virginity. It knew I was crossing into a chapter of my sex life that I hadn't yet explored. The arousal I was feeling was much different than usual. It was euphoric. It felt so good that it almost hurt.

"I want you to enjoy all of it," Izzy said. "I just want to make sure you're ready, okay?"

I nodded, smiling as his hand continued to rub my cheek, and then he was brushing my hair back again, rubbing my forehead.

"You're so beautiful," he said.

I closed my eyes, almost feeling like crying. I actually might have just a little.

"Thank you."

…

"Are you ready?"

…

"Yes."

...

Izzy twisted the white stick at the side of his window, closing the blinds for extra privacy. Before we moved over to the bed, he took a CD from a pile sitting on his dresser and slid it into his boombox. Slowdive's "Blue Skied An' Clear" began trickling lightly from the speakers as I laid down on the bedspread. He had successfully chosen the most tranquil track I could've imagined for this fervid moment between us. The sparse, echoey vocals made it feel as if gods of some kind were speaking to me.

I watched Izzy pull his shirt over his head and then slip out of his pajama bottoms. He climbed on top of me, took my head in his hands, and forced his tongue into my mouth again. He was clad in only his boxer briefs now, and he was clearly aroused, too, as I could feel his erection poking at me through the fabric.

He helped me take off my own shirt and he started to move down, kissing my neck, my chest. It tickled once he started kissing my belly. When he reached my waist, he started undoing my belt and unbuttoning my jeans. I held my breath as he pulled them down, along with my underwear, to my ankles, and I kicked them off.

Izzy took in the sight of my naked body. His mouth appeared to be watering at the sight of it, and I couldn't believe that a boy so amazing felt this level of intense attraction to someone like me.

"You are *such* a beautiful boy," he said, and he started to lean in close to my groin. "You beautiful, beautiful boy."

I could feel his hot breath hitting the sensitive areas down there, and before he did anything else, he looked up at me with a slightly mischievous, but still innocent enough smile.

"Can I?" he asked, his hands resting on my thighs.

"Yeah," I said in an exhale.

I was shaking like crazy, and I must've scared him a little by this because at first, he hesitated, but then his hands slid up my sides and he buried his face into my crotch.

I felt the warm, wet sensation of his mouth taking me in. It was clear that Izzy had gone down on a guy before [which he's told me], but I would've been able to tell just from how experienced he came off with his technique. I could feel his tongue slide up and down my shaft and it felt so good that I worried I would cum before we even had the chance to go any further. I controlled myself, though, soaking in every detail of the moment so that it would never leave my memory.

Izzy's Tony Hawk poster stared down at me, taped to the sloping ceiling over the bed. Across the room, taped to the wall, each of the four members of All Time Low watched us. In another corner, it was Blink-182.

The bedspread was cold against my naked thighs, and I could feel Izzy's nose pressing into my pubic hair while he sucked on me. His tongue tickled the tip of my penis, licking the tiny hole. I jolted at this new sensation. He pulled away after a few minutes, a look of dizzy passion in his eyes as he chuckled, smiling at me while both of us caught our breaths. The moist lubricant of his saliva stuck to my skin where he had worked his tongue, and now Izzy was tugging at his own underwear to slip out of them.

"You want to suck mine?" he asked, sliding his boxer briefs down. His penis popped out, fully erect. It was sticking out and twitching with an excitement like it had a mind of its own. It was so beautiful.

"Yeah," I said, reaching my arms out to him as he bent his knees, pulled off his underwear, and was naked with me at last.

We switched positions on the bed so that he was lying on his back while I straddled him. His penis had just let out an ooze of pre-cum that dangled from the tip, a natural lubricant his body was creating to assist in the sex he apparently wanted to have with me.

I wouldn't be able to describe the taste of it if I tried. I wasn't really all that concerned about the taste, though. It was Izzy's reactions to me pleasuring him that really turned me on. He gave off cute little moans as he ran his hands through my hair, assisting me and guiding

me while I tried what he did and ran my tongue along his shaft. I found the shape of his head, his circumcision scar where I licked and searched for the spot that my touch would give him the most bliss.

"Oh, Kieran," he moaned. "Oh, fuck, that's good."

His sensual, soft tone was so different from what I saw in him when we first met in the theater room back in October. This energetic, friendly, and charming alternative skater boy was now revealing his sensuous and sensitive side. He was revealing the side of him that was a passionate lover who knew how to present his body to someone else who worshipped it, a boy who liked to be touched and handled in such a way that it surfaced in the erotic reactions he had to me tasting the heart of his sexuality.

I pulled away, my spit stringing from his groin as he breathed heavily. His skinny torso rose and fell with each breath, his ribs slightly visible with each inhale while his eyes were fixated on mine in a sedated stare of pure satisfaction. He reminded me of a perfectly illustrated man in an ancient Roman painting, staring off into space and entranced by some unseen spiritual force the artist had been inspired by.

"Am I doing okay?" I asked.

"Fuck me," was his response.

I'm surprised I didn't cum right there and then.

"…What?"

"I want you to fuck me."

…

"Okay."

"Please," he said, rolling over on his belly so that his backside was exposed to me. I had never seen someone look so vulnerable.

"Fuck, me, Kieran," he continued to beg. "Fuck me. *Please* fuck me."

…

"Okay," I repeated, and admittedly, I freaked out a little because I didn't know what the hell I was doing.

I carefully began to mount Izzy's back as he closed his eyes, sighing in preparation for me to enter him.

In all the fantasies I'd done over the past few months in imagining how wonderful it would be to lose my virginity to Izzy, I never once imagined that I would be the one fucking him. I always pictured it the reverse way. I'd lay back and Izzy would top me, but here, as the moment came, he invited me to take charge.

…

This was it.

…

It felt warm inside him. Izzy moaned again, biting down on his lip as I gifted my virginity to him.

I was careful not to use too much force in fear of hurting him. I assumed, unless it was information he kept from me, that I was the first guy to stick a dick in his ass, and with that virginity came an inexperience that would manifest in intense pain at the first attempt. We were successful enough, though, and after a while of being careful, I started to thrust faster once it was clear that he was enjoying it.

He groaned, twisting his arms around behind him to touch the sides of my back as my body fit into his. He sounded almost sleepy with his intimate moans. I was so lost in the moment that I wasn't necessarily occupied by the fascination of losing my virginity to him anymore, but so intent on reaching that impending orgasm.

I could smell him, his sweat, the familiar body odors that would normally be a distaste in the locker room…*arousing* me, making my hunger for him grow frighteningly. It was like I would do absolutely anything to fuck him and to continue to fuck him even if it meant skipping school for days on end. Hell…I'd drop out of school if it meant I could have sex with him forever. I just wanted him and only him. Nothing else mattered.

248

I reached my hands around his sides, pinned them between his hard ribs and the sweat soaked mattress. I instinctively grabbed his nipples and played with them while I kept pushing into him.

"Fuck!" Izzy yelped, his teeth biting down on the pillow his head was resting upon. This startled me into a slower thrust with the fear that I had harmed him, but he reassured me with the sudden begging to keep going, to test his limits.

"No, no," he gasped. "It's okay, it's okay. Keep going. Keep going."

I closed my eyes and pressed my face hard into his back, kissing his skin moist with sweat before I continued thrusting in and out, harder and harder until I thought the bed would break.

It was coming. I couldn't hold it in anymore.

I felt the extreme, tightening tickle pulling the wind from my lungs in a release of all the energy that had built up in me for so long, ever since the first time we kissed, which felt like a million years ago.

I saw stars when I squeezed my eyes shut at the precise moment I came, and opened them after I grunted in a strange, animal-like choking sound that seemed to possess me. Izzy clutched his pillow as I came inside him in an intense discharge that I never witnessed my body do before. I could feel so much coming out of me that it felt like it wouldn't stop. I was practically hyperventilating.

I pulled out of him as Izzy retreated into a fetal position. I fell back in a daze, exhausted and wet with fresh sweat all over me. My pubes were damp like moss, my hair soaked. Semen was still dripping from my dick. Time felt like it was slowing down.

Once he regained some strength, Izzy flipped over on his back again. I watched as he started to finish himself off by jerking off vigorously. His eyes were fixated on me as his already bony frame tensed up, his shoulders hunched, and his pale skin went flush.

He came soon after, and I watched as he aimed his load onto his belly. His thick semen splattered against his navel and sternum while his entire groin area contracted with each spurt. It was the first

time I'd ever seen another boy cum in person. Like everything else about him, the act was beautiful and the look on his face suggested he'd never felt something so intense.

Once he was completely drained, he collapsed back onto the pile of pillows. We were both struggling to catch our breaths for a long while in the cool down of our most intimate moment yet. Despite the exhaustion, I was so stirred by how sexy Izzy looked, naked, covered in his own seed, and beginning to reach his fingers down below his balls. If my body had been ready, my mind would've almost certainly cooperated in getting me hard again at the sight of him beginning to finger himself. I suspected he was trying yet another kinky visual to assist me in getting off again.

After a brief moment, he retrieved his fingers to show me...the vague color of blood.

"My...*God*," he breathed. He stared in complete awe at the lines of light pink that had stained his fingers.

I took his wrist in my hand and studied what I had done to him, shivering as droplets of sweat fell from my hair.

"Jesus," I said, butterflies ravaging my stomach.

...

He offered his fingers to my mouth.

...

Still shaking, and for whatever reason surer that what I was about to do was right [surer than I ever have been about anything in my life], I took those bony fingers of his I had grasped so many times, now smeared with his blood, took them into my mouth...and sucked on them.

I could taste the faint, but familiar flavor that up until then I had only ever remembered from instinctively treating a finger prick. Izzy stared back into me with a tired fade of satisfaction. He looked like he had just run ten miles, but won the race.

"Thank you," he finally said, still breathing heavily, but in more relaxed breaths.

I looked down at the mess that we had both left as he pulled his fingers from my mouth.

"You're welcome," I said, closing my eyes and letting out a deep sigh. "I hope I was…okay."

Izzy patted my thigh and he started to stand up.

"You were perfect."

Izzy crossed the room and opened his closet where he reached into the pocket of his black peacoat and retrieved a pack of Camels. He grabbed a lighter from his dresser, lit a cigarette, and started smoking it as he looked at his naked self in the tall mirror attached to the closet door. He smiled at my reflection in the background, blowing smoke against the glass, but then he held it and let it go without taking another inhale. The thin, cylindrical paper just burned, shedding its skin around a stick of ash that surprisingly didn't fall.

With his free hand, he ran his fingers through the hair on his belly, rubbing the spot just above his navel that was still wet and sticky. His eyes seemed lost, but transfixed…on something new, something he didn't understand, but nonetheless was enchanted by it. We said no words, but…I understood completely.

"I'm gonna go clean up," he finally said, dumping what was left of the cigarette in an empty Dr. Pepper can sitting on his dresser. "Wanna take a shower with me?"

"Sure."

I stood up a little too fast, stumbled away from the bed, and followed him out into the hall.

Instead of using the bathroom at the end of the hall where weeks ago we had bathed together, Izzy led me through the master bedroom to his dad's private ensuite where the house's only shower stall is.

Mr. Murraro's bed was surprisingly unmade, a few original Basquiat paintings decorated the stark white walls, and the intense colors of the offbeat artwork jumped out rather abruptly from the otherwise blank spaces. Vertical blinds were drawn in front of the windows facing the street, a digital alarm clock's green display the only source of light in the dark corner next to the bed before Izzy flicked on the overhead light.

The walk-in closet was open, and I could see acres of dress shirts, business suits, ties, and leather shoes [some still in their respective boxes] making up the wardrobe of Izzy's father. The dresser was cluttered with assorted men's fragrances, colognes in various-sized bottles, and a few framed photos here and there depicting years of the Murraro family from the early '80s up until just several years ago. A few partially melted Christmas candles had hardened over the side of the dresser like icicles. It was a shrine for the patriarch of this broken home.

The bathroom was very similar to my own parents' with its vaulted ceilings and skylights slanting down above a large jacuzzi tub and shower stall, but with original Keith Haring prints framing the shower's entry. It was as if the artist's signature faceless figures were acting as guards.

Once Izzy turned on the lights, he went over to the shower stall to open the pebbled glass door like it was a gate to some exclusive world we were finally being granted access.

"Just gonna let it heat up a little," he said, twisting the knob for the hot water. The showerhead began raining down on the tiles as we stood beside the open stall.

I'm not sure if this is something that happens to all boys or if it's some weird phenomenon only my body does, but my ears started ringing, and it's something I've noticed happens often after I cum. This, along with the constant roar of the shower going, made me feel slightly dizzy, and I almost felt I was going to fall over, but I grabbed the cold wall as Izzy put a hand on my shoulder.

"You good?" he asked.

"Yeah," I exhaled, and then we both chuckled at the same time like a psychic link had merged us. Is that something that happens after sex?

Izzy grabbed my head and kissed me roughly for a quick moment while his hands squeezed my ass. I returned the gesture to him as the room began filling with a thick fog of steam.

We stepped into the shower together. Izzy's wavy and ever so slightly curled hair melted under the water into a wet limp. I stood under the stream with him, and we both rinsed our bodies off, wiping the sweat and drying semen away. I washed Izzy's back for him and he washed mine. We shampooed each other's hair, and Izzy giggled as he lathered his hair into a makeshift mohawk, posing with the heavy metal devil horns before he laughed and rinsed the shampoo out again.

Once the sweat and cum was cleaned from us, Izzy positioned himself so that the shower aimed directly to his backside. I watched him reach behind to clean himself out with a washcloth. He winched as a couple of faint drops of blood fell in blotchy dots against the black tiled floor before they ran and disappeared into the whirlpool of the gurgling drain forever. It made me worry for a moment that I had caused some kind of damage to his body, and like he could read my mind, he reassured me:

"It's okay," he said. "I think you just got a little excited."

His smile invited me to join him. We finished off the shower by embracing under the soothing massage of the water pressure. We didn't kiss, but just hugged our bodies close together, and I held onto him for dear life. I could feel every part of him press into me, and his hand pet my back as if he were saying he would protect me from all the evils in the world for the rest of my life.

"I love you," he whispered in my ear, and we were so engulfed in the hot steam that it was as if we were standing in a cloud.

...

After our shower, Izzy and I dressed into our sleep clothes and headed downstairs for a snack before we moved into the study. We ransacked the old fridge and carried armfuls of food and drink to the study in dangerously oversized loads that nearly fell from our hands.

Leftover pizza, Dr. Pepper, chips, spinach dip, and bagel bites littered the glass coffee table. Izzy popped one of his dad's '80s cassettes into the tape deck of the Beomaster. He turned the levels up to the max, and soon, this band Figures on a Beach was booming over the speakers at concert level. Izzy mouthed the words to "No Stars" as he danced around the room in his boxers and t-shirt. I watched him from the floor, laughing, as I sipped directly from the bottle of Dr. Pepper and laughed at the sight of him grabbing the floor lamp like it was a microphone. He lifted up his shirt a few times, rubbing his chest and imitating some of the dramatic poses singers make when they're performing on stage.

This is how it was for the next hour or so, well past midnight, and we were still snacking and listening to various albums from Mr. Murraro's collection [my favorite being "Angst in My Pants" by Sparks that Izzy danced erotically to for me].

Eventually, Izzy got a fire going in the fireplace while we sat on the couch together and looked through his brother, Giovanni's, senior yearbook from Mt. Olive High School.

This was surprisingly the first time I'd ever seen a photo of Izzy's older brother. The Murraro house, not counting the photos in the master bedroom, was essentially bare of any pictures except for the abstract art everywhere.

The black and white senior portrait of Giovanni from two years ago showed a young man who shared many of Izzy's facial features [especially the eyes], but he clearly had an overall taller and lankier looking stature. His nose was larger, too [not a bad thing; it was a handsome nose that went well with the rest of his delicate facial features and warm smile]. Giovanni's jawline was a bit sharper and more chiseled than Izzy's, and his hair was far less curly, but much longer, and rested at his shoulders in waves that swirled ever so slightly halfway to the ends. I would say that Giovanni had inherited more of the Italian genes while Izzy is more of a balanced mix of this and the Jewish features that come from their mother.

The photos kept coming when Izzy showed me his eighth-grade yearbook from Mt. Olive Middle School. The inside of the front cover and first few blank pages were smothered in different handwriting styles from the various signatures of Izzy's friends and

acquaintances back home. It was clear from the comments that *everybody* loved Izzy.

I felt strangely nervous as Izzy flipped the pages toward the eighth-grade section, as if seeing this picture of him from the past would reveal something I wasn't ready for.

...

The picture of Izzy as an eighth grader made me fall in love with him all over again. While Giovanni's smile in his senior portrait had been so understated and professional, Izzy's eighth-grade smile was the kindest and most inviting expression I'd ever seen. At thirteen, Izzy looked essentially the same as he does now, but slightly more youthful as he was yet to grow any trace of facial hair. His hair appeared more curled than it does now, he was wearing a button-down short-sleeve shirt that looked like it came from The Gap, and...that smile...

I'd never seen someone look so genuinely happy and friendly in a photo. If I'd seen this picture before I knew Izzy, without any context or clue as to who he was or what he was like...I would have wanted him to be my friend. Everything about his smile...his dark eyes so inviting, his teeth visible...it spoke so much about how wonderfully kind he was. It didn't look like a smile staged for a photo. It looked like the smile of someone who was happy with every aspect of his life and the way his world was. He looked like someone who loved everyone and everything.

Ishmael Y. Murraro

I read over his name captioned below the photo several times. I'd never seen his real name written before, and even though I know he hates it so much, while I probably wouldn't tell him this...I think it's a beautiful name and he should embrace it.

After we'd looked through the yearbooks for a while, Izzy and I watched old home movies on the VCR of he and his family from the days when they lived back in Mt. Olive. First, we tuned in to Mr. and Mrs. Murraro's wedding video, a grainy segment in a Brooklyn church in the summer of '84 where all of the women in the foreground had big hair. I caught my first glimpse of Izzy's mother, Rachael, who was an

absolutely beautiful, but petite Jewish woman from Flatbush with curly black hair and a fun smile that never left her face.

The videos moved on to Giovanni's baby shower in '86, and then clips of his brother as a newborn and Mrs. Murraro giving him a bath in the sink of their old house while their father narrated the memory.

"I'm on this one!" Izzy announced as he popped in a second tape labeled *"1990."* The screen was that familiar blue box just before static transitioned the picture into a moving image of Mr. Murraro, sixteen years ago, holding baby Izzy in the kitchen of their old house. His father looked so young and handsome, a commuting Wall Street yuppie from Jersey, bobbing Izzy up and down in front of the same refrigerator that's now in this house while Mrs. Murraro spoke off-screen.

"Talk to him in your language, Vince!" she said.

Mr. Murraro started to stutter out random baby babble to a six-month old Izzy who laughed in delight. Everyone in the room went, *"Aww!"* and Mr. Murraro kissed Izzy's bald head right before it cut to their living room where Giovanni, four years old, was opening Christmas presents under the tree. Mr. Murraro sat on the floor with him and baby Izzy as they were overwhelmed by the mountains of toys.

"This is Christmas Eve, 1990," Mr. Murraro said, smiling up at the camera with baby Izzy by his side. *"This is Ishmael's first Christmas and he's got lots of toys from Mommy and Daddy, Grandma and Grandpa, Uncle Danny, Aunt Jennifer. I don't know where we're gonna fit all this neat stuff. It's like we're livin' in a toy store."*

The camera zoomed in on Giovanni who was engrossed in his new Magna Doodle while the sound of The Eurythimics' rendition of "Winter Wonderland" could be heard in the background of the mono soundtrack. Their TV was on, and a commercial was advertising *Home Alone* now playing in theaters.

"I think we're gonna need to invest in lots of batteries for this stuff," Izzy's mom said as the camera scanned the museum of toys under the tree.

"And, of course they're not included with anything," Mr. Murraro laughed as Giovanni presented his scribbled drawing to the camera.

Mr. Murraro started to stand up and when baby Izzy realized he was beginning to walk away, he whimpered and attempted to go after him.

"What's the matter, Ishmael?" Mrs. Murraro said, her mouth close to the camera's microphone. *"You want daddy?"*

Mr. Murraro groaned as he kneeled down, scooped Izzy up in his arms, and held him close. He patted baby Izzy's back as the camera zoomed out to show him bobbing him back and forth in the middle of the room.

"I think someone's ready for bed," Mrs. Murraro said. *"This little guy has had one busy day."*

"You kiss daddy?" Mr. Murraro asked baby Izzy.

The camera zoomed back in, close to their faces.

"You kiss daddy?"

Baby Izzy whimpered again.

"No?"

Mrs. Murraro laughed off camera, and the smile that Izzy's dad flashed the camera made me realize for the first time just how much the father and son look alike. At a younger age, Mr. Murraro could have easily passed for an older brother to who Izzy is now. He looked so, *so* happy.

Izzy had tears in his eyes by the time we were done watching a good hour of footage. He was crying softly as the video switched to a segment of Mrs. Murraro spooning food to a baby Izzy sitting in his highchair. When she was done feeding him, she held him up to the camera and kissed him, making him giggle.

I offered my hand to Izzy, and he took it as the tape ended, leaving that blue screen again.

"I don't know what I'd do without you, Kieran," he said, wiping away a tear.

"Me? I don't know what I'd do without you."

"I guess the feeling's mutual, then."

He tried to smile, but it was clearly hard, and much like seeing my dad cry, the image of Izzy being sad is simply unbearable for me.

"I know you must miss her a lot," I said. "I'm sorry I never got to meet her."

Izzy snorted and his tears started dropping out of his eyes like a light rain, trickling down his neck and wetting his shirt.

"I wish I could've met your brother," he said.

Outside, a strong wind was blowing up against the side of the house, and we could hear branches brushing at the wall. A light jingling could be heard at the front door, the Christmas wreath probably shaking from the sudden gust.

"What was he like?" Izzy asked.

"My brother?"

"Yeah."

…

"Well…"

I looked up. The ceiling fan was still, its blades casting long shadows against the plaster like a sleeping spider's legs.

"He was…"

I caught a glimpse of the digital clock on the VCR. It was after two in the morning.

…

"He was my best friend."

Another strong gust of wind surged against the house and, simultaneously, the lights flickered. The furnace shuttered, and briefly, the heat kicked off before it picked up again. The clock on the VCR went black before it started flashing *"12:00."*

We were quiet for a few minutes as we listened to the wind. The fridge beeped from the kitchen as its power was restored. The fire still crackled in the fireplace, the warm orange glow of the flames cozy against my still cold feet.

"I was thinking," I went on. "It's weird, but, like…I never would've met you if he hadn't died. I mean, I obviously wish he was still here, but…"

I didn't know how to finish my thought, but Izzy nodded, apparently understanding.

"I never would've moved here if my mom was still alive. I know what you mean. Like, I don't know how I could be without you now, but I really wish she was still here."

My eyes wandered to the blue TV screen. The Beomaster was still on, but with no music, the only sound that emanated from the speakers was a low, slightly threatening hum of the empty channel.

"You know why I signed up to be in the peer program?" Izzy asked.

"Why?"

"I kinda think I did because I didn't know how else I'd be able to meet new friends around here."

He squeezed my hand.

"So, I'm really glad I did."

I leaned over and kissed him.

"Me too."

We cuddled for a while longer before he went upstairs to pee. I heard the toilet flush distantly, and a few minutes later, he returned with some fresh blankets from the linen closet. He laid back on the couch, pulled the blankets over him, and invited me to join him. I slipped under the covers with him, and we held each other as we struggled to stay awake to *Beavis and Butthead* reruns playing on TV.

It looks like this is going to be the last entry I can fit into you, my journal. In just the past four months, I've apparently gone through so much that I was able to fill the entirety of you with experiences I felt unique or important enough to log. At first, I didn't know what I thought about doing this. I'd never kept a journal before, never written anything so personal to go back and read later, but…I think I kind of like doing this. I don't really want to stop, so I guess I'll have to start using that fancy journal my dad got me.

Goodnight, journal. It's been swell.

Chapter Thirteen
Sunday, January 28th, 2007

Dear Journal,

I don't know what to write.

I'm tired. Just so tired.

I'm weak.

Am I dead yet?

dead? Do I want to be

I feel like I've cheated death

So many

So many times lately.

Tristan LaFerriere

What's keeping me here?

I don't know if I have

the energy

to do this anymore.

Let me…

Let me tell you a little story about Kieran Northrup.

...

Kieran Donovan Northrup.

...

He was born on December 4th, 1991, in Los Angeles, California, the second child of Darren and Shannon Northrup, natives of Pasadena and Santa Monica, respectively. His older brother, Justin, was born on May 12th, 1989.

He lived with his family in the same house on Chattanooga Place in Pacific Palisades for the first fourteen and a half years of his life. His father, Darren, worked as senior manager for the Chamberlain & Reed law firm and his mother, Shannon, was a successful realtor in Los Angeles County.

Despite what he might seem like today, Kieran wasn't always the black sheep of the family. Early on, he grew up just like any other kid being raised by white collar parents. His brother failed at piano lessons, but succeeded admirably in soccer. Kieran was a cub scout for two years from the ages of nine to eleven before a disastrous camping trip to Camp Josepho made him declare his desires to *do his best to do his duty to God and his country"* finished forever.

...but maybe it was something more than just the pricking of sticker bushes against his arms and the sleepless nights failing to get comfortable in a sleeping bag sitting over the lumpy, uncomfortable earth separated by only the thin layer of the tent. Maybe it was something more that scared him away from an organization so dedicated to its Lord, a figure who supposedly frowned upon any relationship that would challenge procreation.

Going back to his youngest years, Kieran was a coward.

263

Whether it was the end of cycle signal on the spin dryer or the sizzling shocks and crackles of the bug zapper hanging from the back porch...he feared it. He was born afraid of the world, everything in it, and had to slowly gain its trust through interactions that proved not everything was out to get him.

...but perhaps it was something deeper that made Kieran uncomfortable within the walls of his childhood home. Perhaps it was something deeper that caused him such distress, such threats from even the inanimate objects around him that he felt didn't accept him for the boy he had been born.

Kieran discovered death for the first time when he was four years old.

His maternal grandmother, Marjorie Curran, passed away on May 17th, 1996, after a short, but aggressive battle with uterine cancer. It being his first association with death, his only understanding of another human being who passed had been the television personality Dinah Shore when his father tried to explain the singer died and went to heaven after the news announced her death two years earlier. In his mind, grandma had *"gone to meet Dinah Shore in the clouds"*, and the innocent remark made even his grieving mother crack a smile in the backseat of the black limo following the hearse to the cemetery.

A short time later, he dreamed of her coming back, coming back just to see him, coming back to tell him it was okay because even in the afterlife, Grandma was doing fine. She was watching him grow up even though she was no longer there to cuddle with him in her armchair while they watched reruns of *I Love Lucy*. She was looking down on him even though she wasn't there to catch him in her arms as he ran and jumped into their pool without a usual trace of fear that followed him in everything he did.

As the pages of the calendar flipped, the new millennium came. The Lewinski scandal somehow escaped his young eyes even though the words were printed everywhere, the Twin Towers fell, Matthew Shephard's murder became a distant memory of the decade passed, and Vanna White no longer turned the letters, but touched them.

Justin grew handsomer and handsomer while Kieran sat in the shade of his older brother's shadow. Each day out in the scorching sun of Southern California, kicking that soccer ball successfully into the goals of the opposing teams brought tanner tones to his brother's skin, and frequent visits to the weight room at Pacific Palisades Charter School added muscles to the once shapeless bones of the boy.

Seeing into the future of Justin's short life would have made these preppy rituals seem a preparation for battle that never came…because he lost long before he had the chance to fight.

While his beautiful brother took girls to movies and bragged of reaching second base in the back row of the theater, Kieran stayed home and fantasized. He fantasized of finding, discovering the dormant sexual desires that had been buried away in him for so long that were just beginning to peak at the surface in his early years of puberty.

What were these strange sensations he was feeling when images of Ashton Kutcher beckoned to him in the passing cases of DVDs at the video rental store? Why did he want to undress Aaron Carter with his eyes? Why is it that when Christina Burke told him he was cute inside the staticky slide during recess one day in the fourth grade that he didn't care? Why did he ask Tim Lazenby to see his penis in the boy's bathroom one afternoon when he should have been curious about what girls were keeping under their skirts?

He knew all along, but somehow covered the threatening thoughts with enough layers that he convinced himself he was just like the others.

He wouldn't grow up to be a freak…

The wandering boy of twelve became lost.

Confused.

The sudden changing of classes in junior high made him grow up too fast, and even the tiny group of peers who bothered to sit beside him at the lunch table were beginning to blend in with the crowds of other districts as he approached thirteen. Kieran was not a laughingstock of the school, but he hardly belonged with anyone.

He was lonely.

Tristan LaFerriere

Justin knew everyone.

Kieran knew nobody.

Justin had confidence.

Kieran hated himself.

Justin got any girl he wanted.

Kieran couldn't even get the girls he didn't want.

...

And then the first miracle occurred.

...

As images of Britney Spears, The Backstreet Boys, and NSYNC began disappearing from the displays of CD stores, the former definitions of the industry were abruptly replaced with the likenesses of My Chemical Romance, Paramore, From First to Last, Panic! At the Disco, Death Cab for Cutie, Cute is What We Aim For, Boys Like Girls, All Time Low, The Academy Is... and...

Stay Sweet.

The first time Kieran saw him was shortly after turning fourteen, in the months leading up to the unexpected migration across country when he felt like maybe he could deal with this, maybe he had finally grasped the concept of just being a body in the halls of the school in Pacific Palisades where everyone was supposed to have an identity. Maybe it was best to skip that part and just be there...just be Kieran Northrup without trying to impress the cliques, none of which he ever felt he would fit into...

Maybe it would be best to just not care.

...

But then he saw Matt Daniels.

Heard his voice.

And that sealed his fate.

...

The name of the band had been thrown around so casually during classes as they, along with their genre, grew exponentially in popularity. Emo was in. It was cool to be uncool. Suddenly the girls and boys who covered their faces with hair of red and black didn't cause doubletakes and Hot Topic had become the new Sears for Generation Y.

Kieran "met" Matt Daniels on a Sunday.

With a fresh Myspace account, the lyrics of "We're All Going to Paris" played over and over and over again each time he visited the page of Mason Blanchard, one of the five on his list of friends besides the default Tom. It wasn't like they ever really spoke to each other except for the few times they had done group projects together in science, but still someone who would acknowledge he existed...

And his profile song was by Stay Sweet.

And it was really catchy.

And Kieran, for the first time, found something current he was interested in. Up until then, it had been his parents' Cheap Trick records and posters of Robin Zander that fondled his fantasies of long-haired rock stars.

But that Sunday in January, that boring afternoon in the beginning of 2006 when he searched the music video for "We're All Going to Paris" on YouTube unleashed him.

Matt Daniels was a perfect human creation he never thought could exist...even though he had grown up a short drive from the Hollywood hills where all the beautiful people lived...Matt Daniels was different. Matt Daniels was a long-haired, fair-skinned skinny young man in tight jeans and tattered sneakers. Matt Daniels had green eyes that made Kieran feel faint as his music video character sang, sitting on the moving luggage carousel at the airport while the band

267

furiously strummed and drummed out the notes of their signature song. It was their big hit that made Stay Sweet the next Nirvana.

Kieran found his God.

He slipped into Hot Topic at The Del Amo Mall while his mother matched Cartier earrings to go with her new watch. The walls of band shirts displayed in glass boxes along the faux façade of cardboard brick were selections of interchangeable identities, and Stay Sweet was up there, his new uniform.

But just the band shirts weren't enough.

His mother questioned why he had added a box of hair dye to the shopping cart at Ralph's later that week, and without hesitation, he announced he would be changing his color from the chestnut shade he had been born with...

To black...

And the next day he was a black-haired boy, Stay Sweet's logo a ribbon across his chest on the pre-washed shirt from the emo shop, his pale Irish skin a whiter white against the unnatural darkness emanating from his scalp and covering his face. Stay Sweet was his religion now, and he was a follower of Matt Daniels, copying his look, becoming the image of that boy in the band poster watching sensually from the wall of his own room.

And suddenly those buried desires came back when the thoughts of Stay Sweet's front man and what was hidden well under his clothing were the main subjects of his dreams. He wanted a body to go with that voice, accepted internally that this is what he was interested in, but knew he could never tell another soul that he liked other boys.

But maybe it would be okay because California was a good place, a progressive extension of an otherwise stuffy conservative country that would never let him be himself.

...

But in March, his dad made the announcement in a tone that suggested a new baby was coming into the family.

The Northrups would be moving to King's Valley, Pennsylvania in June.

There was nothing he could do to be ready for what was waiting on the East Coast because his parents were leaving everything behind, starting new in every possible way, this new house on Skyview Drive would be a blank canvas for new furniture, new consumer goods...

Flying first class from LAX to Philly, five hours in the air and saying farewell to the Pacific Coastline he had so rarely departed from...*Batman Begins* playing on the tiny screen in front of the seats while the tiny, cheap earbuds dug into his ears uncomfortably.

Goodbye to California and hello to Pennsylvania, The Keystone State a landlocked rectangle of very little excitement or amenities that would appeal to someone of Kieran's personality. Here there would be no beaches, no frothy tickles of sea at his toes to remind him that there's so much more to the world than the suburban street he felt stuck on.

Their house was the first one built, one of many big homes going up in what was once an open field of farmland. No neighbors for weeks, and towers of cardboard boxes isolated Kieran even more than the lonely lunches back in Cali, but he didn't care because there was nothing to see or do here, nothing better to take part in than unpacking the few remnants of their house back west.

Mom and Dad drove two new vehicles home, bought Justin his own, and surprised the two kids with their very own laptops while a hole was dug in the ground for the pool out back. Stainless steel machines pulsated in unison with the quiet dinners at the table, all the fine china laid out, but no one to impress with it.

Meanwhile, Kieran's thirst for the same sex strengthened and steamed from his insides as he pleasured himself to the printed pages of *Alternative Press* and Matt Daniels with his sensual smirk so beckoning.

He wanted his body, wanted his lips against his, wanted to wake himself up with the one thing he wished for, but never thought would come...

...

Eric Gleason.

...

When Justin brought this boy home, his first friend in this new world, Kieran saw a light that even California hadn't offered him.

Somehow, this seemingly impeccable boy with blonde hair and a surfer's body accepted him...

...but like any piece of good news, Kieran questioned its authenticity almost immediately because no boy of such beauty had ever instantly taken such a liking to the quiet and insecure younger brother of the so much more popular Justin.

Was this a joke?

Did Eric Gleason, the son of a successful grocery chain magnate, really want to play a game of billiards with the emo Kieran Northrup? Did Eric Gleason, the stud who would be inheriting a Lambo, really enjoy playing poker with him? Did Eric Gleason, this otherworldly perfection, really want to sit with him by the pool and treat him like he was a real person?

No.

...because then Tyler Kirkland came around soon after, and all the superstitions, all the premonitions, all the hang-ups, and all the doubts Kieran had that Eric may have been genuine came true...

...because Tyler revealed the real Eric Gleason.

He was just like the others, this Tyler, his brother, Evan, they all...they all...

They were all phonies.

Tyler had teased Kieran with an intimate moment in the woods while they were alone, hiding from the other boys in a game of manhunt. The unspoken understanding between them was that they would watch each other masturbate...

But when Kieran was finished, Tyler ended it and proceeded to bend the truth to tell the others Kieran had initiated this…it was his idea to just expose himself and get off in front of this other boy he hardly knew.

Then Kieran *did* become the laughingstock because in the eyes of all the others, he was a freak.

Perhaps it was their excuse to call him a freak, a confirmation made from a series of events that Tyler had set him up to do.

This is what Kieran thought because…

Tyler didn't like him.

Evan didn't seem to like him.

Eric Gleason didn't seem to like him anymore, that is, if he ever did.

Even Justin seemed to be growing distant from him.

The summer ended for Kieran when the final blow made him gun-shy to even leave his own room for the remainder of August, when he was invited one last time to be a part of one of the many gatherings between Justin and his new King's Valley friends.

Some stupid game which ended in Tyler chasing him with a bottle of piss…

Kieran escaped, but would never trust them again.

It was over.

He was alone in King's Valley now.

He was completely alone.

The first week of high school arrived, and Kieran, terrified to leave the house, was hesitant in making any new acquaintances.

A nerdy Australian boy, Thomas, and his black emo friend, Athena, accepted him into their little group while his brother went on to take over this new school as its leader even though they were fresh to this town.

But that storyline ended abruptly on September 8th.

...

Justin was killed.

...

He drowned when he crashed his car into King's Lake, Kieran alongside him on their way back from the mall...

Kieran survived and he had the scar across his chest to prove it.

He lived with that scar for months afterward, every unfortunate glance toward the mirror a reminder...

Justin was buried and gone for good, and Kieran spent the next weeks in a daze, passively making his way to and from school, staring at the dinner plates each evening while he avoided questions from his parents regarding his recovery from the tragedy.

But being invisible could only work for so long.

King's Valley High School took every little word he said seriously, every little facial expression or eye movement as a sign that he was still grieving and could pop at any second. He had to have been unstable, at least in their eyes.

...so they sent him to the school counselor who listened to him tell the story he didn't need to tell...

And she put him in this program where a peer would begin "assisting" him in getting through the schoolyear.

...

And then the second miracle occurred.

272

...

Izzy Murraro.

...

I could go on forever about Izzy Murraro.

Ishmael Ya'akov Murraro.

Izzy was this boy who hadn't come from this world.

Izzy was beautiful in every way.

He made Kieran feel like a human being.

He was Kieran's first true friend.

He was Kieran's first kiss.

Kieran gave his virginity to him.

And together, they were against the whole fucking world. In just a few months, they accomplished so much. The accident and Justin's death seemed to recede further and further into the distance as each week passed. Kieran slowly started smiling more, slowly started to see that some people singlehandedly were able to make the world a more beautiful place.

He let his dye fade.

And by the end of that year that just never seemed to end...

Kieran felt content.

...

And then it was 2007.

It was a year Kieran figured could only go better than its predecessor.

It couldn't have gone lower than Justin's death.

It couldn't have gotten any worse.

Things had to have improved with Izzy in his life. Things were getting better.

Weren't they?

...

Adam Woolf approached Kieran on January 26th, the last Friday of the month.

Adam Woolf had been persistent since October.

He wanted to, for some reason, hang out with Kieran even though they were so different.

And Adam was friends with Tyler Kirkland.

Adam was friends with Eric Gleason.

Why the fuck did he want to hang out with Kieran?

It didn't make any sense.

He should've known better.

He should've blown him off a third time.

But he didn't.

He didn't because this time he told Izzy.

This time he told Izzy that this supposed former friend of his brother seemed so desperate to get him to come with him to the movies or that skate park everyone was so obsessed with.

And Izzy was the one who told him he should go.

"Go!" he said. "Why not? Why don't you want to hang out with him?"

Kieran knew the answer, but didn't feel comfortable admitting it.

He didn't want to see Adam because he had no interest in anyone else now that he had Izzy.

Saying this out loud…to him…would have been his way of declaring some crossing a benchmark of love between them that he didn't quite understand yet.

Were they in love…or did they just love each other? He wasn't sure he understood the difference just a few months before, but now he very clearly grasped what that meant with his new experience.

They had sex.

They told each other they loved each other.

But what kind of love was that?

Were they boyfriends?

No.

Or were they?

He didn't know.

Why didn't he know?

They didn't keep any secrets from each other.

Why didn't he just…"pop the question"?

He would.

He would later that night.

After he went out with Adam Woolf.

Before he'd know for sure if he had to commit to one boy.

275

He *wanted* to commit to this one boy.

He wanted Izzy to be all his.

But because Izzy was encouraging him to go ahead, to see Adam for the evening...

He'd let the night take him wherever it decided to take him.

For once, just once, Kieran told himself...be spontaneous. Let the night guide you.

And then,

Later,

Later that night,

He could ask Izzy.

He would ask him to be his boyfriend.

...

Darren and Shannon were taking a flight out to Seattle that night to visit Ryan, Darren's brother, who had finally gotten in touch with the family when the news eventually reached him across the country of his nephew's death. He had called the house not crying, but clearly shaken. He wanted to see the family as soon as possible. He needed his big brother, Darren.

The news would have stirred Kieran a bit more if he hadn't been so nervous of how the night's events would go, but so much was happening. So many things may have been about to change.

He'd be hanging out with Adam Woolf.

He'd be declaring his love for Izzy...officially.

He wasn't even that excited that he'd have the house to himself for four days.

He was too nervous.

Something had to fail, right?

Adam Woolf came roaring up the street at seven that night in his Dodge Viper as Kieran waited and watched from the living room windows. The Viper turned and pulled into their driveway where it sat idling between the two lampposts, the sound menacing as Kieran came out the front door.

Down the flagstone walkway…

And into the car.

"Kieraaaaan!"

Adam was more than enthusiastic.

A big, tight, uncomfortable hug that squeezed the air out of his lungs.

"Shall we hit The Skate Park?"

"Sure."

"Sweet!"

Adam threw the car in reverse and squealed away.

Adam kept the windows down, and the cold wind of January blew through the car like a wind tunnel, assaulting Kieran's long hair in an uncomfortably strong breeze on their way through Belmont Hill Estates, out onto the streets of King's Valley…on their way to that fucking skate park.

Castlegate Skate Park.

So, this was the place where Justin met Eric so many months ago?

This place, this bustling building that used to be a Laneco…

Cars pulled up, some stayed, some dropped off depending on the patrons' ages.

Adam parked in the gravel lot, and he and Kieran started for the hottest hangout in town.

A glowing, buzzing red neon sign spelled out the place's name above the front entrance.

Inside…

An old, dated '90s carpet…dingy with stains of God knows what…

More neon lights.

No one really skating.

Just like no one went to the King's Valley home games to watch the game, no one came to The Skate Park to skate.

The fluorescent, flickering snack bar sold that soggy pizza he suspected they sold.

The Pepsi was flat.

The napkin dispensers were empty.

Hot dogs glistening with grease danced in a circle behind the foggy glass of a heated display case.

The roller rink was dark, vast, and windowless.

Questionable employees, King's Valley High dropouts stood behind the skate rental counter that was covered in stickers for Billabong, Hurley, and Neff.

Things glowed in the dark.

There were too many people, and Kieran couldn't recognize a single one because in the dimness, there were no faces.

Just silhouettes.

Just voices of older kids who were greeting Adam.

No one knew Kieran.

Adam didn't bother to introduce him to anyone.

He just made his rounds with him at his side like he was presenting this otherworldly, emo creature to all the skatepark's clientele.

It was disorienting.

The music was loud.

Girls screaming.

Two girls arguing.

Guys talking about their favorite scenes from *Jackass Number Two*.

The faint smell of that soggy pizza…liquidy nacho cheese sauce wafting in from the shitty snack bar up the short flight of steps in the corner.

Cigarette smoke coming from the bathrooms.

"Yo, what's up, Adam!"

"Hey! Dennis!"

Dennis.

Dennis Folton.

Kieran knew that name. He knew that face, but he couldn't see him in this darkened room.

Who were these people with him?

The music was too loud for him to hear.

A messy beach bun of hair crept from the shadows.

Melissa Grandstaff.

That permanent frown on her face had to be there somewhere.

These were all Justin's old friends.

What if Eric Gleason was there?

Or, even worse...

Tyler Kirkland.

...

Something was being passed around in the corners of the roller rink.

Monster?

Red Bull?

It came to Kieran.

Adam pushed it to his lips.

"Drink this."

He took it and winced at the horrible taste.

Not an energy drink, or if it was, it was laced with alcohol because the flavor stung his throat.

...

Something was off.

...

He was tired and he didn't want to be here anymore.

He wanted to be home.

With Izzy.

This place was Hell.

The smell of pot.

A joint was being passed around now.

The music seemed louder, but...

Incoherent.

"Come on, Kieran."

Adam's voice came from the shadowy older kids.

The older boy's hand was grabbing his and pulling him along like an angry parent dragging their misbehaved child.

They passed the arcade where a guy and a girl were violently making out.

His hand was up her shirt.

Her hand was down his pants.

Moaning.

Past the *South Park* pinball machine beckoning to him to insert a quarter.

Past the short girl wearing all black, with piercings covering her face, who was snorting a line of something off the Skee Ball field.

"Come on, Kieran!"

Adam's voice...was it Adam's voice? It was deeper, more assertive.

He was being pulled more harshly. His shoulder hurt.

Eiffel 65 drowned out most other sounds.

Their song, "Blue."

Was he in the bathroom now?

Was Adam taking a piss alongside him?

Everything was red.

A hot pink red.

Was that faded graffiti above the urinal…about him jerking off in the woods?

And then he was out in the cold again, in the parking lot by the Viper…by the little groups of teens congregating and waiting for their rides, planning parties, figuring out where they wanted to spend the rest of their Friday nights. Who could they get to buy them alcohol? Who was holding?

Kieran was in the Viper.

The engine rumbled.

The tires were squealing, and they were leaving The Skate Park.

They were passing the Dairy Queen that wouldn't be open for at least another month.

The green and white lights at the Hess station went out as they flew by.

A car dealership was still lit, but empty for the night. Hundreds of empty, lifeless new vehicles watched them from the slightly raised knoll that the lot sat on.

Immortal Technique was playing quietly on the radio.

"Dance with the Devil"

Something was off.

Past Circuit City…

Past the 24-hour King's Valley Diner...

Away from any street lights and into dark, off beaten path territory.

A turn here, a sharp jerk to the left.

King's Lake Road.

Fast.

Adam was driving *really* fast.

"No," Kieran tried to say...

But his voice was gone before he could say he didn't like this. He hated how they were going so fast around the winding lakeside roads at night.

It was all too familiar.

…

He was going to die this time.

…

Four months ago, he wouldn't have cared.

Four months ago, he would have been okay with dying.

He had nothing then.

But now he had Izzy.

He couldn't leave Izzy.

"No."

But Adam was pressing the brake.

The car was slowing down.

Thank God.

Adam turned the car so that it faced the edge of the road dangling over the lake.

"We're gonna stop and take a look at what you did."

The Viper's headlights focused on the guardrail.

The guardrail…

One section had been replaced.

Its silver was a shade off from the rest of the barrier.

Something was off.

It was where Justin's car had smashed through.

Faded, ruined pieces of paper from the weather, sympathy cards, hearts, crosses, prayer cards…all hanging in the same spot where Kieran last listened to his brother call out his name.

"Look at what you fucking did, Kieran."

Something was wrong.

Adam was yanking on Kieran's hair.

It fucking hurt. He expected to feel blood leak from his roots.

"Look at what you fucking did!"

The Viper was moving again.

"No."

Kieran could no longer speak. Any words he attempted were caught in his throat. It was as if his brain wouldn't let him process what he wanted to say.

"We've got some friends to meet up with."

Friends?

No.

Something was very wrong.

Adam drove to King's Valley Park, home of the town's public pool that wouldn't be open for another five or six months, home of a few playgrounds with swing sets and moon climbers, home of the tennis courts, and home of the baseball field.

The baseball field.

Even though most of King's Valley's amenities were fairly new [the playgrounds, the tennis courts, the high school, Belmont Hill Estates, the shopping centers], the baseball field in King's Valley Park was old.

Very old.

Maybe from the '50s?

The bleachers were contained in an aged, weathered wooded box of a structure where the blue and white paint was peeling.

Once maybe fifteen, maybe twenty years ago, an attempt had been made to spruce up this decaying thing with a painted mural alongside the rear wall that faced the empty lot where Adam was parking the Viper.

The headlights revealed this mural, this faded artwork depicting smiling, friendly residents of King's Valley...the mailman, a police officer, a crossing guard, caricatures of local, small business owners standing outside their shops that no longer existed now that the town had been gentrified in the past few years.

The hardware store was on there, too, the kindly elderly shop owners and their painted smiles standing in front of a depiction of their beloved business that they had no idea would burn to the ground in a decade or so to make way for the outlets, the shopping center with the new Gleason's supermarket...

Gleason's.

Eric Gleason.

There was one other car parked in this lot.

A yellow Lambo.

Eric Gleason.

Something was *very* wrong.

Adam was out of the car.

Adam was opening Kieran's door.

Adam was pulling Kieran out of the car…dragging him…violently.

"Quit dragging your fucking feet!"

Kieran didn't know how he was walking. He felt like he was asleep. He was half walking and half being dragged by Adam toward this old bleachers building in front of the baseball diamond that at this late hour was merely a shadow against the night sky.

A threatening shadow.

The structure was watching him.

It was where he was going to die.

He knew that.

Adam was opening the gate, a tall, rectangular chain-link contraption that made a horrible screech as it swung.

Adam's arm hooked onto Kieran's firmly and pulled him along…

Up the crumbling concrete steps…

Through another chain-link door…

Into the overhang that protected the bleachers from rain.

Darkness.

Darkness except two little glows...

These halos of light drifted up from tiny screens, tiny flip phone screens where two people were texting or looking at photos...or whatever...

Two faces lit palely from their own phone screens' lights.

Eric Gleason.

Tyler Kirkland.

Any feeling Kieran had left went numb.

Something was *extremely* wrong.

The two boys snapped their phones shut, and again the world was plunged into darkness while Adam gripped his arm firmly.

Only the echoing, crunching sound of sneakers against the concrete floor, stepping closer, over broken glass, over gravel and stones...

The first sensation he felt in this dark abyss of terror was a load of spit that hit him in the face.

Kieran closed his eyes.

Another bullet of saliva splattered against his face.

A strong hand was grabbing his crotch through his jeans and squeezing.

"You like that, right?" a voice said. *"You like it when a guy grabs your balls?"*

Tyler's voice.

"You like getting your dick rubbed by another dude, right?"

Eric's voice.

While Tyler's fingers teased Kieran's groin through the denim of his jeans, Eric's stronger hand, at the same time, forced its way through the rim of those pants, pushed down, and began to grope his genitals.

Squeezing.

Kieran winced in pain.

And then, even in the darkness, he saw a million little stars because one of these three boys punched him in the face.

He was on the ground.

He was being pulled back up.

He was punched again.

He tasted blood.

Another blow.

His eye felt wrong, like it didn't fit in its socket the way it was supposed to anymore.

Warm, sticky sensation on his face.

Was it the spit residue?

Or was it the blood?

Or was it both?

A sudden, startling blow to his ass made him fall forward.

"I've got a game...and it's called...Butt Kicks!"

His knees hit the dirty concrete floor hard, and another blow to the back of his head pushed him flat against the ground.

The jeans...the new jeans...torn.

His knees were pulsating with pain, burning...

He was being forced over on his back, grabbed and yanked like a rag doll when a dozen or so more kicks to the belly and ribs lasted a lifetime.

He couldn't breathe.

His ribs ached.

He had no energy to fight back.

"Fucking faggot."

"You fucking faggot."

Through his ringing ears, this is all he heard. Over and over again.

"You fucking faggot."

"Fucking faggot."

Someone was sitting on his chest now, squashing his lungs.

Adam.

He couldn't breathe.

Someone was undoing his belt.

He couldn't breathe.

Someone was pulling his pants down.

He couldn't breathe.

Someone was tearing his underwear away from what they protected, pulling them and his jeans down to his knees.

He couldn't fucking breathe.

Someone was squeezing his balls again.

The pain radiated up his belly, the belly that was being crushed by the whole weight of Adam.

Someone was sucking his dick.

His limp dick with no trace of arousal.

He felt teeth.

He screamed.

He cried.

He was slapped in the face.

The weight of Adam finally lifted.

He was forced over, on his belly, his bare ass exposed.

Someone smacked it.

Hard.

Smacked it again.

Smacked it again.

Smacked it again.

Stinging. Horrible, sharp stinging.

He could imagine the scars, the red handprints on his skin.

Laughing.

A pair of shoes…nice, expensive sneakers…stopped in front of his face pressed against the concrete.

Eric's shoes.

The pantlegs of Eric's designer jeans.

Unzipping.

Laughing.

Another slap on the ass.

A warm stream of piss started hitting his scalp, raining down his face, stinging his eyes. The smell made him want to vomit.

The taste...

The fucking taste...

Laughing.

Another slap on the ass.

The piss dripped from his face and hair, formed and collected into a puddle in front of him.

Unzipping.

"You wanted me to cum, right?"

Tyler's voice.

"Alright. I'll cum."

That unmistakable sound of jerking off.

Kieran was too tired to react, to feel anything anymore.

He knew it was coming.

A few minutes later, it hit him.

Another warm, splatter of body fluids. Tyler's cum dripped onto his face in big, unwanted droplets that mixed with Eric's piss.

The fucking smell...

Laughing.

It had to be over soon.

His mind almost went to oblivion when he felt another hand yanking on his hair so hard, he thought it would tear from his scalp.

"Fucking faggot."

Snipping.

"Faggot."

Snip.

Snip.

Snip.

Snip.

Snip.

Tearing.

Laughing.

The cold, dull blade of the scissors brushing against his scalp, behind his ears.

Snip.

Snip.

Snip.

Laughing.

"Faggot."

Laughing.

The sole of a sneaker stepping on his bare ass.

Snip.

Snip.

Snip.

Someone shoving a stick in his ass.

Unbelievable pain.

Just let me die, Kieran thought. *Just let me fucking die already.*

Snip.

Snip.

Pulling.

Tearing.

His hair was coming out in chunks.

The cold air of January found the top of his head. Nothing left to protect it from the chill.

Snip.

Snip.

Snip.

Just let me die.

"Fucking faggot."

Just let me fucking die.

"This is for Justin, you fucking faggot."

Just...let...me...die.

"You're a fucking faggot."

Snip.

Snip.

Snip.

Kick.

I love you, Izzy…

…

Quiet.

…

Nothing.

…

Just quiet.

…

The sound of the Lambo and the Viper's engines collectively turning over, two beasts growling in the night…

Tires rolling away…

An hour passed.

Black-Haired Boy

Tristan LaFerriere

Maybe two.

Kieran was cold.

...

His hoodie, his beloved red Stay Sweet hoodie...

Was torn from his body, shredded and destroyed.

...

His pants and underwear were in a crumpled knot around his ankles.

...

His Stay Sweet Shirt was torn and drenched...

With sweat...

With spit...

With piss...

With semen...

With blood...

His eyes were swollen.

...

His body ached.

...

His ribs were sore.

His knees were gouged open and bleeding. The blood that dripped down his knees had dried into crusty trails of red and black that stuck to the tiny hairs of his legs.

His ass stung with red hand outlines and black marks of the bottoms of sneakers.

…

His balls were aching, pulsating with pain.

…

His lips were puffy…bloody.

…

The stinking aroma of piss surrounded him like he had been tossed into a urinal.

…

His insides hurt. Blood dripped from his ass where the stick had been jammed.

…

Cold.

…

So fucking cold.

…

His hair was gone.

…

His hair was fucking gone.

Chapter Fourteen
Monday, January 29th, 2007

Dear Journal,

I don't remember writing that last entry yesterday.

I don't know how I did it…

It was a long entry and I have no memory of it.

I must have been scribbling furiously.

The first pages of you, my new journal, are practically torn up from the scratches of the pen.

The handwriting is hardly legible.

I had difficulty reading back what I wrote.

Not just because it looked bad, but…the content…

It made me feel sick.

I've been in and out of feeling sick since I remember waking up…

This morning.

I must've been nearly catatonic.

I didn't even address myself in the first person.

It was like my soul left my body for a while because it couldn't handle being in that crippled, damaged body anymore.

I feel like I was asleep for a month.

I don't know how the fuck I got out of that building at the baseball field. The moments leading up to that nightmare of an hour [or at least it felt like an hour] are very hazy. I don't know if they drugged me or if it was a panic attack because I could sense something bad was going to happen.

They fucking drugged me.

They had to have.

It was in that energy drink, that Monster, that Red Bull, or whatever the fuck it was.

That was when everything started fading in and out of being real.

That was when everything started to feel like a dream, a nightmare…

I *do* remember my whole body hurting, and it took me a long time to even move again. I crawled from the spot where they assaulted me, that big concrete slab that was covered with every body fluid [including my tears], and struggled to stand up.

My legs, as though they had shattered, made me scream out in pain.

They wobbled.

Some fresh blood dripped from my knees.

My hoodie was torn to shreds and my jeans…

I was too muddy to even remember how the fuck to zip them back up, to button them, so I ended up stumbling away, only managing to pull my boxers back up, and limp down the cracked steps in my tattered shirt and underwear.

I either couldn't find my sneakers, or they had taken them. My socks dipped in and out of the thin layer of the last snowfall from a week ago. My feet were wet, soaked, and I clung to the cold, metal railing back down to the sidewalk.

Then I don't remember much except that I must have been aware enough of what was going on, what I was doing, that I took the most desolate path home, away from the main roads where there was the chance that anyone would see me.

My toes were numb, blanketed with layers of slush and snow as I walked half a step at a time through the empty park, along the edge of the playground where two swings swayed in the wind, past the icy public pool, down the white hill to the road less traveled than Main that intersects with Arbor Avenue.

My head...

I felt bald.

There was a cold breeze that should have been blowing my long locks around, but instead, it absorbed into my scalp like a freezing hair dryer close to the roots.

I couldn't think of what I looked like.

I had to block out any thoughts of what I would see...if I made it home...if I ever looked in a mirror again.

A jet passed overhead, its soaring engine sound high above all I could hear on the otherwise desolate suburban street I reached past the park. I wondered briefly about the people up on that plane, on their way to or from Philly, I imagine, some looking out their windows at the firefly twinkles of light far below in King's Valley and Reading and Wyomissing...having no idea that this fifteen-year-old boy was limping home in his underwear.

Some people still had their Christmas lights up.

Some rotted trees were lying dead at the ends of snowy driveways, glistening red and green tinsel entangled in the decaying branches.

Then all I remember is reaching Skyview Drive sometime later, struggling to hike up that steep incline to the pocket where my and Izzy's houses stand.

I noticed for the first time that my house hung ever so slightly higher than the rest, this monstrosity of capitalism looking down on the rest of the world at the end of the high cul-de-sac.

301

I ducked down behind the shrubberies at the bend of the road across from my driveway because I heard one of the garage doors opening, the sound of a car engine coming to life.

Dad's Cadillac came rolling back out of the driveway, the white reverse lights on as the sedan backed up. Very faintly, I could hear the crumpling sound of the tires rolling over compact snow outside the garage. The reverse lights clicked off, I heard a gear clicking, and the car came forward down the driveway. Its headlights were like eyes in the night as Mom and Dad left for their late flight to Seattle.

I waited for the car's red taillights to disappear down the street.

They couldn't see me…

I couldn't let them see me like this…

They wouldn't be home until Tuesday.

Dad had forgotten to press the button again to close the garage, and that heavenly light emanated from the door, shining against the brick wall that lines the driveway.

I started up the driveway, limping, my silhouette, as I can imagine, like that of a wounded warrior returning home from battle.

The house…it looked…for once…so inviting and warm. I had never been so happy to see it. I could've kissed the lawn jockey.

The electric lamps on either side of the garage came to life, revealing a layer of slush that resembled shaving gel against the glass.

Someone was in the house.

For a second, one terrifying second…I thought they beat me to it. Tyler Kirkland, Eric Gleason, and Adam Woolf had broken in, somehow got past my parents before they left. They were waiting for me inside, waiting so they could do more to me.

Maybe they would kill me.

302

I experienced quick, flashing visions of one of them hiding in the pantry as I walked into the kitchen, a butcher knife slashing my throat, and me being left to bleed to death on the kitchen floor. I imagined the horrible things they would do to my dead body and what they would leave for my parents to find when they came home. They would crucify my naked body to the front door or some sick shit...

But as I stepped into the nearly empty garage, the kitchen door swung open...and there stood Izzy.

He had been ready to greet me with his usual happy enthusiasm, apparently surprising me by sleeping over at my place. My parents trusted him enough now to let him be alone in their home.

But that smile, that smile that never fucking fails to make me happy...didn't last for a second.

I had to look down because I couldn't handle seeing his reaction to what I looked like, and then I found I had to close my eyes because in the light of the garage, I could see my legs and feet, all the blood, the red trail following me in from outside. Simultaneously, a warm stream started running down my leg. I pissed myself.

"Oh my God..."

Izzy's voice sounded...inhuman. It was as if his mother had come back to life for a few days, but then he found her dead again.

"Oh, God...Kier-an...Kier-an...what...ughhhh..."

He put his arms around me, and that was when I finally collapsed in a downpour of tears, uncontrollable crying.

"Oh...oh God...ughhh...what...who...who..."

I clung to his shoulders, limp like a dead body as he dragged me inside. His breathing was panicked, short, quick gasps that I never heard him make before.

"Kieran...who...oh my God...what...what happened?"

I couldn't speak. I just cried.

The TV was on far away, in the sunroom…muffled voices incoherent to my ringing ears. An audience was applauding.

…

"Izzy…"

I choked out his name while he held me in the middle of the family room, Larry running up and trying to sniff out who this unrecognizable human was.

I forced open my swollen eyes and quickly regretted it because Izzy, crying, hurt me more than what had happened to me.

"They…they…"

I was stopped by more uncontrollable sobs. The pain returned to my bloodied knees.

Blood…

So much blood on the carpet.

Izzy rushed across the room as he carried me toward the back stairs, my dangling feet bumping into the side of Dad's chess table, which sent most of the pieces crashing to the floor.

Izzy carried me up the stairs, one arm around my back and his hand curled into my chest, the other under my knees and holding my bent legs up while I rested my pounding head against his sternum.

I felt like a small child again; I remembered my dad carrying me to bed in the comfort of my soft pajamas and holding onto the Simba doll I dragged everywhere with me.

The walk to the bedroom was short, but in that brief time, my consciousness faded in and out again. I noticed my breathing changed; I wheezed. I sounded like a dying vacuum cleaner, an overweight man just finishing a marathon and on the verge of a heart attack.

We were upstairs now.

Izzy set me down on my parents' bed and I heard him running the bath in the next room.

The soft memory foam of the mattress and the darkness of the room made me sleepy. I was ready to sleep. I didn't want to be awake for this. I couldn't see Izzy crying. I couldn't take that.

I was lifted from the bed.

Izzy carried me into the bathroom. I kept my eyes closed, the blinding whiteness of the room too much for me to handle. My eyes were still in great pain, something so off about the way they felt.

"It's okay," I heard him say quickly. "It's okay…it's okay."

I was crying again. I don't think I ever really stopped crying from the moment I saw him in the garage; it just came in different sized waves that rolled up and down with the tide.

He helped me lean against the wall, pulled what was left of my ruined Stay Sweet shirt from my torso. It practically peeled away from my damp skin.

"Oh God…"

Izzy's whimpers at the sight of my body made me feel sick. I squeezed my eyes closed.

He sat me on the edge of the tub where I cried out in pain. Everything was sore…more than sore. Everything was broken.

He rolled the soaked socks from my feet.

My feet hurt and they were so cold. My toes felt like they were going to fall off.

When he assisted me in standing again, he helped me out of my boxers. My arms folded, I clutched my sides as I shivered.

Izzy picked me up again. I almost instinctively clung to him more tightly as if I were a recently hatched duckling meeting its mother for the first time. I needed him more than anything. He was all that could protect me.

I cracked my eyes open as I felt the hot water meet my backside. I opened them fully again, seeing the white, white ceiling and black skylights of the bathroom as he set me into the tub.

The water came crashing over my body, over my face, over what was left of my hair, and beneath the surface I sank...the shimmering, distorted image of Izzy on the other side of the water, looking down with that halo of light from the ceiling behind him.

The tub suddenly became massive, the water much deeper than it should have been. I was descending further and further into a pool, and then an ocean...the light was fading away.

Izzy was disappearing.

Soon after, the water turned red...and black...the thundering sound of the water filling the tub disappearing...replaced by the echoing laughs of Tyler, Eric, and Adam...Dad telling me he loved me...Matt Daniels singing "Under My Sheets"...Izzy begging me to fuck him...Justin's scream...the splash of his car falling into King's Lake...

I was in the lake...sinking...deeper and deeper into that black abyss...drowning with Justin...his body floating past me, lifeless...

...

I was joining him in his grave.

...

Sinking.

...

Sinking.

...

Then I remember nothing.

...

I remember nothing.

…

That was when the whole world shut off.

Tristan LaFerriere

Chapter Fifteen
Tuesday, January 30th, 2007

Dear Journal,

Yesterday morning is when I came to, or at least when I remember coming to.

"Kieran?"

...

I was in my parents' bed.

Izzy was sitting on the edge of it, looking directly into my eyes. Behind him, on TV, contestants were bidding on an item on *The Price is Right.*

Late morning sunlight fell into the room from the open curtains of the front windows. Larry was sitting on the bed, too, at my feet where he was curled up in a sleepy ball.

Then I remembered what happened to me…but Izzy looked okay, and that was all I cared about.

"Izzy," I said slowly and hoarsely. My mouth was incredibly dry.

He forced a smile, but already he was starting to tear up.

"Kieran," he said, and reached his hand out to brush my hair.

My hair…oh God…it was all fucking gone, most of it…

None of us said anything for a little while. The TV went to a commercial break, and while elderly actors spoke of how their mobility scooters changed their lives, I tried to sit up. I groaned when a sharp pain in my ribs knocked the wind out of me.

"It's okay," Izzy said gently. He put a hand on my shoulder and assisted me into a sitting position. "You're okay. You're okay. You're okay."

308

I managed to look down. My eyes hurt when I moved them.

I was dressed in an oversized plain white t-shirt that smelled like it was fresh out of the packaging. I couldn't see under the covers, but I knew I was wearing a fresh pair of boxers. My sore feet rested at the edge of the bed, protected by the blankets, too. Izzy had apparently slipped them into fresh socks.

Izzy let out a deep sigh that sounded like it meant relief, but he closed his eyes tightly for a few seconds.

I hated seeing him like this. Seeing Izzy in such a serious, concerned tone made me uneasy and confused. There was something so uncanny about it.

"I was so fucking worried about you," he said through tears. "I didn't know what to do."

"Why..." I swallowed. "Why didn't you...take me to the hospital?"

"I was going to. You begged me not to."

I felt a drop in the pit of my stomach. What the fuck was going on in my brain that I couldn't remember?

"What?"

Izzy let out another deep sigh.

"I cleaned you up in the tub and told you I was gonna take you to the hospital, but you kept saying you couldn't go because they were gonna hurt you again if you left the house. You were...screaming at me not to take you anywhere. You were...you were going crazy."

...

"I said that?"

"Yeah. I wanted to call the police, but..."

He looked away, obviously crying now.

309

"I didn't even know what happened," he continued. "I was just...I was just waiting for you to wake up. You went out for so long..."

"How long was I out?"

"It's Monday morning."

"Monday?"

"I called us both out."

"How...how did you...?"

"I can do a pretty good impression of my dad."

"But...what about...me..."

"I called back, like, twenty minutes later...said I was Darren Northrup." He shrugged. "I don't know...I guess they bought it."

Helps when the average age of the school secretaries is about ninety...

I took his hand.

"Izzy..."

"Please...tell me what happened. Who did this to you?"

With hesitation, I told him everything that I could remember. I told him how Adam picked me up, we went to The Skate Park, it was dark, I drank something, things got hazy. I was dragged out of there, he drove me to King's Valley Park and...God, I don't think I can write that shit down again.

When I was done with my story, Izzy looked broken. I expected him to break down crying again, but he almost immediately had a response.

"We have to call the fucking cops," he said.

I shook my head.

"Kieran!"

It was the first time I saw him get annoyed with me in the slightest. It startled me.

"We can't," I said.

"They assaulted you!"

"They'll retaliate," I said. "And my parents...they can't know about this."

"Kieran..."

"They can't...this would *kill* them...they can't handle another..."

I stalled, looking toward the windows. I remembered my dad trying to get through to Uncle Ryan on the phone all those months ago. I remembered his tears and how shattered he sounded. And my mom...sitting on Justin's bed with tears in her eyes as she brought his old shirt close to her face.

"I can't put them through this," I finally said. "I just...I can't.

"Kieran..."

"I can't!" I snorted, crying. "I just have to...stay away from them." [The thought of even seeing any of their faces again at school made me sick]. "They'll...they'll be gone in June. I just...I just have to wait. They'll...they'll be gone."

Izzy just looked down for a long time. I think the TV went through at least two more commercial breaks. The contestants on *The Price is Right* were spinning the big wheel by the time he finally looked back at me. The tears were dried, and he looked more neutral than I think I've ever seen him. He didn't look happy, he didn't look sad, he didn't look angry. It looked like there was nothing in there.

"I really think you should rethink this," he said.

I didn't say anything.

"But," he continued. "When are they coming back?"

"When is who coming back?"

"When are your parents coming back from Seattle?"

"You said it's Monday?"

He nodded.

"Tomorrow night."

Izzy bit his lip.

"They're gonna see you like this, Kieran. You have bruises all over your face. You're swollen. Your hair…"

Like it was a magic word, he immediately started crying when he mentioned my hair, and I mean really crying. He buried his face into those two skinny hands.

I reached out to touch his arm with my right hand…which he took…and then he hugged me closely for a long, long time.

When he broke the hug, he sniffled and stood up suddenly. Without warning, I watched as he brought a fist down against the end table.

"God…fucking…DAMN them!" he screamed.

Larry scurried away from the bed as Mom and Dad's bedside phone crashed to the floor, the cordless receiver's batteries rolling away as it smashed to pieces.

I closed my eyes with a sob. I was truly frightened of his reaction.

…

I stayed in bed for the rest of the day except for the few times I got up to go to the bathroom. Izzy told me that while I was passed out, he worked at putting the house back together, cleaning up any blood

from the family room carpet, replacing the chess pieces in their respective places, ensuring that the garage floor was washed clear of my blood and piss. Several towels were ruined with blood stains when he attempted to clean me up, and they, along with the clothes I had been wearing, were tossed in the trash.

Izzy went out to Turkey Hill in the afternoon to get us both hot dogs. He brought them to me while the TV continued with its insufferable schedule of daytime programming I've only ever seen in the summer or when I'm home sick from school. After a full hour of contestants guessing the prices of recliners and dinette sets on *The Price is Right*, it was Brad and JT discussing JT's recent breakup on *The Young and the Restless*, and the announcer at 1 pm telling us:

"Like sands through the hourglass, so are the days of our lives."

Izzy tried to cheer me up by telling me that Kody was working at Turkey Hill when he was there.

"He got a haircut," Izzy said, watching me slowly eat my hot dog while we shared fries. Crumbs and ketchup were all over the bedspread.

"Is he still cute?" I asked.

"Oh, yeah."

. . .

"Does it look really bad?"

"What?" Izzy asked.

I just looked at him and he still responded. He knew what I meant.

"No, buddy." He ran a hand across my head, brushing the remains of what used to be my best feature. "No. You're still so, so handsome."

"I'm sure," I scoffed.

"You are!"

...

"Let me see."

Izzy finished his hot dog, left the room for a minute, and returned from my parents' bathroom with a handheld mirror. He handed it to me, and my hand trembled as I prepared to look at myself.

...

I was surprised to see my hair hadn't been cut nearly as short as it felt. I guess that from being used to having it so long for such a long time, it just felt weird having it be what most would consider a "normal boy cut."

Tyler, Eric, and Adam really did do a number on it, though. My hair, which hadn't been even trimmed a millimeter since before we moved, had been well past my shoulders. The dye had mostly faded, but the black still existed at the tips, and this was enough to make the illusion that I was more dark-haired than I appeared.

Now my hair was so boringly cropped, only its natural color left [the brown with its red tint, or *chestnut*, I suppose]. This was any basic haircut my mother would have taken me to the salon to get when I was twelve, when she would tell the stylist, Cynthia, to just give me the "usual trim." Those were the days before I insisted on growing it out...so I could look like Matt Daniels...the days before I successfully hid what I thought to be my ugly face from the world.

I couldn't hide it now. My bangs were nonexistent. I just looked like an average boy, my eyes unprotected and exposed...and my eyes...

I remembered something funny from my childhood that for some reason has stuck with me all the way until now. Justin and I used to play *Donkey Kong Country* frequently on our Super Nintendo when we lived back in California. I loved that game, but there was always a sense of nervousness in me when we played. If Donkey or Diddy Kong managed to fall off a cliff too many times or get stung by one of those deadly bees that were planted all over the game [even in the ice cave

levels], that counter of lives would get shorter and shorter, and soon I knew that "game over" screen would appear.

I would dart from the room in fear because I hated it. Whoever designed the game thought it would be a good idea to freak all the kids out who would play it because when you lost all your lives, Donkey and Diddy Kong would appear in a still shot of animation with the words *"Game Over"* crowning their horrid appearance. They had been badly beaten by their enemies, their eyes swollen purple and shut, their faces covered with bandages as they stared through the screen at you, the player, as if to remind you of how badly you fucked up.

This is what I looked like.

My eyes...my blue-green eyes were blue around the edges, too. It looked as though a bee had stung me at each eye and I had come down with a mild allergic reaction. Something was so comical about how cliched I looked after being assaulted. The animations in cartoons and video games of characters having black eyes weren't really all that unreal. That's what I fucking looked like.

My lip was purple at the top, near that little reservoir leading up to my nose. I pressed a finger to the bulging skin and felt a nerve stir angrily.

"My God..." I said, noticing how I didn't look terrified or even necessarily gory, but just...sad. I looked sad. I looked disappointed that I had been beaten up. I looked sad that my hair was cut and now I just looked like your average, boring, basic boy.

I put the mirror down and stared at the underside of it for a while, all the little scratches and pitted gouges in the black plastic from having been stuffed in the bathroom drawer with other toiletries and beauty tools.

"It's gonna be okay," Izzy said.

"I look terrible."

"No, you don't."

"My hair's gone."

"It'll grow back, buddy."

"My face…"

"It'll heal."

"It fucking hurts."

Izzy shook his head. He looked sick suddenly, like he might throw up.

"We have to get you to a hospital."

"No!"

Izzy was startled by my harshness. I had really screamed when he suggested I see a doctor. Apparently, even in my subconscious speech, I was consistent. I didn't want any authority figure to know what had happened to me because that would mean Mom and Dad would find out…the police…I couldn't put my parents through shit like that. It would've been bad enough if that happened to me under any normal circumstances, but less than six months after Justin died? I just couldn't do that to them. And that's probably how Mom would find out I'm gay. I'd have to testify that this was a hate crime and then…

That's not how I wanted it to be. I wanted to come out to her the way I wanted to. I wanted to be able to have a sit-down with her like I did with Dad and have it all be okay after we hugged it out or something. I didn't want her to find out I was gay because a few jocks decided to piss and jerk off in my face and leave me for dead on the bleachers of the park in the middle of the night. I couldn't let those bastards take that away from me. I couldn't let them win. If anything, this was all I had left. It was all I had control of. I couldn't give that up.

Izzy was crying again. His tears were plopping down on the bedspread.

I took his hand like he was the one who needed taking care of.

"It'll be okay," I said, wincing from the pain in my groin and ribs. "It'll be okay."

Izzy looked up at me, those painted eyes glistening with tears like brown crystal marbles just polished.

I found Izzy's weakness. I found what breaks him.

Seeing me broken is what breaks him.

...

Izzy went out to Burger King to get us dinner. I slept for most of the afternoon, and when I woke up, I was relieved to find that I wasn't quite as sore anymore. The smell of the broiled burgers in the brown bags actually stirred me, woke me up. It smelled so fucking delicious.

"Here you go," Izzy said, pulling out two Whoppers and setting down two large drinks on the "breakfast in bed" tray I had been using all day for eating and writing.

"Thanks."

I unwrapped my Whopper and took in the amazing scent of it. Izzy had just reheated it in the microwave and it was still steaming. Who knew food would snap me out of feeling so bad [sometimes I wonder how I've managed to stay so skinny], but I guess after eating only a banana and a few crackers here and there that Izzy had apparently fed me when I was practically catatonic for a couple of days, I was desperate to scarf down as much junk as I could. The scent of the burger was like smelling salts to my malnourished body.

While we passively watched an episode of *The Sopranos*, Izzy turned to me. He had hardly taken a bite out of his Whopper, but the Dr. Pepper was nearly empty. This was also when I noticed that his shirt smelled of cigarette smoke.

"Why?" Izzy asked.

...

"What?"

"Why? *Why* did they do it?"

317

I swallowed the chewed clump of ground beef, lettuce, ketchup, mayo, and strips of onions.

…

"I don't know," I said after a while. "But…according to me…the entry I…apparently wrote…"

I remembered Adam's words buried somewhere in my brain. I probably wouldn't have remembered if it hadn't been for what I wrote down in my dazed state.

"Look at what you fucking did, Kieran."

"This is for Justin, you fucking faggot!"

…

"They blame me for my brother dying," I said, a disappointed tone in my voice. "They think it's my fault."

Izzy's face, if possible, turned an even whiter shade of pale. His eyebrows moved into a position that suggested anger.

"No," he said, shaking his head. "No…that's…"

"Ridiculous?" I chuckled. "Fucked up?" I shook my head, too, and took a sip of my drink to cool my head. "It doesn't surprise me anymore. That just about sums up this fucking world."

"But why would they blame you for his death?"

"Because I made him go to the mall that night to get that CD."

"What CD?"

It suddenly occurred to me that all the time Izzy and I have spent together, all of the secrets we've shared with each other, all of the intimacy…and I had never gone into full detail about the accident with him. I'd never described the circumstances surrounding it. All he knew was that Justin drowned and I had successfully escaped the car with my long-lasting bruises.

"Mandragora," I said. "The night it was released...I..."

My eyes fixated on the TV, a commercial break advertising Cingular Wireless. A Hallmark commercial followed, Josh Groban's latest CD release available in their stores just in time for lovers on February 14th.

I started crying.

"I made him take me to get it and, on our way back home...that's when he..."

I buried my face into my hands and sobbed.

"That's when he crashed..."

Izzy didn't brush my hair or touch my arm like he normally would to comfort me. He just hugged me. I could feel his tears soaking my shoulder.

"It's not your fault," he said, his voice quivering. "It's not your fault."

I whimpered before he finished his thought.

"And fuck them for putting that shit in your head," he added. "Fuck them."

By now, night had long since fallen. My parents' bedroom was no longer lit by the natural glow of the sun from the windows, but the warm lamp light.

Justin...

What would he have thought of this?

Would this have been it?

Would this have finally been the last straw?

Would he have finally taken my side over theirs if he saw what they had fucking done to me?

Izzy stared at me for a long while. I diverted my eyes to prevent having to see any more expressions of pain inside him. I had noticed that the scruff of his chin was more filled out than usual. His facial hair was starting to grow in, and it made me wonder if he hadn't bothered to shave since what had happened to me.

"Kieran," he said after a long time.

I didn't say anything, but looked back at him as if to answer.

"Wait here," he said. "I'll be right back, okay?"

"Where are you going?"

I almost felt like instantly crying, like being separated from him now would be too much for me. It reminded me of that home video of baby Izzy crying out and reaching for Mr. Murraro when he started to walk away.

"Just to my house," he said, standing alongside the bed next to me. "I'll just be, like, five minutes, okay?"

…

"Okay."

He forced another smile and left the room. I listened to his footsteps go down the stairs and out the front door.

The next few minutes just never ended. I couldn't stand being alone with nothing to focus on except for the traumatizing flashes of memory from the night I was assaulted.

I hate being alone with my thoughts.

I sighed with relief when I heard the front door open. Izzy came in the room a moment later and started to walk slowly toward the bed where Larry was now fast asleep beside me. He smiled again as he climbed back on the mattress with me, and finally, this time, it felt real when he looked ever so slightly happy. I could smell fresh cigarette smoke again.

"You want to mute that?" he asked, nodding toward the remote sitting on the bedside table.

I reached over, shut the TV off, and Izzy started to brush what was left of my hair with his hand.

"I have something I want to give you," he said, and he started to reach into his jacket pocket.

I wasn't sure what the thing was that he raised up in front of me, this gold necklace-like object with a pendant of a symbol I didn't really recognize at the end. It appeared to be old [when I say old, I really just mean from, like, the '70s or '80s, but definitely not something recently purchased. It had a worn, slightly tarnished appearance that suggested it had already been through years of use].

"What is it?" I asked.

Izzy was already starting to cry again. It appeared difficult for him to get the words out as his eyes watered up. He still looked happy as he cried this time, though. He didn't look sad or hurt.

"This was my mom's Chai," he said softly, marveling over the pendant like he was seeing it for the first time, too. "It's a Jewish amulet...this is in Hebrew."

He brushed the symbol with his thumb.

"My parents were never really religious," he continued. "I mean, my mom didn't even care about celebrating Hanukah. We always just did Christmas because she *loved* Christmas, but...she did tell me and my brother things about Judaism and she liked to carry on some of the traditions her family did. Being Jewish was more about family to her than it was about God." He looked real serious as he held the necklace up. "In Hebrew, this means 'life.'"

He looked down for a second and snorted as tears dropped from his eyes.

"When she was dying in the hospital, she took it off and gave it to me," he said as he cried. "And..."

He drifted off for a moment, wiping away more tears with his arm. His body was shivering.

"And…one of the last things she said to me was to wear this and…if I did, I'd always know she was still here with me…to protect me."

I started crying, too. I don't think I've ever cried so much in one day before. I buried my face in my hands as I felt Izzy begin to slip the chain around my neck. As soon as I felt the pendant rest against my chest, Izzy grabbed one of my hands tightly and brought his face very close to mine. I looked up at him.

"I want you to wear it," he said. "I want to protect you."

I tightened my grip on his hand, returning the gesture as if I were returning a hug. I was shivering now, too.

"As long as you wear it….no matter where I am…"

He finished off the sentence in a whisper.

"I'll protect you."

…

After midnight, the two of us were cuddled up close to each other, buried underneath several layers of blankets, the sheets, and the bedspread. Larry was still with us, too, his soft fur in between us.

The room was dark and quiet with only the occasional distant sound of a car passing somewhere, the furnace kicking on, or the deep chimes of the grandfather clock downstairs. With my parents away and Mr. Murraro gone for another visit to Brooklyn, the two of us were the only occupants of the entire cul-de-sac. This was our private world, and thinking about it more made me feel more comfortable. No matter how damaged I was, I was at least in Izzy's arms.

My parents' alarm clock was showing 2:50 am when I heard Izzy sigh, his body stirring and causing Larry to move as well.

Outside, it was another windy night. Shutters were rattling, tree branches casting creepy shadows against the bedroom walls as they were thrown against the window.

Three more deep chimes echoed from downstairs. I pictured the face of that clock, that painted moon with its creepy smile arched high above the hands as we moved into the early, dark hours of the cold morning.

...

"Izzy?" I said, on the verge of falling asleep again. "You're awake?"

"I can't sleep," he said dully.

I didn't know what to say. I just stared over at the digital clock, watching the glowing red numbers.

"What are you thinking about?" I asked.

I expected another long pause, but he responded immediately.

"How I want to take you downstairs," he said. "Get in my car and drive us both away from this place. Forever."

Because he was spooning me from behind, his arm draped over my chest, I took his hand, kissed his fingers, and held on to his hand tightly. I began to drift off to sleep again rather quickly, feeling the cold of his mother's Chai that he had put around my neck.

Izzy's fingers were cold, too.

Dead cold.

Chapter Sixteen
Saturday, March 24th, 2007

Dear Journal,

I can't believe how long it's been since I last wrote something. It's a fairly uneventful night, so I decided I had to get back into my old habit of making a decent number of entries before the muscle memory of it completely vanished. I don't want the only entries I ever logged into this beautiful journal my dad bought me to be all about the worst things that have ever happened to me, so I'm just hopeful that something good will happen soon enough.

I've been so fucking preoccupied lately. The rest of the winter was this constant challenge…kind of like a real-life game of chess where every move I made had to be carefully planned out to satisfy myself and everyone else at the same time. There were so many strategies I had to master to hide, to keep my stories straight, to make my lies convincing and consistent.

The first few weeks after the assault were the hardest. I *did* go back to school, on January 30th, which was the Tuesday my parents returned from Seattle with a whole novel of news about my Uncle Ryan and what had become of him. I'll get to that stuff later.

Izzy drove me to a nearby Eckerd Pharmacy early that morning. I wore a plain white t-shirt I usually sleep in, jeans, and an oversized gray hoodie that used to belong to my brother with the hood up so that I wouldn't stand out in the slightest…all while wearing my Ray-Bans to hide the black eyes and scars.

At the drugstore, we picked up some concealer. It took a good fifteen minutes to get just the right shade. I had to hold my wrist up to the little tubes of makeup and we finally decided on one that seemed close enough to my pale, almost pink complexion.

While walking to the register, we passed the wall of boxed hair dye, all the faces of fashionable women with different shades of locks staring at us while I felt a tear forming in my eye. Izzy grabbed a bottle of Dr. Pepper from a cooler at the front and paid for the stuff.

We hopped back in the Alfa and Izzy drove over to this abandoned shopping center in the "less desirable" part of town where

we were the only car in the center of the huge, empty lot. About a football field's length away, cars were lining up at the drive-thru of a still operating, but outdated McDonald's for morning coffees. Otherwise, though, we were the only souls in sight of the desolate area.

I noticed everything looked gray: the overcast sky of mid-winter, the pothole-infested blacktop of the parking lot, the moldy smudges formed over the former Ames department store location's exterior walls that overtime have gotten dirtier and dirtier. A building that obviously used to be a Pizza Hut had been painted over, in gray, for whatever the latest business that had taken over the location had been before it closed down to the empty structure it is now.

I hate this time of year, and especially now that I'm living in a state that experiences all four seasons. I've discovered that in the Northeast, the few months between the December holidays and the beginning of spring, drag on in this drab, depressing period of nothingness. The skies are always gray, it's cold, and there's hardly anything at all to look forward to until spring break comes around. There are no special events, no exciting holidays, no movie releases worth going to the theater to see. At least in Los Angeles, I could still go to the beach this time of year if I wanted to. Even though I've never been big on lying out in the sun, the warm weather just naturally makes me feel better. I think that's why I especially hated the weeks following my assault. There was nothing in sight that could comfort me. I was trapped in King's Valley like it was this limbo between winter and spring.

Izzy applied the concealer to my face to hide the bruises while we were parked in that open lot.

"Does it look okay?" I asked, my eyes closed while the cold, wet makeup was brushed on.

"So far, so good," he said, but not entirely convincingly. "We just have to hope that when it dries, it still blends in."

"What if it doesn't?"

"Then I guess you'll look like you have a bunch of birthmarks on your face."

This managed to get a slight chuckle out of both of us.

325

It felt like we were in the car for an hour. By this time, we were a little less than twenty minutes away from the start of homeroom, and all the windows had fogged up. I examined myself in the passenger side vanity mirror, shrugged, and put my Ray-Bans back on.

"Thanks," I said. "I just hope no one will notice."

"I think it'll be okay," he said. He fired up the engine and took a sip of his Dr. Pepper, Izzy's substitute for morning coffee. "Just...go to the bathroom between classes to check on it."

I rested back in the seat, sighing. This was fucking exhausting.

When we got to the school, Izzy parked in a space as far away from the building as possible. We were in a corner at the southeastern-most section of the parking lot that was on the border of a chain-link fence separating the property from the inclining hill leading down to backyards of suburban homes on Carlton. I asked Izzy to park here because it would be further away from most people, and I wanted to keep my distance from any crowds with the chance I might run into one of...them...

We got out of the car and started walking at a slightly quick pace to the building. We would have been late for homeroom if we walked any slower, and that would have risked having us being sent to the office for a pass that would only make chances of my wounds being seen even higher.

"You'll be fine," Izzy said between breaths as we neared the main entrance. "Just...act normal. Don't draw any attention to yourself."

"I mean...I never do."

Out of breath, we stopped just before the glass doors leading to the atrium lobby. There were a few students inside, but most of the crowd was gone as homeroom period approached in just minutes.

Izzy looked through the glass and then at me where he gave me a little smile before he put a hand on my shoulder.

"I'll see you at lunch, okay?"

I nodded, he hugged me quickly, and we went our separate ways once we walked inside.

…

I couldn't concentrate at all in any of my classes. Trying to keep my head down as much as I could without drawing attention to myself was fucking hard, so I tried to act all absorbed in my work even though I was just scribbling nonsense in my notebooks. I prayed that it wouldn't be one of the days where Dr. Meller decided to schedule a surprise follow-up to see how Izzy was doing as my peer. At our past meetings, I simply told her he was doing an excellent job and that things were much better without adding that our peer meetings had morphed into us hooking up in whatever empty classroom we were assigned.

…

"Your hair!" Athena cried when we met her and Thomas at lunch. "Kieran! What happened to it?!"

I laughed nervously, Izzy and I sitting down with them in our usual spot. I had been dreading this moment. I could hide from just about everyone except these two. They'd easily be able to tell something was up.

Since I wasn't in class, I stuck my Ray-Bans on and put my hood up in hopes that no teachers observing the halls would notice, but it was still obvious that my hair wasn't what it used to be. Normally, even with my hood up, it would come sprawling out around the sides of my face.

"Yeah," I said, feeling my blood pressure go up with the anticipation of a coming lie. "My mom made me get it cut. She said it was getting too long."

"That's fucking bullshit!" Athena said. "Your hair was so nice long."

…

"Yeah. I know."

"What's with the sunglasses, Northrup?" Thomas interrupted before I could lie again.

"My eyes are red," I said. I had an explanation for everything lined up, but I foolishly hadn't thought them all through as well as I should have.

Thomas and Athena looked at me strangely. Izzy looked down at his sandwich and I thought that even if I looked okay, his sudden change in personality would have tipped them off that something was wrong. Izzy was never this quiet.

"Why?" Athena asked. "Did you, like, smoke weed?"

I almost denied it, but this seemed to be a great opportunity to finish my story that still didn't have a convincing ending.

"Yeah," I said, putting my head down and forcing out a fake embarrassed laugh. "I did."

"What?!"

Athena was laughing so hard that a couple of preppy girls walking by glanced at us.

"Wait...what? Are you serious?"

"Yeah," Izzy said before I could continue the lie. "We both smoked on Friday."

He looked to me as if to be reassured that this fib sounded good enough.

"Yeah," I said, and then finished the lie for him. "We, uh, got *really* fucking high and...well, we passed out in my room and didn't wake up until Sunday morning."

Thomas and Athena stared at us. Athena looked pleasantly surprised. Thomas looked skeptical.

"And your eyes are *still* red?" Thomas asked.

"Yyy-yeah," I said. "It's fucking weird. I don't know."

"I smoked a couple times before," Athena went on. "Alyssa and I got weed from Kody Kurtz. You know him? He works at Turkey Hill. I think he graduated last year."

"Yeah," Izzy said. "He's...who we got it from, too."

"Just be careful. Sometimes he's sketchy. Alyssa swears that one time, the dime bag she got from him was laced with acid or something. She was tripping for hours." She looked at me. "That's so weird your eyes are still red, though."

"I...guess I'm just not used to it."

Thomas continued to study me. He knew we were full of shit. He was smart...and we were terrible fucking liars.

...

I pretended to have forgotten my gym clothes for the rest of that week so I could avoid class. Instead, I decided taking zero credit for four days and sitting on the auxiliary gym bleachers with all the other slackers would be safer. I could at least keep my hood up and my sunglasses on without being noticed, and it gave me time to re-apply some of the concealer in the bathroom.

I also didn't want to see Adam. If I saw him, I might've puked.

If I saw any of them, I probably would've gotten sick, and besides trying to hide my new appearance, putting my head down in the halls also served as a way of avoiding eye contact with Tyler or Eric or Adam possibly passing by. I think at this point, even seeing Evan or Melissa Grandstaff would make me feel sick.

I fucking hate them all.

...

I was sitting in the sunroom in my house, dozing off that night, while I half-watched some old Katharine Hepburn movie on AMC. I ended up putting *Nitro* in my Walkman and listened to Stay

Sweet while I faded in and out of sleep on the couch, a blanket that my grandmother knitted draped over me. Luckily, the CD ended at just the right time because shortly after is when I heard Dad's Cadillac coming up the driveway. Larry had been sitting on my lap and I must've scared the shit out of him because I jumped up from the couch so fast I nearly tripped.

TV off.

Lights in the sunroom off.

Kitchen lights off.

Deck lights off.

I ran up the back stairs to my room, slammed the door, undressed, and jumped into bed just as I could hear Mom and Dad coming in through the kitchen downstairs.

I prayed they wouldn't check in on me. I had no concealer on.

…

Movement downstairs.

…

The fridge door closing.

Footsteps across the tiled floor.

…

Muffled voices.

…

The jingling of keys being tossed on the counter.

I squeezed my eyes shut.

Please don't come in my room. Please…

Five minutes felt like five hours.

…

Footsteps coming up the stairs.

…

The footsteps grew louder and louder until they reached a climax.

…

Nothing.

The door to the master bedroom opening and closing.

…

A long pause.

…

"From New York, the greatest city in the world...it's Late Show with David Letterman!"

I sighed with relief...for now, but still cried silently into my pillow while I clasped the Chai pendant Izzy gave me. The chain was cold on my bare chest, but it made me feel better. Recently, any time that I'm not with Izzy is torture, and this really does make me feel like he's always beside me.

I kissed the Chai pendant and rolled over on my side to try sleeping.

…

To avoid my parents for at least the next few days, I set my alarm early to slip out of the house before they would wake up, and in the evenings, I spent the nights at Izzy's house. Since the night I came out to my dad, he's about as easygoing as can be now, so I communicated with him via text, packed a bag, and basically spent the

rest of that week living in Izzy's basement while I waited for my face to heal enough so that I didn't look like a fucking Halloween prop.

It felt like I was a fugitive being hidden by the Murraro family. Izzy's dad would cook dinner, Izzy would bring it down for me, and I'd eat with him in the basement without ever seeing his dad. Izzy's explanation to Mr. Murraro for the reason I didn't want to be seen was because I had fallen down the stairs at home and gave myself a black eye, which I was very self-conscious about [the lies just kept piling up and up and up and they got stupider and stupider].

It almost seemed too easy. How were we getting away with this? How was it that nobody really looked at my face for a whole week? Is that how little people noticed me in the first place? I couldn't believe how little trouble I had with getting past my own parents and making sure they didn't look at me for as long as I was able to avoid them.

By that Saturday, three nights spent at Izzy's, four skipped gym classes, and probably over a hundred applications of concealer later, my eyes were finally back to normal in that at least they weren't swollen anymore. My face had gone back to its usual shape and structure, but the bruises beneath my eyes still lingered even though they had faded significantly. I could get away with going out in public without the sunglasses on at all now and just hope that the makeup would be enough to cover up any obvious marks.

It was perfect timing, really, because this was the night that Athena invited Izzy and I to join her and Thomas for bowling. After receiving the group text from her, Izzy and I, sitting in his basement, decided it would be safe enough to go out. I just needed a fresh coat of concealer, and as long as I played it cool, nothing would be obvious. The bowling alley, after all, was a dark place. The makeup wouldn't be noticeable.

We were quiet on the drive over after another application of concealer. I looked over at Izzy, behind the wheel of the car with this...I don't know...blank expression as he stared forward. We weren't even listening to any music which was so rare for any drive with him.

He wasn't Izzy anymore.

"What are you thinking about?" I finally asked him.

He looked at me for a second and then directed his eyes back to the road, the exit for Route 222.

"What?"

"What are you thinking about?"

He didn't respond for so long that I thought maybe he wasn't going to, but as we drove along the highway, he sighed.

"This is just crazy."

"…I know."

"No," he said, and he was digging for his pack of Camels. "*This. This* is fucking crazy."

He pulled a cigarette from the pack, stuck it in his mouth, and grabbed his lighter from the dashboard. His hand trembled as he lit the cigarette and then tossed the lighter angrily back on the dash. I cowered in my seat, seeing a side of him I never wanted to see.

"What do you mean?" I asked, not sure if I knew the answer and was just digging for more, or if I truly didn't understand what he was trying to say.

He exhaled a puff of smoke out the cracked window.

"We can't hide this shit forever," he said. "We have to go to the police, Kieran. We have to tell your parents. They're gonna find out."

"I can't do that to them."

"You know how hard you told me it was for you to come out to your dad?"

"…Yeah."

"Because you let it build up for so long, right?"

"...Yeah."

He took another drag.

"But when you *did* come out to him, you felt better, right?"

"Well...yeah, I mean...because he took it well. I don't think..."

"Of course he isn't going to take this well." He was able to finish all my sentences. He knew me so well by now we were practically the same person. "You were *assaulted*, Kieran. No good parent should ever take that news well if it happens to their kid...but you *have* to tell them. They can't get away with this."

The cigarette was still stuck in his mouth, glowing orange at the tip and a light string of smoke escaping from it. He was putting no effort into smoking it. It was just there. Tears were in his eyes, but he looked more pissed off than sad.

He grabbed the cigarette with two fingers and jammed its remains, most of it, into the ashtray where it disintegrated into a cloud of embers. He was still shaking, and there was even a hint of a stutter in his voice when he spoke again.

"They can't fucking get away with this."

He was crying.

I turned and looked out my window, at the other headlights and taillights around us on the highway, the same stretch of road where I spent my last few minutes with Justin almost six months before.

A few minutes later, we were pulling into the lot of King Pin Lanes from the busy avenue it faces, the local bowling alley that's really more of a bar. The music is always pumped up super loud, the lights are always down low, and rather than experienced, professional bowlers serious about getting a decent score, it's just a bunch of drunk people laughing as they toss their balls straight down the gutter and then hurry back to their table to finish off their margaritas and nachos.

I had been there once before...with Justin...at the end of June. It had to have been only a few days after we moved in. The house was

still a mess of unpacked boxes, the pool hadn't been dug yet, the kitchen appliances were still draped with cohesive, peel-away transparent plastic, and my brother didn't even know anyone in town yet. This was before he met Eric at The Skate Park and before he decided I wasn't his best friend anymore, but an embarrassment to his image.

We bowled a few games that night in June, shared a plate of nachos, and actually had a decent time. I was being emo as hell, of course, focusing on the fact that we left California and how much I hated this new place, but it was one of those nights when Justin was really nice to me. I remember him clapping for me when I got a strike or a spare, remember him giving me a high-five, taking me to Rita's for an Italian ice afterward and us both sitting in the car enjoying our treat while we listened to the station that played Van Halen and The Cars…before all the music from the "Tyler Kirkland crowd" took over his playlist.

Izzy parked far enough away from the entrance that I assumed was because he was going to check how my concealer looked before we went in, but after he shut off the car, he just sat there, staring ahead at the beige wall of the building with its cracks and chipped chunks of stucco while a Kiss song pumped at top volume from inside.

Izzy and I have shared a great number of comfortable silences together since I met him, but this ever-growing number of uncomfortable silences was beginning to kill me. I was always waiting for him to break the quiet with whatever he wanted to say of what was on his mind, but that never seemed to happen quick enough for me to be comfortable, so I'd always intercept with something…something that I was afraid to say because I didn't want it to be the wrong thing. I didn't want it to be something that upset him. I had seen him so upset in the past week so many times that it was sadly starting to become normal. I was becoming numb to the idea of seeing Izzy crying. That's something I never thought was possible.

…

"I, uh…I really don't want to go in there," I said.

"Me neither," Izzy said, his hands resting on the bottom of the steering wheel limply like a sloth's claws dangling from a tree branch.

335

Quiet. More uncomfortable silence between the two of us.

I looked out the window at a couple in their 20s, laughing drunkenly as they left the building. Behind them, a lanky guy with glasses who was probably their designated driver followed. On the steps leading up to the bowling alley's entrance was a short and slightly chubby girl who looked a few years older than me, cell phone in one hand and a lit cigarette in the other while she texted someone.

Inside, the roaring music changed to "Slow Ride" by Foghat.

"I should've taken you to the hospital that night," Izzy said.

Long pause. My stomach dropped.

"You could've died."

"I told you not to."

"And I shouldn't have listened to you."

He let out a deep sigh and then took in a deep breath like he was trying to control an oncoming panic attack.

Izzy having a panic attack? I had to be fucking dreaming.

"I'm a bad friend."

This startled me.

"What...?"

"I'm a bad friend." He was crying again, burying his face into his hands and the muffled words, still audible enough, made me start to cry, too. "I'm such a bad friend."

I unhooked my seatbelt and took him in my arms.

"Shhhh," I said. "It's okay. It's not your fault."

"You could've died," he said again, between sobs. "And it would've been my fault."

"No," I said. "None of it's your fault. None of it. You're my best friend."

He cried and cried while I held him, trying to reassure him over and over again that he didn't do anything wrong. He felt like such a baby in my arms as he whimpered. Suddenly, I felt so much bigger than him. His skinny body felt so fragile as he trembled with tears.

"Don't cry, baby," I said softly, patting his head. "It's okay."

"I hate everything right now," he cried. "I hate everything."

…

"I love you, Izzy."

He clung to me tighter after I said that.

"I love you, too, Kieran."

"No," I said. "I mean, I *really* love you. Like…"

I swallowed hard, still holding him. We had both gotten our crying under control enough, but the two of us were soaked from our sticky tears.

"Like," I continued. "I'm…I'm *in* love with you. I want you to be my boyfriend."

Izzy took my hand and we watched as a light dusting of snow, the last snowfall of the season, on February 2nd, powdered down onto the car and around the parking lot of the bowling alley. Strains of classic rock continued to emanate from within the building.

"I thought you'd never ask," he said with one of his cute chuckles that was sadly mixed with tears…but the tears also seemed to be a mix, a mix of happy and sad that was hard to distinguish.

I grabbed him and kissed him.

We kissed for quite a while, and now that I think about it, we were sitting there, making out in his car in that parking lot just like any other couple without a care in the world. People easily could've seen

us. I didn't care anymore, though. I just didn't give a shit if anyone knew. In fact, I *wanted* people to know. I wanted *everyone* to know. I wanted to show the world that I loved Izzy Murraro and that I wasn't ashamed of it.

During our long session of kissing there, I felt his hand slowly begin to rub my crotch, almost hesitantly, as I imagined him being afraid of hurting me after having been injured down there. I let him do it, though, and relief set in when I felt myself get aroused. Thankfully, I wasn't completely broken in that department.

I returned the favor, putting my hand on Izzy's groin and feeling him up while I felt his erection grow. He unzipped his pants, pulled them down enough to expose himself, and lifted his shirt just above his belly before I went down on him. I sucked on his penis, rubbed his chest and nipples, and just lost myself in the moment of it all while I listened to him moan softly.

I felt so much relief when I heard him laugh a little, a tickling laugh that I could feel through his belly while my face was buried between his legs.

I was pleasuring him.

He was happy.

I needed that.

I rose and our faces met. I grabbed him and kissed him again, my body on top of his, his hard penis poking my belly.

He unzipped my pants for me.

The car was rocking.

He started jerking me off, slowly at first, but then quickly as our kisses became rougher. The tip of my penis grew wet around his fingers while I thought about letting him fuck me for the first time, right there in the car for the world to see.

The windows were fogging up.

I was getting close as I took in the pure euphoria in Izzy's face. His eyes were closed, his growing hair disheveled with one of the curls fallen down between his eyes. His facial hair, which has continued to grow, made him look older. He almost looked drugged. I kissed him roughly again.

I wanted us both to climax, wanted us both to cum while we were in each other's arms, but he broke the kiss and looked at me with a real serious expression before we could go any further.

"You need to promise me something, though," he said, out of breath.

...

I stayed quiet, my dick going limp. I knew what was coming.

"You need to promise me you'll tell your parents."

I wanted to argue, but...I literally just got everything I ever wanted in the world. Izzy was my boyfriend now. Was I really going to fuck this up?

"Please, Kieran," he said. "Promise me you'll tell them...when you're ready...it's fine, but...you have to tell them. You can't let them fucking get away with this."

I stared at him, tears everywhere. He gasped for air for a second, obviously out of breath from what we just did, but maybe also because he was just exhausted from everything going on. To be honest, he almost looked like he was losing his mind.

"*We* can't let them get away with this."

...

"I promise," I sighed.

He kissed me again, but any attempt to have sex right there and then in the car failed. His interjection had taken away the passion from me. The pleasure was replaced with dread.

...

Tristan LaFerriere

The bowling alley was jumping with a crowd of drunk partyers ranging from our age to people who were probably old enough to have been at Woodstock. When we first walked in, Pat Benatar was belting out "Hit Me With Your Best Shot" while Izzy and I passed lanes of people attempting to bowl and failing miserably.

Thomas and Athena didn't notice anything out of the ordinary, or at least I thought for the first hour that Izzy and I bowled with them. Despite all that was on my mind, I surprisingly did well for the few games that we played in contrast to Athena who threw a gutter ball on nearly every other turn.

Izzy was quiet most of the time like he has been lately, and it made me wonder how long it would be until one of the others would say something, or maybe they already did notice and just hadn't mentioned it yet. How could they have not noticed how quickly, and overnight Izzy's personality had suddenly changed?

I took a good, long look at him that night and wondered if I would ever see the real Izzy again. Despite all I had been through, I think this was way worse for him in some way. Izzy suddenly reminded me of me, but to an extreme. He never smiled anymore, he kept to himself when we were in public, only answered in one-word sentences when Thomas or Athena would ask him anything. Even all the nights I've stayed over at his house and watched him sleep at night haven't been the same. I used to see this peaceful angel at rest, but now Izzy just looked dead when he was asleep. Every night, he looked as though he'd battled the whole world and was just on the edge of survival or giving up.

He looked more worn out than me.

I didn't know how to help him. If I were to tell my parents, would that actually make him better? I wasn't sure if anything would help. I feared this more than anything. I honestly didn't really care about what happened to me.

He was my boyfriend now, but...not the same boy.

I just wanted my Izzy back...

...

340

"Northrup?"

I had run to the men's room near the end of our third game, close to our time to be leaving, to apply some extra concealer to my face. I felt relieved to find the bathroom empty, but less than thirty seconds into my application and Thomas walked in, visible in the mirror I was looking in to check the status of my fading bruises below my eyes.

I audibly gasped and spun around to face him.

I was caught. There was no point in trying to hide it now.

"Thomas..."

"Northrup..."

Thomas looked down at the tube of concealer in my hand, uncapped and a little already applied to my face. He looked up at me with an expression I've never seen on him before. He looked like he just found out I had been stealing money from him for years and only just found out the truth or something sad like that.

"What's going on, Northrup?"

"Wh..."

"Don't make shit up," Thomas cut me off before I could even attempt at coming up with an excuse. "It's way too fucking obvious."

"...What's obvious?"

He rolled his eyes.

"You really think I believed you and Izzy skipped school to smoke weed?"

...

"Athena bought it, but she's Athena. I could see right through that shit, Northrup."

341

It frightened me to see Thomas being so stern with me. I never expected this to happen. I always saw him as the type to never get offended or angry with anyone. What the fuck was happening to all these people I thought I knew?

"Tell me what's going on, Northrup," he finally said after we stared at each other in silence for a painful while.

...

"I don't know what you want me to say," I started, and I thought I could get more out, but Thomas quickly made it clear that he wasn't in the mood for bullshit.

"Cut the crap, Northrup. Just tell me what's going on. What the fuck happened to your face? Why'd you cut your hair? And since when do you wear polos from fucking Hollister?"

I looked down at the gray shirt Mom had purchased last summer when we first moved, one of the many pieces of clothing she tried to get me to wear that I never would've been caught dead in before what the "Tyler Gang" did to me, but now...it makes it so much easier to blend in with all the other King's Valley preps.

"This isn't you, Northrup," Thomas went on. "I don't know what the fuck happened to you, but I just want you to know that I see it and you're not fooling me. You might be fooling Athena, but you're not fooling me."

I looked down at the floor. I really felt trapped. Something serious was about to happen whether it would be me admitting to him what happened or...I don't know, but it wouldn't be pleasant. I knew that much.

"Are you gonna tell me or not? I don't want any bullshit. Either you tell me, or you don't."

What I ended up doing was really fucking foolish. I was such an idiot.

"Just leave me the fuck alone," I said.

Thomas's expression changed and he didn't say anything, but I could only read it as him saying, *"Oh, okay. Fuck you, dude."*

I left the bathroom, made my way through the noisy arcade where a couple of girls were screaming at one of those claw games to get them the SpongeBob plushie they wanted, and back to our lane where I grabbed Izzy's arm just as Athena was about to toss her ball in the gutter again.

"Come on," I said.

Izzy looked up at me, confused and I think slightly startled.

"What?"

"We have to go."

I expected him to ask questions, but he started taking off his bowling shoes and we were already heading back to the counter when Athena was finished with her second gutter ball in a row.

"Hey!" she said. "Where are you going?"

"We have to leave!" I said quickly. "We'll pay…just…everything's gonna be okay."

"What?"

It was hard enough to hear each other over the ridiculously loud background music of some acid rock song, so I just gave her a wave as Izzy and I ran to the counter to pay and quickly leave. I didn't want to see Thomas again. I didn't want to see him pissed off, or worse, hurt.

I can't believe how mean I was to him…

…

"Your…hair," my mom said when she saw me the following morning for the first time since she and dad's return from Seattle. "You cut it?"

343

I was standing nervously in the kitchen doorway as she and dad looked up at me from the table in their weekend clothes, two cups of coffee in front of them. I had spent the last hour in my room practicing the conversation upon seeing my parents again for the first time since I was assaulted. I had what seemed to be a route for any possible question. Since it was a Saturday and I planned on spending the day at Izzy's house, I hadn't bothered to put on one of my preppy outfits to blend in. That would've really raised mom and dad's eyebrows, so with my short, chestnut hair, I was wearing a Paramore shirt and skinny jeans so that it didn't look like I had completely changed overnight.

"Yeah," I said, looking down at my feet.

"Why?" Dad asked.

"I…just figured it was getting too long. It was…I don't know…getting kinda old."

Mom studied me and then rose from the table with her coffee cup in her hand as she walked over to me.

"Did you…cut it yourself?" she asked in a very concerned tone.

"Um…yeah…why?"

She sighed.

"Kieran…you really should've waited to go to a salon. They would've evened it out better for you."

She took some of my hair in her hand and brushed it through her fingers, sighing again before she took another sip of her coffee.

"I mean, it's too short to do anything with it now, but when it grows out a little more, we definitely have to get it shaped for you."

She was about to walk back to the table, but paused when she got a good look at my face. I froze. I can't even begin to tell you how terrified I felt as she studied my eyes.

"Are those bruises?" she asked.

"Yeah. I...fell down the stairs."

"Oh, Kieran...are you alright?"

I walked away, toward the fridge. I felt so nervous I thought I might pass out.

"I'm fine, Mom."

"You have to be careful, Kieran. Especially when Dad and I aren't home. You could've gotten hurt and if you wouldn't have been able to reach the phone, who knows what would have happened. Are you sure you're alright? You don't feel dizzy or anything?"

"I'm fine," I repeated, and I opened the fridge just to keep my eyes away from them as I scanned the shelves for something, anything to grab to keep me occupied. "I just...put some ice on it. I'm fine now."

The fridge kicked on with a groan, my face getting cold, as I grabbed a Diet Coke to sip.

"Come here, Kier," Dad said as Mom sat back down at the table with him. "We want to talk to you."

I felt a swarm of butterflies in my stomach as I crossed the room and sat at the table with them. Was this going to be some sort of interrogation?

"So, we wanted to tell you about Uncle Ryan," Dad went on.

I sighed with relief inside.

"Oh," I said. "How's he doing?"

Dad shrugged.

"Alright. He was, uh, pretty broken up when he found out about Justin, but he's doing okay now. He's been sort of couch hopping here and there for the past year, but he's been staying with a high school friend for the past couple months."

"Oh."

I pictured my Uncle Ryan, my dad's younger brother...he and my dad are twelve years apart, so he's twenty-nine now. The last time I saw him, I remember his hair being long like mine used to be. His hair is a shade of darker brown than my father's. Rather than a button-down shirt with a tie or a sweater vest, he's just about as polar opposite of my dad as you could get. He has this obsession with Nirvana, so most of his wardrobe, from what I remember, are Nirvana shirts and torn blue jeans. It makes a lot of sense to me why he ended up moving to Seattle when California wasn't working out for him anymore. He's basically the embodiment of the grunge movement. He was at the prime age when Kurt Cobain was at his peak.

It's crazy to think that Uncle Ryan was younger than I am currently when I was born. Somewhere, we have pictures of him holding me as a baby only a few weeks after I was born when he was fourteen. It basically looks like Jimbo Jones from *The Simpsons* holding a baby. Nowadays, he looks more like a young Stone Gossard, which I'm sure he'd be flattered to hear since he also worships Pearl Jam.

"He was asking about you," Mom said. "He really wants to see you."

"Oh," I said. "Yeah...that'd be nice. Are we gonna, like, go back to Seattle to see him again?"

"Well," Mom said, and it looked like she didn't enjoy the message she was about to relay. "He's actually going to be staying with us for a little while...in June...he's coming here for a few weeks."

It actually struck me funny because I knew exactly what was going through my mother's head. Uncle Ryan, my dad's couch-hopping, grunge-loving, jobless younger brother would be staying with us in our idyllic suburban paradise for three weeks at the end of June. Dad had offered this stay to him, all flights paid for. I was unaware if my parents had fought about this decision or not, but at the end of the day, he is family, so regardless, my dad won this time.

"Well," I said, smiling. "That'll be nice." I sipped my Diet Coke.

"Yes," Mom said, unconvincingly. "It will be."

Dad stared at her, disapprovingly, before he stood and walked to the sink to wash out his coffee mug.

He threw it in the sink so harshly that it shattered.

...

For the next couple of weeks, Izzy and I ate separately from Thomas and Athena, and I felt like a complete asshole for it, but I wasn't ready to face Thomas after our confrontation in the bowling alley bathroom.

So, Izzy and I were eating in the library. It was a place where I knew none of the "Tyler Gang" would be since it seemed they were always congregating in the cafeteria, and at least it was quiet. It seemed like the library is where a lot of the outcasts take their lunches. In the back of the room, on several occasions, we saw a few chess games going on at a few tables and it made me wonder why this hadn't been the place Thomas preferred to eat lunch considering it was a resource for all his extracurricular enthusiasm.

The computer lab was full of journalism students putting in extra time for their third marking period articles. I've decided to play it safe with a simple movie review on *Stomp the Yard*, a film Izzy and I went to see before I was assaulted [really just an excuse for us to fool around in the back row of the theater, so I did most of my research by looking up the plot on IMDB].

Since Mrs. Kinney has probably been the most understanding of all my teachers, I told her I needed some time alone to work on my writing because I was feeling down about my brother again [not the real truth; it was just another way to avoid Thomas for a while], so every period I would have normally been in the computer lab with everyone else was me in another empty classroom, alone, while I pretended to be productive.

"You should've told him," Izzy said to me the first day we had lunch in the library.

"I'm not ready to."

"It's just Thomas. You can trust him, can't you?"

347

"He might tell his parents."

"Why would he do that?"

"Because he always does the right thing."

I immediately chuckled in spite of myself. Here, I was basically admitting that keeping it to myself was the wrong thing to do, but…it certainly felt like the easier thing to do.

"So, you guys, like, aren't talking?" Izzy asked. He took a sip from his can of Dr. Pepper, but he had no lunch that day. He looked tired.

"Not…right now," I said. "He's pissed because he knows I'm hiding something."

"Then you should tell him, Kieran."

"You said I could tell when I'm ready."

"I know, but…"

Izzy looked away, over at the chess players in the back of the room. He was wearing a gray sweater with one of his beanies that day, his continuing to grow hair sprawling out of it. His facial hair was longer still, too. There was practically a beard that was beginning to form, a slight tint of red in his otherwise dark brown hair that I'd never seen before since he had always shaved it before it got anywhere close to this long. He almost looked like a different person.

I noticed him shiver a bit as he took another sip of his soda.

"Are you cold?" I asked.

He slammed the now empty can on the table and started blinking numerous times as he fidgeted in his chair.

"I'll be alright," he said, and as he crossed his arms, it was really obvious that he was trying to keep warm.

"Are you sure?"

"It's my anemia," he said. "Sometimes I get cold. I'll be fine."

This was the first time I really ever saw Izzy show any signs or symptoms of his anemia. He had told me about being diagnosed and that sometimes he would feel lightheaded or cold, but other than him being very pale most of the time, he always seemed okay.

"Do you want my hoodie?" I asked.

He was still staring off into space, shivering at an almost violent rate before he finally nodded. I unzipped the gray hoodie that used to be Justin's, stood up, and gave it to him.

"Thank you," he said quietly.

Izzy gave my hand a quick squeeze before he started putting it on. The hoodie was so large on him that it looked like he was wrapped in a blanket, and I was frightened by how cold his skin felt.

...

February 24th...a bad fucking day.

I spent the night before at Izzy's. He seemed to be in a slightly better mood than usual. Mr. Murraro had gone to Blockbuster to rent some movies, so we ended up watching *Clerks II* before we played *Mario Kart* for a few hours.

"Looks like you finally healed," Mr. Murraro said to me when he came downstairs with the rented DVD for us. "Izzy told me you took a nasty spill down the stairs."

"Yeah," I said. "I'm doing alright now."

I never realized lying so much could be so exhausting...

The next morning is when shit got bad. I woke up at about eight, in Izzy's basement room, and found that he wasn't lying next to me like he had been when we both went to sleep. The TV was still on, another news report breaking about the circumstances revolving around Anna Nicole Smith's death and pending funeral.

"Izzy?" I called out.

Nothing.

In my t-shirt and boxers, I climbed out of bed, looked over near the laundry room, the corner where the furnace is.

Nothing. Nothing but Izzy's stuffed Spyro staring at me from the shadows.

"Izzy?"

I started upstairs and distantly, I heard muffled voices coming from the kitchen as I approached the door. When I opened it, I walked in from the hall to find Mr. Murraro, still in his robe as he hugged a crying Izzy beside the counter.

I froze. Had he told his dad what happened to me? What was going on?

Mr. Murraro looked up and noticed me. He had tears in his eyes as well.

"Oh...Kieran," he said softly.

Izzy looked up from his dad's arms and immediately walked over to me with his arms outstretched. He hugged me tightly and sobbed into my shoulder. I hugged him back, still unsure of what had happened.

"Izzy..." I said. "What...what is it? What's wrong?"

"His grandfather died," Mr. Murraro said, swallowing as he tried to hold back his tears. "My father."

"Oh," I said, and I kissed Izzy on the cheek. "I'm so sorry."

Izzy kissed me back as he shivered in my arms. He felt so cold.

Details came to me sporadically for the next hour as I sat with Izzy and his dad in their kitchen. Apparently, Mr. Murraro's father had suffered a massive stroke the night before, was rushed to the hospital,

350

but died shortly after five in the morning. His mother called him, upset and crying over the phone with the sudden tragic news.

"He was doing just fine when I saw him a few weeks ago," Mr. Murraro said. He sighed, playing with a spoon that was still sitting in his bowl of uneaten, soggy cereal. "He was doing just fine…"

Izzy's dad wiped away a tear, tried to smile, and then stood up.

"I'm gonna get dressed and…make my way over to Brooklyn. I have to call Giovanni."

Izzy was quiet, sitting beside me with his hand in mine while he stared at the floor like a zombie.

"Izzy?"

Mr. Murraro leaned down, put a hand on his son's shoulder, and got close to him.

"Izzy?"

He looked up at his dad.

"Are you going to come with me, or do you want to stay here with Kieran?"

It surprised me that Izzy's dad even suggested the latter option, but I guess he knows how close Izzy and I are. I don't think he knows we're technically a couple yet, but telling him it was okay that he could stay home with me instead of going to New York to be with his family during a death was shocking. I almost didn't feel worthy of such.

"I don't know," Izzy said. He looked at me. "I…I think I should go."

I nodded.

"Yeah," I said. "I think you should."

Mr. Murraro headed upstairs to get dressed. I followed Izzy to his upstairs room where he changed in front of me. This was the first time I saw him naked without it feeling sexual in any way. He looked so fragile without his clothes on, his body bonier and paler than ever. The image almost reminded me of one of those horrific photos of holocaust victims who were starving to death. He looked so sick...

He stopped in the middle of putting on his jeans, sat on the edge of the bed, and put a hand to his forehead.

"Are you alright?" I asked.

He nodded, still holding his head.

"Yeah. I'm fine. I'm just..."

He slipped into his jeans and zipped up the fly.

"I have a headache."

He stood up again, slowly, and crossed over to his closet to grab a shirt.

He didn't make it to the closet.

I watched, in what seemed like slow-motion, as Izzy collapsed to the floor. Before I knew it, he was face-down on the carpet.

"Izzy!"

I ran over to him and kneeled, clutching his cold hand and trying to wake him up.

"Izzy? Izzy!"

I rolled him over. He was conscious, but looked too weak to move. His eyes were halfway closed, and I swear, if his face was even the slightest shade paler, he would've looked like a ghost.

"Izzy! Are you okay?"

He blinked slowly and tried to reach his arm up to point out the door, but it looked difficult for him to even do that.

"Get my…dad," he mumbled.

I called for Mr. Murraro, and I must have had a lot of urgency in my tone because he came running into the room, fully dressed for their drive to Brooklyn.

"Izzy…he…he collapsed and…I don't…I…"

I started to cry as Mr. Murraro patted my shoulder.

"It's okay," he said to me. "He'll be fine. It's his anemia. It's happened before."

Izzy's dad leaned down and lifted him up from the floor. With Mr. Murraro's help, Izzy was able to walk back over to his bed where his father insisted he rest for a little while. Meanwhile, I stood in the corner and sobbed, watching the whole thing like it was a scene from a horror film.

"Hey, Kieran…"

Mr. Murraro came over and hugged me.

"He'll be okay. Don't worry. It happens. He's okay."

I sobbed and sobbed into Mr. Murraro's shoulder as he held me.

"Don't cry, Kieran. It's okay. Izzy's okay, buddy."

He patted my back and I clung to him like he was my own dad.

"I'll be right back," he said, letting go of me and leaving the room.

When Izzy's dad returned, he was holding a large tumbler of ice water and there were two pills or something in the open palm of his other hand.

"Here," he said, holding out his open hand to Izzy. Izzy's trembling hand took the two pills, he swallowed them with some water, and Mr. Murraro handed the tumbler to him.

"Drink the rest of that," he said to his son. "I'll go get you something to chew on."

"What are those?" I asked as Izzy's dad started for the hall again.

"They're iron supplements. I'll be right back."

I walked back over to Izzy, who was in a sitting position in his bed while he sipped at the large glass of water. He still looked so sickeningly pale and still without a shirt, I could see the bones of his ribs more clearly than ever before.

"Are you okay?" I asked, still crying.

Izzy nodded as he took another sip of the water.

I sighed and sat on the edge of the bed.

"God, you scared me," I said.

"I'll be okay," he said, his voice raspy. "This happens sometimes."

He set the water down on his bedside table and groaned. I took his hand and he squeezed it to the best of his ability.

"You're so cold," I said.

"Yeah...it's the anemia. I'll be okay."

He looked up at me and gave me a weak, but nonetheless genuine smile.

"Don't worry, bud," he said hoarsely. "I'll be alright. I'm not going anywhere."

He reached out his hand to me, and his trembling fingers brushed the edge of the dangling Chai around my neck.

"I'll...pro-tect you," he said, sounding a bit loopy as he smiled to the best of his ability again. "I gotta pro-tect you."

I took his trembling fingers in my hand and kissed them. Then I climbed in the bed and cuddled up to him, tried to keep him warm with my body heat until Mr. Murraro returned with a bowl of mixed nuts for Izzy to snack on.

What touched me most was seeing Mr. Murraro lean in and kiss Izzy's forehead as he handed him the bowl. He also gave me another pat on the shoulder as he stood back up, went to the hall closet, and returned with a large, ripple crochet stitched afghan that he draped over Izzy's bare shoulders. The scent of cedar rose from the old throw that I was later told by Mr. Murraro had been knitted for him by his grandmother some forty years ago when he was a little boy.

Izzy's dad postponed the drive to Brooklyn for a few hours to make sure Izzy felt well enough to travel. I stayed by his side for the rest of the afternoon, holding him while he dozed off in my arms under the comforting weight of the afghan. I dozed off, too, hearing Mr. Murraro's muffled voice on the phone somewhere else in the house as he called relatives. I couldn't be sure, but I thought on several occasions I could hear his voice break as he spoke, crying over the phone as he talked to Giovanni or another family member about what had happened.

It was around three when Izzy finally started feeling better. He looked slightly better, too. His eyes didn't look so tired, and some color returned to his face. I helped him pack some clothes and toiletries into his backpack for a possible few nights at his grandmother's house in Brooklyn.

Out in the driveway, I hugged Izzy before he got in his dad's Ferrari. He kissed my neck quickly before he got in the passenger side. Mr. Murraro came from the front door after he locked it, wearing his black peacoat and carrying an overnight bag.

"We'll probably be back Monday night," Mr. Murraro said to me. "I'll make sure Izzy calls you."

I smiled.

"Thanks. I'm, uh…really sorry about your dad."

"Oh, Kieran."

He leaned down and gave me a hug.

"Thanks, buddy."

I expected him to break the hug, but he didn't. He actually hugged me for quite a while and even gave me a quick kiss on the top of the head.

"Don't worry about Izzy," he said once he finally did step away. "He's fine. He just needs to eat a little bit more. I think he's been under a lot of stress lately for some reason and…this didn't help."

I nodded as he smiled and put a hand on my shoulder.

"Thank you for caring for him so much."

I smiled, too.

"He's…my best friend," I said. "I'd…I'd do anything for him."

"He'd do anything for you, too, Kieran."

Mr. Murraro looked back at his car where Izzy was sitting and then back at me again.

"I'm so glad you guys found each other," he said. "Ever since you two met…I've never seen him so happy. I mean, he's always been a happy kid, but…he's *really* happy now."

I looked over at the car and nodded.

"He loves you," Mr. Murraro added.

I smiled, a lone tear running down my cheek as my boyfriend's father put his arm around me for a sideways hug, Izzy's mother's Chai cold, but comforting against the skin of my neck. I really felt like I was part of their family now.

"I love him, too," I said.

He gave me another pat on the shoulder before he stepped in behind the wheel and started the engine. The Testarossa's flat-12 engine roared to life at a volume that made me jump as exhaust fumes puffed from the tailpipes. I watched it begin to roll down the driveway, but then the tires screeched, and the car stopped near their mailbox.

A moment later, Izzy was opening his door and running back up to me as fast as his frail body could.

"Kieran!" he said, and stopped right in front of me.

He looked down and shook his head.

"I'm...I'm sorry I pressured you to tell anyone about what happened. I shouldn't have done that. It just made things worse."

"No," I said. "It's okay."

Before I could get another word out, he threw his arms around me and kissed me, one hand on each of my cheeks. When he broke the kiss, he put his face close to mine and spoke at a low volume.

"It's okay," he said. "We'll figure something out."

He put his hand to my chest for a moment, a gesture I'd never seen him do before.

"Love you," he said, and he darted back down the driveway.

"I love you, too!" I called.

Izzy hopped back in the Ferrari, and I watched as it sped away.

I sighed, standing in their now empty driveway in my jeans and gray hoodie. I turned to face their house, locked up and empty for at least the weekend. Without their presence, the place was just a shell, a defunct amusement park ride that still hadn't been demolished.

What the fuck was there to do in King's Valley without Izzy...

…or Thomas…

…or Athena…

…

…or Justin?

I stuffed my hands in my pockets and trudged back over to my house where, later, Mom and Dad announced they were going out to the country club for dinner and suggested I come along.

My mother, disappointed after my several declines, told me it would be nice if I started spending more time with the family before she went upstairs to get ready. My father, giving me a quick and sympathetic smile as he followed her, snuck me a twenty and whispered to me that it was for pizza.

I watched them disappear up the stairs together, and later, after they had left and the sun had long since gone down, I drew myself a bath. While I waited for it to fill, I sat naked beside the tub with several towels draped over me. Larry came into the room and sniffed around, curious why I'd suddenly started laying in a spot normally reserved for him. I soaked in the hot water for a long while once the tub was full, and then sat, alone, at the dining room table in my father's bathrobe. My phone was an arm's length away next to the open pizza box from Domino's while I waited for a call from someone, anyone…

I imagined Izzy sitting in the chair at my side, my head resting on his shoulder while we dug into our breadsticks.

I imagined *him* resting his head on *my* shoulder, tears in his eyes while I ran my hand through his hair, threading through each of his beautiful, dark curls that looked like they'd been sculpted by Michelangelo.

I wondered where he was now, probably in that Brooklyn brownstone where Mr. Murraro grew up, embracing his father, brother, and grandmother.

…

My phone sat silent against the tablecloth.

...

Ten deep chimes from the clock in the hall.

The clock on my phone was a full minute ahead.

How upset Mom would be if she knew.

This entry has gone on damn long. I think I'll keep writing another time.

Goodnight.

I love you.

Chapter Seventeen
Monday, April 2nd, 2007

Dear Journal,

Sunday, the day after Izzy and his dad left for Brooklyn, I went up to my mom who was in the living room, cleaning. Apparently, the cleaning ladies hadn't done a sufficient enough job the day before.

"Hey, mom?"

"Yeah?"

She was leaning over the coffee table, a bottle of Old English furniture polish by her side. I could smell the chemicals as I approached her. I was wearing that gray hoodie again, and a pair of basic jeans.

"I was, uh, wondering if you could take me to the movies."

Mom stood up, looked at the coffee table for a moment to check that her work was acceptable, and then at me.

"What movie are you going to see?"

"*Ghost Rider.*"

"Do you have any money?"

"Yeah."

"Alright. What time's the movie?"

"Four."

Mom checked her watch and nodded.

"Alright. Just let me put this stuff away. I'll meet you in the garage."

My heart pounding, I went to wait for her.

Mom drove me to the Regal Cinemas that's across town in one of those slightly desolate shopping centers. It's in walking distance

from the main road where Turkey Hill is, but besides a Chinese buffet, Linens 'N Things, and a couple of hair salons, there isn't much to do in that area of town.

"I'm surprised Izzy isn't going with you," Mom said as she drove her Chrysler 300 along Edward Martin Drive.

"He's in Brooklyn," I said. "His grandpa died yesterday."

"Oh. That's too bad."

"Yeah."

"What about those other friends of yours? Thomas and, uh…"

"Athena."

"Are they going to meet you there?"

"No. I don't think so."

"So, you're going all by yourself?"

"Yeah."

"How come?"

"I…don't know. It's something to do, I guess."

…

"I'd say coming to the country club with your father and I for dinner once in a while would be something to do, too."

…

"Don't you think?"

…

"Yeah."

…

361

"So, what's this movie about?"

"It's *Ghost Rider*…like the comics."

"Oh." Mom nodded without knowing what I was talking about, and then we were pulling up alongside the theater.

"Thanks, Mom," I said, and opened my door.

"How long's the movie?" she asked.

"It's, like, three hours."

Her eyes widened.

"Three hours?!"

"Yeah. Um, it's…it's a long one."

"Alright, well…"

She checked her watch again.

"I'll be back here to get you at seven-thirty, okay?"

"Sounds good, Mom. Thanks."

"Have a good time."

She drove off, and I started for the outdoor box office windows, but quickly hurried across the lot toward the road when I was sure that mom's car was far enough out of sight.

I was out of breath by the time I made it to the Turkey Hill entrance. I looked through the glass doors to see if I could make out who was working behind the counters. Kody was there, with shorter hair, as Izzy mentioned.

I held my breath and then walked through the door, an electronic *ding dong* alerting the staff that I was a customer. I felt like I was about to rob a fucking bank.

362

Just calm the fuck down, Kieran. Calm the fuck down. People do this shit all the time. It's not a big fucking deal.

...

"Hi."

I stared back at Kody Kurtz, the tall, lanky lip-piercing guy who Izzy and I always found so cute, standing behind the register. I stood stupidly with a bottle of Coke that I grabbed for something to purchase.

"Hey," I said and gave him probably the stupidest smile ever as I held up the Coke bottle. "Just this."

I placed the bottle on the counter, looked over my shoulder to make sure no one was behind me, and then leaned in.

"Hey," I said in a loud whisper.

He looked back at me as he scanned the bottle.

"What?"

...

"Are you, uh...um...holding?"

Kody checked his digital watch.

"I get off in twenty," he said. "Meet me by the old Cavalier outside. It's white."

That's it? That's how easy this would be?

"Oh," I said, and probably smiled an even stupider smile. "Cool. Great!"

I walked away without even paying for or taking the soda.

I waited for Kody outside for the next twenty minutes, sitting on the concrete slab at the edge of the parking lot where this decrepit old, probably mid-80s Chevy Cavalier was sitting. The thing looked

like it was about to fall apart. One of those *"Coexist"* bumper stickers seemed to be holding the front bumper to the frame of the car, and one of the headlights was broken. Another, fresher sticker proudly declared, *"Fuck Bush,"* beside one that said, *"Jesus Sucks Dick"*. Three of the four hubcaps were missing.

While I waited, I looked out in the distance at the rest of the lot, the busy avenue that Turkey Hill faced, and the setting sun in the horizon. I could see the Reading Pagoda atop Mount Penn, one of the few recognizable landmarks in the area.

What the fuck was I doing?

...

"Hey."

Kody walked up behind me, carrying his jacket as he nodded toward the shitty old car.

"Hey," I said. "Thanks for waiting for me."

"You waited for me. I don't have shit on me now, so hop in."

"Oh," I said, feeling nervous again. "Where, uh…"

"Just to my place. It's, like, five minutes away. You cool with that?"

He opened the driver's side door and I suppose he noticed I was stalling.

"You coming?"

"Oh. Um…yeah. Sorry."

He eyed me suspiciously as I attempted to find room to sit in the passenger seat. The inside of the car was a fucking mess. The seat was littered with candy wrappers, the floor in front a fucking landfill of garbage like Burger King wrappers, empty soda cups, and crushed cigarette packs. The ashtray was overflowing, and it looked like the car hadn't been cleaned in a decade.

"Sorry," Kody said, his voice muffled as he had already stuffed a Newport 100 in his mouth. "I don't usually have passengers."

"It's cool," I said, trying to get comfortable with one of the seat's springs sticking out into my ass. The ceiling upholstery was sagging and brushing against the top of my head.

Kody started the car, and I seriously thought the engine was about to explode. The frame of the old Cavalier shook, and the muffler had obviously fallen off at some point, or at least had a hole in it, because it sounded like we were riding a motorcycle.

I gripped the handle on the door as Kody pulled out of the lot and cruised onto the road. The car rumbled and shook as he picked up speed, and to let his cigarette smoke out the window, he opened the window on his side completely, which let in an uncomfortable amount of chilled February wind.

"So, what's your name, kid?" Kody asked.

"Kieran," I said at a volume loud enough to be heard over the strong breeze and rumbling car motor. "Kieran Northrup."

He nodded.

"Kody Kurtz. How'd you hear about me, man?"

"Um, my friend."

"Does she have a name?"

"Athena Rhodes."

Kody took a drag and tapped the steering wheel with his fingers.

"Can't say I remember her," he said. "I got a lot of customers."

He pressed a button on the dash for his aftermarket CD player.

"Mind if we listen to some tunes?"

"No. Go ahead."

I was nearly cut off by the ear-splitting sound of "Through the Fire and the Flames" by Dragonforce blasting over the ancient car's shitty speakers. Kody pounded on the steering wheel so hard to the beat of the song that I'm surprised it didn't fall off like everything else on the car seemed to be on the verge of doing.

"So, you went to King's Valley High?" I asked as loud as I could over the music.

"Yessir."

"You graduated last year?"

"Yessir." He nodded and took another drag. "Well, almost two now. Class of '05."

"Nice."

We stopped at a stoplight and at a complete stop, the car vibrated and shook even worse than when it was in motion.

"Sorry, man, Kody said. "She's on her last leg."

"It's alright."

"Mind if I grab some Taco Bell? I'm fucking starving. Didn't have time for a fucking break today."

I shrugged.

"No, that's fine."

"Cool, man."

The light turned green, and we jolted forward, passing a number of fast food restaurants on the avenue. This was a part of town I had never really been to. It didn't seem "run-down" necessarily, but it certainly didn't have the wealth that Belmont Hill Estates and the surrounding communities near the high school have. All the restaurants were the outdated versions, designs that hadn't been updated since the early 90s perhaps.

We pulled up to the Taco Bell drive-thru where a smudged menu with missing letters greeted us. Two teen workers were sitting outside the back door in their jackets and smoking cigarettes as a female voice on the crackling speaker asked for Kody's order. He ended up getting two burritos and nachos.

"You want anything?" he asked me.

"I'm good," I said, surprised to find that a drug deal could be such a friendly experience.

He got his food, and then we continued up the road, pulling onto a side street where there were a number of older rowhomes. Kody parked the Cavalier outside one of them, killed the engine, and we got out. He was already munching on one of his burritos as I followed him up the front steps to his front door. The front porch had a pair of old, green plastic lawn chairs stacked next to a TV tray that was holding an overflowing glass ashtray.

"Hey, Mom," Kody said as we passed through the living room.

I felt awkward as I found Kody's mom, a middle-aged woman with graying hair, lying on the couch in her pajamas with a plaid blanket over her as she watched *Judge Judy*. A lit cigarette was sitting in her nearby ashtray and a glass of wine was within her reach on the end table. There was something sad, but at the same time, sort of cozy about this place.

"Hi, honey," she said, sounding tired, or maybe she was medicated. "Who's this?"

"Just a friend. We're gonna hang for a bit."

"Alright. Nice to meet you, honey."

"Nice to meet you," I said, and Kody brought me up the stairs to a hallway that, like the rest of this cluttered house, smelled of cigarettes. Some old family photos stared at us from the wall.

"Sorry we had to come here," he said as he led me into his messy room. "I was late for work this morning, so I didn't bring any of my stash. If I'm late one more fucking time, I'm gonna get fired."

"It's okay," I said, looking around the room. It was pretty stereotypical for what I would imagine someone like Kody's personal space to be like. A glow-in-the-dark peace sign poster was hanging over the bed, some Bob Marley merchandise was here and there. A glowing green lava lamp was switched on in the corner beside an old tube TV where a dusty Xbox was sitting on top of the console. The twin bed was unmade, and I could smell body odor in the air. I would have guessed that he furnished the entire room at Spencer's Gifts.

Kody switched on his TV, and it warmed up with sound before the image came clear: the "Knights of Cydonia" music video.

I watched as he took off his Turkey Hill uniform shirt, tossed it in a pile of clothes on the floor, and walked over to his dresser drawers where he opened the top drawer. His ass crack was visible at the rim of his black work pants that were nearly falling down from his skinny frame.

He started rummaging through the drawer while I stood there awkwardly, unsure of how the whole process works. Was there etiquette with drug dealing? God, I hate calling it that...I mean, it's just...pot.

"So, how much do you want?" Kody asked me.

He retrieved a plastic bag that was crumpled up to a smaller size, the little space inside filled with weed.

"Um," I stuttered. "How much will...twenty bucks get me?"

Kody's expression went from fairly neutral, possibly even a bit on the happy side, to annoyed.

"Twenty bucks?" he said flatly.

I chuckled, embarrassed.

"It's, uh, all I've got right now."

Kody sighed, closed his drawer, and walked over to a littered desk.

"Why are you here, dude?"

…

"What?"

"Why are you here?"

He opened his desk drawer and pulled out one of those glass things you smoke weed with [a bong, I guess?].

"You don't seem like the type to smoke weed."

"I…don't?"

"No."

Kody sprinkled some of the pot into the end of the bong.

"Why, uh…why do you say that?"

"Because I know every type. Let me guess; this is your first time buying weed and you have no idea what you're doing. You probably come from the rich side of town, and you could probably buy a fucking yacht if you wanted to, but you've only got twenty bucks on you cuz you're morally straight. You don't want to disappoint your parents by stealing from them to get your first fix. You have no idea what you're doing. Is that it?"

I looked down at the floor, so fucking embarrassed.

"Well…uh…yeah. I mean…"

"It's cool," Kody continued. "Just give me your twenty and we'll share this light."

"Really?"

"It's best you don't go spending all your cash at once your first time, anyway. The first time is always a hit or miss."

I felt slightly better as I fished into my wallet for the twenty and handed it to him.

"Thanks," Kody said, and he stashed it in his pocket.

Kody and I sat on the floor beside his bed, in front of the TV, while we shared hits. The newbie I am, I stereotypically coughed like crazy each time I took a drag. It reminded me of movies where the dorky kid tries weed for the first time and makes a total ass out of himself. That ass was me.

Kody laughed after a few hits and shook his head.

"You're something, dude."

…

"Oh? Am I?"

"You're a nervous kid."

There was no use denying that.

"Yeah…I am, I guess."

On TV, Ronnie Radke's face filled the screen as he screamed out the lyrics to "There's No Sympathy for the Dead" in a new Escape the Fate music video.

"How'd, uh…you know that I was a…rich kid?" I asked [I hate calling myself that].

Kody took a drag and chuckled as he looked me over.

"Those sneakers you're wearing," he started. "Air Jordans, right? XX1s? They're, like, almost two hundred fucking dollars, dude."

I looked down at the new sneakers I had only started wearing after my Converse went missing the night of the assault. These had been a pair Mom bought me that collected dust in our closet for a while before I had no other choice, but to start putting them on.

"Oh," I said. "I guess so."

"And your hoodie, man. That's one of those nice ones from, like, Bloomingdale's. It isn't that cheap Forman Mills shit that I got."

"Oh...well, this was my brother's."

Kody passed the bong back to me and nodded.

"Makes sense why you're fucking swimming in it, dude. What the fuck are you doing with it?"

I took a drag, held in the smoke for a moment, and then let it out with another cough. Kody took the bong back from me.

"He died," I said.

"Oh, shit, man. I'm sorry."

"It's okay."

"What happened? How'd he die?"

Kody took another drag as I repeated the same story for the hundredth time. I make it shorter on each subsequent telling.

"Car accident. He drowned."

"Wait, man...was your brother the one who crashed his car in the lake?"

"Yeah."

"Shit, man. I remember that. It was big news. I'm...I'm sorry, man."

"It's okay. It's been almost six months. I'm kinda numb to shit now."

We were awkwardly quiet for a while until we finished up the last of the weed. I wasn't feeling anything at all.

"I don't feel anything," I said as I took my last drag. Kody immediately grabbed it back from me, presumably to get as high as possible from what was left.

"It's your first time," he said. "Usually, you don't feel shit your first time. That's why I told you it'd be a fucking waste."

I shrugged. A waste of an hour? Maybe, but at least I tried.

"What are you doing here, anyway?" Kody asked again as he started to pack his paraphernalia away. "Why'd you just decide today that you wanted to get some weed?"

"Um...does it matter?"

Kody shrugged.

"Just curious, man. Like I said, you really don't seem like the type."

"What's that supposed to mean?"

"I already told you; you're like that innocent, rich kid who doesn't want to do anything illegal." He stood up and crossed back to his drawer to stash the bong away. "So, what made you decide to break the rules?"

"You don't know me," I said, feeling slightly offended. "Maybe I...like breaking the rules sometimes."

Kody held his hands up as he crossed back to me and sat down on the floor again.

"Not trying to be an asshole, man. Just saying..."

I sighed. The Escape the Fate song was over and now it was Gerard Way singing about how teenagers scare the living shit out of him.

They scare me, too, Gerard. They scare me, too.

"Okay," I said. "You want to know why I'm here?"

Kody shrugged as he checked his phone.

"Sure."

"My brother's friends think it's my fault that he died because he was driving me somewhere I wanted to be when he was in the accident, so they blame me for his death, and to get back at me for it, they beat me up, stuck a stick up my ass, pissed and jerked off in my face, and cut all my hair off. My boyfriend is so traumatized by it that he stopped eating and he's a fucking wreck, and on top of all that, his grandpa just died yesterday, so he's in New York and I'm alone, so everything's pretty fucked up right now and I figured maybe smoking would calm me down a little bit."

Kody stared at me for a while. He looked uncomfortable.

"So, you were raped?"

"I wasn't raped. I was…"

"They stuck a stick up your ass and jerked off in your face. You were raped. That's fucked up, man."

I felt like I was going to be sick. I knew it all along, but never used the term. Kody saying it confirmed it. It made it real.

"Well," I scoffed. "What can I do about it now?"

"When did this happen?"

"Last month."

"You go to the police or anything?"

"No."

"Why not?"

"Because I don't want my parents to know about it."

"Why not?"

"Because that would fucking kill them."

373

"Is that enough to not go to the police?"

I looked down as Kody lit another cigarette.

"It's complicated," I said.

"Sounds like it."

"I'm gay."

Kody shrugged.

"That's cool. Who cares?"

"A lot of people care."

"Like who?"

"Well, I mean, look at the fucking world."

Kody took a drag of his cigarette.

"But, like, who have you come out to? Who knows you're gay?"

"Well, my Dad, my boyfriend…my two friends from school." I shrugged. "You."

"Okay. And how many of them cared?"

…

"Well…none of them really…"

"Exactly, so I think what you're doing is spending too much time worrying about shit that never happens. I'm pretty sure if you went to the police, you'd feel a lot better, but you're just afraid of what's gonna happen."

…

"I don't know."

"What if you just got someone else to fuck them up for you?"

"I...I can't do that."

"Why not?"

"I don't know. I don't really want to get involved in shit like that. And, besides, it's not like I know anyone who'd do that."

Kody flicked some ash in his ashtray.

"I would."

A dog could be heard barking outside somewhere. A grumpy old lady neighbor was yelling at the mutt to shut up.

"Who did this to you?" Kody asked.

"Oh, I don't want to..."

"Dude, I'm a fucking drug dealer. I'm not gonna say shit. I don't tattle."

"I don't know if you'd know them."

Kody flicked his ash again.

"Try me, dude. I've lived in King's Valley my whole fucking life." He coughed. "Word travels very quickly in this town. I know everybody's secrets. Even yours now."

...

"Tyler Kirkland."

Kody looked out in space for a moment, cigarette in hand, and shook his head.

"Jesus Christ." He laughed to himself.

"What?"

375

"Tyler...fucking...Kirkland."

"What about him?"

Kody shook his head again.

"That fucking kid. When I was a senior, he was this annoying little fucking sophomore. He came to me once for weed, took two fucking drags, and started rolling on the floor claiming he was high as fuck. That's total bullshit. He's a fucking moron. His brother's a fucking basket case, too, man. He's fucking weird."

"Evan?"

"Yeah, I guess that's his name. I don't know; I just know he's fucking weird. He used to fucking stare at girls all the time in middle school. He was a total creeper. The whole family's fucked up. The mom's a fucking crack whore and the dad's got a fucking meth lab in the basement."

"I wouldn't be surprised," I chuckled.

"It's true."

...

"Wait...really?"

Kody nodded.

"They have a meth lab in the basement?"

He nodded again.

"You're shitting me."

"Nope." Kody dumped the last of his cigarette in the ashtray and leaned back against the bed. "Trust me; I have connections. I know. You ever been to their house?"

"Yeah...once. A long time ago."

"Did you see their basement door?"

I remembered; there was a piece of paper taped to it with the words *"Keep Out"* or *"No Entry"* or something like that written on it. Was this for real, though? It could've just been a rumor.

"Yeah," I said. "But, are you sure…"

"Fucking positive, man."

"What about Eric Gleason and Adam Woolf?"

"Huh?"

"They're the other two. The three of them did this to me."

Kody scratched his side and looked up at the ceiling as he thought.

"I know Eric Gleason," he said. "But not Adam Woolf. Eric Gleason…he's, like, the richest kid in town."

"Basically."

"Yeah," Kody went on. "And his fucking dad, that fucking corrupt supermarket CEO. You know, he paid off the mayor to make sure the old hardware store was burned down so they could build that new shopping center that's going up on Main."

"Well, that's…speculation, isn't it?"

"No." He shook his head. "It's totally true. My friend's dad is on the town council. He knows shit. The hardware store was a protected landmark and the only building left out of, like, a dozen they tore down on the old main strip. The only way they could get rid of it was to burn it down and cover it up as an electrical fire. The fire department's in cahoots with Town Hall. Someone was hired to burn down the building, the fire department was paid off to fight it as slowly as possible, the place burned to the ground, the chief firefighter was told to report it as old wiring, and now they have their land to put in the new Gleason's. They're trying to make this place as appealing as possible for the rich by shoving all the poor people like me out. That's why our space is getting smaller and smaller every fucking year. You know, the new high school was built where there used to be a horse

farm. The poor old guy that owned it couldn't afford to run it anymore, so they drove him out, knocked down his buildings, and put that big, fucking ugly monstrosity in its place. It's the same with all those nice new homes over in Belmont Hill. You know that area?"

"…Yeah."

"Same shit. That was all farmland. This town was about as fucking rural as it gets and in just the past couple years, they're trying to turn it into a fucking mini mall and McMansion city. It's bullshit."

"Shit," I said, feeling like part of the problem. "I thought those were all just rumors."

"That's what all the loaded people around here want you to think. They don't want that shit exposed because it would mean they wouldn't get their new country clubs and golf courses."

He grabbed another Newport from his cigarette carton and lit it.

"Fuck King's Valley," he said, blowing out a puff of smoke. "Fuck King's Valley." He turned to me and offered the pack of smokes.

…

"Uh…sure."

I hesitantly took a cigarette and he lit it for me. As he took another drag, I attempted to do the same without coughing up a lung. I was almost successful.

"You're not like the others, though," Kody said after we smoked in silence for a minute.

"What do you mean?" I coughed.

"Like, you're a rich kid, but you're not a douchebag. I can tell you're a good kid."

I shrugged.

"I've always tried to be. And look at where that's fucking gotten me."

"Don't feel too sorry for yourself, man. It only gets worse from here."

"Great."

"I'm sorry about what happened to you, though. That's fucked up. I would've hired a fucking hitman to kill off those fuckers if they did that shit to me."

I put the cigarette back to my lips, inhaled, and felt the cool menthol fill my lungs. I finally didn't cough this time. I actually kind of liked the taste.

"So...you gonna tell your parents?" Kody asked.

"I don't know."

"What's stopping you?"

"I told you."

"They'd take it really bad, huh?"

I didn't say anything. Kody and I looked over at the TV for a little while. It was dark outside now, and soon I'd have to get back to the theater before mom figured out I wasn't really at the movies.

"Let me ask you this," Kody finally said. "Would it kill you that much not to tell them? Like, do you feel like it'd drive you crazy if you didn't tell them?"

...

"I don't think so."

"And you don't want to go to the police?"

I shook my head.

"So, would it do any good to tell your parents if you don't actually want to do anything about it?"

"What do you mean?"

"If you told your parents, would it do any good? Or would it just make them feel like shit? Would it be better that they never know or would telling them in any way be a good thing?"

...

"I...don't think it would."

"Then why bother telling them if it's just gonna hurt them? If you can live with it, there's no point."

I smiled.

"Thanks, Kody."

He shrugged and tossed his second cigarette in the ashtray.

I wished Izzy could have been there to see this, Kody Kurtz shirtless and hanging out next to me. I thought about all the times Izzy and I checked him out behind the counter at Turkey Hill and how cute we thought he was. Now here he was chilling with me like I was his friend, and giving me advice like some wise soul, this native of King's Valley who's seen it all. I guess that twenty dollars bought more than just my first smoke.

"Do you think you can drive me over to the theater?" I asked him, dumping the rest of my cigarette in the ash tray with his.

"Sure, man. Let me get a shirt on."

Kody went to his closet, put on an August Burns Red shirt, and I followed him back down the stairs. We passed through the living room again where his mother was now snoring in front of the evening news doing yet another report on Anna Nicole Smith's death.

...

380

"How long have you known you were gay?" Kody asked me as he drove me back to the theater. He was smoking another Newport.

"Um...I don't know, I feel like I've...always kinda known. It's hard to say. Like, I didn't really fully realize it until a few years ago maybe, but...I think I've always been gay."

Kody nodded.

"I don't get what the big fucking deal about it is. Who cares who you're fucking?"

"I know."

"People are so fucking uptight, man."

"Yeah."

"But fuck those people, man. It sounds to me like you've got a pretty good support group."

"Yeah. I guess I do."

"You said your dad knows?"

"Yeah."

"And he's cool with it?"

"Yeah."

"That's awesome, man. Your dad must be fucking chill."

"I guess, yeah."

"If I were gay, my dad would probably knock my fucking teeth out."

I didn't know how to respond to that remark.

"Where, uh...where's your dad now?" I asked.

Kody shrugged.

"Who the fuck knows, man? Probably in jail."

"Oh...I'm sorry."

"It's cool, man. I don't give a shit. I don't really know him that well. He and my mom were never married. The only present he ever gave her was a fucking black eye three days after I was born."

I stayed quiet.

"So, you said you have a boyfriend?" Kody asked.

"Yeah."

"Cool. What's his name?"

"Izzy."

"Izzy?"

"Yeah."

"Like Izzy Sparks?"

"...Who?"

"The *Guitar Hero* character."

"Oh. Uh, I guess."

"That's kind of an unusual name."

"Well, it's not his real name."

"What's his real name?"

"...Ishmael," I said with hesitation, feeling like Izzy would kill me if he knew I was revealing his real name to someone.

"Ishmael," Kody repeated, nodding his head as he took a drag of his cigarette. "*Ishmael*. That's a badass name."

I chuckled.

"He from around here?"

"Yeah, he and I both just moved here. We live next door to each other."

"Well, that's convenient, dude. Is he that kid I've seen at Turkey Hill with you?"

"Oh...so you remember me?"

"Yeah. Your hair was longer before...and black."

"Yeah...before those fuckers cut it."

"Shit, man. I know you don't give a shit, but I'd really like justice to be fucking served. Fuck Tyler Kirkland. Fuck Eric Gleason and whoever that other rich kid is. Let me guess, they're all jocks?"

"Yeah."

"Doesn't fucking surprise me."

Kody pulled into the parking lot of the movie theater. Now at nightfall, the marquis and neon lights were all lit up. There was a small line outside the box office.

"You waiting for someone?" he asked me.

"Yeah...what time is it?"

He checked his watch.

"Seven."

"I have half an hour, then."

"They've got an arcade in the lobby there. You want to go in and do a couple games of DDR or something?"

"Sure."

So, we did. Kody and I went inside the theater, and just like he said, there's an arcade beside the snack bar that was mostly empty. Besides the huge Dance Dance Revolution machines, a few pinball machines and a Ms. Pac Man cabinet were all this little game room had. We ended up facing each other in a few rounds of DDR.

I did surprisingly well, beating Kody in three out of the five rounds we played. When we were done, we sat at one of the few empty tables in the lobby of the theater that's right beside the front windows so I could see if my mom was coming. Since it was a Sunday night, the place really didn't have many patrons, and a cleaning guy was already mopping the floor while we waited. An '80s hit echoed through the cavernous, neon-lit room as we talked.

"It's nice talking to a genuine person for a change," Kody said to me. "Everyone around here is so fucking fake. I mean, I get that I sell weed, but…it'd be nice if people treated me like a fucking human being. Most people just know me as the weed guy and that's it. They don't actually want to hang out with me."

"Well, you seem nice," I said. "I like making new friends, you know?"

"Well, consider us friends," he said. "Hit me up. You know where to find me."

"Thanks."

"Anytime."

I glanced out the window. Still no sign of my mom. I was relieved. I was enjoying my time with Kody.

"So," I said. "All that shit you told me about Eric Gleason and his dad…that's all true?"

"Yep."

"You're sure?"

"As sure as I can be, man."

"I have a friend who writes for the school paper and this shit is just the kind of stuff he'd want to write about."

Kody cocked an eyebrow.

"Yeah?"

"Yeah. Definitely."

"Would the school even let you publish something like that, though?"

"I don't know."

Kody shrugged.

"I guess it's worth a shot, right?"

"This person you know who has inside info…you think they'd be down with an interview or something?"

"It's hard to say, man. Probably, if the price was right…and as long as it was anonymous."

"I'm sure that can be arranged."

Kody nodded.

"I'll see what I can do."

"And what about Tyler Kirkland?"

"What about Tyler Kirkland?"

"You said his dad has a meth lab in the basement."

"Yep."

"And you're sure about that?"

"One-hundred percent positive. I know several people who have seen it first-hand."

"And...you think they'd be down for..."

"I don't think so, man," he cut me off. "Unlike the shit with local politics, which no one gives a fuck about...this would get a lot of people in deep shit."

"How so?"

"Dude! It's a fucking meth lab. All it'd take is one phone call."

...

I looked up.

"What do you mean?"

Kody chuckled.

"Dude...if one person fucking tipped off the cops about it and they raided that place..."

He stopped and looked at me for a moment. He must've seen it in my face.

"But," he started. "You didn't hear that from me."

...

"Thank you," I said.

That was when Mom's Chrysler pulled up to the curb outside and my phone simultaneously vibrated.

Chapter Eighteen
Tuesday, April 4th, 2007

Dear Journal,

I approached Thomas at his locker that Monday morning, February 26th. Izzy was scheduled to return home from Brooklyn that night. My heart was pounding the whole drive to school. It was my first time without having Izzy to drive me, so I asked my dad for a ride when I found him in the kitchen. He had just been finishing his coffee and appeared to be more than just a little excited when I brought it up. I suppose, in a way, it was me fulfilling his wish to drive me all those months ago right after Justin died.

He let me back his car out like usual. When we got to the end of the driveway, Dad stayed in the passenger seat. He offered to let me drive the rest of the way to the school since I have my permit now. I felt like passing on the offer since I was already nervous enough. I was worried about what Thomas might say to me when I walked up to him, but I decided not to make myself seem suspicious [suspicious in that I used to be very adamant about getting time behind the wheel].

I ended up driving the whole way, my hands squeezing the steering wheel as I drove a daring fifteen miles an hour through town. I glanced over at Dad a few times. He seemed to be keeping his cool, but also in a position that suggested he was ready to pounce if I put us in a life-threatening situation.

My reflection caught me a few times in the rearview mirror. I still practically didn't recognize myself. The short, auburn-like hair was one thing, but the green and white long-sleeve polo shirt and khakis I threw on were almost too preppy for something even Justin would have worn. Mom had bought the outfit at Benneton's back in L.A. As it was my first time wearing all of this, I had to rip the tags off. My tan jacket, zipper open, topped everything off. It reminded me of something my dad would've been photographed in when he was that poster child of a WASP in high school. I definitely didn't look like someone who would be listening to Stay Sweet. I looked more like someone on their way to a tennis match at a country club.

I pulled the Cadillac up to the school's front entrance. We left a little earlier than Izzy and I normally do, so I had some extra time to kill before homeroom started. There were others being dropped off by

their parents. Some were sitting on the brick wall that lines the wheelchair ramp. Further, beyond the school grounds, the "punk" kids had already congregated in their smoking spot. For a brief moment, I nearly considered joining them because just about anything seemed better than facing Thomas. I didn't like the thought of him possibly shutting me out for good and...I honestly could have gone for another cigarette.

Dad shook my hand as I parked the car, which was his gesture to tell me I did a decent job. He got behind the wheel, drove away, and I limped up the front steps. I still occasionally feel pain in my legs ever since *that* night, and especially when I'm going up or down stairs, so I gripped the cold railing and carefully made my way inside.

...

"Hey, Thomas."

Thomas was putting away his messenger bag and carrying a stack of books for his morning classes when he looked up at me.

"Hey," he said, monotone. He shut his locker and spun the combination lock. "What's up?"

I looked down at the floor.

"Not much," I said, still unsure of how to mend things. There were too many people in the hall, and I wanted this to be private. "Can we, uh, talk somewhere else?"

It took him a moment to respond.

"Sure."

I led him up a few steps, past my homeroom, and toward a rear corner of the building where the woodshop classrooms are. We went through a set of double doors that lead outside, closer to the student parking lot, but near the greenhouse where some of the science classes grow plants and stuff.

As homeroom approached, the outside was basically abandoned, so the two of us had the corner all to ourselves. Thomas

stood in front of me, arms crossed like a pissed off teacher, and I tried not to cry as I began to speak.

"Listen," I said. "I...I know that you're probably pissed at me." I looked down. "I...I don't blame you. You *should* be pissed at me. I was...I was a total ass to you. I was a complete dickhead and...I'm really sorry."

Thomas just continued to stare at me. His expression didn't budge. This was more awkward than I imagined.

"Something," I continued, fidgeting as I tried to find the right words. "Something...happened to me. I...I didn't know what to do. I was, like, all fucked up in the head and lost and afraid. I was going crazy, man. I wasn't thinking. I'm...I'm sorry, Thomas. I just...I just feel so bad and I don't know...I don't know what else to say. I'm sorry."

...

He looked down at the ground for a moment. Much like those few seconds between me coming out to my dad and his response, I felt nervous as I waited to see if Thomas would accept my apology or tell me to fuck off. I relaxed when he looked back up, but this time with a brief smile. It was the smile that would normally accompany some random political fact of his.

"Northrup," he said softly. "You're my friend."

I looked down again because I felt the tears coming this time. One dropped down to the sidewalk and formed a dark circle on the concrete.

"The only reason I was harsh with you is because I care about you a hell of a lot," he went on. "I do, Northrup. You're a good kid and you've got a good heart. I was worried about you." He put a hand on my shoulder as I started to quiver from crying. "I love ya, Northrup."

I immediately hugged him and burst into tears into his shoulder.

"Are you mad at me?" I asked.

He responded by squeezing me tighter. At the same moment, a chilly breeze blew through the corner, tossing a few of the last remaining fallen leaves of the season from the sidewalk and messing up our hair. We finally broke the hug when another bell sounded from inside the building. We were officially late for homeroom, but neither of us cared.

"Northrup," Thomas chuckled, looking me and my WASP outfit over. "What the fuck are you wearing? This isn't you."

I wiped the tears from my eyes as he continued.

"What happened to you, Northrup?"

My stomach dropped a bit. I looked back at the doors we had just come through and then back at Thomas. Something took hold of me and suggested I just seize the fucking moment. If there was any place in the entire world I wanted to be, King's Valley High was definitely not that place.

"You want to get out of here?" I asked.

Thomas looked back at the school, the idea of skipping school a discomfort in someone like he's DNA.

"Where would we go, though?"

"Anywhere. Anywhere but here."

...

Three hours later and I was sitting next to Thomas in the back row of the nearly empty theater at the Regal Cinemas. After some minor convincing, I was able to get him to agree to cutting school with me for the day. Luckily, for both of us, it was a day that he didn't have any quizzes or tests, and, as of just a few weeks ago, his parents surprised him with a '99 Camry for his first car. So, we took a drive across town, had breakfast at McDonald's, and bought a couple of matinee tickets to see *Norbit*, a movie that we could ignore so I could bring him up to date on everything that had happened to me.

"Jesus, Northrup," Thomas whispered to me about half an hour into the movie. I had just finished telling him everything that

happened from the moment Adam took me to The Skate Park to when Izzy left for Brooklyn. "Are you sure you're alright?"

"Yeah," I whispered. "I'll be alright."

...

"Are you sure you shouldn't go to the police about this?"

"It wouldn't do any good. And besides..."

I paused to take a sip of my Coke.

"I'm over it."

We stared at the movie screen for a little while longer, and then I felt Thomas's hand take mine. He gave it a squeeze and it felt as if Izzy were sitting with me there, but this gesture felt more friendly than romantic. This was the first time I was seeing the vulnerability in Thomas, the first time I was seeing the true amount of warmth that can come from his heart.

"I don't think I could ever get over something like that," he finally said. "Fuck those guys."

I chuckled, amused at how "normal" Thomas has come to sound as opposed to the overly intellectual demeanor he gave off when we first met so many months ago.

"Yeah," I said. "But, really, I'm okay now."

"You're sure?"

I nodded.

"Yeah. I'll be fine." I sipped my Coke again. "Besides," I continued, hesitating a bit. "I, uh...I might have some pretty interesting inside info for your next article."

"Let's not worry about that right now, Northrup."

"Why not?"

"I don't think you need to be worrying about the paper right now."

"That's the first time I've ever heard you say that," I chuckled.

Thomas gave me a look.

"Believe it or not, Northrup, I actually care more about you than I care about the paper."

"Well...I don't really care about the paper, but...this might just be a way to fuck with the people who fucked with me...passively."

...

"I'm all ears."

"My friend, Kody, can tell you more about it than I can. Maybe we can hit him up after this."

"Whatever you say, Northrup."

He looked at me for a while as I continued to sip my Coke. I knew he didn't believe me when I said I was okay, or that I was over it. To be honest, I'm not even sure I believe myself, but all I know is that I'm doing better than I thought I would.

About midway through the movie, Thomas put his arm around me and rested his hand on my shoulder.

Chapter Nineteen
Tuesday, May 29th, 2007

Dear Journal,

Around three this afternoon, it suddenly dawned on me that I hadn't picked you up to write anything in over two months. I'm sorry. I've been trying to get everything in order lately. I've been trying to live as normal a life as I can without thinking too much of all the shit that's happened to me this past year. I've been trying to take care of Izzy and, vice versa, let him take care of me when I need it.

Yesterday was Memorial Day. The senior class just had their prom, so rumor has it that most of them wouldn't be in school today. The rumor turned out to be true; it's a tradition for the seniors to skip the next day of classes following the prom weekend. If Justin were still around, he would've most likely been down at the New Jersey beaches where most of the other class of '07 people were spending time getting drunk and getting laid.

Izzy, Thomas, and Athena came over to my house for the day. Mom and Dad haven't re-opened the pool yet, but Dad has started skimming it and dumping various chemicals into it in preparation for the oncoming summer. The jacuzzi, on the other hand, is all set to go, and the four of us spent a good hour in the bubbling water after Dad cooked us some burgers on the grill.

Izzy is looking so much better these days. Since the weather has gotten warmer, we spend just about every afternoon outside whether it be for taking walks or just lounging out on the deck. All the sun has put some color in his otherwise sickly pale complexion, and since his anemia scare from February, he never hesitates to have a good meal. He started shaving again, too, so that beard of his that was growing in is gone and he's back to looking like the young and healthy boy that I know.

Despite all his improvement, Izzy seemed slightly different following his return from Brooklyn. After his grandfather's funeral, it wasn't that his happy-go-lucky energy was gone, but I could tell, just in his eyes, that he was tired.

It was my time to take care of him for a while, so since then, I've tried to keep it together by not letting my emotions get the better of

me every hour on the hour like usual. Instead, I try to remind myself of all the good things that are going on in my life right now.

My dad [and probably my mom, even though I haven't come out to her yet] is cool with me being gay.

I've recovered mostly from my assault injuries with the exceptions of that slight limp I have once in a while and my left eye sometimes feeling sore when I turn it. All of the bruises have finally faded away.

My hair is growing back...

...and I'm dating the most beautiful boy in the world.

Like Kody Kurtz reminded me...I have it pretty damn good compared to someone like him. I have a nice home, a nice family. I'll never have to worry about being hungry.

My parents recently surprised me with my first car. It's a stick shift, so I'm a little nervous about driving it, but Izzy promised he would teach me. It's a used 2001 Volvo S60 that, until I get my license at the end of the year, has been sitting in our garage...in the same spot where Justin used to park his car. It feels a little strange, almost like I've taken my brother's place, but my parents buying me my own car sort of feels like the concluding chapter of that part of my life. Them finally coming to terms with the idea of me driving on my own after what happened to Justin is like the final say on the matter. It's in the past now, and we're finally moving on.

Speaking of Justin, I finally introduced Izzy to him. A few weeks ago, on what would have been my brother's eighteenth birthday, he and I took a drive over to Gethsemane Cemetery in Reading where Justin is buried. It was my first time visiting his grave, and I felt nervous, like seeing his headstone would be the final confirmation that he was gone even though I've been without him for so long now.

We stopped at a local florist to get some flowers to put on Justin's grave at Izzy's suggestion. The bouquet of carnations sat on my lap as Izzy drove the Alfa down Kutztown Road toward the cemetery. Seeing the headstones appear off the side of the road made my stomach drop. The remains of my brother were closer to me than

they had been since the funeral, and I worried I wouldn't be able to keep it together when we finally approached his marker.

We parked the car and started walking, Izzy holding my hand as we made our way across the field of graves, away from the busy adjacent street and further into the natural greenery where the headstones stuck out around us. The early spring breeze teased at my growing hair, and I shivered as we passed markers for veterans, American flags and badges of honor memorializing the deceased. Izzy gripped my hand tighter as we neared Justin's grave, and I felt slightly dizzy as we walked up to the fresh, dark marble headstone.

"Justin James Northrup
Beloved Son and Brother
Forever in Our Hearts
May 12th, 1989 – September 8th, 2006"

The words, along with a simple image of a soccer ball beneath them, were etched into the marble. The grass below, while grown, was still a rectangular shade off from the rest of the field. This was still, in a way, a freshly dug grave.

"Hi, Justin," I said, like he could hear me. "Happy birthday."

I kneeled down in front of the grave and laid the spray of carnations against the marble. Izzy kneeled beside me, a hand on my shoulder.
"This is Izzy," I said. "He's my boyfriend."

"Hey, Justin," Izzy said, patting the marble of the headstone like he was shaking my brother's hand for the first time.

I stared ahead at my brother's name, the bookend dates of his birth and death, and the cliched words honoring his memory just like every other marker in the cemetery. Surprisingly, I suddenly didn't feel the urge to cry. Even though his remains were only six feet below us, the real Justin felt so far away.

Other than the memories, this was all that was left of him. In a hundred years, if someone was walking by and saw this hunk of marble, this was all they would ever know about him. He died when he was seventeen and he liked soccer. He had a brother. That was it. No one would ever know he held my hand and tried to comfort me when I

was four and we were lost in the mall. No one would ever know that he used six weeks of his allowance to buy me a Game Boy Advance for my tenth birthday. No one would ever know that when our grandmother died, and I subsequently dreamt of her coming back that he was the one who explained to me that death was permanent. No one would ever know that I cried in his arms when his explanation of death made me realize Grandma wasn't ever really coming back. No one would ever know that he hugged me to comfort me only a few days before he died, even when we were probably at our most separated.

"I miss you," I said quietly, rubbing my hand along the edge of the cold marble, caressing the top of his head in my mind. "I miss you a lot."

"Kieran's a good man, Justin," Izzy said. "Your brother's a good man. He's told me a lot about you."

My hand continued to brush along the marble, my fingers touching the etched words of his name until I sat back on the grass beside Izzy. We held each other for a long while in the quiet breeze, the three of us boys together at last until we finally stood and made the long walk back to the car. I looked over my shoulder a few times at Justin's grave, at the fresh carnations laying beside it, and I wondered how long they would last until they would wilt or blow away.

...

"You okay, bud?"

Izzy and I sat in his car for a while, still parked at the cemetery.

"Yeah," I said. "I'm okay." I looked over at him. "Are you?"

...

"I don't know."

"You don't know?"

Izzy laughed a little.

"I don't know what I'm feeling, but…I'm feeling a lot right now."

…

"I feel like I finally got to know your brother."

I smiled, imaging if the two of them had ever met in real-life. Would they have gotten along? I like to think they would have. I like to think of Izzy coming over to our house and Justin greeting him with a hug. I like to think of the three of us hanging out together, Justin smiling as he watched Izzy and I kiss and cuddle.

"He would've loved you," I said as a final thought, my eyes focusing out the windshield, past the acres of headstones trailing up into the vast field. "I'm sure he would've loved you."

Izzy smiled and ruffled my hair. Then he sighed as he followed my gaze.

"Well…" he said.

"Well, what?"

Izzy shrugged.

"What should we do now?"

I shook my head, and we were quiet for a while.

"I don't know," I finally said. "What *should* we do?"

Izzy shrugged again, appearing to be on the verge of cracking up laughing because the moment was so cliched.

"I don't know," he chuckled. "It's Saturday. The options are endless."

I nodded, unzipping my jacket as I was starting to feel warm.

"That's true," I said. "But there's nothing to do around here."

I looked over at him and he looked at me like we both knew the answer we were digging for.

"You want to kiss me?" I asked.

"I always want to kiss you."

We kissed for a long time, two boys in that parked car, next to the cemetery in Reading, with only a few weeks left of school and a free summer ahead of us. Finally, I felt like I had something to look forward to. Finally, it was like the cold darkness of winter had passed away and we could together escape this town for as long as we liked.

I held him and told him how much I loved him.

I lost track of how long we embraced.

All I know is that as long as our arms were around each other, everything was okay.

It'll always be okay as long as I have him.

...

We finally broke our hug.

"Do you want to meet my mom?" he asked.

"Where is she?"

"Washington Cemetery."

"Where's that?"

"Brooklyn."

...

I nodded.

Izzy smiled and started the car. The Alfa rumbled to life, and we started driving... onto Kutztown Road...onto Route 222...onto Route 100...onto Route 78.

As we drove and drove along the highway in silence, into New Jersey, en route to New York, Izzy started his iPod...

"Here we are in your unmade bed,
fully clothed and with a feeling of dread...
You have your suitcase...
and I don't know where we're going from here,
is this really what you want to do, my dear...
The tears in your face tell me all,
the sudden gasp in your voice is a call...
I can't let you go now..."

I felt a chill just before the chorus of the song that up until then had reminded me of the worst night of my entire life. But now, it'll forever bring me back to the moment Izzy put his hand into mine as he drove me along Route 78, east through New Jersey, toward Brooklyn in a moment I felt consummated our relationship even more than when we had sex for the first time.

"Under my sheets!
It's where I find you,
all we have
are the memories left between them.
I still dream of you,
I still dream of you,
I still dream...
I find you under my sheets..."

...and, for the first time, I heard the second verse...

"I remember the first time I saw you,
laying low with the thought that I loved you..."

Izzy's grip tightened.

"I could see the world through your eyes..."

I turned to face Izzy, the side of his beautiful face lit by the red glow of taillights as day turned to dusk.

399

Tristan LaFerriere

"The smile on your face told me all,
the laughter in your voice was a call...
I could never let you go..."

Izzy turned to me, his smile softer than ever as he mouthed the words that a year ago, I never imagined another boy could ever say to me...

"I love you."

...

"I LOVE YOU, TOO!" I yelled at the top of my lungs.

Izzy and I both screamed and hooted, rolling down the windows of the car and bumping our fists out into the air as the chorus repeated:

"Under my sheets!
It's where I find you,
all we have
are the memories left between them.
I still dream of you,
I still dream of you,
I still dream...
I find you under my sheets..."

Made in the USA
Middletown, DE
06 January 2023

20738699R00239